FLIGHTS

FROM THE ROCK

A COLLECTION OF SHORT STORIES

FLIGHTS
FROM THE ROCK

EDITED BY CURTIS, DALY & VANCE

ENGEN
BOOKS

Library and Archives Canada Cataloguing in Publication

Title: Flights from the Rock : a collection of short stories.
Names: Curtis, Ellen, 1993- editor. | Vance, Erin, 1992- editor.
Description: Edited by Erin Vance and Ellen Curtis.
Identifiers: Canadiana 20190127570 | ISBN 9781989473054 (softcover)
Subjects: LCSH: Flight—Fiction. | CSH: Short stories, Canadian (English)—Newfoundland and Labra-
dor.
  | CSH: Canadian fiction (English)—21st century.
Classification: LCC PS8323.F55 F55 2019 | DDC C813/.0832161—dc23

Distributed by:
Engen Books
www.engenbooks.com
submissions@engenbooks.com
First mass market paperback printing: July 2019
Cover Image: © 2019 Kit Sora

Engen Books thanks Kit Sora Photography and Sci-Fi on the Rock for helping make this collection
possible.

CONTENTS

Introduction
Lisa Daly

We take flight for granted. Today, we can fly around the world, sure, not as quickly as when the Concord flew the supersonic flights that allowed a person to get from London to New York and back again in time for tea, but we can fly from Newfoundland to Tokyo, with a few layovers. Before the jet age, aircraft had to stop frequently to fuel. Making that New York to London flight would have involved a refueling stop in Gander, Newfoundland: The Crossroads of the World. In fact, throughout the Second World War, Gander and Goose Bay were the hubs of trans-Atlantic aviation, with thousands of aircraft stopping to refuel and for one last check before flying across the ocean.

Airplanes flying overhead were not always a common sight. When the Hindenburg flew over the St. John's on July 4th, 1936, it was the talk of the town for the next few days. Some were in awe of the massive airship, likening it to a flying whale. Others thought it was a harbinger of the end of the world, and some took cover under whatever was close! The dirigible passed over Newfoundland and Labrador 13 times before its ill-fated flight of 1937. In fact, on that final flight, the passengers were amazed by icebergs sparkling in the sunlight off the coast of Cape Race. In 1928 and 1932, Amelia Earhart twice made history,

Flights from the Rock

first in bring the first woman to travel the Atlantic by airplane. She complained that she was merely cargo in that
flights from Trepassey, so later she returned and left Harbour Grace to become the first woman to fly solo across
the ocean. The Harbour Grace Airstrip saw aviators from
around the world who wanted to fly across the ocean, and
were willing to risk their lives to make new records in the
early decades of flying. These aviators were strong characters, captured by the dream and thrill of flight.

Less than 20 years earlier, all eyes were on Newfoundland for the Trans-Atlantic Air Race. A competition put
forward by *The Daily Mail*, aviators could win the £10,000
prize by flying the Atlantic Ocean in under 72 hours. As
Newfoundland was the closest point of land to Europe,
the aviators headed there in the spring of 1919 expecting the moderate temperatures of an English spring, and
instead finding the snow, rain, and heavy winds of a
Newfoundland spring. Teams set up in St. John's, Mount
Pearl, Harbour Grace, and Trepassey. Planes were flown
in, others shipped in to be reassembled, and even a blimp
entered the race. Some aircraft met with misfortune: the
blimp broke her moorings in high winds and drifted out
to sea, and one team in St. John's attempted to take off,
but went against the wind and crashed on the runway.
Other aircraft left Newfoundland, but didn't make the
full hop, like the flying boats in Trepassey. Three left the
island, two made it to the Azores (one just barely), and
only one made it right across to Portugal, after borrowing
parts from the others. And then there is the exciting story
of Hawker and Grieve, who left from Mount Pearl and
crashed in the Atlantic, were picked up by a passing ship,
and thought lost until the ship came close enough to signal their safety. Some, like the aviators in Harbour Grace,
didn't get to leave before the race was won.

In amongst all of this excitement, John Alcock and Arthur Whitten-Brown prepared, and took off from Lester's Field in St. John's on a June day, and flew 16 hours and 12 minutes to land in Clifden, Ireland, becoming the first people to fly non-stop across the Atlantic. In honour of this achievement, we have compiled stories about the fantastic feat that is flight.

These stories capture the magic and majesty that come with flight. Stories like John Burnham's tale of bush pilots, *Halley's Comet*. Often overlooked because they rarely broke records, bush pilots flew in all conditions, innovated to keep their planes in the air, did the impossible, and survived. Bush pilots continue to play an important role and this story tells of one such feat. Or like JRH Lawless's story *The White Bird Dives*, a historical fiction that questions what really happened to the *Oiseau Blanc* on her attempt to cross the Atlantic. Or *The Triumph* by Amanda Labonté, a steampunk story wherein the reader is introduced to the newest vessel built to protect the British Empire.

The allure of flight is still strong today. While we sit in small seats on a commercial flight, improvements are being made to make aircraft faster, safer, better. Records are still being set, for speed, distance, and innovations are making aircraft greener. While we may never experience the luxury of early commercial aviation, even if we can afford a first class ticket, in this century we have seen supersonic commercial flights, aircraft that can circumnavigate the globe without stopping, and robots landing on Mars. Flying is still firmly in the realm of the fantastic, and flyers are characters in their own science fiction stories. *Per ardua ad astra*: the way to the stars.

Lisa Daly
Editor

Ali House

A native Newfoundlander, Alison is a graduate of the Fine Arts program at Sir Wilfred Grenfell College (MUN), and past recipient of the Golden Crescent Wrench Award. Her short story, 'The Price of Beauty' won the December 2018 Kit Sora Award.

Her first novel, *The Six Elemental*, was released in October 2016. Its sequel, *The Fifth Queen*, was published in March 2019.

She is the only person to have short fiction published in all of Engen's open-call short story compilations, including *Sci-Fi from the Rock*, *Fantasy from the Rock*, *Chillers from the Rock*, *Dystopia from the Rock*, *Bluenose Paradox*, and *Kit Sora: The Artobiography*.

She currently resides in Halifax, Nova Scotia, where she works in arts administration and spends more time than a person should in and around theaters.

The Risk of Dreaming

As I looked out over the cliff's edge, at the vast ocean waters below, my thoughts turned to Icarus. I'd learned about him at a young age, thanks to a book of Greek myths that my aunt had gifted me on my eighth birthday. The story said that Icarus and his father had been unfairly imprisoned on the island of Crete by King Minos, and in order to escape, his father made them wondrous wings of feathers and wax. Before taking off, his father warned him that if they flew too low, the water would make the feathers too heavy to fly, and if they flew too high, the sun would melt the wax that held everything together. Icarus listened intently, but as they flew away, he became so enamoured of being up in the sky, that he didn't heed his father's warnings and flew higher and higher, getting so close to the sun that he melted the wax and fell into the sea. It was a children's book, so it didn't touch on Icarus' mortality, but I learned the whole story a few years later.

It probably wasn't the best subject to be thinking about at this particular moment, but the sun was shining, the sky was clear, and I was preparing to fly.

The design was my own invention, inspired in parts by a bicycle, a kite, and birds. I'd spent over a year working on it, starting with smaller models and testing them rigorously before working my way up to a full-sized prototype. Once I'd built it there was still a lot of trial and error, but I never lost hope. Every test offered new knowledge, more confidence, and brought me closer to my dream.

Months were spent testing my craft over and over, racing down hills and jumping off small ledges, gliding on the wind like a bird. After each successful trip, I'd search for a higher ledge, but eventually I ran out of places to jump from. I considered my parent's roof, but it would have been impossible to get the craft up there. Besides, the angle was all wrong.

Finally, I realized what I had to do. I had to take a risk.

Standing at the cliff's edge, I steeled my nerves. It was a long way down, but the weather was ideal, the wind was strong, and my craft had been tested. There was no better time than now.

"You've got this!" Eliza cheered enthusiastically. "It's gonna be great!"

Jimmy opened his mouth to say something, but then thought better and closed it.

Jimmy wasn't a fan of my ambition, but he was an only child and had inherited his mother's constant worrying. He'd fretted about this plan every step of the way, worried about what would happen if I fell or if the craft broke apart. Despite this, I could see in his eyes that there was a part of him that wanted to fly just as much as I did.

Meanwhile, Eliza was as excited as I was, if not more. She supported all of my crazy ideas, and if my craft had an extra seat, she'd be right next to me. Eliza was the fourth out of seven children, and she was the most reckless and headstrong person I knew. If it hadn't been for me, Eliza and Jimmy never would have said two words to each other, let alone been friends, but somehow I managed to bridge that gap.

They'd been present for all of my previous tests, and their input was invaluable towards making my craft better and safer. I couldn't think of anyone else I'd want with me on a day like today.

Giving the cliff's edge one last look, I walked past them and headed up the hill to where my craft sat, waiting. It looked like something out of a science fiction book, with its laid-back seat, pedals, wheels, ropes, and huge wings on top, but I had faith that it would do what I needed it to. After all, I had built many strange inventions over the years that had succeeded, despite their appearance. Lowering myself into the seat, I stretched my legs out before me and slipped them into the pedals. I did a few quick tests, making sure the chain was well connected to the wheels and that the rigging was moving the wings properly, before looking down at my friends and giving them two thumbs up.

Eliza let out a whooping sound while Jimmy gently put a hand on her arm and safely pulled her back from my intended flight path.

Putting on my helmet and lowering the goggles over my eyes, I took in a deep breath. I could see the path before me, laid out as clear as the cloudless sky above. In my imagination I had already done this hundreds of times. I would start pedalling, racing down the hill at a great enough speed that the momentum would keep me from falling into the ocean after I went over the edge. Once airborne, I'd ride the wind on those large, sturdy wings, steadying my craft, before using the ropes to tilt the wings, letting the wind lift me higher and higher. With enough skill, I'd soon be soaring far above the ground.

There were a lot of people in town who thought I was

crazy. They said that I would never succeed and I should leave flying to the birds. Often they would laugh and say 'Remember Icarus!' I know that they were trying to mock me, but it was actually good advice.

See, when other people thought about the story, they focused on Icarus' fall. They considered the myth to be a warning from the gods; a reason to be satisfied with what they had, and to keep their feet firmly on the ground. If you dared to fly, then you would surely fall.

But what I thought about was Daedalus – Icarus' father. When it came to him, people only thought about what he'd lost. Yes, he'd invented something amazing, but it had cost him his only son. Still, they didn't know what his life must have been like as a prisoner, knowing that he'd never be free again. And, honestly, you can't put Icarus' death on anyone but Icarus. His father *had* warned him.

So, yes, Icarus fell, but Daedalus made it to safety. He flew over the sea and made it all the way to Sicily, finding safety from Minos. No other human had done such a thing before, but he did, wearing giant wings of feathers and wax. Daedalus lived because he understood the risk.

I thought of all my tests and theories, and everything that could go wrong.

And after that, I thought of everything that could go right.

Some people would never fly because they were too scared of falling. They would never feel the wind in their hair or gaze at the world so far down below or know that they were doing something incredible. The only way to do that was to swallow your fear and doubts, and jump. And that was exactly what I was going to do.

I took another deep breath, focused on the horizon, and prepared to fly.

Fortune Favours The Bold

The temperature outside was freezing, but inside the Kaminnyy Klub it was warm and toasty. The fireplaces were blazing, the food from the kitchen was piping hot, and holding a mug of warm cocoa could almost make a person forget about the sub-zero temperature outside.

"You know, if most bosses had a choice, they'd give their crew time off on a warmer planet," Levi remarked, taking a sip of cocoa. He'd unzipped his large, down jacket, but had yet to take it off, despite the woollen sweater he was wearing underneath. His dark green hair was stuck up on one side of his head, but he didn't seem to notice or care. Or maybe he didn't want to risk losing any warmth by taking a hand away from his mug to smooth it down.

Captain Pilar Argus smirked in response, unconsciously smoothing her own silver hair. "You knew what I was like when you agreed to work for me," she replied. Her jacket was hanging on the back of her chair, as she was perfectly content with the amount of warmth coming from the fireplace.

"Well, I have a lot of regrets," he muttered.

She didn't take his remark personally. Argus had grown up with Jonas Levi and worked transport with him for over fifteen years, so she knew how much he hated being cold. Unfortunately, his being her second-in-command plus her oldest childhood friend meant that she got a certain pleasure out of tormenting him.

"You know, you could have stayed on the ship," she said.

He shook his head. "Not until Banu manages to get his super-heater invention up and running. It's much warmer here."

They were on Klatch, the outermost planet in the Rossija system, which meant it was the coldest and least populated. Earlier in the day they'd finished their current job by delivering a shipment of goods to one of the speciality stores a few blocks away. While she could have taken off for a warmer destination, Argus had decided to stay on the planet for a little break. It was partly to torment Levi, and partly because she wanted some different scenery after spending the last five and a half days in hyperspeed, travelling here from the Diota System.

Although Argus wouldn't want to stay too long, she liked how quiet it was. On warmer planets, there were always so many people going around at all hours of the day, and everything was so crowded and loud and annoying. Being on Klatch was like a breath of fresh air. Really cold air, but still fresh.

"Um... I think we have might have a situation..."

Her mug was halfway to her lips when Levi spoke. Sighing, she put the mug down and looked at him. He motioned his head towards the left. Even before she saw it, she knew the problem had something to do with her pilot, Aja Kanto, and the ship's doctor, Vera Quintas. Sure enough, they were part of a group of people who had all risen to their feet and were talking angrily with each other.

"What are those two up to now?" Argus said under her breath. Any time Quintas went out in public there was a chance of a brawl breaking out, but she'd been hoping that this restaurant would be relaxed enough to avoid any misunderstandings. The doctor, despite being in her mid-forties and small in stature, managed to find offence in almost everything, and one night in particular a bar had almost burned down after someone remarked that she'd look good in green. Argus had been hoping that Kanto, despite being only twenty-two, would be able to keep the doctor in check, but apparently that had been asking too much.

As Argus drew closer to the group, she picked up on the conversation, which was a heated discussion about who was the better pilot. And now she knew how Kanto had become involved.

"Any place! Any time!" Kanto yelled at the red-haired woman standing in front of her. The woman was half a foot taller, so she had to stand on her tiptoes to make up some of the difference. Quintas was standing next to Kanto, her arms crossed over her chest, grey eyes narrowed in anger.

"Tomorrow," the woman said. "Solnechnyy Restoran on Istra. First one to arrive wins."

"Bring it!"

"Yeah," Quintas said, jutting out her chin. "Bring it!"

"We'll see who brings it at noon tomorrow," the woman replied, smirking.

Argus quickly placed herself between Kanto and the red-head. "Hold on. What's going on here?"

Kanto paled at the sight of her captain, but Quintas wasn't as worried.

"We're going to kick their butts in a race tomorrow,"

Quintas said, her voice filled with arrogance.

"Or, we're not," Argus replied pointedly.

The woman laughed. "Should've known you two would have an excuse."

Kanto glared at the woman before putting an arm around her captain's shoulders and leading her away from the crowd. "We have time to fit this in, right?" she asked in a low voice. "You always have a few days buffer between jobs, so we've got time, right?"

"That's not the point," Argus said. "We're a business, not a bunch of bored space-racers."

"But she's *really* annoying," Kanto replied. "I want to wipe that smirk off her face *so* bad. I mean, she didn't believe that we outran pirates in the Daehan System last week, but we did."

Argus held back a sigh. "And racing her to Istra will make her believe that?"

Kanto shrugged. "It's worth a shot."

She looked over at Levi, who was shaking his head. They'd done their fair share of racing in the past, but now they were too old and responsible to get caught up in petty squabbles. It'd be best to put the brakes on this and go back to their drinks.

"Look," Argus said, walking back to the crowd. "Unfortunately, we've got better things to do than race some stranger across the system. So, on behalf of my crew, we're going to have to decline your offer."

"Sorry about that," Levi added, not sounding sorry at all.

The woman smirked. "No apology needed. I knew she'd find some way to weasel out of this." She laughed wickedly. "I mean, look at your ship. There's no way you'd win any kind of race with a lowly EOS-class. It's no wonder they stopped making those piles of junk."

"Excuse me!?" Levi and Kanto shouted in perfect unison.

Argus' violet eyes narrowed. "You'd best choose your next words carefully," she said in a low voice.

The threat did nothing to the woman, who rolled her eyes. "Either your ship can handle a race or it can't. It's not my fault if it or your crew aren't good enough. You know, you should've consulted someone who knew a thing or two about ships before making such a terrible purchase."

Argus stepped forward until she was directly in front of the woman. At six feet tall, Argus was the tallest member of her crew and, unlike Kanto or Quintas, she was able to go eye to eye with the stranger.

"Name and ship."

"Ilia. The Rumble. It's a Zeus-class." She smiled confidently.

Argus knew that those ships had a better speed than hers, but she also knew that her ship had something the Rumble didn't – something that would give them the winning edge. "You've got one chance to take back what you said about my ship and walk away. If you don't, then you'll end up having to eat those words."

Ilia closed her mouth and remained silent.

Argus' eyes narrowed. "I'll see you tomorrow at noon." She turned and walked back to her table, to get her coat. It'd be best to get out of the restaurant before she did something she'd regret.

As she moved to the door, the rest of her crew were quick to catch up with her.

"That was so amazing!" Kanto cheered quietly as they bundled up. "You were so powerful and commanding! You were awesome!"

Argus didn't respond. Truthfully, she hated that she'd let herself be goaded into a race by the other woman. Ilia had played them all like fiddles, knowing exactly what to say to get them riled up, and she hated that it had worked so well. Although she had no doubt that her ship would be able to win this race, she had better things to do than get caught up in petty bets.

When they reached the ship, they were greeted by a wall of heat. It was such a change from the outside temperature that they started peeling off their many layers, lest they sweat to death.

"Banu?" Argus called out to the ship's mechanic, hanging her coat up along the wall.

The door to the galley slid open and a pale face with blond hair and white eyes looked out at the group. "You're back."

Argus nodded.

"There was a bit of a situation," Levi said. "Best for us to leave quickly."

"Nice job getting the heater going," Argus said.

Banu looked down at the floor. "It was more difficult than I thought it would be, but I figured that it was important for us to have a warm place to sleep tonight, and I didn't know how long we wanted to stay here."

"Well, as luck would have it, we'll be travelling to Istra tomorrow," she said. Istra was the closest habitable planet to Rossija's sun, so they'd have no need for heaters out there. "Although 'luck' might not be the best word."

"I think the word you're looking for is 'spite,'" Quintas said helpfully.

Confusion crossed Banu's face. "I thought our next job was in the Walh System."

"This isn't a job," Kanto interjected. "This is all pleasure."

She filled Banu in on what had happened at the Kaminnyy Klub as they all moved into the galley. It was the communal area of the ship – part kitchen, part dining room, and part living room. Argus and Levi sat down on one of the couches, while Kanto and Banu took the other. Quintas went over to the fridge to get a drink, before sitting down at the table.

"So, tomorrow we're going to race to Istra and teach this Ilia whose ship is the best!" Kanto finished, smiling triumphantly.

Banu frowned. "But you said her ship was a Zeus-class."

"And?"

"And those ships have thirty percent more speed than we have. Considering the distance, it'll take us almost three hours longer to get to Istra."

Kanto laughed. "You're forgetting about CIRCE! With her, we'll be able to jack up our speed and leave them in the dust!" She mimed dusting her hands off before raising them in the air. Quintas laughed under her breath.

Banu looked down at the floor and Argus immediately sensed that something was wrong.

"Banu?" Kanto asked, finally picking up on his lack of enthusiasm. "What's wrong?"

"I... may have..." he took in a deep breath and closed his eyes. "I may have short-circuited CIRCE in my attempts to get the heater up and running."

The words came out in a jumble, but every person in the room heard them. When he finished speaking, it was so silent that you could've heard a pin drop.

"...Oh..." Kanto's eyes went wider than Argus had ever seen. "Oh, no."

"Can't you just fix it?" Quintas scoffed as she took a drink, already shrugging off the revelation.

"If it were that easy, he wouldn't've said anything," Levi threw at her.

Quintas shrugged. "I should have known we'd find some way to mess up a sure thing..." She picked up her drink and left the galley.

As Quintas walked away, Argus tried to remind herself of all the good work she had done, and how many times she'd stitched up her and Levi after some bad run-ins. Honestly, she knew that the doctor was likely putting on airs to hide her disappointment, but it didn't help the situation. Still, as much as Argus wanted to be angry at Quintas, it was her own fault for not diffusing the situation properly.

It would be easy enough to pack up the ship and move on to another system. In the long run, who'd care if they skipped out on a race with a random person in a bar on a planet they rarely visited? The answer was: she would. Her pride would remember.

Most people throughout the five systems knew better than to insult someone else's ship. It was a low blow, and one that Argus would never forgive Ilia for. She'd purchased the Aurora – or Ror, as they affectionately referred to her – when she'd started up her own transport business. After working in transport for almost a decade, she'd finally saved enough money to buy her own ship, and she'd fallen for Ror. Sure, the model was being phased out, and she wasn't as fast as other ships, and her weapons weren't as impressive, but they didn't need any of that for transporting. She loved that the ship was designed to look like the old shuttles that transported people around the universe, and the fact that it was solar-powered was a huge cost-saver. Batteries didn't come cheap these days.

Ror was also the only home she had left. After the moon she grew up on had been attacked by the Vanguard, the scourge of the universe, and her family and friends killed, Argus had nowhere to turn to but her ship. And she sure as heck wasn't going to let some other pilot insult her.

She'd thought that they would show up tomorrow and blow past Ilia's ship, leaving them so far behind that they'd have to spend hours in space knowing that they'd lost to a "lowly EOS-class." She wanted to teach Ilia that you couldn't judge a ship by its stats, and that if you wanted to goad someone into a fight then you'd better make sure that they have no chance of winning.

But none of that would matter if they couldn't fix CIRCE. She was one of Banu's many inventions, and one of Argus' favourites. She transferred power from one function to another, so if they were being chased by pirates and needed to go faster, they could take power from their weapons. Or if they found themselves in a particularly terrible asteroid field, they could boost their shields. CIRCE's energy transfers could be a real drain on the battery, but she'd gotten them out of so many scrapes that Argus couldn't hold it against her.

"How long do you think..." Argus finally said.

After a few seconds, Banu shrugged. "I'll need to purchase some items when the stores open tomorrow. I don't have all the materials I need here, and I can't really do anything until then..."

Factoring in when the shops opened, Argus calculated that they'd have about two hours to get CIRCE up and running before the race started. Considering Banu's hesitation, she knew that it would take him that long, if not longer. After doing some more mental math, she came out with a rough estimation of how long they could go without help and still manage to win.

"Could it be done in five hours? Maybe five and a half?" she asked.

He shrugged again. "Probably. If there isn't anything too terribly wrong. Now that I know how to build her, it won't be like creating her from scratch."

She nodded. There was still an opportunity to back out, give up, and run away, but on the other hand, there was still a chance that they could win. She looked over at Kanto, who still had hope in her eyes, before turning to Levi. He looked like he was doing mental calculations, his eyes darting back and forth, and his mouth screwed up in a frown. After half a minute, he looked at her and nodded.

"If we don't win, at least we'll be close enough to the sun to refuel," he said.

Argus nodded. "Banu, go make a list. As soon as the shops open tomorrow, you go out and pick up anything you think you might need."

He nodded and headed for the door.

"Kanto, Levi," she continued, "we should spend some time plotting the fastest, cleanest route to Istra. Kanto, can you get the long-range scanner from the cockpit?"

Jumping up from her seat, Kanto nodded and rushed out of the room.

Once it was just her and Levi left in the galley, Argus let out a loud sigh.

"It's gonna hurt if we lose tomorrow," she said quietly.

"Then let's not lose."

She glared at Levi. "Can't you say something useful?"

He paused to think. "Maybe the Vanguard will show up and we'll have to call the whole thing off."

Slumping onto the couch, Argus let out another sigh. It wasn't a good sign when she found herself secretly hoping for the Vanguard to appear.

The sun was high in the sky, but Klatch was just as cold as ever. Earlier in the day, Argus had done some scouting to find out where the Rumble was parked, which wasn't far away, and then figured out the half-way point between the ships. At fifteen minutes to noon, Levi and she bundled up and headed out.

It was her last ditch effort to get out of this whole mess. If Ilia didn't show up, then Argus could say that she'd tried and leave with a clean slate. They hadn't made any specific meet-up plans, but Argus wasn't about to take off on an hours-long race without knowing her opponent was prepared to do the same.

As the time moved closer to noon, she found herself hoping that Ilia wouldn't show. Banu had arrived back at the ship around nine-thirty with a box full of supplies and had been working diligently since then, but CIRCE still wasn't fixed. Although she trusted Banu's technological capabilities, she didn't feel good taking off without being prepared.

Taking in a deep breath, she checked the time. There were still five minutes left, but the second it went past noon, she was out of here. Levi let out a groan and she looked up to see someone walking their way. Swearing under her breath, she tried to push back all of her doubts and project the confidence she didn't feel.

"Didn't expect to see you here," Ilia smirked, her mocking tone evident despite the winter wear covering most of her face.

"Wanted to give you one last chance to back out," Argus fired back.

Ilia laughed. "I hope you're ready to lose."

"I hope you're ready to eat those words."

The two of them turned away and headed back to their ships, Levi following Argus closely. Nobody wanted to be late starting the race because their ship had to wait for them to get on board.

"One minute to takeoff, Cap," Kanto informed Argus. She'd already warmed up the engines and was ready to go.

Argus shrugged out of her jacket and dropped it on the floor. "As soon as it hits noon, you get off this planet as quickly as possible. And let me know if the Rumble tries to skip out early. We don't race cheaters."

"Gotcha!"

Leaning on the control panel, she went over their plan again. They'd completed numerous long-range scans last night, trying to pick up on any asteroid fields or high-gravity areas or anything else that might slow them down. They had a good, clean path to Istra, but it still wouldn't be enough for them to win without help.

Finally, the clock hit noon and it was time. As Kanto guided the ship off the planet, Argus hoped that she wasn't making a mistake.

Once they'd reached space and stabilized, Levi picked up Argus' coat. "I'm going to go check on Banu, see if he needs a hand."

Argus nodded. "I'll call you if I need you. Otherwise, give him all the help he needs – whether he realizes it or not."

"Aye, aye." He walked out of the cockpit.

Argus sat in the co-pilot chair. She knew that Ilia's ship was already gaining on them, but there was still a chance that they could win. Looking up at the clock, she put her own count-down in effect. They had three and a half hours to fix CIRCE before suffering a humiliating loss.

"Kanto…"

"Yeah, Cap?"

"If this plan fails, promise me that you'll fly us straight into the sun."

They were more than three hours into the race and it hadn't been the smoothest ride. One of the asteroid fields had ended up being bigger than they'd anticipated, so in order to not lose time, they'd had to go through part of it. Thankfully, their shields were stronger than their speed.

There wasn't much for Argus to do as they flew, other than calculate how far behind they were. Kanto was holding to the plan, flying her best, and Banu and Levi were still trying to get CIRCE up and running. Quintas was staying out of everyone's way, which was greatly appreciated.

Every minute that passed was one minute closer to failing. Ilia was about twenty-five light-minutes ahead, and in less than an hour she'd be on Istra. As much as Argus wanted to go and see what was taking Banu and Levi so long, she knew that they were doing their best. Next time she'd have to let Banu know that a warm ship wasn't as important as a functional one, and never to do anything that might risk their existing equipment. Still, she had to admit that his heater had worked wonders. He'd made the ship feel like it was on Istra instead of Klatch.

As the clock neared the zero-hour, she started fidgeting. Soon they'd reach the point of failure, where they couldn't win no matter how fast they went. Why had she thought that they could do this? As soon as Banu told them about CIRCE, she should have withdrawn and given up. Her stupid pride was going to be the death of her. Instead of taking a break between deliveries, she was wasting time trying to race a faster ship. Maybe it would be best if Kanto flew them into the sun.

Soon, there were only five seconds left before everything they did was for naught. Four. Three. Argus closed her eyes and prayed that CIRCE would be finished soon. Two. One.

It felt like time had slowed down, but the clock and ship kept going. The point of no return had been passed. Argus slumped back in the co-pilot's chair. There was no way they'd catch up now. Heck, the Rumble would have almost three hours to gloat about their win before Ror landed.

"Cap…?" Kanto said quietly.

"Yeah?"

"Did we just lose?"

She sighed. "Yeah."

"So, do we keep going?"

Argus paused. Right now she wasn't sure which would be worse – to keep going or to give up. If they gave up, then Ilia would have the satisfaction in knowing that they were quitters, and if they kept going, the next four hours were going to be painful – filled with dread for what would be awaiting them once they landed. Neither option sounded good.

Although she didn't receive an answer, Kanto kept the

ship on course.

The mood in the cockpit shifted drastically to one of resignation. Usually, Argus enjoyed watching the flight through space. As long as they weren't dodging space junk or other ships, it could be peaceful with darkness all around them. She wished she could pretend this was merely a normal journey and enjoy it.

Suddenly she heard footsteps running towards the room. She turned just in time to see the door slide open and Levi burst in.

"Punch it, Kanto!" he said, smiling despite his heavy breathing. "CIRCE's back!"

The two women stared at Levi.

"Can't you see the clock?" Kanto asked. "We lost."

Levi looked up. They were now eight minutes past their three and a half hour deadline. He shook his head. "We've still got time."

Argus gave him a flat look. "How? Are you going to get out and push?"

"No, I did the math. We've got time."

She was confused. "I did the math, too."

"And how many decimal points did you go back?" He raised an eyebrow.

Something clicked in her brain. "Kanto, punch it!"

Levi laughed as Kanto pushed the ship to the highest speed. "You're good at math, Captain, but not as good as me."

"Shut up, Levi," she shot back, but it was impossible to keep the glee out of her voice. Her heart started to race as she sat up in the chair. "How long until we reach Istra?"

"Approximately 45 minutes at top speed."

"And the Rumble?"

"Approximately 50 minutes." He smiled brightly. "See, we even managed to give you a few to spare."

The rest of the trip went faster than it should have. Quintas and Banu joined them in the cockpit to watch the scanner as they closed the distance on the Rumble. There was one tense moment when they hit a patch of space debris outside of Yasny, but the prospect of winning seemed to have renewed Kanto's vigor and she flew through it with no hesitation.

Forty-two minutes after they'd reached top speed, they caught up to the Rumble. Argus wished that they could fly up next to them and wave as they passed by, but instead she had Kanto keep a good distance while instructing Banu to hide their ship ID. She wanted Ilia to think that they were still behind them, and to not realize that the ship that'd blown past them was the very one she'd mouthed off about.

"The minute we hit the ground, we book it to Solnechnyy Restoran," Argus informed everyone. "We've got a five minute head-start, which isn't much time, and I want us to be laid back and relaxing when Ilia's crew comes in."

"I've reserved the landing spot closest to the restaurant," Levi said. "It'll be faster to walk than to take the ATV, so be ready to go as soon as the ship's parked. Clear?"

Everyone nodded. The competitive spirit had infected the entire crew, including Banu, who hadn't even met Ilia, and they were practically vibrating with excitement.

When the ship touched down, everyone except for Kanto was standing next to the exit. As soon as the engines turned off, the door was open and they were gone. Kanto caught up to them a minute later, having promised Argus that she'd followed proper shut-down protocol and locked the door.

The hostess at Solnechnyy Restoran was startled by the group's sudden appearance, but found them a table and brought them all drinks. Argus looked around the room, at the unfamiliar restaurant goers, and felt all the tension drain out of her.

Seven minutes later, the door to the restaurant opened and Ilia strolled in with her crew. They were laughing and smiling, but then Ilia saw Argus and her crew, and her expression changed to utter disbelief.

"How did you get here?" Ilia asked as she stormed over to the table.

"I could have sworn that we told you about our ship," Argus replied.

Ilia shook her head. "No. You cheated somehow. You were way behind us."

"Guess our ship's better than yours," Kanto gloated.

"But I've got a Zeus-class!"

"Maybe next time you shouldn't judge a ship by its class," Argus said helpfully.

Ilia opened her mouth to say something, but then she let out a frustrated sound and stomped away.

Argus laughed and raised her glass for a toast.

Lindsay Kitson

From Portage La Prairie, Manitoba, Kitson has had several stories published in the past, including 'The Maelstrom at the End of the World' in *Athena's Daughters Volume Two*, 'Cod Liver Oil' in *Parallel Prairies*, and, 'Two Foxes' in *Keycon Chapbook*.

She has been honoured with the First to Solo award, given by Women in Aviation. She holds a commercial pilot's license, float and multi-engine instrument ratings, and currently works as a bush pilot in central Manitoba.

Aurora One

The skies have been empty for thirty years.

I walk out onto the apron to gaze at the faded orange and white striped windsock at Saint James Richardson International Airport. It's horizontal, in a wind straight down runway three-six.

Good old CYWG. Here is where I started my career as a young man, flying air taxi forty years ago, in an age when people still patted women pilots on the head and said, "That's wonderful that more women are getting into aviation."

And then five years into my career the oil wells dried up. Biodiesel has never been a viable option – all the arable land in the world couldn't produce enough fuel to keep North America running.

They managed to keep some of the small refineries going – there's still trucks on the road, but not many. The roads across the country are in such disrepair with no fuel to power the equipment to repair them that anything on them nearly has to be all terrain. No one's making Avgas or Jet-A anymore. Thousands of planes sit in hangars, rusting their great hearts out, paint peeling, leather seats cracking. Nothing but dust in the fuel lines.

Until now.

I look over my shoulder at the Cessna Caravan on the apron. It shines with a fresh coat of paint still curing, but dry enough for today. There's no Air Canada anymore, or any other airline. They all dissolved when the fuel ran out. We were all shocked enough that Canada managed to hold together as a country at all. The US broke down into city states and small nations – not enough of them could agree on enough things to hold them together. They tried to annex Canada early on, before things broke down, but then winter came and they went home.

Canada's a big country, and collecting taxes is kind of a bastard when everybody's all spread out like they are. But then they noticed the roads were getting even worse, and people kind of realized the socialism thing maybe wasn't so bad and ponied up for the most part. Six months ago, they had a referendum on getting planes back in the air.

Now, they whined about the cost of roads, and sewer maintenance, and telephone line maintenance, and what not else, but there's something about a plane that says to the world, "We're not just okay, we're rockin'." Got people right in the feels and the referendum approved funding to start work.

I love the smell of Jet-A in the morning. Used to have a t-shirt that said that.

No Jet-A smell today. The Caravan is converted. New tech: miniaturized molten salt reactor replaced the turbofan engine. They didn't want to bother getting the old Pratts running again, with no fuel to run them. They want something sustainable. Not just a plane for today. A plane for tomorrow.

And they put out a call for pilots. Thirty years ago, there were seventy thousand pilots in Canada. Three quarters of them had been set to retire in a few years – now most of them are dead, and a good bunch of them too old to fly. There were no new pilots, but they put out a call, and every pilot who still thought they could fly answered. Who among us wouldn't? Thirty years grounded, and a chance to get back in the sky? If you think we wouldn't, you don't understand pilots.

Most of us didn't pass the medical. Only two of us did: me and Joey. We drew straws, and I got the short one, making him pilot and me co-pilot.

After Joey's heart attack six months ago, they almost imported another pilot from god knows where. I convinced them not to. Instead, they pulled together a group of youngsters with lofty dreams and stuck them in old flight simulators. They narrowed it down and let me pick a co-pilot from a group of ten young men and women. Well, nine young men and one woman.

The mechanics wave us over. I turn to my co-pilot. "Ready?"

"Hell yeah," says Jill.

See, what us old airmen know, is woman pilots have to work twice as hard to get taken half as seriously. I picked Jill.

Once in the plane, I adjust my seat and wait for the mechanics to clear the area. Jill hands me the checklist. She's businesslike – got a safe attitude, steady nerves – she'll be a good pilot.

I follow a checklist pieced together from the original Caravan checklist and steps added special for the new engine. The reaction keeps going even when the prop is disengaged; it just slows down. There's a lever that engages the prop shaft, then electric switches to control the flow of Thorium into the reactor. I flip some switches and the engine engages with the reactor. The prop starts slowly at first, like a turbine. People say it doesn't sound that much different from a turboprop, but for a pilot who used to fly them, it does. It's hard to describe, but it starts smooth, without the screaming whir of turbine vanes. Still a roar, still very much alive. I wish I knew more about the insides. Jill knows more. She's all up on that stuff.

A group of photographers from news agencies all over the country – some even further – snap pictures while I raise the wing flaps and turn on the avionics. My heart's pounding, but it has nothing to do with the photographers.

I know the engine's been tested; it's been run eighty times since they finished installing it. The mechanics know what they're doing, and every millimetre of this aircraft has been inspected. And still I've got nerves like a goddam student pilot going on their first solo.

I don't let Jill suspect.

"Winnipeg tower, Aurora flight number one, on apron six ready to taxi," I say, my finger on the radio button.

"Aurora one, Tower, clear to taxi charlie, uh, hold short three-six."

I laugh. He sounds like a new controller on his first day. There's no other planes in the sky to make it worth even classifying airspace, but they still want to use all the old procedures. They're planning for the future.

I lift my feet off the brakes and let the plane roll forward. I can't hear them over the engine, but the crowd gathered goes nuts. It's the first time in thirty years anyone's seen a plane move under its own power. Actually it's not – we've been taxiing around the apron for months testing things, but the crowd don't know the difference.

We roll out onto the taxiway and sit short of runway

three-six to finish the last checks. Hold the brakes and gun the engine, check fuel, check suction, check oil. I pass my hand across the instrument panel, old habits returning. Check instruments left to right, to keep from missing one.

The engine checks out fine.

"Tower, Aurora one, holding short of three-six, ready for take-off."

"Aurora one, Tower, cleared for take-off."

"I can't believe how many people are out there," says Jill.

"You want to do the take off?" I ask.

"Really?"

I smirk. There'll be lots of time later to fly myself if this goes well. It feels good to be able to give this moment to her. I take my hands off the controls and prop my arms up, one on the window and the other on the back of Jill's seat. "She's all yours. Once around the circuit."

Jill bites her lip. She's nervous, but I'm not worried about her. We roll forward onto the newly paved runway and turn to line up on the centre line. This runway is four times as long as we need to take off and land, but it's funny seeing the mile of runway ahead of us, looking like it goes on forever. Because it does. There's a quote, damned if I can remember who said it, but it goes, *"A mile of highway will take you a mile, but a mile of runway can take you anywhere."*

Jill pauses, looks at me.

"What are you lookin' at me for?" I say. "Let's get this bird in the air."

Jill nods, takes a deep breath, and pushes the throttle forward to full power. The engine roars, and we surge forward, yawing to the left just a little before Jill gets the rudder in to correct it and keep us on the runway. Sims don't hold a candle to actual flying – it'll take her some getting used to yet. But she'll be fine.

The airspeed indicator kicks in, reading thirty knots, forty knots.

"Airspeed alive," Jill acknowledges, like I taught her.

Seconds feel like minutes as we gain speed. We're loaded light, all but empty, so we can lift off at around sixty-five safely. Fifty knots goes by. Fifty-five. Sixty. These are the moments when, even when you've taken off hundreds of times, every once in a while, you remember you're surrounded by nothing but a well-organized bunch of aluminum and fibreglass with a giant fan stuck to the front, and that thing's supposed to take you up in the air, and it all seems so goddam insane for that one moment and then…

Jill hesitates again, and I prompt, "And rotate."

Jill keeps her eyes forward, glancing again at our airspeed, and pulls back on the control column. Gently at first, then firmly.

And the wheels leave the ground.

Jeff Slade

A resident of Salmon Cove, Slade is a prize-winning author and avid reader who enjoys both making and hearing puns, playing the guitar, and cats.

Slade has previously been featured in 2018's *Chillers from the Rock* with his short story 'The Culling,' and in 2019's *Dystopia from the Rock* with his story 'Anchored.' His award-winning story, *Extinguished*, was featured in *Kit Sora: The Artobiography*.

Flight of the Puffin

The ocean was always angry.

An endless, impossibly dark blue undulating body of water, rippling and shimmering as far as Alice could see. Periodically a whitecap emerged and fumbled about for a few seconds before the hungry sea swallowed it whole. So dark she could've sworn it was a swarm of shadows, they wrestled and struggled with each other beneath an infinitely stretched navy sheet. Silent as the grave, it constantly moved and shuddered before her eyes.

Each morning Alice had the same dream. When she'd finally rouse from her slumber, the night would be surrendering its grip on the sky, bleeding from a deep purple bruise into a pale mixture of light blues and whites, a bandage for the previous evening's wounds.

She didn't need to set an alarm. Decades of living on a farm had instilled a natural clock within her. Each day she woke at the same time, put the same kettle on, made the same cup of tea. The only thing that had changed in recent years was the number of cups she'd had to make.

Sighing to herself, Alice got up and made her bed, then made her way to the kitchen to put the kettle on. The wooden floorboards and stairs creaked in protest as they always did. She ignored them like she always did.

While each day started the same, Alice's day-to-day life had changed significantly since Fred had gone off to the war. Her niece had taken in the few farm animals they'd had left; Alice just wasn't capable of keeping proper care of them. In exchange, her niece provided her with regular supplies of fresh eggs and milk on her weekly visits.

She removed some of those very same eggs from the fridge and broke them open over a pan on the stove. A glance at her calendar, the top of which was emblazoned with 'Compliments of Purity Factories, all the best in 1943,' reminded her that she was due for another visit from her niece any day now.

Those visits were the only regular human contact she had any more. She and Fred had been unable to have children, so there were no kids or grandchildren of which to speak. Alice had only had one sibling, who'd passed away in a car accident some years ago, leaving her with the one niece.

Aside from her lone relative, no strangers came to visit either. She vividly remembered the last one who'd knocked on her door over a year ago: the crispness of his uniform, the strained look upon his face, the thin manila envelope clutched tightly in his hands.

That envelope had turned Alice's world upside down, had brought it all crashing down around her. She clucked her tongue at the memory, and that particular choice of words. Missing in action, it'd read. Fred had been flying a supply run, carrying troops and much needed provisions to remotely located soldiers along with several other planes when they'd been ambushed, caught unawares over the ocean with no ground support to assist them. It'd been like shooting fish in a barrel.

Alice looked out the window at the water in the harbour, colloquially known as Torbay Bight, the harbour that connected directly to the Atlantic Ocean. The same ocean in which Fred's plane went down, though a vast number of miles apart. He nor his plane were ever recovered.

The hissing from the stove told her the eggs were ready. Turning off the burner, she slid them onto an old plate before she fetched a fork and knife. A few rolls remained on the kitchen counter, and she took those to the table too. They'd been Fred's favourite; he'd snatch one off of the tray as soon as she'd removed it from the oven and eat it plain, no butter at all. *Sure you're sweet enough as 'tis, he'd say, and you made 'em with your own hands.*

Fred. He'd gone to the war because he wanted to go, needed to go. He was well into his fifties when he'd left, signing up for pilot duty. He'd flown all his life, mostly chartered flights on smaller crafts on the mainland before he'd retired and bought the farm here back home, and he knew they needed experienced pilots.

Don't you worry, Ally, he'd said, no fighter planes for me. They need someone to bring supplies to the boys, and who am I to say no? It was no use talking to him, he'd had his mind made up before he'd even told Alice.

The worst part was that Alice didn't blame him.

Little did most people know, but she had been bitten by the flying bug herself. When they moved back home to Newfoundland in the mid-1930's and acquired the farm, Fred had also purchased a small plane for crop dusting purposes. While she knew he'd loved flying, his times crop dusting on the farm had been the first time Alice had actually seen him in the air, and his enthusiasm was infectious.

When he bought a Piper J-3 cub that came standard

with tandem seats, she forced him to take her with him. Before long, she made him give her flying lessons, and in no time, she was able to fly the plane herself. They never told anyone, and if anyone had asked, she was just the passenger -- most people around those parts wouldn't know the difference.

Some of her favourite memories with Fred took place in their plane, which they'd christened *The Puffin*. Spraying the crops required a little diving; the plane had to be fairly low in order to maximize the delivery of its payload. They'd made a game out of it, seeing who dared to dive the lowest before pulling up and over the crops. Once she'd gone so low, she swore the plane's wheels had brushed against the carrot tops. Fred had joked if he'd have reached out, he could've plucked one up with his bare hands.

The plane, a factory chrome yellow model, lay dormant in a garage on the outskirts of their farm, having laid that way since Fred left nearly two years ago. Neighbours had helped Alice out after Fred's departure, but since she received the news that fateful day nothing had grown in their fields.

She gazed out through the kitchen window at the barren landscape that had once been their livelihood. Alice knew she should make an appointment with the bank soon, that she should come up with a plan, something, anything. She didn't want to, not today anyway.

Standing up, she put her dirty dishes in the sink next to the pan and rinsed them off. The washing could wait. Instead, she felt an impulse she'd not felt in some time. So she got dressed and headed outside.

It was a short walk to the shed, and the early morning June light helped Alice find her way once she'd thrown the double wooden doors open. Inside, nestled amongst several barrels of fuel, pesticide, and a table of various tools, was their plane. While it hadn't been airborne since Fred left, she would come and visit it every now and then, keeping it clean and in working order, ready for the day he returned.

Even after she'd found out that day would never come, still she visited. It brought her peace of mind, thinking of soaring through the blue skies and not lingering on the cold, dark ocean which haunted her dreams.

She ran her hand along its cool metal exterior, peering into the empty cockpit as she walked past it. Her fingers slid down lower, running over the black lightning bolt that was slightly faded from years of use. It still energized Alice, however, and reminded her of better days. Less lonely days.

Her foot banged against one of the wooden blocks placed in front of the plane's wheels, keeping it in place. There was one on either side, and she stared down at the one nearest her. The wood had aged, but was still strong, still did its job, holding things back.

Alice kicked the block out from under the wheel, then went to the other side and did the same to its counterpart. With both blocks gone, it wasn't hard to wheel the plane out of the garage far enough for her to open the cockpit. A quick check of the fuel gauge showed it was still full, the indicator bobbing high, and the trim was still properly set.

Once she checked the oil, she leaned into the cockpit and turned the fuel on, then primed the engine. Alice moved back to the propeller and turned it once, twice, three times. *Third time's a charm, after all,* Fred's voice reminded her. She gave it a hard turn the fourth time and the engine roared to life.

Alice quickly popped back into the cockpit and took a deep breath. Her hand went for the brakes, slowly releasing them and moving the plane completely out of the garage at long last. It felt good to feel the sun on her face, different somehow than moments earlier when she'd been on her feet.

She taxied out along the well-worn path they'd always used for takeoffs and landings, which also doubled as their driveway. They owned several acres of land, their nearest neighbour being several miles away, and the ocean ran along the entire eastern side of their Torbay property.

Once she'd picked up enough speed, Alice pushed forward on the stick, raising the tail of the aircraft, and then pulled it back, lifting the plane up into the air. It wasn't the fastest of aircraft, but she was thrilled nevertheless to be soaring through the air once again. Alice took a few laps around the farm, going higher and higher with each turn, until her home and its surroundings shrank to the size of her hand.

That's how you know you're high enough, Fred's voice echoed in her memory, and she pictured him holding his hand up and over their house on the ground below them. She mirrored the action, squinting as the morning sun reflected off the windows before her hand blocked it out. *There we go, just right.*

Alice took a wide right turn, soaring over her property and heading for the nearby harbour. She'd occasionally flown out there with Fred, but never on her own. There were going to be several ships visiting St. John's harbour that week, even some visiting from the Royal Navy fleet according to the newspaper, so maybe she'd catch a glimpse of one of them coming in or out of the Narrows.

The air almost immediately felt cooler on her skin as she flew over the water. It mixed nicely with the warm summer sun, and Alice briefly closed her eyes. The hum of the engine, the gentle swaying with the wind, brought her a modicum of peace she'd not felt for some time.

When she opened her eyes, she found herself surrounded by blue, as water stretched out below and before her almost as far as she could see. A slight finger of land stuck out on the right side, the last outstretching part of the harbour before it surrendered to the Atlantic. Even the copse of trees, so thick and huddled together on the land, receded into dots and dashes the further out they got before fully yielding to the water.

A flash of light once again caught her eye, not unlike the glare she'd seen earlier from the windows of her home. Alice leaned forward and squinted, trying to make out its source. It appeared to be a dark outcropping of rock, jutting just off the harbour's edge, or perhaps it was a whale? It was large and cylindrical shaped, floating and --

She froze once she realized what it was.

A U-boat.

It had breached the surface and was sitting there, while one of its crew appeared to be looking around the harbour with a pair of binoculars. Alice recalled that the submarines needed to resurface every so often to refresh their air supply, and this probably had seemed like a remote enough area for them to do so, even in the early morning hours.

Why were they there though, she wondered. The war had always been a European affair in her mind, all the more reason why she'd been perplexed at Fred's insistence to serve. Sure, there had been a handful of reported instances in the newspapers where U-boats had been spotted around the Maritimes, but surely there was nothing of value here, in Alice's home, for them to take?

They'd already taken her Fred. What more could they possibly take from her?

Then she recalled St. John's harbour, the Royal Navy. Could this boat be part of a sneak attack?

Before Alice could ruminate on it any further, the German sailor had spied her sailing across the harbour. *The Puffin* moved slowly at the best of times, and even as she yanked the stick to bank away from the boat, it was too late.

A hail of fire from the sub's exterior mounted flak gun peppered her, tinging and pinging as metal met metal and perforated the fabric portions of the plane. The aircraft shook and wobbled, unsure of itself, and Alice looked down to try and gauge the damage.

Her eyes stopped when she saw the mess of her right leg, and the trail of blood that flowed freely from it. Shrapnel from the plane had sliced her open; if the guns had struck her directly, it would've caused far more damage, but this still looked pretty bad. *Funny*, she thought, *I don't feel anything*. Moving her head back a little, she saw spurts of red as they plumed behind her, spilled down, down, contrasted starkly against the blue waters below.

Is this what Fred saw? Alice snapped her head back forward, moving the stick back in the other direction to avoid going into a tailspin. The U-boat was coming back into sight now, and the gunfire ceased for the moment. She could still make out the sailor, doing something with the flak gun.

There was no radio on her plane, and no way for her to contact anyone about what she'd found. It would only be a matter of time before she crashed and the U-boat slid back underneath the waves, bound to take St. John's harbour by surprise.

Alice knew what she had to do.

She gripped the stick tightly and, with a jerk, put *The Puffin* into a nosedive, aiming for the U-boat ahead and below her. The sailor stopped whatever he'd been doing and was gesticulating wildly; Alice figured he was yelling and ordering whomever was listening to dive or move out of the way or something.

It'd be too late for him, she thought. Just like it was too late for her. Too late for Fred.

She closed her eyes again and thought back to her dreams, to the angry dark blue waters and the shadows that wriggled underneath. She thought again for the thousandth time about what Fred might have seen, crashing into the waters of the same ocean, only at its other end. About how, despite the physical distance, she'd finally be reunited with him.

The wind roared louder and louder. Alice smiled, her eyes still tightly shut.

The ocean finally became calm.

Sara Burke

An Alberta native, Burke is a prize winning author, winning both the May 2019 and August 2019 Kit Sora Flash Fiction Prizes with her stories 'Bubbly' and 'One Up, One Down.' Both were featured in *Kit Sora: The Artobiography*.

She is a volunteer for the organization committee of Sci-Fi on the Rock, and in her spare time crafts, draws and paints.

Burke brings with her her short story 'Grey Jay.'

Grey Jay

This was it. This was the time she would do it. She would run to the edge and leap. Jayne's eyes were fixed on the end of the branch, her heart pounding in her chest. She could do it, you know. The other chicks made fun of her for being so small. She was not as developed as her peers, and she still had a few tufts of baby down sticking out from the top of her head.

"What do *they* know about flying anyway?" Jayne thought to herself. Most of the other hatchlings had only managed to flutter down to the southern branch of the home tree, but they didn't hesitate to rub it in her face. Jayne was a fair bit younger than the other birds in her year. Usually, her kind do not lay twice in a season, but then little Jayne arrived. Mister and Missus Grey were thrilled to have Jayne -- having lost their first clutch of the year -- but being small made her an easy target. Unbeknownst to her her parents, Jayne had snuck down to a solitary branch every day and tried her hardest to practice flying. However, unbeknownst to Jayne, on this particular morning, the older nestlings happened to see her hopping down the tree and followed her.

"*I can do this*," Jayne whispered. "I *know* I can do it this time" She attempted to smooth her tufts down, but they did not like to behave. Her eyes narrowed, focusing on the end of her runway. It was much larger than she thought, but this was it. She had tried before and had almost made it to the end, but lost her nerve. This time it was all the way to the end. She took a deep breath and started to run.

"CAT!" squawked Cadence, the oldest and most nasty of the group. Jayne whipped her head around, and as she did her foot caught a small wrinkle in the bark. She tumbled beak over tail feathers, landing at the foot of the small crowd. Her folly was met with a cacophony of laughter.

"Aww, poor Jayney can't even walk, let alone fly!" cackled Cadence, to the snickers of her friends. Jayne's eyes brimmed with tears.

"What's the matter, cat got your tongue?" one of the others had shouted, leading to another round of laughter.

Jayne's cheeks burned red through her grey feathers. She scrambled to her feet, but her words became tangled in her throat. She *couldn't* do this. Fighting back the tears, she swallowed hard, and began to run.

Jayne spent the next two days in her nest with a knot in her stomach. Her parents urged her to go back out and try again. They offered to teach her. To be there in case "*those miscreants*" returned. This idea was immediately dismissed, as she knew the only thing more humiliating than being teased by your fellow yearlings is having your parents fight your battles for you. No, Jayne was going to stay in the nest, where it was safe.

On the third morning, Mister and Missus Grey left earlier than usual to gather the stored food from their favourite harvesting tree. When Jayne was smaller they would take turns going out, but lately they had been going together. They would usually return around mid morning and give Jayne some insects to snack on, but on this day they did not return. When the sun hit high noon, Jayne peeked out of the nest, and by mid afternoon she began to worry. She poked her head out of the nest, craning her neck around in vain, trying to catch a glimpse of her parents. She hopped up on the edge of the nest and down to the edge of their branch, but the forest was blocking her view. She climbed all the way to the top of the tree, then all the way to the bottom branches, but still she could not see them. She did not in fact see anyone. She called out, but no one answered. It became apparent to Jayne that it was eerily quiet for a forest full of birds. She found her way to the southern branch and hopped all the way to the end, peering down to the forest floor. She saw the lacy shadows of the ground and realized just how far down she could have fallen. If she had failed to glide on her first leap, she might not have survived the fall. Perhaps it was a *good* thing her practice session was interrupted by the others. Her stomach unknotted slightly.

"Hello?" she whispered to the earth, but she could hear nothing except the spring breeze slipping by.

"Is anyone out there?" she said to the bushes, but there was nothing.

"They probably lost track of time," she thought, turning away from the edge, the absence of the community weighing on her, "perhaps they are all off flying together without me…"

In her distraction, she almost missed the pair of wide glassy eyes staring at her from the base of the southern branch.

A large, brown, and rather gnarled looking tabby cat was perched flat on the branch, eyes locked on Jayne. It had slunk silently up the trunk and stalked her for several minutes. Its great green eyes adjusted rapidly, triangulating its target. Jayne had no time to think before the beast leapt towards her, its wild paws slapping the branch in an attempt to trap her.

Jayne leapt back, flapping as hard as she could. She tumbled down towards the dark underbrush. The wind ripped past her face as she tried to hold her wings steady. The air rushed into her arms, catching her just before she hit the ground. Gliding was not flying, but under the circumstances she would take it. She managed to travel several feet before landing in a thick evergreen bush. Heart pounding in her ears, she looked back to see the cat beginning to climb down the tree. Jayne tried to flap her arms, but they were not yet strong enough to create lift, so she did the only other thing she could do: Jayne began to run.

The beast was fast, much faster than her. She clambered farther and farther into the thick brush, until the passage became much too narrow for something as large as the tabby.

"What's the matter?" Jayne called to the cat "Can't fit?"

It paced back and forth eyeing her, its tail twitching in annoyance. It tried scratching at the wood and digging at the earth, but it could not find its way into the safety of Jayne's evergreen grove. The beast chittered and chirped, yowled and growled, and finally made a disgruntled chortle and sulkily slinked away.

Jayne's chest swelled with excitement. Not only did she glide, she escaped a bloodthirsty beast completely unscathed! She could not wait to get home and tell the older nestlings about her harrowing adventure. She would no longer be made fun of for being small and weak. Her colony would hang off her every word, asking her to repeat their favourite parts for weeks to come. She took a step in the direction of home.

Jayne looked around. She remembered going left, perhaps... Or was it right? The excited bubble ready to burst in her chest quickly deflated, hanging heavy in her stomach. She was utterly lost.

She hopped hopefully up the entwined limbs of her bushy fortress, but she did not seem to recognize anything. The cat was gone, but the terror of the encounter crept slowly up her back, and she shivered. It could still be out there. She wanted to go home, but there was no indication of which way would take her there. The trees all looked the same. She sat defeated on the tallest branch of the thicket and began to weep. She would never find her parents. She would never fly. She would likely starve, as she had not yet been taught to forage.

Her stomach growled, and Jayne realized she had not eaten today.

"But, I glided," she told herself, "I did that on my own. I escaped that mongrel in the tree, and I am alive. I can do this, too. I just need to think about what to do next."

Jayne thought back to all the food stores her parents had brought back. Insects and spiders, berries from last season, bits of fungi, and some strange meaty substance that she could not readily identify. She had remembered her parents telling her they stored food under bits of bark for the winter, so she decided that was a good place to start.

Jayne picked at bark, looked behind rocks, and turned over leaves and twigs. She wandered all over the forest looking for bits of food, but to no avail. She thought perhaps she could try flying, and let from some branches of a small shrubbery flapping her wings. She was weak at flight, and weaker from lack of food. She had began to lose hope, when she spotted a plump hen eyeing her from a fair distance away. She swiftly traversed the forest floor in Jayne's direction, and to her amusement Jayne noticed she had behind her no less than eight young.

"Why Hello there!" called the hen, "You look like you could use some help! Did you lose something?"

"No, I'm… I'm fine" said Jayne "I just need to get home."

"Home? Well, you won't get there unless you live under that twig!" she said cheerfully.

Jayne furrowed her brow. "No, I don't live down here, I am just… looking for something to eat."

Jayne explained her predicament to the hen, who had now introduced herself as Mrs. Willow, and by the end of the story the children stared at her in awe.

"Can she join us for dinner momma?" peeped one of the children.

"Yes! That would be so much fun!" chirped another.

"Please, can she?" squeaked a third, and by then all eight children we excitely chatting over each other about their new hero Jayne.

"Of course!" clucked Mrs. Willow. "If Jayne would like to join us in a forage she is more than welcome. Maybe we can even help her find her way home!"

As it turned out the Willows and Jayne shared some common likes, and dined that night on a variety of insects and plants they found on the forest floor. Jayne felt very welcome here, and for the first time in her life was delighted to have friends. She raced the children around the floor, laughing and chirping whenever she'd get close to catching them, but they were quite swift. Jayne considered a life on the ground. It wouldn't be so bad if she could live with the Willows, but she would miss her parents greatly. That evening they nested together in a place Mrs. Willow had arranged.

Jayne fell into a deep sleep, finally feeling safe.

"Momma?" whispered Ava, the smallest Willow child. "Is Jayne going to live with us?"

"No, child. She has her own momma. We have to bring her home," cooed Mrs. Willow, putting her wing over Ava.

"Momma, do you think we will find sister Mary with Jayne's momma?" she said as she began to drift to sleep.

"Wouldn't that be nice," she said.

Jayne lived with the Willows for several weeks, learning the life of the grouse. The summer had come, and the warm air was ripe with the scent of flowers and spruce trees. The eight Willow children had grown considerably, and without realizing it so had Jayne.

Over the time she had spent with her adoptive family, she learned a lot more than she would have at home in her nest. She learned some quick turn maneuvers for running, how to forage for different types of plants, and how to tell directions by the sun. She was content with her new flock.

On the hottest day of summer, Mrs. Willow suggested they take a trip to some chokecherry trees that should be fruiting by now. She described them as a deliciously bitter treat, so of course all nine children agreed excitedly. When they reached the chokecherry alcove, the children exploded in every direction, picking the berries as fast as they could. Jayne was suddenly hit with a memory of this flavour from her nestling days. She remembered her parents occasionally bringing back these berries from their food caches.

"I know this!" she said, "I know this flavour! Maybe we are near my home!"

With that a group of very familiar birds came swooping down from the treetops.

"Oh My GOSH!" squawked Cadence. "Is that Jayne?"

"We thought you *DIED*!" gaped another.

"After that cat chased you out of the tree, we thought you were a goner for sure!" called one from the back. An excited murmur reverberated through the crowd, and Jayne almost didn't notice the Willows coming to stand beside her. She had found her community, albeit the ones she missed the least. It turned out her home tree was due north of the chokecherry grove and she could be home within the hour.

Mrs. Willow hid her sadness well. Although she knew it wouldn't last, she had enjoyed Jayne being a member of her flock. Jayne turned to the Willows with a smile.

"I get to go home!" she beamed. "I will see my parents again!"

She paused. "Where is Ava?"

They frantically searched the trees. The jays searched above, the grouses searched below, but Ava was missing.

Unknowingly to them, Ava had gone looking for her lost sister Mary.

Unknowingly to Ava, Mary had been taken by a large brown tabby months earlier.

Jayne ran between the trees, darting, turning, running as fast as she could. She called Ava's name as she leapt into the air, flapping, taking off into the sky.

"Ava!" she called, "AVA!"

She spotted the smallest Willow child wandering

south of the alcove. She saw a large brown tabby as its ears perked up, and turned its head towards Ava. Jayne's heart sank. The beast was going to strike Ava down at any moment, and she had no idea.

"Mary!" Ava called "Mary! Are you here?"

The wide eyed beast slowly approached the unattended Ava, its haunches raised as it poised itself to attack. It moved with purpose -- and only when Ava moved -- its paws inching closer.

"You don't need to hide Mary!" Ava said "It's me! Come out!"

The cat pounced.

Jayne dove as fast as she could, twisting at the last moment. She spread her wings on each descent trying to make herself larger in appearance. She quickly turned, and swooped back at the tabby again and again. She screeched and scratched, and pecked in desperation.

Ava, startled by the sudden appearance of both the tabby and Jayne, ran and hid behind a tree. She watched in awe as the battle ensued.

The cat swiped its claws at Jayne, catching her in the leg. Jayne tumbled, but caught herself before she hit the ground.

"Back off!" she yelled "Stay away from my sister!"

The cat jumped up and grabbed Jayne by the wing this time, and she fell to the ground. The scene was silent for a moment. The beast had paused and readied itself to pounce once more. Jayne breathed heavily, and tried to get up. She was exhausted and stunned; she just hoped Ava was safe.

The cat raised and wiggled its back legs. This was it.

The Jays and the Willow family emerged suddenly from the tree line. They descended upon the tabby, surrounding it. They chirped, and chattered, and screeched, and cackled. They flapped, and swooped, and dove, and scratched. The beast became so disoriented it did the only thing it could. It ran.

And they cheered.

Jayne flew. She didn't have to think about it; she just did it. She tumbled and soared to the tops of the trees, perching happily on the top of the tallest one she could find. It was there she saw it, her home tree.

"It's there!" she called down to the Willows. "Follow me!"

All nine of the Willows sprinted between the trees, glancing up at Jayne to keep on track. They reached her home tree just as the sun began to sink behind the skyline.

"Mom! Dad!" Jayne called "I'm home!"

Mister and Missus Grey ran to their daughter, embracing their lost child, not letting go for several minutes. The community of Jays had all gathered at the news of the lost Jayne returning home. They invited the Willows to stay in their territory as long as they liked, and they happily agreed.

The young Jays who had once mocked her were now astounded by what Jayne had grown into. They complimented her flying and her bravery against the cat. Jayne thanked them, but had come to realize that their opinion didn't matter much to her anymore.

She spent her time now with her parents, foraging and storing food, or with the Willows running around with the now almost fully grown children.

She left her nest, and soared.

Matthew Daniels

Matthew hails from the mythical village of St. John's, where he gave up his youth in exchange for a quiver of ghost arrows. They include short stories written in local collections such as *Paragon, Kit Sora: The Artobiography, Sci-Fi from the Rock, Fantasy from the Rock, Chillers from the Rock,* and *Dystopia from the Rock.* He has since misplaced them, but he has really nice slippers. It is rumored that his beard sometimes volunteers with Sandbox Gaming. Long story.

Matthew is one of only three authors to have his work featured in each of the five modern *From the Rock* anthologies.

Rooftop Statistics

It was finally Scrawl's turn today. She'd flown the seas many times, but never before had she been allowed to approach any of the continents. Above her was still the shuffling light and weight of the sky-pierced ocean. Her community, the Cluster, was a kind of half-industrial, semi-ruinous Atlantis; a floating underwater dome; a refugee camp of Humans and crashed crystal aliens. And they needed help.

:Why are you showing me this?: Scrawl didn't have to speak her words. She thought them, and they were heard. In the present, she stood – but her mind was transported to the past.

:You asked why I've been feeling heavier lately.: Ballast answered. He was a Lenu, one of the sapient crystal people, and he was a father to her. :Well, these thoughts have been weighing on me lately.:

Scrawl was in Ballast's telepathic memory projection. In it, a Hindi woman was breathing heavily. A white man Scrawl recognized as her birth father stood worrying nearby. She was seeing this from an adjustable stool on which Ballast had been set.

Next to Ballast was the Dragon known to the Cluster as Vega. Scrawl had never met – nor even heard of – any other Dragon. In this memory, Vega looked much more powerful than she did in the present. They had a presence. Even with newborn Scrawl before them, a gravity of awe coaxed her parents' attention in Vega's direction.

Back then, Vega was a blue-tinged, molten light. Lining her back were many long pairs of winged arms. The upper pairs were spread out in a majestic pose and her tail encircled the group.

Others were with the parents, one or two Lenus and at least one more Human – probably a doctor or midwife. Most of the past Ballast's attention (and, therefore, Scrawl's) was directed at the newborn. Once the child had been cleaned, the father and the midwife helped her mom sit up a little better to see. They hadn't handed the baby to the mother yet because something was…different.

"Her name is Scrawl," the mother said.

The father kissed her forehead and then walked around the baby, who'd been set upon a soft, mossy bed. "Why does it look like she's surrounded by…well…a scrawl?"

The midwife shrugged helplessly.

"Never have I seen wing or fell like this," Vega said. "Yet this looks like a Dragon transformation, as impossible as that sounds."

Because Scrawl was experiencing this through Ballast's perspective, she felt his telepathic comments from the past, but didn't know to whom they were directed. :A Human is born. The forty-eighth in the Cluster since the Lattice lost us.:

The Lattice was how the Lenus connected as a group. It was a binding mental energy, above and yet related to their other feats like telepathy. These concepts still hadn't entirely made the translation to Human thinking. It had been something like two hundred years since the Lenus crashed on Earth. Since their technology was the product of the Lattice, having it fractured in the ocean was like a Human losing their education from a blow to the head. The Lenus still had their mental energy, but lost most of their ability to use it – like having a computer but not knowing what a keyboard is or what the images on the screen mean.

Overcoming the language barriers between themselves and the Human strays and castaways was a slow and difficult task.

No language or education they knew of could explain baby Scrawl. The parents huddled together, whispering in fear. Baby Scrawl, after pawing at the air and investigating her surroundings, seemed to be studying the watery sky above her more than the Dragon, the Lenus in view, or any of the Humans. Since the weather of this stretch of the ocean was calm that day, the sky of the Cluster wriggled with billowing daylight; the Lenus must have shifted the Cluster up closer to the ocean's surface.

The mother asked through a haze of fatigue: "I thought Dragons came from eggs."

Laughter from Vega's pearly bulk sounded like a cross between the whooshing of a seashell and the clattering of precious gems run through the fingers. Then she shook her head and said: "A myth. Many are the amusing Human legends, spanning uncounted years, about my kind. Some say we sprout from volcanoes or come fully-formed by the will of the gods. The power that changed me from a Human into what I am now is partly love and partly a great primal need for freedom. Becoming a Dragon is a grief as oft as not." Vega spread all her arm-wings wide, encompassing the group, and leveled her gaze upon the mother.

Since the Lenus had no eyes and lived in a very different way from Humans, they had a wholly different response to the Dragon. One that was hard to understand from a non-telepathic, protein-based way of life. Their awe came from a different place and meant different things. Nevertheless, most of the Humans looked upon this form not as a deity or a great lizard, but as a mountain. A living testament to the scale and truth of nature, and almost more landscape than person. Scrawl's mother was the only one there who could look the Dragon in the eyes.

Today's Scrawl, watching these events from Ballast's projection into her mind, saw her mother looking the Dragon in the eye. Ballast's attention in that moment had been on the mother, so what was in the Dragon's eyes was out of reach. Gratitude was one of the floods that ran through Scrawl, and it was hard to separate one from another. Wonder. Joy at seeing her mother's real-

:How am I seeing your memories? You don't have eyes!: Scrawl clasped her hands together in the present, just to remind herself of her own reality, since all her hearing and sight were now her age ago.

:I'd have thought you understood by now.: Ballast replied in the present. :We Lenus had to learn to translate our mental energy to yours just to make it known that we weren't jewelry or tools for cutting!:

Scrawl was mortified. :Did my ancestors-:

:It's in the past. A Human saying. Rather odd, really. We Lenus have what you call time a little bit more...how to say...*now* than you do. More lines and less flow. But I digress. What you are seeing is my best effort to turn my memory into something your memory can understand. Most of your kind know this by now, and so it is too normal to be noticed, but there were decades when we struggled to match up how we know the world enough to use telepathy.:

Scrawl took a moment to absorb this. Then she said: :Why are you showing me all this now? You had my whole life here, and I've asked about my parents so much!:

Ballast hid his emotions, but he was wrestling with how to answer. Or if he should.

"Am I intruding?" Lockheed asked as he approached. He was dressed like a '30s air yacht pilot. His was a common greeting in the Cluster, as telepathy was daily culture here.

Scrawl said: "I was just chatting with Ballast." Technically true. "I was saying that I've flown above the waters so much, I've almost given names to all the waves!"

Lockheed laughed a parchment laugh, made of cigars, a jovial spirit, and more than sixty years of life. "I know the feeling."

"But you can't fly," Scrawl pointed out with a furrowed brow.

"I wasn't born here, remember?" the man replied. "I've covered a lot of sky in three different air yachts, one of them mine. I called it the *Ivory Flower*. Did I ever tell you-"

"Yes!" Scrawl laughed. "A dozen, dozen times!" She was nervous and didn't know how to feel about Ballast's attitude right now, which she could only describe as momentous. "It's a shame we couldn't build you another." She looked around at the Cluster as she spoke. Water walled it in as a dome, but there was no visible barrier to tell the community apart from the surrounding ocean. Newcomers always struggled with that.

"I used to get flight jitters too, you know," Lockheed remarked. He laid a warm, gentle hand on Scrawl's shoulder. But Scrawl noticed him glance in the direction of Ballast, whose crystal form was strapped to her lower back.

:What are you not telling me?: she asked Ballast.

:I'm disappointed in Vega,: the Lenu replied. :She should be here, attending your first continental flight, not gallivanting-:

:That isn't fair.: Scrawl cut him off. :Vega has given so much for the Cluster. And it's not like she can swap out with another Dragon for shift work.: Vega's arm-wings conveyed a power no one in the community – including the Lenus – fully understood. Most thought that Vega had "built" (for lack of a better word) the dome that kept the community intact and that the Lenus were sustaining it. In fact, the reverse was the case.

:Your people have created as much here as anyone else by now,: Ballast retorted, :and nothing mine have done will crumble in the time it takes for Vega to give you a hug.:

Ballast had raised Scrawl after her parents had died during a failed rescue mission. The community took in crashes, refugees, and any other lost souls who had no hope of seeing land. All their differences were held together by survivor love. Scrawl knew and loved Ballast well enough to know when he was using one trouble to veil another. Vega's behaviour was also strange; it wasn't like the Dragon to get lost in work when anyone was leaving the Cluster, never mind Scrawl's first fully-fledged attempt to secure help from humanity.

Despite all the Dragon's support, and the compassion and ingenuity of the Humans, the Lenus were slowly fading away.

"Scrawl?"

She realized she'd entirely tuned out Lockheed. "Sorry, sorry," she said. "It's just-"

"Jitters," the man said with a smile. Despite having lived in the Cluster for a couple of decades, his pilot's outfit was in great shape: leather coat, a scarf of an outmoded pattern, a flat leather cap and even the traditional goggles lifted so that they were strapped to his forehead. "Where are your wings?"

She shrugged. "I don't need them yet." Cluster fashion was its own beast, informed by the stragglers they rescued from the ocean. After a few dozen births in the community, and rescues of Humans spanning five continents and well over a century, they were the epitome of all things eclectic. Scrawl wore a ghagri – a sash/shawl Punjabi article that extended from her left shoulder to her left hip. It was secured with a wide cloth belt. Under it she wore a long-sleeved silk shirt and baggy slacks.

"You know," Lockheed said, "of all the things I've seen you do with those wings, the queerest thing to me is that you don't need to adjust your clothes."

Scrawl tilted her head. Where was he going with this? :I'm sorry,: she said to Ballast in her head, :you've been interrupted.:

:We've all the ocean,: the Lenu answered.

"You can't just put wings wherever you want," Lockheed continued. "They have to be in the right spot, with the right size, shape, and angle. Unless you're a Dragon."

"What do you mean? Vega seems natural enough to me." Scrawl was quite serious.

"Those wings are almost more like arms," Lockheed said, "and nowhere near as big as they should be to lift such a body. I can't begin to guess how that sublime creature flies."

:Do you know how we communicate,: Ballast projected to them both, :or how the Lenus got separated from the Lattice?:

"Fair point," Lockheed conceded. He met Scrawl's eyes. "I've had leathers prepared for you. You won't get far in the winds above the ocean dressed like that!"

"Yes," Scrawl replied, "I've been getting a whole rainfall of advice since it was decided that I could finally go to land."

But it was what he wasn't saying that she found the most disconcerting. Why not him? Why now? Who was this young woman, Human but for her wings, and why did she stay Human after a lifetime if what the Dragon says is true? Vega has talked about Humans becoming Dragons, the slow but inevitable process. Always a process, though. It was like she was born with wings and stopped there.

Or had she?

"I am grateful," she said to Lockheed. Before she could elaborate, the ocean above them began to shift. It was broad daylight, and the sun was sharp. Great glass slivers rose in the air, wrapped in a liquid scintillation as they led the chorus of Lenu wills that altered the energy technology surrounding the community. Ocean wind swirled down on them. Forces most of the Humans didn't understand parted the water in peninsular grips so that the people contained in the dome of air could adjust to the wind and light. The great slivers were practically wizards among the Lenus of the Cluster, but quite small compared to citizens of the Lattice. Each appeared to Human eyes as a different glassy material: ruby quartz, obsidian, white crystal, and something so transparent its surface was iridescent.

Few of the Lenus levitated or otherwise moved of their

own power anymore. They couldn't spare the energy. The community filtered its people out of every crevice and nook. Numerous vestiges of Human technology merged with Lenu-guided life, Human-crafted stone, and coral to create the Cluster. Plane parts, car and gun components, railroad tracks used as binding or support poles, all manner of rafts, lifeboats, and ship assemblies, wooden constructions from a dozen decades. So much mish-mash was evinced by the buildings and landscapes of the Cluster that the fashion of its people seemed almost homogeneous and bland by contrast.

But today was different.

Most of the Humans stepping into view carried crystal people in their arms or strapped to themselves. One person even had a Lenu worked into a kind of peg, so that she could walk despite losing her lower leg in cannon fire and the Lenu had a way of getting around and staying in contact with his lover.

Scrawl never did ask how love worked between that woman and her crystalline partner. She'd grown up with the species. Only the Dragon stood out as being one of a kind in a way that even she was not. Wasn't love just a spark between two unique people?

The woman approached carrying leathers. "Cutting it close, aren't you?" she said grumpily. "You could have taken some of this yourself, you know."

"I didn't come straight here," was Lockheed's laconic answer.

The woman with the crystal sighed with reproach, but turned a grin toward Scrawl. "We been hearin' a lot 'bout you," she said. "We made this stuff, had to scrounge. Not a lot of cows around here for makin' leather, y'know."

Scrawl began undressing and taking the articles in

turn. Newcomers always struggled with this, but the Cluster put a priority on helping people lost at sea. Modesty was less important since losing clothes or having to remove them to deal with injuries was the norm. Scrawl chuckled as she went. "Thank you. And don't mind Lockheed."

"I don't."

"I'm right here, ladies," he said with his most disgruntled air. The other two made a "pft" at each other in a way he found conspiratorial.

"I heard they're not giving you food because you can get energy from the Sun," Lockheed started then. She knew something else was happening here. By now, the crowd comprised most of the Cluster's population, and the majority of them were avoiding eye contact with her. But they seemed excited, happy, proud.

"The Lenus had a long meeting with Vega about that after my...discovery," Scrawl answered, pulling on the last of her flight gear. She strapped Ballast back into the same spot. He wouldn't obstruct her, but she couldn't see him or the slight colour changes that could reveal his emotions. That made her uncomfortable, but she was probably just self-conscious because of the crowd avoiding her gaze. "I've heard before," she went on, "that my wings can absorb energy. But I don't feel anything." When she flew outside to save some stragglers or stretch her wings, everything was great. But when she spread them in the community, while the Humans enjoyed the view, something was different about the Lenus. Even Vega gave her mixed feelings. But everyone insisted everything was fine.

"I guess it's good that you won't need to carry food, though I doubt you can just eat daylight," Lockheed said with a curl of the lips.

"I'll have Ballast with me," she said, tapping her hand behind herself. An amorphous warmth filled her mind from his presence. It was a telepathic hug.

:Did you know Lockheed was the one who named me?: Ballast said suddenly.

Scrawl blinked.

"What?" Lockheed asked.

"Why did you call him Ballast?" she asked Lockheed while simultaneously asking her Lenu foster father, :How did you live here for so long without a name?:

"I liked the pun with the boating word. It's an electrical contraption for controlling fluorescent lamps," Lockheed answered.

:Names are a Human construct. We don't need them because every Lenu feels the personality of the ones we're talking about. It's hard to describe,: Ballast answered.

"Good luck with your flight," said the woman with the Lenu leg.

"Thank you!" Scrawl said again.

"About your discovery…" Lockheed started.

Scrawl closed her eyes and cast her face skyward, taking in a slow, deep breath. Easing herself back into a conversational posture, she looked Lockheed in the eye. "Sorry. Too many coming at me at once."

Lockheed nodded. Daylight flooded them all as the Cluster's dome opened fully to the sky. Scrawl lifted an upward palm at him, and he proceeded: "The way I hear it, your wings helped you to…sense something in the dome. And because of what you were able to tell them, the Lenus could work with Vega to stop the way the Cluster has been losing energy."

Scrawl thought this was common knowledge. "Well… yeah." She hesitated. "I'm almost ready to go. Why are you coming to me now, at the last minute? What are you getting at?"

Lockheed fidgeted with his outfit, tugging at the scarf or shifting the goggles every now and again. "I, well, now that we know – I mean, that is, we can, well, the Cluster can fix its problem now. We don't have to keep draining the Lenus and slowly dying. So why are you leaving at all?"

"They need more energy to make it happen," she said as though this were obvious. "We don't need innovation or people power, and no one we've sent home from the Cluster has ever come back. None of the ships have believed us, the ones we could find intact. No one would speak for us or with us. Geysers and gills, some of them even shot at us! But you know all of this. Why are you asking?"

As the dome opened completely, her back sprouted the tracery of a set of Dragon-like wings. But they weren't the thin arm-wings of Vega; they extended to a full bat-like breadth. Each was almost as long as she was tall, the highest and lowest points being above her head and below her waist. They were segmented as though made of stained glass. The black outlines sheened and limned like spider silk, and each segment was the sky – clouds and all. The segments were not directly aligned, however; they were a picture of the sky cut up and rearranged so that the physical pieces still fit together but the image was randomly chopped up. As her wings filled in, she felt something from Ballast at her lower back. It was not a physical sensation, but an emotional or psychological backlash. Like the vacuum that pulls water up a straw, but in her mind. She knew many Lenu conversations were happening right now, and she knew her wings were having a stronger and stronger reaction to the energies of the Cluster every time she produced them. But there were so many reactions from Ballast alone, so powerful and numerous, that she wondered what it all meant. She still had Lockheed before her, though, and waited for him to say something.

Lockheed clasped and unclasped his hands. Scrawl looked up as Vega descended upon them and collected Lockheed onto her back. "You dotard," Vega teased, "My wings hunger for sky. Aren't the arrangements made?"

Scrawl brightened. "You're coming!?"

Lockheed shook his head. At the time, Scrawl thought it was sadness in his eyes. "Where's Shimmer?" She meant the Lenu who spent the most time with the odd sky yacht pilot.

"This flight will be for us two alone," Vega said.

Lockheed tried to say something, but it was lost in the wind of Vega's takeoff, and they went into the southward sky. Scrawl was directed to go east. Her wings didn't flap because that wasn't how they got her aloft. Lifting into the air was more like sinking upwards. She waved to everyone, and many waved back or cheered. But she noticed that most gazes followed the Dragon, watched the opening to the dome, or looked around at their bustling home.

As soon as they passed the threshold, the ocean sealed over and the community was once again beneath the waves. Scrawl looked down before she sped to the east. From above, through the thin veil of water, the Cluster resembled vast gem-encrusted lichen. Like cloud-watching, the more she gazed upon it the more it took on shapes. A face crowned in Medusa hair, a glittering trilobite, some mountainous underwater tree.

Then she was gone.

Her flight path leaned into thermals and sought less resistant pathways. Otherwise she soon found herself trusting in the motions of her body and the bloodflow – so to speak – of the world around her. Even as she brought up her arms to guard her face against particularly intense gusts, patches of unavoidable clouds, and phalanxes of birds, she slipped into Zen.

:Okay, Ballast.: she thought. Her mental tone was firm and expectant.

Instantly, she was watching her own birth again. Vega had just spoken, a fact that she knew with the kind of dream logic that comes with such telepathic projections. Scrawl's rage at this answer had a creamy quality, frighteningly soft and indulgent even as it choked, and the visual imagery of the memory actually bent under its force.

Ballast spoke over the memory even as he retained its projection. :Vega has taught us much since our crash here twenty of your decades ago. Did you know that she is from here? Vega was already in the ocean, undirected but not lost. We never did learn what the Dragon was doing in the ocean, or if it needed to do anything. We were too late to realize what her hoard was.:

Scrawl was not appeased. This brought on far more questions than answers. :Why hold me back for so long, when I could have reached out to my fellow Humans on the lands of the world? It would have been much easier than all the boats and the messages and the waits for hope.:

:The Lattice has seen Dragons before coming to Earth,: Ballast replied, :so we knew what your existence meant. So did Vega, when you were born with your wings. Do you not know that a person must age and lose and love much before they mature into Dragon kind?:

:I've heard countless tales about Dragons, where they come from, what they are. We have hours before I reach the shore and we talk at the speed of thought. You owe me answers. There's too much happening that I don't know about, and those last hours in the Cluster were full of riddles and hints. What aren't you telling me?: Scrawl's body was held on an almost perfectly flat plane by the speed of her flight and the tension of her leg, back, and core muscles. Her wings only moved to tilt or roll her for less air and humidity resistance. The segments of the wings did not change as she moved, so she both blended with the surrounding sky and stood clearly apart from it. It was all ocean below her, in every direction, but she'd never seen it like this – for so long and so fast. Living within the ocean's bosom all her life, she'd seen the churnings of its dreamlike vastness and all the innumerable flutterings of the things that lived in it. But to see it from flight like this was like looking upon the scales of a Dragon's back and seeing that they were soft and alive, hard and invincible, endless and majestic, all at once.

:Vega knew she was dying when you were born.:

Scrawl didn't attempt words. Her reverberating emotional shock was enough.

:The World Dragon needs only one Dragon to ascend in order to be free. This is a truth of Dragons of any world. So, when the Earth's Dragon brought you about-:

:We have hours,: Scrawl interrupted, :not weeks. Did Vega do something to my parents?:

:What? No!: Ballast was mortified. :I said the World Dragon and I meant it. Vega was mighty before the Cluster sapped her strength, but a World Dragon is not a thing you can see. It is the world.:

:I don't care about that! Did I kill Vega?:

:It's not like you to be this impatient, my dear.: Ballast's grief in this statement was real. Lenus have never been known to project false emotions.

:Something's wrong. I thought the insights I gave you through my wings were helping!:

:They have and they are. You have no idea how much.: Ballast's thoughts came with a shading of shame so faint that the conversation continued before Scrawl could put her finger on what was bothering her about his words. She was reminded of Lockheed's last glance before Vega took him away, and realized what she'd seen that had been so off-putting.

Pity.

Ballast pushed on. Scrawl wasn't even seeing the surrounding ocean and sky anymore – it was all Ballast's memory. The first time her mother held her. :The World Dragon only makes a new Dragon when the current Dragon has little chance of ascension. But to make you partly Dragon straight from birth…: even now, Ballast was trying to raise her.

:You're saying you're not the only one who's been a father to me?: she asked.

:In a way, the Cluster was your mother and the Dragon your father. But I'm getting poetic.:

Scrawl actually laughed. She'd never mastered how to bring that completely within the mental space of conversing with a Lenu, so it happened with no one but the sky to hear her. A whale broke the surface below, which she only noticed because the laugh broke the surface of Ballast's projection. Then she was back with her parents, the midwife, the Dragon, and the Lenu. As she watched her infant self, she said to today's Ballast, :I love you, Dad, but you can be terrible.:

:I know, little one, I know.: He was letting show a weariness she'd never felt in him before, so she didn't have the heart to follow through on a joke about his size.

:So I was too important to let go?: This offended her, but not angrily. :If I'm so much more powerful and destined than other people-:

:Careful, my daughter. Pride can carry you too high to breathe.:

:Should I not be proud?:

:Scrawl.: Ballast almost never actually used her name. It came with a mental footfall that dissolved the memory projection. They were in a cloud, a world of pearl. :A true Dragon like Vega can fly with the sheer power of impossibility. It matters not the size and shape of her wings, or how many wings they have. A creature of a Dragon's size should not be able to fly through the flapping of wings. Yet they do. Vega shared that impossibility with the Cluster. That is how the Cluster lasted so long. But it was not enough to get us back into space.:

:I know that. That's why-:

:Hear me. You were born part way to the flight of a Dragon, but ever under Vega's shadow. That shadow is like this cloud.: And the pair emerged, light blue above and dark blue below.

Suddenly she recalled Lockheed today, dressed as a pilot as he hadn't done in many years. Of all days, in the air again – but with a dying Dragon. Her grief and dread seeped a hint of grey into her wings. Land was sneaking up ahead of her. She thought to turn.

:No.: Ballast said. :Let them have their final flight.:

:That's what you weren't telling me!: A sick kind of relief came with that. Guilt, but also a vague awareness of having been cheated. :It should have been my choice to say goodbye!:

:You're the only one who could chase them, argue with them about their last sunset.: Ballast pointed out. :Even an ill Dragon moves well. Would you spoil their dignity, their last joy of being true to themselves?:

:But Lockheed's old, not dying.:

:Cancer,: Ballast replied.

Scrawl stopped. Her knees were slightly bent to take off the strain, and her toes dangled. Otherwise she was upright and held securely by her wings, so closely matching the sky that she could have been knitted into it like a badge on a sweater. Before her stretched leagues of shoreline and the island state of Hawaii was too far south for her to see from here. As her wings took in energy from the Sun, they kept her warm and strong even at high altitude. They also took the edge off the trouble breathing, though it still felt uncomfortable, and she wasn't nearly as hungry as such a flight would have left someone travelling under their own power.

:Is it safe to assume,: Ballast started, :that you're not just hesitating about our dearly departed?:

:We're going to have to talk about that,: Scrawl replied distantly. She was watching the vague blue-brown edges of the land of the United States as though it could tell her something. :Never mind all this Dragon talk. I'm a grown woman. Not telling me about the cancer, that I get.:

:Really?: The Lenus had radically different ideas about death. They did not attend Human funerals in the Cluster. Humans didn't know what was done with a deceased Lenu among the crystal people, and didn't ask.

:His body, his choice. And it breaks my heart,: Scrawl went on, :but only a fool would be surprised about Vega. She looked the wrong kind of pale even when I was a kid.:

:Then…?: Ballast prompted.

Scrawl turned slowly on the spot with the rigid position and precision of a well-anchored, hanging ornament. :I always thought the Cluster was about trust and sharing. I thought spying and deceit were part of this "Cold War" the lost have been talking about for the last…how long has it been?:

:Too long, my daughter.:

:Can your people really have daughters?:

:We covered that with the birds and the bees.:

:There aren't any birds in the Cluster.:

:Now you're just being cute.:

:What is cuteness like if you can't see?:

:Does seeing have something to do with it?:

:You're trouble, Daddy.:

:I love you, too.:

:I don't think the Cluster needs me. Not now, here, like this.:

Scrawl wondered what colours Ballast must have been showing. He hesitated. :We didn't – don't – have enough energy.:

:But what can the Humans – I mean, the land Humans – give us that the Cluster can use? I've seen the oil and gas stuff that some of the sinking ships have managed to salvage when we saved their crews. If it was any good to us there, we'd have used it already. Are we looking for a submarine?:

:You're not asking the questions you're really wondering about.: Ballast was reproachful.

Scrawl retorted with a brute emotional undertow – a telepathic glare. His shock at such a gesture was like the oily sheen of a bubble's surface pressing against the backs of her eyes. What she'd done was quite possibly the most intense moment of disrespect and young rebellion she'd ever levied against him.

She flew then. As the edges of land and sea passed beneath her, she was reminded of mental pictures different Lenus had conveyed to her of fault lines, crevices, fissures, and volcanic geysers on the ocean floor. The association was brief but hard to shake. Beautiful and catastrophic, it brought to mind memories of Vega in rare moments of excitation.

Long after that boundary had faded into the horizon behind her, Scrawl was still looking upon the rooftops of American communities. :I should have known.: She said at last.

Ballast's words were bordered with fissures of simmering apology and dew-laden anger. :Always you took such pride in giving to the community, in striving to learn. Was that not what drove you to study the boundaries of the Cluster? Sometimes I wonder if you made your discovery through the gift of your wings, or sheer inspiration.:

:Do you see my people the way I see those rooftops?:

:What do you mean?:

Using the very connection Ballast had created for them, Scrawl transmitted her mental imagery. She was one of few Humans who'd spent their whole lives with the Lenus and worked hard at being party to their mental translations. :As seen from above,: she said.

She performed a U-turn and began a slow descent. Now that she was here, after years of stories, daydreams, and plans, she wasn't sure where to begin. Ballast was troubled. :Should this not be a joyous day for you?:

:You always told me that the waves, the powers, the energies – whatever you want to call them – of my wings were rude to the Lenus. But they also understood that I am what I am, so unfurling my wings was always a delicate thing to do. Complicated and almost...: she struggled for the right way to wrap up her thoughts. :...momentous.:

:I was not lying.:

:I've looked down on the Cluster from heights well above the waves.:

:What are you trying to say?:

:I knew what the Cluster was like. Born there, lived there, spoke with its people.:

:But that-:

Scrawl pressed her point. :When I get under those rooftops, they won't be distant points anymore. Whole worlds, ways of thinking you'd never see no matter how far you fly.:

:We did our best when we crashed here, young lady. Your people broke us down, tried to make jewellery out of us, attacked us with bullets and clubs and everything in between. Until we fled to the sea. Do you know how hard it is to move without the Lattice?:

:I'm a woman, Dad. Not a lady. Not all the trappings you have with this Dragon stuff of yours. Woman. Girl, but grown up?:

:No need to be snarky.:

:If you think that my wings and my inspiration are two different things, father, then you do not understand my people.:

:You are a people of one.:

:Wrong, Dad. I-:

She would always remember that first shot more than all the others. It was really more like the first tap in an elaborate drum performance, but the shift of her world-view happened in that one tragic pop. It missed her body, but it hit home. She was Human. In the air, yes, but Human. Why were they-

:SCRAWL! Flee!: Lenu emotion, when at its strongest, did not surge with adrenaline even when they were at the peak of fear. Ballast's fear for her now was the most robust Scrawl had ever felt of anything from him, save for the ever-abiding fatherly love. Intensity of Lenu feeling came through to Humans as a sense of time. She was embedded in a prism of fear, four-dimensional and extending into future and past.

She hastened back toward the shore. Large, odd devices and huge klaxons and sirens ignited the sky with noise instead of light. Scrawl did not know the term Skysweeper, but she knew enough about weapons to avoid it by flying low. Then Ballast experienced fear the way a Human does. Not well-fitted into a mental framework of energy lines and a reality made up of radiance and surface tension, but an abominable now of body awareness and surging environmental violence. "STOP!" she screamed at the Humans. She remembered stories and shouted all the translated phrases she'd ever heard. "STAND DOWN! CEASE FIRE! PARLEY!"

Several times as she swooped and dodged, avoiding buildings and the people firing their guns, she got in closer despite Ballast's warnings and pleas. She heard the people shout many things, but they would not listen to her.

Wasting no more time, she made a mad aerial dash for the only safety she knew: the Cluster. Ballast was exerting himself mightily. Only when she'd left the coastline behind, thinking of its boundary with the sea like a kind of scar now, did she begin to get her bearings again. Her ears contained gunfire the way a shell contains the sea. There was a redness in the back of her mind, or a humming buzz from her nose. Perhaps a visual tickle. Then a burst of her own understanding.

:Dad! You're exhausted!:

:I...I was in their heads, trying to understand.: Scrawl's silence prodded him to continue. :Your wings blended with the sky. They kept saying and thinking something about stealth. Communists. Proxy wars. There was too much to sift through. Your skin colour confused them, but they still think you're Russian.:

Enough people from all walks of life had found their way to the Cluster that Scrawl had learned many basics like language and geography, but current events were a little harder to follow. She knew what Russia was. She knew about wars, mistrust, racism, and the like. But to be fired upon before she got a word in was still a shock. Every now and again she looked behind them as she flew. Dots were in the distance.

Something was ahead and high, high above them. Glistening, massive but small with distance. Not yet a form she could name. :Your mind touching takes work, but it shouldn't be this draining. What's going on, Dad?:

:I'm sorry. Forgive them. You're a threat, they're only doing what they can.:

:Is that what the dots are? Are the Americans chasing us?:

:Yes,: Ballast said. His thoughts were like watercolour, but too thin to form an image. She had to concentrate to "hear" him. :But that's not what I mean. You're draining me, my daughter.:

Her eyes darted about and her brow furrowed. Then her eyes widened and her stomach sank. Her gaze zeroed in on the mass floating high and getting higher with every moment. Too many questions were clicking into place. Tears slid down her cheeks.

:I thought you only seemed bigger when I was young because I was small.:

:We really are grateful for all you've done, my daughter, and we couldn't have saved the Cluster without you.: They both shared mental images of Vega, the pale dying Dragon of many arms. Rarely did Vega fly during Scrawl's lifetime, and she understood now the cost the community must have demanded of the Dragon. Lockheed atop Vega, in one final flight, was the best memory Scrawl and her father could use to express their feelings to one another.

But amidst this bitter love and grief was an outrage like magma on the ocean floor, flowing and seething and obscured by its own mists. Betrayal. :You knew. They all knew. The Cluster is leaving me behind.:

But she had to tear her heartbroken gaze away from the Cluster as it flew into space and back to the Lattice, fleeing her, humanity, Earth. She had to turn from the home that was abandoning her, because the dots were now the savage machines of American fighter pilots.

Her flight was different from theirs. She was like a thread in the tapestry of the sky, woven into its being and so more natural and able to sift herself within it. But they were brute force, like the artlessness of a sewing machine. Faster, tireless, but less creative in their problem solving. She swam among their ranks, causing two collisions and one of them to accidentally gun down one of their own.

Ballast was too tired to interfere with or even read the minds of the pilots. Scrawl's mind was racing. She couldn't run from them. She couldn't attack them. :It was never about rudeness, was it?:

:Please, daughter, you must live.:

She dodged, rolled, and dove in every direction. Diving up was natural to her, because she did not fly by fighting gravity. But she'd never danced with violence, so she didn't know its steps. :I've been draining your energy. You said I wasn't taking from people!:

:I'm sorry. But what was I to do?: Scrawl's ears were screaming with her own blood flow, lost to the sky-shivering cacophony of the war machines. Only telepathy got through now. Ballast went on. :I kept it secret. The Lenus didn't know, Scrawl, and neither did the Humans. Only I, Vega, and a few others had any idea. The Cluster loves you. Only by promising that we would come back for you did we get everyone to agree to go, and to say nothing to you. Lockheed led the arguments against the plan. But your wings, and their energy thirst, would have consumed too much for the Cluster to safely escape Earth.:

She couldn't take it anymore.

The remaining planes whirled about her, having learned from her tactics. They wouldn't allow crossfire, and stayed too far away to collide. But they maintained a perimeter. She couldn't get out. Scrawl shrieked, and as she let loose it became a roar. She began to change, scales sliding over the surface of her skin and a tail rapidly emerging. Clothing tore and Ballast sprung loose, twirling into the emptiness of either sea or sky.

A bullet grazed her.

It went by her lower back. It didn't even make contact. But this was a 0.30 caliber M2 AN mounted machine gun round. Its force was enough to shatter her lower spine, even in mid-transformation. Pain flooded all of her senses, invading her memory and imagination, and she became as a living static of agony.

When she came back to herself, nothing made sense

at first. :Dad?:

She called out with her mind, but could hear no thoughts. Without a Lenu nearby, she had no telepathy of her own. Her senses were lying to her, surely. She waited. But there was no denying it – Scrawl was at the bottom of the ocean. She was breathing water and she could see in the darkness, but not how she would have expected to. When a person wears light amplification goggles, they translate the dark into something the eye understands. This vision had no losses in translation. It was her own.

Scrawl was a landscape now, but at first did not understand her shape. Her head was so far away from her body. Even her wings were different. Before they were not entirely a physical truth, or perhaps they were more true than her body. They were bigger now, and no longer woven into her surroundings. She could not cause them to dissolve into her body or disappear or however it was she'd retracted them when she'd been-

Her eyes shot open.

Agony took musical form. She wailed, but it was something else, a cry born of the world itself. Her home, the Cluster, saved itself. With her, but also from her. Everyone was dead, lost, gone. Several breaths spanned the lifting of her neck. With care and trepidation, she turned her head and looked upon herself. Her wings were like her body now, scaled and of such a dark cyanic splendour that she knew in a deep way that no Human could see her. Not so far beneath the waves.

No sensation came from her legs or tail.

That was why she could not make sense of her form by feel alone.

No injuries were in evidence. Her tail lay curled upon itself in an undignified knot. She could do nothing to straighten it. Being so wrapped up in the ocean was a rapture she could not explain, and so natural was its world to her that it did not press upon her with crushing weight. Her forelegs were functional, and her wings moved at will.

:Dad? Ballast? I'm scared.:

Somehow the susurration of water around her, and the occasional slips and gurgles of distant hydrothermal vents or creatures made wise by their fear, served as an echo to her failed telepathic call. She tried to feel bitter about the fact that she'd helped make the Lenus spaceworthy again. Scrawl had a desperate need for wrath, something to take the edge off the abyssopelagic depths.

But that was not her.

To no avail, she strove to recall the moment she'd been separated from Ballast. Had he been destroyed? Why wasn't she panicking about being paralyzed? There was just a cold, lightless calm. And heartbreak. Shock sifted about under her scales as she realized she'd never seen a Lenu in the water. Could they be unconscious and still live? She knew they didn't sleep.

Scrawl could not see the surface of the ocean from here. No light, of the day or anything else, reached her here. She strove to make sense of the difference between what she knew and what she understood. Maybe it was just vertigo, but she started to think she was far above and looking at the underside of the ocean as though it were a rooftop at the bottom of a different world.

Peter Gillet

Peter Gillet was born in Oromocto, New Brunswick; and is the author of many celebrated independently published books of short fiction, including *Mind Full of Prose* and *In Dark Corners*. Peter was the first author to be listed as non-binary in the New Brunswick library system.

Peter has a long history with flying, as an air cadet, flying gliders, and small planes (with assistance).

First Flight

Lassen rubbed his bruised shoulder as he set down another bundle of sticks gathered from the forest. Mother was boiling rock-root, dropping the heated stones into the bag of water, and lifting out the cold ones to return them to the fire pit.

She looked at the sticks and frowned. "I'll need more than that. Go again, and be quick about it!"

His sister, Dara, sat quietly, cleaning dirty roots to prepare for boiling. Their eyes met for an instant before she bent to her task. He turned to leave.

"And don't let me catch you grumbling about Garten and his friends. They didn't beat you half as much as you deserve, you lazy boy!" Lassen winced at her parting words.

He followed the familiar, weaving route through the round huts of their village and then started down the path through the rock-root and sweet-vine fields. He felt the heat in his face as he thought about his older brother and the men of the village gone hunting. "Next year, I'll be on the hunt too. I'll be big enough and no one will hit me." He looked up to judge the distance left to the wooded slope and spotted someone ahead of him.

"Matta." He gritted his teeth. The younger girl had often joined his sister in taunting him. When he could catch her alone though, he let her have it. This morning, she was headed into the woods and no one was with her. She was carrying what looked like a bundle. He picked up his pace, but not too fast. She hadn't seen him yet.

"You'll get more than firewood, you little brat," he whispered. His aimless anger had found a familiar target and it felt good. She disappeared into the bushes at the edge of the woods, and Lassen started a loping stride to gain ground. It wouldn't do to lose her.

He paused just inside the bushes to let his eyes adjust to the relative darkness. The sun was behind the hill at this time of morning. The paths through the woods criss-crossed up the slope. He and the other children had explored almost every part of this hill. Just when he thought he had lost her, Lassen heard the telltale crack of a twig being stepped on further up the path.

He moved as his father had taught him, avoiding twigs and loose dirt. He slowed whenever he spotted movement through the leaves ahead. Lassen's heart was pounding in his chest. "I'll be the strong one," he thought, and grinned as he clenched his fists.

It was easy to keep up with her shorter legs. He wondered though, why she was climbing so high. They were passing more than enough dead, dry branches within easy reach. He let his frustration feed his anger.

She paused up on Lookout Ledge, so named because from the edge you could see all the way up and down the valley. Small birch trees grew thin on the rocky plateau. When Garten had dared him last summer, Lassen sat on the edge and dangled his legs over the cliff. He remembered looking down the drop to the pile of rocks far below, and how it had made him sick.

Instead of earning their respect, his brother had only laughed at him and called him a coward and a baby.

Lassen watched through the bushes as Matta unrolled the bundle she had been carrying. It looked like a deer hide, cut into a shape like an arrowhead. He stood up and strutted into the little clearing. "Awfully high up to be gathering branches."

Matta let out a yip and scrambled back as he approached. "Are you using this to carry more sticks? Seems too big for you to carry." He kicked the edge of the hide with his toe.

"You leave that alone!" Her protest was cut short when he glared up at her.

The boy squatted and felt the hide with his fingers. "Too thin. This couldn't hold much before it would just split, stupid girl." He looked up at her, and noticed her little fists at her sides. He narrowed his eyes and held the edge with both hands. "I think I could rip it easy."

She opened her eyes wide. "Please don't, Lassen."

"What's it for?" He stared at her, but didn't remove his hands.

She relaxed her fists, and spread her fingers, palms down. "I can't tell you."

"So you want it ripped." He lifted the edge slightly higher, and smiled at her groan.

"Please just leave it alone. Leave me alone."

"I can't do that, stupid girl." He moved to pull the edge tight.

"No! That's the only one!" She contorted her face into a snarl. "Just leave it alone. You wouldn't understand." She pointed right at his face. "You're the stupid one!"

Lassen dropped the hide and closed on her in two leaping strides. He realized he had slapped her only when she reached up to touch her face. His right palm stung.

He grabbed the front of her tunic and raised his open hand. Tears fell from her eyes. "Never call me stupid. Tell me what it's for, or I'll slap you again." She made a small gurgling sound, and closed her eyes. He shook her, hard. "Tell me!"

"You would never believe me." She shook her head. "Just slap me again and leave."

He pushed her to the ground. "You think I'm stupid? You think I wouldn't understand?"

He lifted his foot to stomp on the girl, and she yelled, "Wait! I'll tell you!"

Slowly, Lassen lowered his foot and then took a step back. "So tell me then."

She sat up, and wiped her eyes. "I have to show you. Let me stand up again, please."

"Go ahead, Matta, but don't think I'll let you run away. You know I can run faster."

Matta stood up, and went to one of the birches. She plucked two leaves and brought them over. "These leaves are the same, right?"

He nodded, but narrowed his eyes. "Yeah, so what? Is this some kind of trick? You know if it is, I'll just smack you for it."

Her lip trembled, and then she swallowed. "No, it isn't a trick. Watch how they both float to the ground." She let them go, and he watched them.

He looked up at her. "So what? Leaves fall."

Matta held up a hand, and retrieved the pair of leaves. "Just watch." She carefully held one leaf by its stem in her mouth while she crushed the other, rolling it into a little green ball. She then held them both out. "They are the same two leaves as last time, right?"

"Yeah, but you've smashed that one." He pointed with his chin as he crossed his arms.

She held them both out like last time, and let go. The ball fell straight to the mossy ground and bounced. The flat leaf was still making its slow descent. Lassen watched it the whole time. He looked back up, and Matta had a little grin. "Do you understand?"

He frowned. "Why don't you tell me what that was all about?"

She picked up the ball and leaf. "The only difference is their shape!" She was smiling now. Lassen shook his head. "The flat, thin leaf didn't drop as fast as the crushed up leaf."

"So?"

She pointed to the hide on the ground behind him. "I thought about it when I watched the leaves fall last year. I thought about it even more when the wind blew them around and kept them from falling."

He shook his head. "The wind blows leaves around. Everybody knows that."

She pursed her lips like she was chewing on something. She suddenly smiled. "You know how the fish swim in the river and we always find the pinchers on the bottom, under rocks and logs?"

"Yes." He uncrossed his arms. "I think you're just trying to get out of a whooping."

"Don't you see? The pinchers are like this crushed leaf, and the fish are like the flat leaf." She dropped them again. "The pinchers can't help but sink, but the fish swim."

"Of course fish can swim. So, can we. What does this have to do with anything?"

She nodded her head quickly. "Yes! You just said it. We can swim, like the fish can swim." She pointed to the flat leaf. "In the water." She then pointed to the crushed leaf-ball. "But out of the water, we're like the pinchers."

Lassen felt dizzy, and shook his head to clear it. "Things float in water. Nothing floats..." He waved his hands around. "...out of water."

She pointed up at the birds flitting from branch to branch. "What about birds? They fly around like fish swim in the water."

He put his hands on his hips. "Birds fly by magic. Everyone knows that."

Matta looked at the ground. "What if we learned that magic? What if we could fly?"

Lassen took another step back. "That makes no sense. We don't have the magic of birds. If you don't make sense soon, I'm going to give you a beating you'll never forget." He realized as he said it, his brother Garten had used those exact words.

"What if a spirit told me about the bird-magic?"

Lassen touched his left ear, just like his baba had taught him. "Don't talk about spirits! You're just a liar."

"The wind, Lassen." She pointed at the highest branches, where the leaves were moving in the breeze. "The wind for us is like the river current for the fish. What if we're in our own kind of water and all we have to do to swim in it is to look and act more like a fish than a pincher?" She pointed at the large, thin hide. "To be shaped more like a fish?"

He shook his finger at her. "Fish don't fly."

"Wing-mice fly."

He looked down at her, but remembered the time last summer the children of the village had managed to knock a wing-mouse out of the dusk sky with rocks. Its front legs had wings shaped a bit like birds' wings, but made of thin skin. He looked back at the hide, and then turned back to Matta. "It can't work like that. There has to be magic."

"It does work, Lassen. It worked twice already."

His eyes opened wide. "What do you mean? Have you already flown?"

She nodded quickly, her mouth breaking into a smile. "It was after dark, and from the jumping rock by the swimming pool. The first time, I only made it halfway across. The second time I got a good running start, and I landed on the pebbles on the far side. That's how I got this scratch on my forehead." She lifted her hair for him to see.

Lassen felt his heart pounding in his chest. "You're going to jump off Lookout Ledge."

She nodded, more slowly this time. "And when I fly over the village, and everyone sees me, they'll know I have powerful magic. They won't make me do stupid chores like fetching firewood and water ever again. I'll have more respect than any hunter." She smiled, and had a funny look in her eyes.

Lassen turned and looked at the hide-wing, and then looked at Matta. "How does it work?"

Matta opened her mouth slightly and then looked hard at him. "No. This is my plan. I get to fly, not you."

"I could just rip it up, like I was going to do at first."

"You wouldn't. It took me weeks to make that wing, Lassen."

"Then no one gets to fly."

She balled her fists and furrowed her brow. "Will you tell them I helped you? So I can at least get out of some of my chores?"

"I'll think about it." He grinned as she fumed.

"Fine." She relaxed her shoulders and dropped her chin. "I'll have to show you how it works." She waved her hand for him to step back, and then she walked over to the hide. She pointed at two small holes near two of the points. "These are where I hold on with my hands." She held her arms out wide. "Like this."

He nodded. "So I hold onto it there, and it lets me fly?"

She shook her head. "There's more. You have to… here." She picked up a leaf. "You see how the stem goes up the middle, with the leaf on each side?" He nodded. "You have to make yourself like that stiff middle." She pointed at a slightly larger hole near the third point of the hide. "You have to stick one foot through there, and then… just watch."

Matta lay down on her stomach, with her arms stretched out, and her right leg straight. "Like this, and then when you are in the air, tuck your other foot behind your ankle. Like this." She stood up, and wiped the leaves from the front of her tunic. "Do you think you can do that?"

He nodded. "I can do it."

With Matta's help, Lassen slipped his foot through the rather tight hole, and then she passed him the other two points. The hide hung loosely behind him. He practiced holding his arms out wide. "I can feel the wind catching the wing!" He smiled at Matta.

She nodded. "You need to get a run at the cliff, to get flat like I was. I fell straight into the swimming pool twice because I wasn't brave enough to run at first."

He puffed up his chest. "I'm brave enough now."

"Run with your arms crossed on your chest, so the wing doesn't slow you down. Remember to jump off the cliff like you're trying a shallow dive into water, and spread your arms wide. And don't forget to tuck your left foot." She paused. "I can't believe you're taking this chance away from me, Lassen. Maybe you picked on me and slapped me, but I never thought you'd be so mean. You're going to be so powerful, maybe even made the leader of the village."

He laughed. "You thought I was stupid. Everyone thought I was weak and stupid." He faced the cliff and smiled. "They'll all see how smart I am." He ran as fast as the wing would allow and dove head-first off the cliff.

Matta closed her eyes and touched her left cheek with gentle fingers. "Are you there, Nanka? Did you see?" She opened her eyes and cocked her head to the side, listening. She smiled. "I did it just like you said and now he's gone. Thank you."

The girl picked the remaining forest litter off the front of her tunic, while nodding. "Are you sure though? Just like smoke rises from the fire?" She frowned, and looked around at the birches shivering from a sudden gust. "No, I believe you, Nanka. Of course I love you. I'll try that next."

Matta glanced towards the cliff, and then walked back down the hill, gathering firewood as she went.

Paul Carberry

Paul Carberry works for the Canadian Armed Forces and is a proud member the Royal Newfoundland Regiment. He is a huge proponent of the horror genre and its place in literature. He has two children, daughter Dana and son Rick, with his wife Leah.

Paul has published two novels with Engen Books: *Zombies on the Rock: Outbreak*, and its sequel *Zombies on the Rock: The Viking Trail*. On August 18 2018, his first novel attained Bestseller status.

He has also had numerous short stories featured in publication, including 'The Light of Cabot Tower,' 'Into the Forest,' and 'Halloween Mummers.'

Harmon Field

Captain Cyril Jones walked across the tarmac of Ernest Harmon Air Force Base in Stephenville, Newfoundland. Quickly, clouds drifted overhead, rays of sunlight poking holes in the white fluff, letting the blue sky shine through. *The American Beauty*, a B-17, waited at the edge of the terminal. It was an impressive air-fortress. *American Beauty* was a four-engine heavy bomber, designed to rain hell into the ocean from the skies. The huge collection of metal was a marvel to witness in person. Standing at twenty feet tall and with a wingspan over one hundred, it was a miracle it ever flew. When glimmers of sun struck the silver frame, radiant morning light shimmered back. Someone had scrawled "American Beauty" along the nose in florescent yellow. The manufacturer had placed the image of a nude woman with flowing blonde hair lying on her stomach, enveloped by a red sunset, just below the cockpit. The plates that held the plane together were visible. Different sized sheets of polished alloy stood out prominently over her body, with the countless rivets holding them together running along the lines. Each wing harnessed two massive cylindrical engines, hanging beneath the arm. Each turbine had a black propeller with three blades spanning over eight feet long and a foot wide. Someone painted the tips of each wing and tail a bright yellow while dark green highlights accented each motor. A white star encircled by a blue circle rested just behind the door and on top of both wings.

Cyril climbed up the ladder, entering the belly of the air fortress, the rest of the ten-man crew hard at work loading six-hundred-pound depth charges into place. Barrels filled with Torpex explosive, a substance fifty percent more powerful than TNT, waited inside the drum. Command had received reports of a German U-boat patrolling the Atlantic Ocean, heading towards a convoy of supply ships that had left from New York City. Cargo ships loaded with weapons, ammunition, food, and medical supplies were headed for the Allied Troops who had pushed further inland from the beaches of Normandy. The German U-boat had been trailing them for over an hour, quickly gaining on them. *The American Beauty* would now have to race against time to destroy the threat. Cyril ducked as he shuffled along the edge of the B-17, the exposed metal frame threatening to strike the taller man in the skull. "Excuse me," he said as he passed between the depth charges, the crew giving the captain enough room to wedge past them. Cyril reached the door to the cockpit and was required to twist sideways to fit his vast shoulders through the narrow door.

"What took you so long, Jones?" Sitting in the hardened leather chair was Richard McDonald. Short, black hair covered his head. Looking much too young to be an aviator, Cyril couldn't help but stare. Muscle mass had yet to build up on his lanky frame, and his jawline was rigid and strongly defined. He looked like a fresh recruit, making Cyril long for his old partner.

Cyril grumbled under his breath, lumbering into the

tight fitting pilot's chair. "For something so grand, they didn't allow adequate space."

Young Richard spanned his arms out, illustrating how much room he had on either side. "Speak for yourself, giant."

Jones slid into his chair, the dashboard littered with gauges, dials, toggles and knobs. Cyril had never flown a bomber into action before; he was used to the simplicity of a two-seater jet craft. They drafted him into the Air Force at the outbreak of the war and he had just completed a tour abroad as a fighter pilot. They assigned him to the Harmon Air Base in Stephenville yesterday and he didn't have time to test-fly *The American Beauty*. "Turbines are ready now."

"Roger that." Richard went through his pre-flight checks. "All good on my end, sir."

Cyril flicked the engine's power toggle up and the four engines roared to life one at a time with a growing thunderous growl that grew louder with each passing moment. The massive propellers started slow, sending heavy vibrations through the metal structure as the blade swung down, rocking the whole plane. Once the instruments reached full strength, the propellers spun so fast they blurred into a circle, then vanished, but their raw power surged through Cyril's veins. The four engines sent an immense amount of energy coursing through the metal frame, establishing a force field that ran through his body. "Make sure the exit is closed."

"The light is green." Rick flicked the switch above his head, locking the door in place.

Cyril powered up the thrusters, the wheels bumping the airplane up and down as he taxied the bomber towards the runway. Her heavy payload put a great amount of strain on the landing gear. The craft rolled down the path slowly as Cyril moved it into position, the long strip of pavement stretching endlessly into the horizon. Looking down, he could see the red needle hanging just above the capital F on the fuel gauge.

"Ready?" Cyril asked, a swarm of butterflies fluttering in his gut.

"All systems go," Richard said sternly.

Now, with the throttle fully forward, *The American Beauty* lurched ahead and accelerated down the long span of asphalt. The plane felt like it was being held to the runway, fastened to the earth by a force pressing down hard on them. Cyril checked the odometer; they had reached one hundred miles an hour, not nearly fast enough to achieve lift off yet.

"Call out the speeds," Cyril demanded, his voice becoming gruff as the edge of the runway appeared in his view.

"One hundred and twenty," Rick called out, the plane gaining speed faster now as the engines thundered, the rumble nearly deafening as they contested against the constraints of gravity.

"One hundred and eighty."

The tree line blurred into one giant green streak on the left, the ocean turning into a blue stream on the right. *The American Beauty* started to bounce up and down, her wheels leaving the ground a bit longer each time.

"Two hundred and thirty."

The force pinned Cyril into his seat. The grey had all but disappeared, the green grass rushing towards them as the airplane's landing gear still lingered over the asphalt.

"Two hundred and sixty."

Captain Jones felt weightlessness washing over his

body as they defied gravity. *The American Beauty*, and her sixty-thousand-pound payload, soared into the horizon to meet the sun. They soared high into the sky with the earth looking so far away. The trees and grass swept out of view, and the dark blue waters of the ocean stretched as far as the eye could see.

"Would you look at that." Richard's voice was full of awe.

A scatter of clouds laid in a heaping, chaotic mess over the deep blue ocean. The clouds constantly flowed, an oddly transparent drifting thin mist.

"It never fails to amaze." Cyril had been flying for thirty years and couldn't remember being disappointed. "What's our bearing?"

Richard looked at the compass, inspecting it with a grim expression. "Our relative bearing is nine o'clock," His tone lacked confidence.

Cyril nodded his head and confirmed the altimeter. "We are flying at ten thousand moving at two hundred and sixty miles an hour." He continued to scan his dials. "With this strong tail wind, we should arrive in thirty minutes."

"I hope that's sufficient time," Richard whispered, his voice trailing off.

"It will have to be. We won't get there any faster." Captain Jones corrected him, "I'll hold the course steady, you go back and make sure the depth charges are in place."

"Aye aye, sir." Richard drove his arm up in a half-hearted salute before he hopped out of the cabin.

Cyril shook his head at his young co-pilot. "Damn kids," he muttered to himself, examining the dashboard for the oscilloscope, a high-frequency direction-finding device used to spot the U-boat. Once turned on, the U-

boat's signal flashed over the speaker, the radio operator clicking away on his Morse key sending a broadcast
to another German vessel nearby. Clouds passed by the
cockpit in translucent sheets as Cyril lowered his eleva-
tion -- he wanted to be as low as possible before dropping
those depth charges. It was conceivable a powerful breeze
could alter its direction far off course from greater alti-
tudes, and he couldn't afford to miss his target. It wasn't
just the crew aboard the vessels below that were at risk;
there were thousands of soldiers counting on him. Cyril
gripped the wheel tightly as the steady winds at the lower
altitude began to tear at the wings.

The whole plane vibrated violently, and the B-17
seemed to jump up and down without warning as it entered pockets of air. The strong winds blowing off the
ocean tried to adjust the craft's course. Cyril Jones had
dropped the bomber down to just two thousand feet as he
approached the U-boat, leaving no room for failure.

"How deep do you think they are?" Richard in-
quired.

"I'd say fifty meters. They are nearly within torpedo
range." Captain Jones struggled to keep *The American
Beauty* steady, the turbulence wreaking havoc on the
air-fortress. "Tell them to set a short fuse on those depth
charges. We will be dumping them in five minutes."

Richard unbuckled his seatbelt, nearly toppling over
as the plane dropped just as he stood up. He braced himself against the door frame. A loud explosion sent Richard
flying into Cyril's lap, the vibrations rocking the plane.
The plane rocked to the left as the wing rattled furiously.
Richard tilted his head up, shoving his raven black hair

from his face, his emerald green eyes large with dread even though he couldn't see the complication. "What was that?" The words spilled from his mouth, terror pushing them out.

Cyril looked behind, black smoke billowing from the first engine. Fire inside the turbine glowed bright orange and red beneath the black soot-covered cowling. The propeller ceased turning.

"It's nothing to fret about," Cyril lied in an attempt to calm the inexperienced pilot. "Just tell them to set the depth charges for shallow depth and get back here as soon as possible."

A boisterous, mechanical hiss screamed out, drowning out all the other noises of the engine. A loud bang chased the terrifying screech, an engine on the opposite wing sputtered and gasped as it failed. Cyril felt *The American Beauty* losing altitude, the wind groaning as gravity grasped the sixty-thousand-pound airplane, trying to haul it down into the ocean.

"Not yet, you devil," Cyril said calmly as the B-17 cried out in rebellion. The whole plane rattled viscously while the two remaining engines buzzed loudly as they struggled to keep the plane up long enough to reach its final destination.

"They set the depth charges," Richard startled Cyril as he turned up in the door frame. His face was ghost white, all the colours drained from his skin. "We aren't going to make it," he said matter-of-factly.

"I have an urgent mission to carry out and nobody will stop me," Cyril said defiantly, not aimed at Richard but glancing up towards the heavens. "Get your parachutes on and make sure the crew follows you. Leave before it's too late."

"But sir…" Richard stammered but stopped when Cyril craned his neck to look at him. His steely blue eyes filled with energy, burning brightly like the spark of a fiercely hot blaze.

"That's a direct order," Cyril barked as the plane groaned, the wings ready to rip apart as the screws began to wrench loose. "You have to lead them now; I'll be right behind you." Cyril yanked up on the gearstick, tilting the nose of the plane up just enough to let the wind support her at one thousand feet, "You're running out of time."

Richard nodded his head, a tear rolling down his face "Grab your parachutes, boys. Move it," he bellowed as he disappeared into the cargo bay.

The two working engines were being taxed far beyond their capacities. They hacked out dense clouds of black exhaust as the propellers continued churning, aviation fuel flooding them both.

"Keep it together, girl." Cyril watched as the red gauge of the gas line drifted towards empty at an alarming rate, the altimeter bouncing up and down. Each time the gauge dipped a little lower than the last time, the sky started to raise high into Cyril's point of view and retreated beyond the cockpit window. A surge of wind ripped through the cockpit as the cargo bay door opened, the pressure creating a vortex inside, depressurizing the plane. Cyril looked down towards the ocean. He could see the dark outline of the German U-boat beneath the surface. He flicked the plastic guard from the release trigger, his thumb hovering over the red button.

"Just another few minutes until you can sleep, girl." His heart beat faster and faster, his hand probing for the ejection lever underneath his chair. *The American Beauty* soared through the sky, holding onto her last moment of glory until it petered out. The outline of the German ship coming closer and closer.

An eerie silence crept over Cyril, the last two engines dying together. The wind whistled loudly as *The American Beauty* rapidly lost altitude, the ocean rushing up to greet her. Cyril watched as the black form beneath the ocean raced towards the nose of the plane.

He pressed the red switch. The bay doors clacked loudly as they sprang open, the depth charges plunging into the ocean. The water dampened an enormous explosion as the ocean burst skyward beneath him. Cyril yanked back on the ejection lever at the exact moment the nose impacted the water. A formidable force pounded against Cyril as everything went black.

The sky was so intense it appeared to be white. A pleasant breeze lifted the unpleasant bite of salt spray. The elegant tones of the waves crashing against the shore lulled Cyril into a relaxed state. He glanced around: the snow white surface of the beach ran into eternity, disintegrating into the crystal clear blue wash. Cyril found himself laying back comfortably in a cabana, an ice cold beer in his hand. Someone had pressed a wedge of lemon into the rim of the transparent glass bottle.

"Where am I?" His surroundings confused Cyril.

"You know where you are Mr. Jones," a hearty voice said from behind. Delicate footprints scrunched the sand beneath his feet as the stranger stepped into view. He was an aged man with a long grey beard, his hair drawn into a long braid that flowed lightly in the breeze. His jaw was square, but his skin was smooth and he had a sympathetic smile. With skin clear of any blemishes, his blue eyes stood out, fixated on Cyril, an absolute calmness pouring out.

Looking down at his feet, Cyril asked, "How long have I been here?" It was a question he demanded more to himself. He was sporting a pair of sandals, his sinewy legs covered up by a pair of tan khaki slacks. He wore a white dress shirt with all the buttons undone, the fabric opened and lay sprawled open against his side.

"We brought you here after the crash." The man offered his hand. "I'm Peter."

Cyril accepted his outstretched hand, his grip firm and full of calluses. "The last thing I recall was striking the bath."

"That was an eternity ago." Peter grinned, a luminous smile on his lips, "You've been at this institution ever since. We believed this place would help you heal quicker."

"How long have I been here? What happened after I crashed?" Cyril sat up, his mind racing as he recalled his mission. "Did the convoy make it?"

"Your actions were heroic, Cyril." The smile lingered on Peter's face, "The convoy made it to the shores of Normandy."

"How is the war progressing?" Cyril asked.

"Why would you burden yourself? It ended long ago." Deliberately, the smile withered from Peter's face, a vast sorrow in his eyes.

"Our war is over? Did we win?" Cyril took a swig of his beer; it burned his tongue, the bottle filled with salt. He scrunched up his face in disgust.

Peter chuckled, swinging his head back and forth. "You could say that you won but does anybody really win at war?"

"Of course people win. The world is a safer place now." Cyril slammed his beer down on the table next to him, wondering why the chair was turned down like that. A plate and glass rested upside down, salt sprinkled over the white setting. The chair was tilted down, the back of the chair leaning on the table. The centre-piece was a candle that had burnt halfway before being snuffed out, the blackened wick long extinguished. "Where am I?"

"Cyril, you know where you are," Peter responded.

"I don't think I want to be here." Cyril tried to sit up but discovered that he couldn't. An imaginary force glued him into the chair, compelling him to face Peter.

"Where are you?" Peter pleaded with a grin, each word dragged out and extravagant.

"Am I in hell?" Cyril shuddered.

"No," Peter shook his head. "Do you think you're dead?"

"Am I?" Cyril's heart sank deep in his chest, buried underneath the fear and dread whelming up inside. "Please, I don't wish to play this game."

"This isn't a game. I just need you to accept." Peter knelt down beside Cyril. "You can leave whenever you please or you can remain here." His hand gripped Cyril's shoulder. "It's your decision. After what you accomplished, we agreed you can have another chance."

"Another chance?" Cyril brushed Peter's hand away. He clutched his beer and took an enormous draught, anticipating that it would be better this time. "I'm in limbo," Cyril stated. He watched as Peter bowed his head in approval. "Who are you?"

"That's not important; we will meet again and when it's time, you will understand." Peter pointed behind him. A tall building rose in the distance, created from white sandstone, the sun glistening back at them in tiny sparkles picked up by the rough surface. The windows mirrored the bright blue sky back at them, obscuring the interior from Cyril. "You can walk back there and join your old acquaintances and family, or you can experience your life. You've earned that."

Cyril could hear the familiar laughter of friends, their joyful voices carrying on brilliant conversations. He could smell his grandmother's homemade bread warming in the oven, the crisp smell of apples picked from the tree in his garden growing up as a youngster.

"Then this war isn't over yet?"

"It will never be over."

"Take me back, I'm not finished."

Saltwater spewed past his lips and he could taste the harsh brine of the deep as it charged up his throat. Cyril tried to breathe, but there was too much water seeking to make its way out of his breast. Feeling his chest compressing, he opened his eyes to find Richard hovering above him, his shoulders pumping up and down as he thrust his clasped hands into Cyril's chest.

"You're alive, Jones!" Richard cheered as he rolled Cyril over onto his side and patted his back. Cyril coughed as the last of the ocean water left his chest. Cyril looked up at the puffy white clouds high above him in the bright blue sky. He wondered when the next opportunity to fly above the clouds would be.

Michelle F Goddard

Goddard is originally from Trinidad and currently living in Ontario, Canada. She has been an honorable mention in Writers of the Future and has had her short fiction included in both the *Water* and the *Blood is Thicker* anthologies.

She brings with her her short story 'To Soar Above a Fearsome Road.'

To Soar Above a Fearsome Road

Over the edge of our floating sanctuary, the world spread before us in all its grim testimony. The jagged teeth of dead cities sprouted from barren swaths of desolation, rising up to bite us as we floated by. Conch shell swirls of destruction crept across the landscape, proof of the tornados that had swept aside what was left after the wars. The wind whipped electromagnetic bands of energy that snaked across the sky, pulsing and writhing and ready to strike. Man had battled man and nature had joined the fray.

In desperation we had prayed. We had prayed and our god had answered. A mist had spread across the length and breadth of us. A many-tentacled form plucked us up from the earth; town and fields, rocks and streams, all that we were. Our god slithered and slunk below to support us upon its back. We had been a patch of land near the sea. Now we were an island in the sky.

As we were borne upward, peace descended; we were divested of our hostility as easily as changing from a soiled garment to a clean one. We were saved from our past to start anew. Generations later we were still safe. Do we now shake our fists and bemoan our fate? Is it right to envy the birds when they glide past? Of course it is. We are human. Perhaps that is why our god does not understand why we chafe. We live among the clouds, yet flight is forbidden.

It was the agreement we made. For when one has seen rockets fly to splinter the earth, and jets scream across the sky to deliver death to huddling clutches of humanity, when wars are launched from the air, that accord could only be inevitable. But those are stories told by stoic elders to impatient children.

Some days, after I have trekked to the farthest boundaries of our sanctuary to search for salvage, I climb out of my mech-strider, beating dust and dirt from my dungarees, and stand at the end of the main road; a road that now leads in a direction that can no longer be taken. There, ragged edges of grass cascade, roots and branches claw at wispy clouds, concrete and tar crumble. It was as if they, like me, wish to reach beyond our carefully constrained world. My unbound hair would rush over my shoulders and snap at my cheeks, to lash me to obedience. Those days I would return home red cheeked and unrepentant, yet resigned.

Then you crashed and my world tilted.

I ran to you. Fear turned my mech-legs into trundling rubber wheels and my heart a rusted hinge as I clanked across the terrain. I climbed out through the metal carapace to find you on your back laughing. It made my stomach churn. Was that the punishment for your trespass? Madness? But you looked at me, your eyes wide and clear, this stranger with twisted braids black as tar spread around her head so like our god's tentacles. I wondered if you were a messenger. Or a gift. "Hello," you said smiling up at me. "I'm Bertie."

My lips silently caressed your name. Then I saw the

debris. You did not understand my fear, mistaking it for concern or confusion. But though it looked nothing like the war-crafts of history, so slight and delicate like a dragonfly, I knew it for what it was. I should have smashed it, raised a mighty mechanical fist and let it fall upon the fragile frame. But that repentance, even now, is but shadow.

I helped you to your feet. "I'm Majel," I said.

Against your chest, you cradled your left arm. Bruising ran along it, seemingly bone deep even on your dark skin. Any pain you carried, however, was down feathers, diminished by the transcendent light in your eyes as you examined your wreckage. I could not stand by, drawn by your magnetic resolve.

You stayed my hand as I approached the delicate wires that ran along the wings. "Don't touch. You could get a nasty shock." You turned your attention to a battery behind the seat. "I have to shut down the power supply."

"Are there weapons?" I asked.

"What?" You shook your head and smiled so disarmingly. I felt a fool to have doubted you at all. "It's a single-seat glider. A plane? Not a weapon. It is propelled by electro-aerodynamic propulsion. But you probably don't understand—"

"You're using electricity to propel it. That's why I didn't hear anything."

Your eyes shone brighter. "That's right—"

"We still have to get rid of it."

Your face fell so hard it almost broke my heart. "Why? What's wrong?"

"These are forbidden." I scanned the area, my gaze flitting like a bee until it alighted on your face. My resolve softened. "Then we must hide it. It can't be found."

"But I need to fix it," you said. I saw you wince even as you gestured toward your plane and knew that was impossible. "Please help me." You took my hand with your uninjured hand and pulled me close. "Please. I'll fix it and then go. I won't be any trouble. I promise."

You captured my gaze and I felt myself burned. I searched your dark iris and pupil and looked for flame. Was this passion? Desire? I wanted it and feared it. You laid your injured hand over mine, your gaze never wavering though you must have felt great pain, as you tightened your grip. I marvelled that your ardour could lend you such strength and was compelled to meet it.

We folded the wings and secured your plane behind my mech-strider. I marched toward the wildest part of the forest, gentling my gait to not damage it further, while scanning the horizon for unwelcome eyes. The weight of your plane behind me was next to nothing, unlike the stone on my heart. The plane's thick wheels bounced along the shaded path while the delicate material stretched across its body flapped, barking as if to protest its injuries. I wished for silence, not breathing easy until we reached the forgiving pine needle floor.

"Where are we going?" you asked. "I thought I saw a town in the other direction."

"And you had best hope no one else saw you."

"Why?"

"They would wonder how you got here." And they would look into your eyes and see what I see and know. Somehow they would know you were not supposed to be here. And they would take you from me. But I could not speak those words and you did not ask. I thanked our god and prayed for him to turn his many eyes away from me, promising to be good if I could have this, for just a little while. This exhilaration would be enough to last my life. I would be content to fix and repair and nothing more. I would never again stand at the end of the road and look over the edge. Searching. For more.

By the time we reached my cabin at the very edge of my family's acreage, you were shivering and pale. I abandoned your plane to see to you. Once inside, you scanned my house as I gently probed the severity of the injury. Your wrist was not broken, but the sprain was serious. I spread healing salve and bound your injury. I felt the touch of your gaze and looked up into the dark pool of your eyes, languid with the mild sedative. "I already feel better," you said. "Thank you, Majel."

"You're welcome, Bertie. You must rest here. Stay here. You understand? Don't leave. I'll hide your plane. Then get us something to eat."

When I returned, you had already stoked the fire. I could see the smoke curling from the chimney as I approached the cabin. I expected you to be resting in my chair, not investigating my tinkering strewn around the space.

"You *can* help me," you said. "I thought no tech was allowed but you've got tools. You even knew what I was doing—"

"Yes, we have tools," I said as I laid out bread and cheese. "But to repair. To repair only. We can fix what we have, but nothing more. And planes are forbidden. No flight." I ladled soup into a pot and put it to heat on the stove.

"But why?"

"You clearly have never been bombed out of your home."

"And you have?" you asked, sitting at the table.

"Not here." I poured water into glasses and placed one before you. "Never here."

"And why is that?"

"Didn't you see it? Below us? Holding us up?"

"I saw a mist. I thought it only strange clouds. But when I rose higher, the land spread out before me. But how are you floating in the sky? What is behind the mist? Tech from the wars?"

I shook my head and looked away. It was not a subject we discussed easily. How was I to explain it to a stranger? And she had seen nothing but a mist. Had our god remained hidden to unbelieving eyes? Then how to make her understand the need for secrecy? "We prayed for help. Our god answered." I ladled out soup into bowls and brought them to the table.

"And your god lifted you into the sky?" You peered at me, your bandaged left hand lying limp in your lap as your right held your spoon. "But you are not allowed flight. You are trapped here."

Before I could answer, I heard a knock on my door. We froze like deer in a thicket.

"Majel," Tomas called, from behind my front door. "Majel. I know you're in. I can see the smoke from the chimney."

I rose and beckoned to you to follow me to my bedroom. "I'll get rid of him," I said. You nodded and for the first time I saw fear in your eyes. Probably a reflection of my own. "Don't worry," I said, forcing a smile to my lips.

Tomas pounded with thick fists on my door. I opened it, but not wide. "What is it, Tomas."

His gaze invaded the room behind me. "What were you doing?"

"What business is it of yours," I said, bristling.

He turned his glare on me. A light flashed in his eyes, sending a jolt of fear through me. "My business is the god's business. As yours should be."

I held my ground as if I hadn't seen the sign, as if this was nothing more than Tomas, a childhood irritant, badgering me as he always did. Though, of late, as adulthood seemed a destination just over the next hill, his attention on me felt more pointed, more precise. More covetous.

"And why must you stay here when you have a perfectly nice house in town with your family," Tomas said. "Where it's safe."

"I enjoy my peace and quiet. Which you are disturbing. Good day, Tomas."

"But I came to check on you." Tomas tried to push his way through. I did not let him get far, but my cabin is small. His gaze fell on the dining table behind me and he frowned. "Why are there two bowls?"

"I was very hungry," I said pushing him with strength fuelled by fear. "Now leave me alone, Tomas." At first he fought me. "Violence, Tomas?" That was enough to make him pause.

He staggered back, but regained his footing, and glared at me his face growing red. "Someone said they saw a plane. Everyone was scared. I was just making sure you were all right. You don't have to be like this."

"I'm fine. Goodbye, Tomas." I shut the door, and spun around to press my back against it, relieved when I heard the mechanical hiss of his strider moving away. I hurried back to you. "I will help, but we must hurry. They saw your plane."

We took our meals to my workshop. I had stored your plane in the barnlike structure with doors wide enough for it to pass through once repaired, yet secure enough to keep it hidden. I stalked the contraption, excitement and fear creating a frisson that set every nerve tingling. I could not help but look on in wonder.

"I take it you've never seen the like?" you said, noting my expression. "It's experimental. Everything optimized."

Optimized. The word sent a shiver through me. Optimization. Not just repair. Experimentation. Change. Improvement. I was dizzy with the thrill of touching something new. I scanned each component before me; the power converter, the battery, the caps and fuselage. The shining sheet like material stretched between the braces and over the delicate frame. A few of the support bars had not survived the landing, being not as sturdy as the rider.

You patted a small metal box and grinned at me. "But it wasn't until we found a light weight battery system efficient enough, yet powerful enough, to generate sufficient voltage, that we knew the solution was close."

"We? There are more of you?"

"A group of us. Working on all sorts of projects. But I think you and I can handle this fine."

We began to disassemble the plane, you directing me with sure succinct instructions that I followed with less certainty. Your easy manner, however, quickly inspired more confidence, and soon we had laid out three damaged struts; one that, if it were hale, would be key to bear the weight of the airplane's frame.

"I think I can help you fix these," I said, "but I wouldn't trust them to hold forever."

"They only need to hold for as long as it takes me to get back down. I could fly this blind and one handed."

"You may have to," I said, making a show of glaring at your injury.

You laughed, that wild, mad laugh of yours, a laugh that soared, that made me dare hope.

We turned our attention to the damaged struts and began to repair them. Once I hammered them straight, I wrapped each rod at its weakened points with thin sheets of metal. It was hot work, and you grinned as I wiped sweat from by brow. "If only my wrist were this easy to fix."

"You should count yourself lucky your injuries weren't more serious. All of this so that you can fly."

"What is wrong with that? To travel? To escape?"

"To where? The world I see below us does not look very welcoming."

"Yes. Yes. There are still conflicts. Perhaps there will always be wars."

"Not here. We're safe here."

You tilted your head and stared at me, your eyes narrowing. "But that's not enough." I could not lie to such frank regard and returned to my work. You chuckled. "You're not fooling me," you said waving your finger in my direction and then at my workshop. "I've seen your secret place." Your grin held no malice. It was warm and I found myself smiling back. "Why have this, if you don't want more."

"For privacy. Peace and quiet. Unlike some people, falling like a star from the sky. You could have died."

You laid your hand on mine. "It's not enough to just survive." When I looked into your eyes my heart flinched. You pitied me and in that moment I pitied myself.

In silence we finished the repairs, bolting the struts back into position, testing the braces and running the battery while the hairs on my arms rose in sympathetic excitation. Even though I had not created it, even though I had only helped to repair it, I felt a thrill to have my hands on something new, something I had never touched before, that no one in our sanctuary had ever touched. My hands trembled as my gaze caressed the thin wires and the shimmering material that hung over head.

Outside, the sun had set. Darkness filled the space beyond the few windows of my workshop. I was surprisingly not tired, buoyed by an exhilaration I had never had before.

"I'll need a trial run before I throw myself off this floating island," you said.

"At least you have some sense," I said, trying to lighten a heart that had grown weighty with your words.

"Is there a hill?"

"There is a rock cliff. My mech-strider can pull the plane up the incline but we must be careful—"

"Or you'll fall over the edge of the world," Tomas said, from where he stood in the darkness of the doorway. "This is why you pushed me away?" Tomas strode into the room and yanked you to your feet. "And who are you?"

"Please don't," I said. "She's hurt."

"And why is that?" Tomas said, giving you a shake with a cruelty that had not been so evident before. Or perhaps it was fear, I could not tell. "She shouldn't be here."

"Please, Tomas. Please."

Tomas regarded me with dawning clarity; a puzzle whose solution was suddenly evident. The light in your eyes, one of our god's many eyes, shimmered. "We must make this right, Majel."

"She'll go," I said. "We'll never see her again."

"No," Tomas said, his voice strident with authority. "Our god permitted her to land. There is a reason. Of course, she must stay."

"But I don't want to stay," you said, your voice stiff and commanding.

I shivered as he turned to glare at you. He pulled you closer. His eyes shone brighter. I could see you had no choice but to be ruled by him.

"You will be happy to stay," Tomas said. "Our god guides us to peace. Helping us to forget the woes of the world below."

"Or you could make her forget us," I said, the words gushing from my mouth like a river straining against its banks. "Yes," I said putting my hand on Tomas's arm. "You could do that instead. Please, Tomas."

"No, Majel," you said, breaking away from him to take my hand. "I won't forget you."

You did not see his rage as he came up behind you.

"There will be peace," Tomas said, as he laid his hands on your head. A light flashed from his hands. The air around us contracted and then expanded so violently we stumbled back, almost falling to our knees. You straightened slowly, gazing around with a blank look upon your face. Tomas gave no more time to recover. He pushed you ahead of him toward the large workshop doors. "Come. We will take your malefaction and cleanse ourselves of it."

We guided your plane to the edge of the world. You strolled beside us, a beatific smile upon your face. The trees swayed in the pre-dawn breeze. The sky warmed, the indigo curtain of night drawing back to reveal the glow of day. I shivered even as I sweated with fear and exhaustion. Your gaze upon my face was empty.

Finally, we stood at the end of the road, your plane balanced precariously, the wind pushing up the sail-cloth wings. You reached out and ran your fingers along the edge, your gaze distant but full of marvel and longing.

"Are you all right, Bertie?" I asked, touching your arm. You looked at me but I could sense your struggle; a feeling that something had been misplaced, lost. "It's me. Majel."

Tomas stepped up beside me. "Soon, you will be able to start your friendship properly. In the grace of our god. Do not worry yourself. She will never miss her old life."

Your hands caressed the braces. Both your hands. You continued to smile with no sign of pain as you stroked the plane like a lover.

"But will she be happy?" I asked.

"Is happiness worth all of our safety?" Tomas asked. "Would you risk that?" He stepped toward me and took me by my shoulders. He brought me close, almost an embrace. Perhaps he wished I would fall into his arms. When I didn't, he stiffened though he did not release me. Tomas leaned close to my ear. "I could push them both over. First the sinner, and then her sin. It would be my right as the hands of our god."

I jerked away from him and bumped into you. You staggered, but steadied yourself on the back of your chair. You moved to sit, perhaps a trace memory reasserting itself, stronger than fear or doubt. It leant me hope.

"She is dizzy," I said. "Let her sit for a moment." I did not wait for Tomas's permission and guided you into the plane. I saw your hands settle as your gaze became resolute.

During the wars, there had been a reason to lift us up. Out of the devastation and destruction. All the reason in the world. But reason did not rule here. Even when laundry was hung to dry and flew brazenly in the breeze, we watched the sky and listened for rumbling admonishments. Make-shift kites soared in secret by children too smug and innocent to know fear, only to be hastily and completely destroyed by parents. I could not diminish the light in your eyes so easily. I could not be the cause of that. If this was madness, sanity felt like death.

I leaned to whisper in your ear. "Survival is not enough." I ran to the back of the plane and pushed you and your plane over the edge of our world.

You disappeared. Beside me, Tomas stood, arms hanging limp, mouth agape as shock overrode anything else he might do. I scanned the sunrise for you and prayed the light to hide my hope. But as I saw your plane rise into the air, as it turned and glided, a delicate outline against the dawn, I could not help the tears that ran freely down my face.

I turned and walked back to my cabin. But I knew I would find myself taking the road to the edge of our world, to stand with toes hanging over the edge, to feel the wind fill me. Someday to lift me. Not today, but soon.

Shannon K Green

A gifted author with a talent for the strange, Green has been recognized in both the genre community and the contemporary literary community for his pursuits. In the past, he has been shortlisted for the 1996 Arts and Letters Award, and later won the 2015 Audience Choice Steampunk Newfoundland Showcase.

Green's short fiction has appeared in *Fantasy from the Rock, The Hamthology,* and the bestselling collections *Chillers from the Rock* and *Dystopia from the Rock.*

Sadie's Mechanical Bird

"Will she go?" the little girl asked solemnly from the doorway, pointing at the device as he stepped back.

He mopped his brow with a rag that seemed more effective at leaving behind grease than removing sweat before he stepped out of the work shed and countered, "What do you think, Dee? Will it fly?"

Dee stood to her full three feet and eleven inches and gave the odd device a long look. He could see her going through a checklist in her head as she examined the gleaming brass contraption. Walking the length of the tube-shaped body, periodically tapping the sides with her fist, pausing to test the up and down motion of the wings as well as the back and forth motion of the tail fin. She repeated the process on the far side of the device, her progress marked only where he could see her feet beneath it and her irregular tapping on the body. As she stepped around the portion of the craft that he called the nose (she called it the pointy end) she said, "Nope, Mr. Vert. I don't think she will."

Vert seated himself on a nearby crate and began to pack his pipe, steadily regarding the confident child. She returned the look with equal steadiness and calm. It had become one of their games in her head: he would look at

her waiting for an answer while she waited for him to figure it out on his own or for him to ask what it was that she
had seen and he had not. Scratching a match and puffing
his pipe alight, he said, "What do you see this time? It's as
light as I can make it, the body is paper thin except at the
braces. The boiler is small enough to stay contained and
the motion of the vehicle should self-stoke it...."

Overhead a seagull cried. Dee looked up at it calmly, a
smile on her face. Vert looked to the girl and then looked
up to see the bird wheeling overhead. The girl pulled
some crumbled ship's biscuit from her pocket and threw
it on the ground nearby. She fetched herself a cup of tea
from the small coal stove in the shed and took a seat on
another crate outside the door.

The pair sat in silence, he thoughtfully smoking his
pipe, she sipping her black tea. Vert looked to her again,
then resumed smoking his pipe. He was constantly amazed
at this seven-year old girl. She was precocious and bright,
but not what most educators would consider exceptional.
In fact, from what he had heard from most of her tutors,
she was slightly above average for her age in most subjects, but that was all. Yet the child had a remarkable ability for sketching and an undeniable knack for seeing the
errors in Vert's machines. It was this girl who had helped
him solve the problem of his trackless train by telling him
to mount the track to the vehicle rather than the ground.
She had perfected his box mover by adding larger wheels
at the fulcrum. In fact, he had presented Miss Sadie "Dee"
Volant with no less than nine patents he had registered in
both their names in the past year alone. Dee was an engineering prodigy who left him back in the 1850s while she
was decades ahead in the 1900s.

The little girl giggled as the seagull swooped down

for the scattered biscuit "D'you see, Mr. Vert?" she asked, excitedly pointing at the bird. "D'you see why your metal bird won't fly?"

Vert gasped as he finally saw what she meant. "Dee!" he said excitedly. "We're going to need a larger work shed."

Over the next few months, pieces of the device were stripped from the frame and left beside their workshop. The ten by twelve work shed was expanded twice. First to fourteen by twelve. Later, when this proved inadequate to the needs of Mister Vert and Sadie "Dee" Volant, Vert had an entirely new building constructed and moved their contraption under cover of darkness, leaving only the discarded portions of the first attempt abandoned in the original shed along with blueprints that had been heavily annotated, broken spanners, and at least one handle-less hammer.

One morning when Vert went to open the workshop doors, he found Dee stood outside. Dressed in the smallest coveralls they had been able to find for her, still many sizes too big for the young girl, she was freshly washed with her long hair tied in a ponytail and tucked into the greasy collar of the boiler suit, smiling brighter than the midday sun.

"Today she'll fly, Mister Vert. Today we make history," she said, excitement plain in her solemn voice.

"Indeed, we will. Or we'll die horrible flaming deaths," Vert replied.

"It'll fly," Dee laughed.

As she entered the workshop, Vert shook his head, muttering, "At least we'll be remembered for trying."

Sadie threw open the double doors at the front of the new workshop, folding them flat against walls. The pair then entered the shed and began pushing out a second fold on the doors until it seemed they had removed the entire front wall of the building. As the sun shone into the newly opened workshop, the highly polished brass surface of the new metal bird reflected the light back into the world.

The new metal bird looked very much like the older version, a tube roughly ten feet long, more or less pointy at one end terminating with a horizontal fan shape at the other. The body was broken by a small dome set slightly before a pair of vaguely corkscrew-shaped wings which extended nearly sixteen feet on either side. The wooden supports of the frame were visible in places beneath a sheath of brass hammered to the thickness of paper.

Dee beamed as she began hitching a cart horse to the bird. "She'll go. She'll fly." Dragging the behemoth through the doors, the wings spun slightly: small pinwheels of red and yellow centrifugal force that caught the eye like the black and white spinning disks used by hypnotists and mesmerists at street fairs. The nose of the bird bucked upward as the wheels of the carriage it was mounted to crossed the threshold of the workshop. Vert instructed Dee to stop the towing and confirmed that the bird was safely secured before allowing her to continue. He repeated the process when the aft wheels of the carriage caused a similar bump for the tail section.

"The cradle cushions worked just as you said they would, Mister Vert," Dee proclaimed as she began the process of loosening the straps that bound the bird to the carriage. Vert nodded as the pair tested the motion of first one wing, then the other, and finally lit the fire in the small boiler box. As the steam began to build, the pair raised the dome and entered the cockpit. Sadie busied herself with multiple levers and switches, looking all about the odd avian device to observe the results. Satisfied with the outcome, she told Mister Vert, "Everything is performing properly, check your systems please."

Vert went through a similar process before turning to his young co-pilot and saying, "A moment to brace myself and we may begin." With an impish grin, he immediately set to work, releasing the stops on the steam engine.

The wings began to turn, slowly at first. Then they started gaining speed as they began to transition from horizontal to an almost vertical position. Dee pulled a lever, and the wings lost their corkscrew shape, becoming rigid blades. Another of Dee's levers was pulled to flip the final six feet of each wing perpendicular to the already extended blade. Vert now pushed a knob in while flipping a toggle causing the wings to spin faster. To an outside observer, the bird now resembled an individual spinning two tea towels in their upraised arms.

The tea towels steadily gained speed as Dee watched them intently. When they had reached what she thought was a sufficient velocity, but Vert was certain was far faster than desired, Miss Sadie Volant released the last anchor binding the bird to its carriage.

At first, nothing happened. The wings spun. The blades spun. The bird sat. Vert opened the stops on the steam engine further and the bird shook like a hay cart on a poorly cobbled road before finally throwing off the ties of gravity and lifting free of the carriage.

When they had reached a height of approximately twenty feet, Sadie and Vert began throwing levers, returning the wings to their rigid formation and setting them to descend and ascend in rapid motion, mimicking the flapping of a bird wing.

"See!" Dee shouted above the engines, and flapping wings. "We're flying! Just like I said we would."

In response, Vert pushed a knob in, pulled a lever, and set the wings back into their corkscrew motion. The bird surged forward. A push of the four-way lever between his legs to the left caused the bird to swerve right. He followed the roadway outside the workshop. Pushing the same lever right caused them to turn leftwards, towards the beach Vert had paid so much to rent from Dee's family. Grinning, he shouted over his shoulder to her, "Now we're flying! Shall we try the self-stoking mechanism?'

In response, the diminutive engineer climbed over the seat, grabbed his hand on the lever and pulled it as far back as she could. The bird lurched and began to climb nearly straight upwards. The pair heard the satisfying rustle of coal shifting backwards, and felt the fire growing hotter behind them. Sadie pulled a knob and looked back with panic on her face. She held the lever in her hand, free of any connection.

"I think it broke before the boiler could close!" she shouted as she pushed the four-way lever forward and climbed back over Vert's seat, then climbed under the seat she had just vacated.

Vert grabbed the four-way lever, forcing it into the central position, attempting to coax the metal bird into a semblance of level motion. He had no idea what the genius lass could do with the contraption while it was in flight, but he knew she would most likely find it an easier time if it was at least oriented as she would have found it on the ground. Glancing over his shoulder, he hoped that whatever corner of the metal bird she had crawled into would protect her in the event of a full system failure.

From behind him, he heard the familiar clanging of

metal against metal, accompanied by what he thought were words not meant to be uttered by innocent children. Sadie poked her head into the cockpit,

"I need something like a screwdriver, blasted hinge is buggered!" she shrilled, panic in her voice. "I'm going to try to remove the durn thing."

Vert reached into a pocket of his shop coat and produced a small, metal handled screwdriver. "Hopefully this one is the right size. And watch your language, young lady, there is a level of decorum to maintain." He thought he heard a "yessir" as she disappeared into the belly of the craft.

He angled lower, heading toward the ocean. Better a cold wet landing than a hard rocky one, he thought. They had just made it over the waves when he heard a loud bang from the rear portions of their contraption. With the belly of the craft skimming the harbour waters, he shouted, "Was that a good noise or cause for further concern?"

"Good noise, fire box is closed but full," Sadie replied as she climbed out from under her seat again. "This view is amazing but can you get us above the waves a little? I want to see more of it."

The pair soared over the ocean, keeping the coastline in sight on their right-hand side, starboard Vert kept telling himself. Occasionally Sadie would disappear into the belly of their vessel. Invariably she would return with a grin that filled her face. The sun was lowering when she returned from of such jaunt and shouted, "Time to head back, the coal is burning down!"

Vert pulled some levers, pushed some buttons, and hauled on the rudder stick; their route altered so the metal bird pointed directly at the workshop the pair had been working out of for most of the previous year. That was when the behemoth shuddered in the sky.

"Might it be that I should have gotten that warning ten minutes ago?" he shouted to Sadie. She nodded sheepishly in reply and forced the wings into a full horizontal, gliding position. A flurry of knob twisting and lever pulling followed as the pair steadily lost altitude on their approach.

All their steam spent, Vert angled the new contraption towards the sandy shore, pulling the nose sharply upwards as the vessel plummeted more rapidly. As the belly of the bird struck the ground, the pair were thrown out of their seats, only to resume them as the metal craft bounded into the air, like a stone skipped across a calm lake. The motion repeated itself several times, each rebound granting them less lift until finally they screeched to a halt where the sand changed to rocks.

Blood running down her face from a wound under her tightly fitted cap, Sadie grinned smugly. "Told'ja it'd go; now we need to figure out how to make it stop."

Paul Moffett

Paul is originally from Ottawa, Ontario and currently lives in St. John's, Newfoundland. He holds a PhD in Medieval Literature. He also used to work as a professional clown.

He brings with him his first published fiction, 'First in Flight.'

First in Flight

It seemed only appropriate that Francis should invite Judith to witness the big moment. He called round to her house on Friday evening and told her to meet him at the bottom of the hill on Sunday morning.

"I can't, Francis," she said. "I can't be anywhere on Sunday morning but church. You should be too."

"Just be there, Judith," he said. "Just…"

He left without any promises that she would come.

Sunday morning was cold and foggy. Francis used the removable wheels to pull his flying machine to the bottom of the hill like a cart, and waited, willing himself to be still.

"I wasn't sure I'd be coming until… well, here I am," said Judith, emerging out of the fog.

"I had no doubts," said Francis. "Come on. You need to… you should be a witness."

"Does it work, then? You actually got it to work?"

Francis smiled shyly. "That's what we're about to find out."

He started walking up the hill.

Judith followed. "Are you saying you don't *know* if it works?"

"I know."

"Francis, you can't…."

"I *know*."

They walked together in silence for a few minutes, then Judith spoke, quietly, "I'm sorry about your dad."

Francis kept walking, eyes forward. He didn't so much as turn to look at her.

Judith let the silence linger for a moment, then pushed on, "We're all sorry, Francis. My mother asked me to tell you."

"The critical problem is conceptual," said Francis. "Everyone else who's working on the flight problem is fixated on stability."

"When we heard," said Judith, "I went to your house to pay my respects. But you didn't answer."

"Everybody thinks of a flying machine as a kind of a boat in the sky," said Francis. "They think of tipping over as a tragedy."

"Francis."

"But why? Bringing your nose too far forward would be tragic, I agree. You would be aiming for the ground. I don't advise it."

"I hoped I would see you in church, but I guess you've stopped going."

"But what if your nose was still pointing toward the horizon but you started to keel? What would be so bad? A flying machine can't capsize."

"The funeral was lovely. It was strange that you weren't there, but I think people understood. You're grieving."

"I wrote letters to everyone I could think of who is working on building a flying machine, but nobody wrote back. Everyone wants to be the one person who figured it out. Nobody wanted to collaborate."

"I was really glad to see you'd gotten back to working

on your flying machine. But…"

"Well fine then, I thought. If they don't want my help, I don't want theirs."

"… but don't be upset, Francis. I'm really glad you've come to a breakthrough, but…"

"I was standing on the top of Signal Hill here when it came to me. I was flying a box kite, of my own construction of course!"

"… don't you think you're avoiding things?"

"The kite pulled on my line like a fish on a hook. It bobbed and wheeled. It wasn't stable, but it flew."

"Have you even visited the grave?"

"Stability is over-rated."

There was a pause. Francis stopped walking. He was panting from the climb. He took a deep, slow, breath, and looked at the machine, not at Judith.

"There's nothing in the grave. He's not even there. He's somewhere out…"

"I know," said Judith.

Francis started walking again.

"You helped build my very first kite. I thought you should be here."

"I'm honoured," said Judith. "Really I am."

They reached the top of the hill, a rocky slope covered with short scrubby grass and overlooking a grey, choppy ocean. The fog was thinning, but it was still thick enough that the horizon was invisible. Judith helped Francis push the machine up the edge of the precipice, its nose pointing towards the ocean. Francis climbed into his machine.

"Are you sure about this?" asked Judith. The wind rose, and whipped Judith's hair around her face. She looked worried. She looked beautiful.

"I'm sure," said Francis, and pushed off.

Heather Reilly

Heather Reilly is the author of the *Binding of the Alma-traek* medieval fantasy series, and has written and illustrated several books for children.

Reilly is the proud recipient of the Noble Artist's Author of the Month award for February 2015 for her short story that appeared in *Fantasy from the Rock*, 'In the Moonlight.'

Reilly currently teaches music in Newfoundland, Canada, where she lives with her husband, and three beautiful children.

The Fifth Leg

The dials began to spin wildly, no longer able to give any kind of accurate reading. There was a flash of lighting around the small plane that lit up the clouds, though it did nothing to improve the frantic pilot's view. The altimeter showed that they were in a flat dive and losing altitude, although the flying ace was almost certain that she could still feel the plane solidly beneath her on the level. Couldn't she? Another flash and she screamed at what the lightning revealed coming out of the clouds towards her.

Everyone had said that Rosalie had had too much spunk to ever settle down. She had been born into the spotlight of Amelia Earhart's failed flight, and she had the bug in her to succeed where her hero hadn't. From the moment she had heard the female aviator's name, Rosalie had lived and breathed flying with the determination of a stubborn mule. It hadn't hurt that her family was rich. Her father owned a plane, and she had been proudly flying since her fifteenth birthday. She hadn't been legally allowed to pilot a plane until then, but she had gone up lots of times to observe and begin her training to lead up to the main event. Once she had been allowed to take control in the cockpit, it wasn't long before she had soloed for the first time. The plane had started to move down the runway, picking up speed as it went. As the nose had tipped up and the G-force had pushed her back into her seat, Rosalie had felt the freedom of an eagle as her metal bird left the runway behind. The horizon had dropped below her and as she had levelled the plane out and the G-force had abated, she had whooped with glee alone in the tiny plane. The rush she had felt at being the only one up there had well outweighed the fear that anything would go wrong. She had taken off and landed enough times with her instructor that she thought she could land the bird blindfolded. The result was a beautiful landing at the end of a perfect flight. After that, Rosalie had flown every day the weather would allow. She had been a natural, and her raw talent had caught the eye of an equally ambitious navigational student named Tommy, who had often flown from the same airstrip himself.

Rosalie could be found at the airfield on a very predictable schedule, and Tommy had made sure to be there whenever possible to watch her fly. Rosalie had never even noticed him; she had only had eyes for the sky and the adventures it held for her. But he had made sure over the years to always sort of be in her vicinity when she was making ready to take off, or he would be there to walk her from her plane once she had landed. He had wanted her to equate flying and the feeling of exhilaration it brought on with him. Whenever she had left the cockpit, she had worn a smile that had blazed like the sun, and eventually, that smile had turned his way.

It was the most important day of Rosalie's life; her seventeenth birthday and the day she would be able to finally hold her deeply coveted pilot's license. She wasn't afraid or nervous, this was just another day up in the sky and she was brimming with confidence and excitement. She stood at one end of the runway and watched the sun rise. She squinted and smiled as the first rays hit her dark brown eyes as they peaked over the horizon. A slight breeze gently ruffled the edges of the brown curls that sat otherwise at peace across her shoulder blades. It was a beautiful day for flying. She could smell the soil and grass from the land that lined the runways. She heard footfalls on the tarmac behind her and recognized the gait of Tommy's steps. She turned to face him with an excited grin on her face.

"Today's the day!"

"I know." He shot her a cockeyed smile and his eyes dropped shyly to the tarmac before finding her face again. He always seemed to reserve that just for her. Whenever he grinned like that it made her feel giddy inside, like the two of them had some sort of conspiracy that no one else was privy to.

"I figured you'd be here early; I just didn't realize that you'd be up before the sun."

She had always suspected that the handsome older boy had been keen on her and in her sheer enthusiasm for what was to come, she threw her arms around him—it was an all-or-nothing kind of day. "I'm glad that you're here, Tommy."

It only took a split second of surprise before she found herself folded into his arms in a secure and warm embrace.

"I wouldn't have missed it for the world."

The sound of more footfalls approaching startled her, and they quickly released each other and took a quick step apart for propriety's sake. A man in an expensive, tailored business suit strode confidently across the tarmac toward them. His pompadour hair style was slicked back with Brylcreem that glistened in the morning sun. Although his hair was greying a little at the sides, and minute crow's feet sprouted at his temples when he smiled, he carried himself like a young man.

"Father!" she greeted him affectionately with a kiss on his cheek. "I thought you had a business meeting that you simply couldn't get out of," she chided suspiciously.

"And miss my little girl's big day?" He endured the kiss and smiled down at her before turning his attention to the navigator standing beside his daughter.

"Thomas," he made the acknowledgement while holding out his hand for the young man to shake it. "I think you're at this airport almost as much as my daughter."

"Yes sir, Mr. Brown. I think I love flying almost as much as she does."

The plane that Rosalie would be using for her test in was brought to the end of the runway and Rosalie's instructor waved to them from the windowed wall of the airport. They were ready to go.

Mr. Brown put his arm congenially around Tommy's shoulders and began to guide him away saying, "I have something I hope you can help me with over in hanger two." As the two men walked away, Brown half turned back to his daughter. "Good luck, my dear, not that you'll need it. I'll see you when you get back."

Rosalie's test flew by and as her instructor handed her pilot's license to her back in the pilot's lounge, she thought that nothing could top the feeling of accomplishment that seemed to light her up from the inside. Her father and Tommy wore identical smiles of pride. Mr. Brown had been confident in his daughter's ability, and to commemorate the occasion, he had prepared a surprise for her. He winked at Thomas across the room to signal the young man to head out to the hanger he had indicated before. Then he drew his daughter aside and presented her with his arm. "Come, my dear, I'd like to have a word with you outside."

She went with him, expecting him to bid her farewell before departing for the business meeting he must have put off for her sake. But instead, he led her to face the closed loading door for hanger number two. Mr. Brown raised his forefinger and thumb to the corners of his mouth and blew a shrill whistle. The loading door instantly began to rise as Thomas hit the button from the inside.

"I got a little something for you." Mr. Brown confided, "I knew you could do it."

The sunlight worked its way into the crack under the door and then moved further and further into the hanger as it lifted. Inside, it revealed a brand new Piper PA-23 Apache all of her own.

"Happy birthday, princess."

"For me?" Rosalie couldn't believe it. The brown and gold design shone brilliantly in the sunlight. She squealed with delight and hugged her father. "Can I take her up?"

"Of course, she's yours. She's gassed up and ready to go."

"Tommy, you want to come for a ride?"

After her birthday she began taking longer and longer flights. More times than not, Tommy went up with her, and she discovered that he really was wonderful at navigating.

When the weather spoiled her airtime and she was forced to spend her days indoors, she made calls to multiple air fields, and began plotting a flight plan to follow in Amelia Earhart's footsteps. She figured that she would have to modify her plane a bit and removed a couple of the seats to make way for ferry tanks to hold the extra fuel she'd need to cross the longer branches of the journey across the Pacific Ocean. The extra tanks meant more weight in the plane, but they would also allow her to make less frequent stops, possibly gaining her a couple of world records. Finally, after months of planning, she thought she was ready.

When she showed the plans to her father though, he had nearly lost his mind. He forbade it, citing that Amelia Earhart had died, and that Rosalie was only half the age that Amelia had been. She was too young, too inexperienced, and too ambitious. He had tried to ground her in fact, but she ran off in a state straight to the airport. She was only slightly surprised when Tommy intercepted her on the way to her plane. She figured her father would call ahead to the boy and would probably ask him to 'talk some sense into her.' When Tommy tried to block her way through and slow her to talk to him, she just circumvented him and carried on, with tears still streaming down her face in anger and frustration. She found her way barred again. He was as stubborn as she was, and he held her by her upper arms.

"Let me go, Tommy!" she warned. He released her, but he didn't move.

"Rosie, you can't fly like this, you can barely see!"

She used her arm to swipe away the tears that decorated her face. More threatened to fall but she held them back with sheer force of will. She put up a strong front in her determination, but her voice cracked when she said, "I can too see! I'm going up, you can't stop me!"

She could feel her nails biting into the palms of her hands as she stood with her fists clenched tightly. He held her blazing gaze for almost half a minute as he seemed to evaluate his next course of action. In that time, she calmed considerably, and most of the anger had begun to drain away. She was left with just a deep sense of sorrow and injustice.

"Please," she pleaded. He broke.

"Fine, but I'm going up too."

They took to the skies in her plane; the only place she felt truly alive. Her anger and even her grief began to abate. She had never let anything stand in her way, and she wasn't about to start doing so now. She would show her father that she wasn't a little girl anymore. She and Tommy traipsed across the sky, and though she felt more at peace inside, the flight did little to help her come up with a solution to her problem. Her father was used to running his company and family, and like Rosalie, he wasn't used to having his wishes rebuked. In short, neither father nor daughter was used to being told they were wrong or couldn't get their own way. Upon making her final descent, Rosalie was astonished to see her father's car at the airport. She had half a mind not to land at all, but she knew that she couldn't stay up there forever.

"Play it smart," Tommy urged as they returned to the pilot's lounge where they knew he would be waiting.

They found the usually calm and collected man pacing back and forth across the floor in an agitated manner. When he finally saw the pair approaching, he ran to Rosalie and took her up in his arms. He was clearly distraught. "Oh, thank God you're alright. See, this is why you must give up this foolishness."

"Actually, Papa, I'm not alright. I have been training for this my whole life, you know this. It's time."

"Rosalie, try to see reason. You said that you were going to follow in Amelia Earhart's steps, but her route was flawed! She didn't make it, even with Fred Noonan to help."

She wouldn't be dissuaded though. Her father stared down into her hard brown eyes and knew she was serious. She tossed her head emphatically and her chestnut ringlets danced across her back. "Fred Noonan liked to drink," she said pointedly. "I don't."

Her father tried to look stern, but he was about to crack, "I don't know what I'd do if I ever lost you."

Tommy sealed the deal by surprising them both. "She won't get lost. I'll navigate; it's what I do best. I promise, Mr. Brown, I won't lead her astray. I helped her plot half the trip, I suppose that I'm as ready to see this thing through as she is."

"But what about your job? You said your boss would never give you the time off," Rosalie reminded him.

It was the only thing that had held him back. His brow furrowed only for a moment before it smoothed. He had been so taken up in the moment that he had forgotten. But he was decided now. "I'll just have to find another one. You're more important to me, Rosalie."

Mr. Brown stuck out his hand for Tommy to shake, "Thomas, my boy, you bring my daughter home safely, and there will be a position for you at my company worth twice as much as you're making now."

Tommy shook it and thanked him as Rosalie looked up at him in gratitude and joy.

With that, their future became set in stone, and something dark on another plane of existence chuckled.

Rosalie's stomach was a bundle of nerves but to Tommy she looked as cool and as collected as ever. They had all of their provisions on board and they waited at the head of the same runway that Amelia had used in Oakland for their clearance to take off.

Their radio crackled, accompanied by the voice that finally set them free. Rosalie grinned and scrunched up her shoulders briefly. "This is it!" The hum of the twin engines rose to a higher pitched drone as the propellers began to spin at the necessary velocity. Rosalie felt the cool plastic of the round knobs of the side-by-side throttle controls and pushed them forward. The plane began to move up the runway and quickly picked up speed. In only a few seconds, Rosalie felt the familiar dipping into her seat sensation that accompanied the moment the wheels left the tarmac. They seemed to even out for a moment, flying only a few feet above the runway before pulling up to a higher altitude. The land around the airport seemed to fall away below them and vehicles very quickly seemed to be as small as toy cars.

The knot in Rosalie's stomach loosened and all she was left with was pure exhilaration as they lifted above the clouds and evened out. She was happy to have Tommy with her, and felt more secure knowing that he'd be her navigator. She trusted his skills implicitly. She took a moment to reflect on how he had been willing to trade in his job for her dream. That proved that his belief in her was unwavering, and showed how much he truly cared for her to support her in that way. If the moment that her crush had blossomed into full-fledged love could be pinpointed, it would have gone down in history as being right then and there.

They made it to Burbank and to Tuscan, Arizona without a hitch. The short flights were a great warm up, and crowds of people welcomed them as they landed. Evidently, her father had spoken to the press, and as they entered the plane to depart early the next morning, news journalists called out questions as cameras flashed to capture the couple in their last moments before takeoff. Rosalie and Tommy buckled in, and sat there anticlimactically as they waited for someone to clear the area of the reporters so they could move the plane. Eventually they were able to take off for New Orleans, the longest leg of their journey so far at over one thousand miles. The couple was cleared to come in for a landing, and as always, Rosalie held her breath until the wheels touched down. As they taxied to a stop, Rosalie was ready for a short rest and another kind of adventure. She might be tired, but she was excited to be in a place with such a different culture from the other states they had been to. She and Tommy dined on gumbo and listened to jazz, and even ventured out onto the dance floor to cut the rug before heading off to bed. Rosalie was in her glory. She just loved the music. The ragtime seemed to make every one of her nerves jitter with wanting to dance. Surprisingly, Tommy showed an aptitude for picking up the moves he saw around him. When Rosalie was in his arms, she thought that it was almost as good as flying. She could have stayed up all night quite happily, but knew she had to show some self-discipline if she wanted to be able to finish what Amelia had started. Her emotions were heightened, and the thought fleetingly crossed her mind for her to ask Tommy to stay with her for the night, but she had always been a good girl, and she didn't want to leave a legacy that would be shadowed in scandal. She begrudgingly went off to bed, making a vow to come back this way again sometime soon.

The flight to Miami was considerably shorter, and Rosalie found herself back in a state that was very much just like home. But she almost didn't want to leave. The next leg of their journey would take them not only to another continent, but Tommy had planned a flight path directly through the edge of the Bermuda triangle. It was an area over the ocean where planes and ships had been experiencing instrument malfunctions and many had disappeared, leaving no trace behind. In fact, only five years before, a Douglas DC-3 flying in the opposite direction along the same route went missing along with its three crew and thirty-six passengers. She never mentioned a thing to Tommy; she didn't want him to see her with such a superstitious weakness, and she just had to stay true to Amelia's route. It was silly, really, she told herself over and over. However, only the vow to herself to finish what Earhart had started allowed her to carry on. She decided that if Amelia hadn't worried about it, then neither would she.

And so, with the sun hidden behind some fluffy, white clouds, the Apache took them up into the wild, blue yonder. The world didn't end. The plane flew smoothly above the city and then out over the water on a completely ordinary flight for almost the first half hour. That was when Rosalie saw the first signs of irritation in Tommy's usually calm demeanor. He was frowning as he checked his charts, rechecked the instrument panel, and looked out the windows. They flew into what appeared to be almost an alleyway of clouds. They ranged from white to darker grey, and as they hung suspended in the air, Rosalie thought that it was like flying through the layers of a tasty pastry. Tommy made a sound of frustration though.

"What's wrong?"

"We were supposed to have just flown over the Florida Keys, but I didn't see them. I'm trying to get our bearing, but I can't see a thing with these clouds. Can you take us lower?"

"Sure."

Rosalie was worried now. She prepared to take them down and glanced over at the altimeter. Her blood froze in her veins. The dial was swinging wildly clockwise and counter-clockwise, back and forth. She checked the compass—same thing. A baseball sized sphere of white light formed off to the left of them and lightning zapped out from it in three directions. It missed them, but seconds later there was another flash of lighting around them. The altimeter showed they were in a flat dive although Rosalie had yet to drop the nose of the plane. There was none of the lightness that one feels when a plane is in a dive, and Rosalie could still feel herself solidly in the seat as if the plane were flying on the level.

"Take us down, now!" Tommy yelled.

Without knowing how far from the water they were, she pointed the nose down and began a fairly steep dive. It was like flying blind. The cloud seemed to go on forever, and Rosalie's fear grew as the plane continued to dive. The fear was like an itch that grew more persistent by the second.

"Rosalie," Tommy warned. It frightened her even more to hear the nervous jitter in his voice.

"I know, just three more seconds."

The itch grew and her blood seemed to run cold. She broke out in a sweat. Then, just when Rosalie was about give it up there was another flash of white light and the cloud set them free. Like a brick wall, the ocean was racing toward them. She quickly pulled up and levelled out frighteningly close to the surface of the sea. But all their efforts seemed to be in vain. The sea looked eerily calm. Not a whitecap or wave was visible. The entire ocean was a still mirror that reflected the underside of the tiny plane and the vast expanse of purplish, angry looking clouds above them.

At first glance, Rosalie had to do a double-take. She was thrown off by the fact that the water wasn't blue, green, black, grey, or any other colour that she had ever seen it before. It took her a moment to realize that it was the colour of the clouds echoed back up at them. The sea slowly released a bubble about six feet in diameter, and when it popped at the viscous surface, yellow steam radiated upward from it and disappeared into the atmosphere. Rosalie had no information to base her first impressions on, but whatever the gas was, she was sure that it was poisonous. The sea appeared to be as thick as molasses.

"What is this place?" Rosalie was now terrified. "Find me somewhere to land, Tommy."

Tommy tried for a while to get their bearings. With the heavy cloud cover, he couldn't even use his sextant or find any celestial markers to figure out their position. Nothing below them looked right. He threw the charts over his shoulder. They were useless. Wherever he and Rosalie were now, it wasn't on any map he had in the bird. He scanned the flat liquid surface on all sides and finally pointed to a place ahead and to the right. "Head that way. I see something on the water."

About half a minute later, Rosalie grinned at him, relieved. "I think it's an island, and it appears to be big enough for a short landing."

"It looks pretty small. Do you think you can do it?"

"I'll make it work."

"I've never asked if you know how to swim."

"If we end up going into the ocean, I think swimming will be the least of our worries."

She lined the plane up to make the most of the ovular island. As they got closer, she saw the way it shined like black, wet asphalt. A sense of dread gripped her. She was going to do her best and she knew that they could land in that amount of space. It was almost awe-inspiring how quickly her Apache could speed up and slow down when it came to takeoffs and landings. However, what concerned her now was that slick runway. If her wheels began to skid upon landing, they wouldn't stand a chance at stopping in time.

The hum of her engines was like a security blanket as she lowered her landing gear. Perfectly lined up for their landing, she slowed her speed and began to raise her flaps. She held her breath. In a couple hundred feet, she would kill the engines completely and they would touch down, for better or for worse. That's when the island rolled.

"Look out! Pull up!" Tommy yelled and pointed to her left.

A great, shiny, webbed paw with claws curled up out of the gelatinous ocean and slowly swatted at the buzzing plane. It was half the size of the Apache, and it was covered in slick black fur. She yelled at Tommy to turn the crank on the ceiling to lower the flaps and she hit the switch to raise the landing gear. She pushed the throttle forward to speed up the plane in an effort to dodge the deadly impending blow. She instinctively leaned away from it and the plane began to bank as it pulled up. The paw just missed their tail, and she continued to climb, not wanting to see the maw that would be attached to the slowly surfacing head of that thing.

With the cloud cover so low, she had no other choice but to fly up into it. Just before they entered the lowest clouds, she saw what looked like two fireballs falling one after the other to the sea on the horizon. When the first touched down, the thunderous roar of an injured monster rolled through the air. The small plane continued upward and was once again enveloped in thick purple clouds.

"Maybe I can get above them," Rosalie hoped wildly. She didn't ever want to go back down. She thought that she might actually lose her sanity if she ever had to face what had made that horrific noise. The clouds were illuminated a light purple for a moment as lightning flashed behind them. Rosalie didn't know how they were going to get out of this. A ball of lightning formed right before the Apache and Rosalie screamed and instinctively raised an arm in defense as a blue, scaly tentacle whispered out of the cloud beside them. Just as the lightning began to reach out from the ball and forked toward their nose, the tentacle snaked out toward it, snatched the ball of electricity out of the sky, and disappeared back into the cloud.

Two more flashes in quick succession blinded them with white light. When Rosalie opened her eyes, she was flying out of a white cloud into a recognizable blue sky. Below them, the blue ocean surrounded yet another island, but this one was recognizable as having normal cities and neighbourhoods below.

"That's not possible," Tommy said sceptically. He looked at his watch, held it to his ear to hear that it was still ticking along properly, and stared at it again. As he grabbed his charts, he told her, "According to my watch, we were only gone for an hour."

"Something's wrong with your watch, it couldn't have been more than thirty minutes."

He easily found their bearings now, and reported, "Then you're not going to believe this. We've reached our destination. That's Puerto Rico down there."

Rosalie flew over the island to the city of San Juan that housed the airport where they had planned to land. She hailed the tower with her radio and asked them for clearance to land. The surprised voice on the other end gave them the go-ahead, but said that they hadn't been prepared for their arrival. This time when they landed, there were no reporters or cameras waiting. The young couple disembarked and headed inside to find a phone. She called her father at work and was very politely told that her father was in a meeting. The secretary asked if she could take a message. Rosalie didn't recognize the voice. Was her father training someone new? She sincerely hoped that nothing had happened to Ethel, she had always been kind to the boss' girl.

"I need to speak with him immediately. Please tell him that his daughter is on the phone."

There was a pause before the secretary came back to her in an admonishing tone. "You really shouldn't say such things, miss. How awful. I'm going to hang up now. I will not be telling Mr. Brown that you rang."

"Wait!" Rosalie called into the receiver. The secretary hesitated before hanging up. "It is Rosalie! Please, get my father."

The secretary covered the receiver of the phone and muffled tones could be heard as she spoke to someone in the background.

A moment later, she heard her father on the line.

"Rosalie?" came the hopeful voice.

"Yes, Papa, it's me."

Cries of joy and celebration came from the other end. Rosalie felt a shiver down her back and the hairs at the back of her neck stand on end as her father recounted how her plane had been lost and she had been missing for the last four years.

Stacey Oakley

Stacey Oakley is an author originally from Moncton, New Brunswick who became a vibrant part of the local Newfoundland writing scene after the publication of 'The Sorrows of War' in the 2016 edition of *Sci-Fi from the Rock*.

She has since gone on to independently publish her own novel, *Hunter's Soul*, and in 2018 was crowned the winner of the 48 Hour Novel-Writing Marathon.

Stolen Wings

Nyx's happiest dreams were also her worst nightmares. They were the dreams where she soared through the sky, the wind moving over her feathers like a lover's touch. She could feel the push of air against her wings and made tiny adjustments for optimal flight, enjoying the sweet pull at her shoulders when she banked hard, her body almost vertical in the sky. She soared high above the forests, coasting on thermals, watching for dangers to her flock even as they played in the sky around her, calling out to each other.

She never wanted to wake up from those dreams.

But she always did, and she always found herself trapped in her human body, a form that had become her cage because she dared to defy the Sorcerer King. She'd also been cut off from her family, afraid to face them since they'd warned her against going near his palace in the first place. She was alone and trapped on the ground. There was no crueler punishment for one of her kind.

"Flying again?" Nyx jumped slightly and turned over to look at Lilith, though she could barely see her face in the dark of the room. She hadn't realized she wasn't the only one awake.

"How do you know?" She tried to keep her voice as normal and level as possible.

Lilith gently stroked her cheek, and Nyx could feel the still-damp tear tracks spreading. "You're crying."

She leaned into the touch even as she wiped her eyes. "Sorry."

"Why?" Lilith pulled her close, clever fingers tracing absent patterns over the fine, faint blue lines that were slightly raised on her back, lines that covered her body just under her skin. They made up an odd pattern, like feathers. It was a common trait among bird shifters, like the feathers that grew in her hair.

She'd heard endless "chicken and egg" debates on whether her kind were human first or animal. She didn't feel it was that simple, but then again, she was pretty sure most of those people hadn't been trapped in one form like she was. Birds were meant to fly, to be free. To know no borders and no cages. Yet, for her, it had become the opposite. She could barely remember what freedom felt like.

She just shrugged in answer to Lilith's question, but spoke as the silence dragged on. "It's been five years. I should be handling it better." Instead it felt like she was slowly losing her mind.

"You're allowed to have bad days," the witch pointed out. "You're allowed to be not okay." Nyx burrowed in under the blankets to be closer to her, the covers almost coming up over her head.

"How much longer until we can face him?" Sometimes it felt like they were right on the cusp of that final battle, and other times it felt like it would be years before they were ready. But they had the sword, and now all they needed was a plan.

"Soon." Lilith sounded certain. "Soon it'll be over.

You'll fly again, Jared will avenge his people, and Alira will take her crown and free her country."

"And what do you get out of this?" It had become a bit of a joke over the past year they'd been traveling together, all of them running to or from something, finding a common goal in their need to get rid of the Sorcerer King.

"Well... I get the library of my dreams and I can spend the rest of my life reading." Nyx couldn't make out her face, but she knew from Lilith's tone that she was smiling. "But don't worry, I'll leave a window open for you to come in whenever you like."

Nyx leaned up to kiss her. "I suppose I will have to make a nest somewhere."

"Not in my books you won't!" She sounded as scandalized as any scholar, but still returned the kiss.

"Then fill a shelf with books you don't like and I'll stay there."

"I can't have you nesting among terrible books. That's just cruel." She wasn't entirely certain if Lilith was joking, but, then again, Lilith likely didn't know either. "I guess I'll just have to give you your own shelf," she said at last with a sigh.

Nyx raised a brow at that. "You'd give up a full shelf for me?"

There was a long pause. "Yes, I would give up a full shelf for you."

She grinned despite everything. "Now I *know* you love me."

Lilith held her close. "I must. For no other being would I make this great sacrifice." Lilith carded her fingers through Nyx's hair. "Try to get some sleep. Once you wake up, you'll be closer to taking back the sky."

Nyx closed her eyes and prayed to powers she wasn't

sure she believed in that Lilith was right.

The next morning they met with the other half of their group in the common room of the inn. Jared was sharpening a dagger while Alira looked over several maps and made notes in a small book she'd carried with her their entire journey, which was spelled to open for no one but her. It contained information about allies, enemies, places -- anything the exiled princess thought might be useful later. Though, since Alira's parents were dead, she was now the queen.

"Have you figured out the checkpoint problem yet?" Nyx asked, glancing over the maps. They were essentially stuck circling the border until they figured out the checkpoints and how to make it to the secret entrance to the palace. It wasn't a big country, but it was perfectly placed for defense and an important point of trade, and the capital city was well-fortified. She sat down on the bench next to Alira while Lilith took the seat next to Jared. The innkeeper brought over food and tankards of a light, spiced ale popular in the area, keeping Alira from answering. The maps themselves gave little away, and the group didn't stand out, especially since the legendary sword had been disguised with a poor leather wrap, beaten scabbard, and coal dust. As long as they didn't encounter any spells that detected magic, there was no way to tell there was anything out of the ordinary about them. Shifters like Nyx weren't common, but not too rare a sight in more remote towns and villages.

"Not quite," the exiled queen replied, clearly frustrated as she glared at the map in front of her.

"We can get close to the spot we need, but it looks like

a place that would be heavily guarded," Jared elaborated, his heavy accent becoming more pronounced as his own annoyance showed through. "If the forces her brother has gathered strike in three days along the southern border like they're supposed to, that could make things easier because attention will be turned away from the capital and the palace, but it's still going to be for nothing if we can't get near the city." Alira knew ways into the palace that only the royal family knew and were protected by blood and magic, including one that led outside the city walls from the palace. But she hadn't been near the city in over a decade and they didn't know how heavily guarded the walls and the palace were under the rule of the Sorcerer King. If Nyx could still fly, the problem would have been long solved. But she couldn't.

"And we can't just disguise ourselves because they have spells for that, which is how we almost got killed a few days ago! Not to mention the Seeker Spells for magical items," Alira added.

"Those disguises were magical. What about something more mundane?" Lilith tried, guilt in her expression. It had been her spells that had disguised them. Nyx took her hand and gently squeezed it. It wasn't her fault. None of them had known about the spells, which were a new tool of the soldiers patrolling the countryside. They could only assume that someone had discovered the sword was missing from its hidden location and alerted the Sorcerer King.

Alira rubbed her face with her hands. "I'm sorry, I've just been at this a long time."

Nyx took a deep breath. "I could see if there are any hawk or eagle shifters willing to help us. Their aeries aren't far from here." Neither were her own people, the

Flights from the Rock

ravens... but that wasn't something she wanted to deal with. Not now. Not until she had her wings back.

Alira frowned slightly. "I always heard that ravens and eagles don't get along."

"Among our animal cousins, ravens will steal eagle eggs for food," she replied. "And there are many differences among our kinds, but taking down the Sorcerer King is more important than petty feuds." She hoped they'd listen long enough to understand that. "Are you sure your allies in the city are still on our side?" It was a rather pathetic change of subject, but she did it anyway.

Alira nodded. "The only people benefiting from the Sorcerer King's rule are the upper nobles. The rest of my people are afraid."

"Fear is still a powerful motivator," Jared pointed out.

"Yes, but everyone we've spoken to is on our side, and the people just need hope, which the sword will give them. And hope is even more dangerous than fear," she argued. "Look at us for an example: we're taking on a powerful sorcerer because we found out a legendary sword is real and works like it's supposed to." They'd tested it a number of times with Lilith's help after adding her to the group, discovering that it really couldn't be stopped by magic or armour. Jared hesitated, clearly searching for an argument, but relented.

"That sounded very queenly," Lilith said, grinning as she sipped her ale.

Alira gave her a wry grin in return. "I might as well start practicing now, since the end is in sight and we might actually win this." She looked at Lilith and Nyx. "I hope I can count on the two of you to be around after it's over." Jared had already pledged his sword to her as a sworn knight.

"I'll think about it," Lilith said. "I do want that library, after all."

"If you ask me to be a messenger I *will* steal the crown jewels and not give them back," Nyx replied. Alira rolled her eyes while Lilith and Jared snorted. "I'm not a pigeon."

"I do hope you have more faith in me than that," Alira said in a dry tone.

"I'll visit," Nyx promised. "My family isn't that far from the capital." Though she hadn't seen or spoken to them in five years. "And since Lilith is willing to give up an *entire* bookshelf so I can have a nest in her library, I can't really stay away."

Their companions turned to stare at the witch, who blushed faintly as she protested. "There are people worse than me!"

"I'm sure there are, we just haven't met any," Jared replied as he checked the edge on his blade.

"I could turn you into a toad," she threatened.

He raised a brow. "You keep saying that and yet here I am."

"I'm starting to regard it as a term of affection," Alira said, pulling another map to the top of the pile, and looked over at Nyx. "If your family is nearby, why not just go to them? Ravens flying over the capital would likely attract even less attention than an eagle or hawk, and you speak of them fondly enough."

Nyx ran a hand through her hair, smoothing down her feathers. "They are nearby..." she confirmed, speaking slowly as she stared at the rough wooden grain of the table. "But... they don't know about... well... this." She gestured to herself, her current state. Her curse. "I was told not to go near the tower, to stay far away. I was six-teen and stupid and I ignored what they said and they were right about what would happen." She took a deep breath, all the despair from the night coming back to her. She heard Lilith rise and move around to her side of the table to sit next to her on the bench. "I was ashamed, and scared of what they would say. Being grounded, losing the sky… it's not something taken lightly among my kind. I was afraid I would end up an outcast unless I found a way to get rid of this curse and went back victorious." Lilith had tried everything, but in the end, it seemed only the Sorcerer King could remove the spell. Or his death.

"I thought you said before that bird shifters need their families as much as birds need their flocks." There was no judgment in Alira's voice, just concern. It still stung.

"I did. I wasn't lying." There were so many different colours within the wood of the table, and they all start-ed to blend together as tears started to fill her eyes. She missed her family, and it was lonely as hell, but she was almost certain it would be worse watching them spread their wings when she only had human arms.

"Aren't you worried that they think you're dead?" Ali-ra wondered, not letting it go. "Wouldn't it be better for them to know you're alive?" Her tone was gentle, but her words still made Nyx flinch, and she couldn't meet the other woman's eyes.

"I don't think you understand. This is a fate worse than death to my kind, to be barred forever from the sky." Her voice broke a little. They couldn't understand. They'd never flown before, never felt the wind beneath their wings or the freedom of the open sky. If they had, this wouldn't be an argument.

There was a pause. "Okay," Lilith said at last, breaking the silence, and putting a hand on Nyx's shoulder in silent support. "Would it make things easier if we spoke to them together or if you went alone?" Nyx took a peak at the others through her lashes. While Alira and Jared looked troubled, she could see that they weren't going to push this any further at the moment.

At least she had something else to focus on. A problem with a more immediate solution: the eagles. "All of us, but I think that once they know how easily he can ground them on a whim they'll be more than willing to help." Provided she could get the discussion to that point.

"Is there a chance they've joined him to avoid that?" Alira was hesitant, but Nyx understood why she needed to ask the question.

"Unlikely. They tend to prefer keeping to themselves and won't serve another."

"I have noticed that in my travels," Jared remarked.

They plotted out the fastest route to the eagles' aerie as they finished eating, no one commenting when Nyx wanted to divert it at certain points. She was certain they figured out she was avoiding her family's territory, but at least none of them called her out on it.

"I guess you'll split your time between the forests and my library?" Lilith asked playfully as they saddled their horses shortly afterward.

Nyx looked over at her. "I'm a raven, Lilith. I'll wander, but I'll always find my way home." She gave her lover a crooked grin. "Besides, you'll be so busy reading you won't even notice I'm gone."

"Now's the part where you kiss her," Jared whispered loudly to Lilith over his horse's back as he made some adjustments to his saddle. She made a rude gesture in turn, though she was smiling as she got on her horse.

"Is there anything we need to know about the eagles before we get there?" Alira wondered, pulling them back to the matter at hand once they were on the road, her little notebook out and a pencil in hand. "Anything that could help us convince them or that could give them a reason to kill us and ought to be avoided. Both are helpful."

"They're a bit snobby, uptight, and proud, but then, I am biased," Nyx replied, trying to avoid sinking back into depression.

"How do they see your kind?" Jared wondered.

Now there was someone asking the right questions. "They think we're nuisances. Tricksters and thieves. Will do anything to get something shiny or glittering. More than a little vulgar and unrefined," she replied. "However, what they see as annoying, we consider to be part of our undeniable charm."

"But will they be willing to listen to you?"

"I'll make them listen," she replied, and turned serious. "When you're dealing with them, be honest. They're usually not as good at picking out lies like us or the crows, but if they find out you've lied to them, they don't tend to forgive. Tell them our chances, tell them about the sword. Let them make the decision to help us."

"And if they want to know why you didn't go to your family first?" Lilith asked.

"I'll deal with it. Like I said, they're proud. They'll probably understand." She hoped. She nudged her horse to go a little faster. "Mostly, just be polite and they'll do the same, and don't show fear."

Two days of hard travel later, they made it to the base of the mountains where the eagle shifters made their homes. There were no birds in view, but Nyx didn't find that surprising. More than likely they'd already spotted the approaching party.

"So, what now?" Alira wondered as she looked around.

Like her wild cousins, Nyx had a certain skill for mimicry, and put it to use, echoing the cry of a fledgling eagle in danger.

"Are we going to find out that's another reason they don't tend to like your kin?" Jared asked, raising a brow.

Nyx shook her head. "Not even the worst of my cousins would sink that low. But in this case... given what the Sorcerer King can do I wouldn't say it's inaccurate." Sure enough, two eagles dove towards them, shifting as they landed. The feather pattern under their skin was a light brown, similar to their feathers.

The taller of the two glared at Nyx. "I hope you have a good explanation for this, raven."

As it happened, she did. Nyx and Alira did most of the talking, once Nyx discerned that the other shifters were not only not sided with the Sorcerer King, but already afraid of what he would do to their peoples. It seemed that in the time she'd been gone searching for a solution, he had been starting to encroach on their territory. It also seemed that she wasn't the first to lose her powers at his hands. Alira proved that she was right about how dangerous hope was to their enemy when she showed them the legendary sword that no magic could stop, and their wish to stay away turned into a desire to help. However, that did not extend to the group's quest. Scavengers like ravens and crows lived within the city. Raptors did not, and would draw too much attention at a precarious time. Still, they would offer aid in other ways, which Alira was happy to accept.

For Nyx, the final blow came when they revealed that the ravens had been searching for her. She had guessed that her family would try to find her, but to actually hear it from another… somehow that made the guilt far worse.

"They have a point about being spotted," Lilith remarked after the pair left. Nyx turned to look at her. "I'm sorry, Nyx, but they're right…"

She opened her mouth to argue, but couldn't. Lilith was right. She was being a coward. "I know. We'll go to my family for help."

"We'll be with you," Lilith reminded her, slipping her arms around Nyx. "You're not alone."

"I think that went quite well," Jared remarked.

"We're alive, Alira will have some of the more powerful shifters on her side once she takes the throne, and I have to face my family. It depends on who you are," Nyx replied, raking a hand through her hair, tense. "Let's go. If we ride now we can find them in a few hours."

Nyx led them into the forests near the base of the mountains she'd avoided before. It didn't take long before things started to get familiar. She'd grown up in this forest, in the village her people had created in its heart. She remembered with painful clarity flying through the trees, showing off to friends by flying as fast as she could and twisting around branches and through small spaces. Sometimes she would hide in the trees and try to startle others when they passed by. As she grew older, she'd ventured farther and farther from the nest.

Until one day she'd gone too far.

"How much longer until we get to the village?" Alira wondered, speaking in a low whisper. "This place is… eerie."

"Well, given what they name groups of ravens and crows, it's not surprising," Nyx remarked. She could feel it too, that they were being watched. "Conspiracy and murder. Not exactly cheerful."

"How did that happen?" Jared wondered.

"I'm not sure. I'm sure there's stories. A lot of cultures seem to associate us with death because our wild cousins are scavengers and carrion birds." Granted, in bird form she had nothing against a rotting carcass either when hungry. "And my people are about as widespread as well."

Jared nodded. "I saw raven and crow shifters passing through my village on occasion."

"I've always wondered, are there any dove shifters?" Alira asked. Lilith groaned, already familiar with how this went after asking the same question.

"Doves are just pretentious pigeons," Nyx replied, ignoring Lilith, but a familiar caw stopped her rant.

"Nyx?"

She held up her hand to warn them to stay silent as the noise grew--other birds answering the call, spreading the word. She could understand them as well as if they'd been speaking human languages, could still pick out familiar voices after half a decade away. She heard at least one flying off towards the village.

"I take it we've been seen," Alira murmured softly, looking around. "What are they saying?"

"That I'm home." She swallowed hard and kept going.

"Nyx!" She barely had time to dismount before her younger sister ran at her, almost knocking her over as she threw her arms around Nyx's neck, burying her face in her shoulder. "You're back!" Nyx hugged her tight, fighting tears. Five years... Mina had been much smaller then, only ten years old. Now she was almost grown. "Where have you been? We thought you were dead!" Mina sobbed, holding her tight. "What happened to you?" She pulled back as Nyx's older brother shifted and landed in front of them, his expression a heart-wrenching mix of shock and relief.

Nyx couldn't help it, she started crying. "I'm sorry... I'm sorry..." She backed up against her horse and covered her face to try to hide the tears.

"Let's go home, Nyx," Caelus said, his black eyes damp. "Mother and Father will be waiting for you."

"I can't," she sobbed. "I can't go home."

"Why not?"

"I'm cursed." She finally looked up at her brother. "The Sorcerer King took away my shapeshifting." Like the eagles, her siblings were shocked, but it was quickly replaced by fury.

"Then he dies," Mina hissed.

"Working on it," Alira informed her. The ravens finally took notice of the trio of humans. "I am Alira, exiled Queen of Tavalor. I'm going to kill the Sorcerer King, reclaim my throne, and restore your sister's wings."

Caelus was quiet for a moment. "Then you'd best come with us as well." Nyx hesitated, still not ready to go home. But then, would she ever be? She mounted her horse, and Mina shifted and flew to her shoulder, pressing in against her neck so she could stay close. The feel of feathers was achingly familiar, a reminder of what she'd lost. But she couldn't push her little sister away. Caelus shifted and flew ahead, leading them back. As they drew nearer, the sight of a bird flying by became more frequent. She yearned to join them, but she couldn't.

It wasn't long before they crossed a stream and came

to the small village. Her parents ran over and she had to dismount quickly again as she was pulled into their tight, familiar embrace. She wasn't sure if she was the one shaking, or if they were. She couldn't stop crying and trying to apologize. Her parents held her and murmured reassurances.

Nyx wasn't quite certain how, but she did end up home, sitting in front of her parents' fire. Lilith was at her side while Caelus and Mina were as close as they could get. Like many of the homes in the village, the windows were large and many, but the shutters were pulled for now, giving them some privacy, though Nyx had no doubt their entire village and the crows' village nearby knew she was back by now.

Her mother handed her a cup of tea and Nyx nodded her thanks, the scent of the herbs and spices one she hadn't realized she'd missed. Introductions seemed to have happened at some point, though she couldn't recall them. Lilith gave her a slight smile when they made eye contact.

"So…" Nyx's father said after a long moment, eyes still a little red. "What happened?"

She told them everything; how she hadn't listened and had flown into the capital, wanting to see the busy city. She'd only been to smaller towns where they were used to seeing shifters on a regular basis. Apparently, that wasn't so in the capital. She'd been captured after shifting to human form in the market and brought to the Sorcerer King, who asked that she work for him. She refused, certain she would only be helping something awful happen. So he threw her in the dungeon for a while. An underground cage was the perfect torture for someone like her; they didn't need to do anything else to hurt her. Then he asked her again. Scared but still rebellious, she refused and tried to escape. So he bound her in human form and gave her a choice: bring him the sword that would kill him and he would return her abilities or be trapped in human form forever. After that, his guards threw her out into the streets.

Nyx had decided to find the sword and kill him with it instead. However, the powers within the sword would only work for the first person to grasp it after its last owner's death, and Alira beat her to it. Then they found Jared when he tried to steal the sword a little while later. Lilith had healed Jared when he'd been poisoned by a bandit's arrow during a fight, and decided to come along with them. She wanted the Sorcerer King's library with its books of spells and arcane knowledge to learn all she could.

Once she got to the more recent parts of their adventure, Alira took over. Feeling drained of energy, Nyx finished her tea and curled up against Lilith, resting her head on the witch's shoulder. Her lover wrapped an arm around her shoulders. Despite her exhaustion, she was certain she saw approval in her mother's dark eyes as she handed them a blanket and sat down again. Lilith wrapped it around both of them.

"So, it's spies you need to help you into the secret passage," Nyx's mother said once Alira finished.

The exiled queen nodded. "I don't want you to take any unnecessary risks, but we need help. I'm hoping that once my brother's troops start the attack the palace guards will have their attention elsewhere. I have supporters in the city, and, given even a chance of hope, they'll start a rebellion. Outside the capital they're just waiting for word to rise up, dividing the King's forces. From what we've been able to find out, the armies only stay loyal because he has prisons full of their loved ones. Once we gain control of the palace and kill the Sorcerer King, it won't take much to regain the rest of the country."

"How many of us do you need and how soon?" Caelus wanted to know.

"Not so many as to draw attention, but enough to make sure the door we need isn't covered by guards."

"Can you show us the entrance you want us to use?"

"Yes…" she pulled her maps out of her pack and spread them out on the floor. "There's a door here, along the northern wall. Traditionally it's only been known to those of the royal bloodline, and we're the only ones who can open it."

"We can make sure it won't be guarded," he replied, dark eyes flicking over the map. "How long will it take you to reach the city?"

"Four days if we push it," Nyx replied, uncertain if her words were slightly slurred or if she'd imagined it.

"Give us a week," he said, glancing at their parents. "Our leaders won't question that we need to do something."

"Go to the crows as well. An attack on us is an attack on them," their mother advised.

"I'll deal with our leaders in the morning. For now, rest." Their father looked at the group. "Gods know you'll need your strength."

One week later they waited in the forest not far from the city's walls, tense as they listened for any sound that could mean someone was approaching. The horses had been left in a nearby clearing with a stream to drink from and plenty of grass. Nyx looked up when she heard a raven's croak, and grinned.

"Caelus is coming," she said softly when the others looked at her. Her brother landed in front of them a few moments later and shifted into his human form. Nyx tried to ignore the pang of envy. She'd be able to join him in the sky soon.

Alira wasted no time. "What are we working with?"

"The city is in a bit of a panic thanks to your brother's forces, all the soldiers on the gates are worried about getting sent to the front lines and it wasn't hard to sneak into the tower office and change up the roster." He pointed to two spots near them on the map. "The door can only be seen from these two posts, and they'll be empty until someone realizes they shouldn't be, but that should give you enough of a window to get in." The hidden door was camouflaged by magic and mechanics to blend in perfectly with the wall. If the Sorcerer King had found it... Nyx knew what they would do, but it would be even more dangerous than their current plan.

Alira grinned. "That's perfect. What are people saying?"

"Nothing where they can think others can hear," he replied with a slight grin. "But there seems to be hope. They're afraid of what will happen, of course. But there is a little hope mixed into it."

"Well, that makes our lives a little easier," Lilith murmured.

"Are we sticking with our plan of attack?" Jared wondered, looking up from the map.

"I can't think of anything better," she replied with a sigh. "It's risky... but it's probably our only shot."

"Let's face it, this isn't the kind of situation where a

duel would work," Nyx added. "We need to have the element of surprise as long as possible."

"And you're sure you can play your part?"

She grinned. "A flock of ravens is called a conspiracy."

"How much longer?" Alira wondered, her fingers tapping at the hilt of her sword the only thing betraying how nervous she was.

"Just waiting for the signal," Caelus replied. Both he and Nyx looked up as a raven called in the distance.

Alira jumped to her feet. "Is that it?"

Both siblings shook their heads. "No, that's a call for caution. The guards should be changing now." She could tell that her brother hated that he couldn't go with them, but she refused to risk any of her kin getting the same curse she had to bear. As much as she didn't want to think about it, victory was not certain.

Another call sounded, the all-clear they'd been waiting for.

"That's the signal," Caelus said. "Once you're in, we'll get out." The four nodded and rose. Nyx's brother wrapped her in a tight embrace. "You'd better make it out alive. I'll be watching the skies for your return."

She returned the embrace. "Tell Mother, Father, and Mina that I'll be home soon." She sounded more certain than she felt. Her younger sister had already made it clear that Nyx wouldn't be forgiven if she didn't return. He let her go and stepped back. She could feel his eyes on her as she followed the others to the door. Alira pulled out a dagger and sliced open the palm of her hand, pressing it against a stone that had a faint pattern etched into it. Nyx wasn't sure if a normal human would be able to spot it unless they knew what to look for. She murmured something in a language that sounded familiar, but Nyx didn't understand the words.

A seam appeared around the door, and when Alira pushed it moved it aside and revealed a passage in the wall.

"Let's do this," the exiled queen said, her voice low and determined as she went into the darkness, the others following.

There was a soft rustle when the door closed and the narrow corridor lit up as Lilith pulled out one of her spelled crystals, illuminating the narrow space.

"Didn't I steal that one?" Nyx whispered in an effort to break the tension as they made their way forward. She also tried to hide her own discomfort, feeling trapped in the narrow space, though she was certain it would only get worse before they made it out.

"You did," the witch confirmed. "I figured out where to look for my crystals in your pack a few months ago."

"They sparkle..." she said in the way of an explanation, falling silent as they went down one staircase and into another hall. It was dry and full of cobwebs, but hopefully that was a sign it hadn't been used in a very long time. The passageway would let them out in between the library and the door to the tower the Sorcerer King was using. Nyx had no idea what it was about sorcerers using towers for everything. Was it just part of the flair for drama? She allowed the oddball thoughts to slip through her mind. Better to distract herself than to start panicking about the enclosed space and lack of air. It was too late to change things now.

She wasn't sure how much time had passed, or how many stairs they'd climbed, or twists they'd taken before they reached the end of the passageway. Alira held up a hand for them to stop and Lilith extinguished the crystal, leaving them in pitch black. There were footsteps coming down the hall, and they all held their breath, staying perfectly still as they waited for them to pass, as if that might help keep them from being discovered. A few minutes later, Alira eased the door open and they slipped out. Nyx drew both her blades, lightly rotating her wrists to loosen them as she prepared for a fight. Jared drew his longsword. Lilith readied her spells. Alira had a hand on the hilt of her sword. Better to keep it and its etched spells hidden until the last moment. Thankfully, the hallway was both empty and far wider than the hidden passage.

Nyx opened the door that led to the tower's staircase, trying not to remember when she'd been dragged down the long spiral staircase and thrown into the dark, cold cell where the air tasted of blood, fear, and death. A shudder ran through her, but she pushed it aside. Never again. If they didn't win, she doubted any of them would live long enough to see the dungeon.

"Remember the plan," Alira murmured as they reached the top. There was another door and they burst through it, ready to fight. The Sorcerer King whirled around at the noise, clearly shocked as he looked over the group, his blue eyes lingering on Alira before going to Nyx. She'd forgotten that he was handsome with a charismatic kind of charm. But it was only a veneer, and beneath it lay a monster. He straightened and smirked, raising a brow.

"What do we have here? A crownless queen, two companions who look like a poor witch and a mercenary, and a little bird without wings." His tone was light, arrogant, and mocking. Nyx didn't look at her companions to see their reactions to his words, forcing herself to stay calm, her expression as neutral as she could get it.

"Does your promise to return those wings stand?" She asked, stepping forward. She could feel the eyes of the others on her.

"That in exchange for the sword you get your powers back? Yes. I like to think of myself as a man of my word. Hand over the sword and the princess."

"No!" Jared snarled, lunging at her. The Sorcerer King waved a hand, and both Jared and Lilith were frozen in place. "Nyx, don't do it!" For someone usually so honest, he was a very good actor, his fear and anger at the possibility of betrayal almost genuine. Of course, some of it likely was. There was a chance she could just hand everything over and fly away.

"How rude," the Sorcerer King remarked. Nyx grabbed Alira and dragged her across the stone floor. "I must say, Alira, you leave much to be desired."

"I could say the same about you," she hissed, glaring at him.

He sneered and reached out to grip her chin in one long-fingered hand as Nyx stepped aside. She felt the ripple of power go over Alira, freezing her in place.

"There, payment made," she said in a neutral tone, her expression hard, like someone who had betrayed her friends.

He gave her a sidelong glance. "Yes, I suppose it is, and more." He waved his hand and she felt another ripple over her. It felt like a massive weight was lifted from her, like she could breathe again. "Go on, little bird. I know where to find you if I have need of anything else."

Nyx took a deep breath and sheathed her swords before walking towards the door as the windows all had glass. This was the moment, to choose to stick with the plan, or to actually betray them and leave with her life and her wings. There was a chance she could betray her friends. But she wouldn't. She shifted forms, black feathers covering her body, arms transforming into wings. She flew straight at the Sorcerer King with a shriek, her claws aiming for his eyes. His expression twisted into one of rage as a blast of magic hit her, throwing her back into a wall with what should have been bone-breaking force.

But Lilith was there with her magic. Nyx's attack had distracted the Sorcerer King from his spells, and her frozen companions were free. Lilith caught Nyx as she fell, winded but otherwise unharmed, and they looked at the sorcerer. As soon as the spell broke, Alira had stepped back and drawn the sword she'd fought so hard to obtain, slashing deep into the Sorcerer King's chest in the same movement. He stumbled, hand pressed over the bleeding wound. He raised a hand to cast another spell, but Lilith shouted a word Nyx didn't understand, a crystal in her hand glowing bright for a moment, and he froze.

"Make sure this one counts. The sword will cut through my magic as well as his and break the spell," the witch cautioned. Alira nodded and ran him through. It was like a marionette's strings had been cut and the Sorcerer King fell, yanking the blade out of Alira's hands.

She withdrew the sword and pressed the edge against his throat as he twitched, life slowly draining from his body. Alira looked at Jared. "He killed my parents and took my crown, but he destroyed your people." The warrior stepped forward and plunged his blade into the Sorcerer King's heart, twisting it to deliver the death blow. He let out a slow, shuddering breath as he breathed his last. Alira slowly sank down to her knees, staring at the corpse that had loomed over her life, over all of their lives, for so long.

A heavy, stunned silence fell over the group.

Lilith stroked Nyx's feathers with hesitant fingers, the deep black showing hints of blues and purples in the light coming through the window. Nyx pressed in close against her neck, shaking slightly.

"It's over…" Lilith murmured at last.

It was over. It was really over.

Later they would talk, they would figure out what came next.

Now, though, before everything became complicated again, Nyx just wanted to fly. She hopped off of Lilith's shoulder and ran to one of the windows, shoving it open, feeling the wind against her skin as she balanced on the wide windowsill and pushed off, shifting before her feet left the stone. Five years. Five long years she'd waited and fought for this moment, to feel the wind against her feathers, the push of the air, adjusting for the currents beneath her, just like in her dreams. Only now, she didn't have to fear waking up, because she was free at last.

JRH Lawless

J.R.H. Lawless writes Science Fiction full of dark humour and hope.

Lawless is a multiple award-winning Canadian SF author who blends comedy with political themes — drawing heavily, in both cases, on his experience as a lawyer and as Secretary General of a Parliamentary group at the French National Assembly.

A member of SFWA and Codex Writers, his short fiction has been published in professional venues, and most recently in the Third Flatiron Press *Terra! Tara! Terror!* anthology, to great reviews, placement as 2018 Recommended Reading, and an award for Best Positive Future Story 2018.

Lawless is also a craft article contributor to the SFWA blog, the SFWA Bulletin, and Tor.com.

Lawless' tale recounts the story of *L'Oiseau Blanc*, a historically famous lost plane.

The White Bird Dives

The night was cold, foggy, and calm, but the open Atlantic still rocked Pierre Etchegaray's dory. The precious whiskey, cognac, and champagne bottles rattled in the dark, despite all the straw padding their sacks.

The small, wiry Saint-Pierrais let go of the oars for a moment to check Caillou, his red, white, and black hunting beagle. The dog still slept, tucked away between sacks of liquor from far-away lands like Scotland, Charente, and Champagne. Nodding, Pierre picked up the oars again and crossed the final distance. Ahead, the American schooner lay waiting for him, all lights out.

Just like usual, the *Arethusa's* crew threw him a line as soon as he got close. The burly Bostonians didn't make a sound as they hauled his dory closer and closer. He gave the sleeping Caillou one last pat, then climbed onto the rim of the dory and jumped. A single, rocking leap was enough to take Pierre onto the schooner's low rear deck. Rough hands grabbed the canvas of his coat and pulled him across — not out of courtesy, Pierre knew, but only to get him out of the way. They were always eager to start offloading the liquor, and get back to international waters as soon as possible.

Nothing more or less than expected. A few more rifles

sitting around the deck than last time, sure. But weapons were a common sight: in case some customs official decided his latest bribe wasn't good enough, or a rival bootlegger tried to muscle in on Bill McCoy's territory. That's what the big machine gun turret on the forward deck was there for, too. It was all business as usual.

And yet, Pierre felt a tension on the air tonight. Something wasn't quite right. But 1926 had been a hard year, followed by an even harder winter. His family and friends depended on the windfall of the prohibition trade. He was in no position to let a few jitters get in the way of a delivery. Fastening his beret against the sea breeze, he made his way up the ladder to the cabin, to speak with the *Arethusa's* Captain. He was expected.

"Monsieur Etchegaray," boomed the larger-than-life man inside, mangling his Basque surname. He waved Pierre into the shelter of the shadowy, tobacco-saturated cabin. Ben McCoy was an imposing man, with the arms of a shipwright and the mind of a businessman. People in Saint-Pierre had worried for their new-found prosperity when they heard about his brother Bill's arrest in the States. But when Ben showed up to take over operations, those fears evaporated.

"Mister McCoy, a pleasure as always." Pierre had always taken pride in his English accent. But the bootleggers seemed to prefer it when he spoke with a French accent thick enough to butter a baguette with. It was closer to their expectations, and Pierre was happy to oblige. "The bottles are safe, and all accounted for."

The good Captain chuckled, then clenched his teeth and let out an ear-piercing whistle. "Not that I'm doubting your word now," he said when Pierre had lowered his hands from his ears, "but you know the saying. 'The real

McCoy.' Can't pay you until we've sampled the merchandise, now can we?"

The night was cold for early May, with the long winter lingering on far past its welcome. The fog had teeth that gnawed at the bones. Pierre could use a bracing cup or two before he set off back to port. And it wasn't as if he had any choice in the matter, anyway.

Both men waited by the dim light of the Captain's pipe, the only light on the ship, for the *Arethusa's* bos'n to clamber up the ladder. He laid a bottle of amber Monnet cognac on the shelf next to the big iron speed control lever with reverence, then headed back down to the deck. McCoy pulled out a knife and spun it around the bottle, removing the seal with one deft movement.

The pop of the cork was like a small explosion in the quiet of the cabin, making Pierre jump. But a swig of fine liquor soon calmed his nerves.

"Ah, that's the good stuff," said the Captain, smacking his lips in appreciation. Pierre nodded in agreement, as the rich vanilla and walnut notes washed through him. "All present and accounted for, as you say."

"Well, you have chosen a good night for the delivery," Pierre replied when the silence became awkward. "It is so calm and silent out here tonight. I see why you wanted to delay the drop-off."

The Captain coughed, then took another sip of cognac. "The weather was part of it, sure enough. But you're right. It is the perfect night. The men and I like it quiet."

And there it was again. That sense of unease. Why was McCoy acting so dodgy? And why were there so many men with guns out there? Even in the diffused, fog-filtered moonlight, he could see the whole crew from the cabin. Half of them weren't even helping to offload the dory, for some reason. The way they stood around with their rifles close to hand, they almost looked like sentries on one of the old war boats.

"So, what's the talk in Saint-Pierre?" said the Captain, forcing Pierre to turn away from the deck and crew.

"Oh, nothing new. All old stuff. But I suppose you might not have heard about the *Bessie C. Lake* yet. That was an English schooner. It ran ashore in the big storm last week. Nothing much to salvage, but the crew is all safe, and they are the talk of the town right now."

"So it's just local gossip, then?" McCoy smiled, and sounded almost relieved to Pierre's ears. "Nothing about the rest of the world?"

"Not much, no. Well," Pierre added, as an after-thought, "there's the aviators, of course."

Captain McCoy's face froze faster than the Pain de Sucre pond. "What aviators would those be, then?"

"Nungesser and Coli. They are great men, you know. The first to fly from Paris to New York in one go!"

"You don't say," replied the Captain, the sudden tension in his demeanour reflected in his voice. "And what do you folks in Saint-Pierre know about them?"

Pierre shook his head in confusion at the bizarre turn the conversation had taken. "The same everyone knows. That they are great men. War heroes. That they are making all France proud. Not that your Monsieur Lindberg is not a brave man as well," he added in a rush. Maybe the American was jealous France was going to win the great race? "But our boys will be beating them to it. The news from the telegraph station says the *Oiseau Blanc* should be arriving in New York any time now. Everyone loves Nungesser and Coli. It is a pity they are flying so much further north than here."

Pierre must have said something right, because McCoy unclenched his fists, and smiled again. A wave of relief coursed through the Saint-Pierrais, just like the ebb and flow of the waves rocking the *Arethusa*.

It would not do to anger the bootlegger. Out here, anything could happen to him, and nobody back home would ever know.

"So they're a long ways away from here then, huh? That's a shame," McCoy said, with his usual, genial grin.

"This is true! Some of the veterans in Saint-Pierre know Nungesser and Coli from the war. They sent messages, and we hope they might come visit Saint-Pierre on their way back to Métropole. After all the celebrations in New York are done."

McCoy refilled his glass from the cognac bottle. He didn't offer to refill Pierre's. "Yes, I heard all about the big party they're planning to through those two down in New York. Thousands of people waiting in Battery Park for a French plane to land in from of the Statue of Liberty. Damn fools, if you ask me."

Pierre raised an eyebrow under his beret. "I am not sure I understand."

The Captain swung back his cognac — such a waste, not savouring it on the way down — and slammed the glass down onto the shelf. "You heard me. Those two aren't even doing it right," he spat. "Flying from Paris to New York when the winds blow west to east. And they don't even care about that Orteig prize. It's all damn nonsense from the get-go. Pride. Symbols. The old world versus the new. Their heads aren't on straight. Never would have made it in the first place, is what I say."

McCoy said those last words in a mumble, and he was starting to slur his words a bit. Too much strong liquor in too short a period. But Pierre was pretty sure he'd heard the words properly. Only, they didn't make any sense.

"Well, we are still hoping Nungesser and Coli will come to visit us here on their way back home. The Marine could send a boat for them, and we would give them a hero's welcome!"

At this, the American glared at Pierre, then burst out into raucous laughter. He reached over with a meaty hand to thump the Saint-Pierrais on the shoulder, laughing the whole time.

Pierre had no idea what he'd said that was so funny. Was it a language thing? But with the cognac singing in his veins, the laughter was too infections not to join in.

"A hero's welcome, indeed!" boomed McCoy, wiping a tear from his eye. "You've got that one right, Pierre."

The Saint-Pierrais opened his mouth to respond, but was cut off by a high-pitched buzz that broke through the fog, invading the silence. Both men froze, alert, as they strained to listen. It sounded far off, but it was like nothing Pierre had ever heard. Maybe some sort of outboard motor?

Sound acted strange when the fog was this thick. Pierre knew it all too well. But this almost sounded like it was coming from above them.

Across the cabin, face half-lit by his dying pipe, Captain McCoy looked almost as puzzled as Pierre. "Well I'll be damned. Ol' Mister Keys was right," he whispered, surprise and resignation mixed in equal parts in his voice.

"Do you know what that—" started saying Pierre, but McCoy ignored him completely. Instead, he reached over to the tall tube of the ship's fog horn, by the open cabin window. He grabbed the horn end, thrust it out the window, and plunged down on the handle. The deep, low bellow echoed out across the sea, and silenced the French-man.

Out in the fog, far off, a second deep bellow cut through the night. Then another, off behind the *Arethusa*. And a fourth.

It made no sense for the Americans to have more than one ship out here tonight. They never brought more than one boat when doing a run. More ships meant more chance of getting caught. With this many ships, it was more like a military operation than a rum run.

The blare of the foghorns died down, and was replaced with a clatter of movement from the deck. As one, the crew stopped all work and grabbed their rifles. More firearms than Pierre had ever seen in one place before.

Up on the forward deck, the machine gun operator snapped a fresh drum of ammunition into place with a sharp click. Then he tilted his muzzle skywards.

"What the hell is going on here?" demanded Pierre, forgetting for a moment where he was, and who he was demanding information from.

"You stay down and shut your mouth, if you know what's good for you," growled the burly Captain. "We're just preparing a bit of a hero's welcome of our own. That's all."

Pierre shook his head in stunned silence. No, it wasn't possible. He couldn't mean...

The high-pitched buzz grew stronger all around them. It seemed to be heading straight for them in the fog. Drawn to the foghorn and the promise of land perhaps, like a bee to a sugar-baited trap.

Then, all of a sudden, it was straight overhead. With two dream-like steps, Pierre joined Captain McCoy at the window. He made it just in time to see a dark, fuzzy-edged shape appear through the moonlit fog above them. Like the world's largest, noisiest, and most tragically lost albatross.

"Fire, lads!" bellowed the American, straight into Pierre's ear.

It was a good thing the Saint-Pierrais had already lifted his hands to protect his ears. The staccato detonations that followed might have deafened him otherwise. Rifles fired off near and far, and the machine gun turret bathed the night in noise and muzzle glare.

McCoy stood next to him the whole time, unflinching, his jaw set and his face grim. Pierre's head rang with the din, but even that could not drown out the whine that fell from the fog-blanketed sky. The gunfire finally came to an end, but the screech of the straining engine — it had to be an engine — only grew louder. There were other sounds mingled in with it, too. Muffled cries in tones that sounded almost familiar to Pierre.

Then came a wet crack of thunder. The sound of something hitting the sea at terrible speed. It was over in an instant.

On the *Arethusa's* deck and beyond, everything went silent. Only a wave of acrid smoke, overwhelming even in the tobacco-steeped cabin, bore witness to the event. It was all that proved it hadn't all been some cognac-fuelled nightmare.

After a moment, a mourning howl rose up from somewhere at the rear of the ship, breaking the silence. It took Pierre a moment to recognise it was Caillou. The beagle, true to his placid nature, had slept all throughout the gunfire and the crash. But now, something else had woken him up. Something mournful.

He always had been a very sensitive dog.

"You'd better shut that mutt up right now," said Mc-Coy, grabbing the dwindling bottle of cognac by the neck. "Or one of my boys will do it for you."

The Saint-Pierrais hurried to lean out the open window. "Caillou! C'est bon! Arrête!" he cried.

The dog hollered on for a second longer, then stopped. With a reproachful look up at the cabin, he shook out his fur and flopped back down onto the bottom of the rocking dory.

Back at the ship controls, the Captain had already polished off half of his fresh glass of amber warmth. Pierre's empty glass still lay on the shelf, forgotten. "Good man. Now tell me. Times have been good for you since the Volstead Act, haven't they, Monsieur Etchegaray?"

"What?" replied Pierre, his head still ringing with those terrible cries he'd heard, if only for a moment. The words he might have understood, if only he'd tried a little harder.

McCoy swirled the liquor around the bottom of his glass. "I hear you've built yourself a nice new house with all those empty whisky crates. You like living there?"

Pierre clenched his teeth, and kept his silence. The American fixed him with a look colder than the fog outside the cabin window. He glanced over towards his rifle for a split second, and then stared back into Pierre's eyes.

"And what about your children? How old are they now?"

Clenching his teeth to stop them from chattering, Pierre replied with a tense, "Twelve, Fifteen, and Sixteen." He forced himself to maintain eye contact, and not to glance at the Captain's rifle as well. It leaned close to McCoy's hand, beside the control lever.

"Still planning on sending them off to studies in Montreal? Expensive, that."

Pierre nodded. There was no sense denying it.

"So I'd say it's important for everyone involved that our business here carries on nice and smooth. It's got to stay on the QT, right?"

Again, Pierre nodded.

"And that means everything stays secret," carried on Captain McCoy, never breaking eye contact. "Or else there'll be repercussions for everyone involved. Especially you and yours, Monsieur Etchegaray. Do I make myself clear?"

Pierre gulped. His throat felt dry all of a sudden. "Like spring water, Mister McCoy."

McCoy stared at Pierre for a tense moment longer then smiled. He chuckled, and twisted the cork stopper out of the cognac bottle. "Good man," he said again, pouring Pierre a fresh glass and topping up his own. "There's going to be plenty more opportunities around here for a man who knows how to keep his priorities straight, you know."

He passed over the glass, and Pierre took it with hands that barely trembled at all. He clutched it to his chest like a lifeline and stared down into its amber depths, not daring to look anywhere else. Not at McCoy, not at the rifle, and most definitely not out the window, at the roiling sea.

"Prohibition business, good as it is, can't last forever. They're bound to realise their 'noble experiment' is a complete disaster, sooner or later. Probably sooner, if what I hear from D.C. is true." The Captain paused to take a sip. "And when the end does come, we'll make sure to take care of our own. Tell me Pierre, what do you know about the air transport business?"

The Frenchman looked up at that, startled. His mind

reeled. "Air transport?"

McCoy nodded, his ruddy cheeks flushed with drink again. "It's the future, you know. After our Lingbergh makes it from New York to Paris, everyone'll be lining up to invest in the new aircraft lines. Air mail. Coast to Coast travel in only two days. And then Europe!"

McCoy raised his glass to Pierre, and the Saint-Pierrais joined him. These stunning images of things to come chased any thought about that terrible impact out of his head, if only for a bit. And he was grateful for it.

"American planes are going to dominate the skies, my friend. We've made sure of that. And when the time comes, we'll need people like you, and places like Saint-Pierre, to make the future happen. Why, once you're here, you're half-way to Europe already! So what do you say? Partners, in rum and beyond?"

Pierre swigged the last of his cognac in one go, and planted the glass back down on the shelf, with a thunk.

"Partners," he said, with a smile he didn't feel, and cursed himself for wearing.

"Good man," said McCoy, once again. "So, same again for the next delivery in two weeks' time?"

"Of course."

In a dream, Pierre took his leave. He descended the ladder, crossed the damp, silent deck, and clambered back aboard his empty dory. It had never felt so big and lonely than at that moment, as he grabbed the oars and cast off from the *Arethusa*.

Caillou let out a sharp, disgruntled breath at his feet, and Pierre smiled for real this time. He was glad for the company on the long, cold ride back to port.

He rowed and rowed, staring back into the roiling damp and the hungry dark. One pull on the oars after another, he would get back home, to hearth, and to family. And if, now and then, strange, broken objects bobbed off the side of his boat, within easy reach, he didn't let them stop him.

He had people waiting for him. He didn't want to see the white boards. He refused to see the bit of metal with half of a skull-and-crossbones motif, over a ripped, black heart. And he categorically did not see a third piece of wreckage bob by, with the word "Alambic" printed across it.

It was better not to know.

And it couldn't have been the *Oiseau Blanc*, anyway. Not really. They were heading for New York, half a world away from Saint-Pierre. Great men like Nungesser and Coli wouldn't come here.

At long last, the lights of the Petit Saint-Pierre and Galantry lighthouses pierced through the fog. Beyond them, friends, family, and plenty of drink awaited. The docks of Saint-Pierre lay piled high with more alcohol than a man could drink in a hundred lifetimes.

Surely, there was enough drink there to banish any haunting spirits. Of St. Louis or otherwise.

Teresita Dziadura

Dziadura has steadily been making her voice heard in the Newfoundland writing scene more and more over the last two years, making her presence known at NaNo-WriMo writing events and seminars as a force to be reckoned with, bringing wit and insight to every conversation she's a part of!

She made her first mark in the world of published fiction with her short story 'Beyond No Man's Land' in *Chillers from the Rock*, a chilling tale that cemented her as one of the fresh new talents in the industry.

Dziadura describes herself as a sci-fi and horror nut, but is also a longtime fan of British comedy. She has studied Marine Biology and has four children with her husband of twenty-five years.

Flight 520 to London

21:55

"Now boarding rows A22 through K43. Please take your carry-on, boarding passes, and passports, and come to Allied Skies boarding desk where our friendly attendants will get you situated. Again that's rows A22 through K43."

"About time," Jade muttered as she wearily grabbed her carry-on and joined the heard of human cattle that had queued in front of the blue and red desk.

The people slowly shuffled forward, one sleepy step at a time. Business travellers chugged coffee and Red Bull, talking on their cell phones as they waited. Others looked vacant and glassy eyed, like Jade, just waiting their turn to be processed.

Her phone buzzed as she had joined the crowd. She scowled down at her phone and turned it off before she joined the mindless shuffle of the queue. She quickly lost herself in thought, running through everything that had happened. Today had sucked.

She lazily gripped her now cold coffee, boarding pass and passport clutched in one hand and her carry-on in the other. A sudden bump from behind sent everything flying from her grasp; coffee sprayed everywhere, including all over her bags, passport, and legs.

"Fudge it," she growled flicking coffee from her pants and hands.

"I am so sorry miss!" a gruff voice said in a conciliatory tone. She turned to give him a piece of her fatigued mind, but stopped cold when she saw him.

He was big. Well over six feet tall and broad. His long greying hair was tied back in a queue behind his neck. A big scruffy beard covered a pale grey t-shirt, so she was unable to read whatever was on it. It looked like the Rolling Stones tongue but she couldn't be sure. He was wearing a leather vest over his shirt sporting several patches down either side. One stood out to her. It was an American eagle with a bike clutched in its talons, superimposed over Old Glory. "Bikers for Vets" was proudly displayed under the bird and the patch below that was a big Harley Davidson. He completed the ensemble with faded jeans and heavy black boots.

He looked nervous and flustered as he dropped his own bags and stooped to gather her things, using his denim jacket to try and sop up the coffee.

"Just great, a biker," she thought as he awkwardly handed her back her things, apologizing the whole time. *"I hope he isn't sitting next to me."*

"I'm so sorry," he said again.

"Don't mention it," she replied, giving him a press-on smile that never reached her eyes.

"I'm not usually this clumsy."

"It's okay."

"Is there anything I can do to make up for it? Get you a new coffee? Antyhing?"

"You can leave me the heck alone," she thought as she turned back around. A gap had opened between her and

the people in front, and she moved forward hoping the small distance might stop the conversation.

It didn't. The odd man laughed self-depreciatingly, "I am terrified of flying. It makes me twitchy."

"So I noticed," Jade said over her shoulder.

"Why did I respond?" she thought. *"It'll only encourage him."*

The line shuffled ahead.

"That obvious?"

"Yeah."

"My name's Nick."

With a sigh Jade said, "Listen, Nick, I don't meant to be ru-"

"Passport and boarding pass please." A business like woman in the trademark blue, red, and white Allied Skies uniform cut into the conversation. Her hair was in a painfully tight bun and she'd long since given up any pretense of "friendly attendant."

Jade, grateful for the interjection, handed over her things, still damp with coffee. The woman took them gingerly and looked disapprovingly at Jade.

"Sorry, there was a spill."

"Completely my fault!" Nick said from over Jade's shoulder, making her jump.

"Sorry," he said again, smiling sheepishly.

Jade rolled her eyes as the attendant handed her back her items and said "You are in A43."

Nodding her thanks, Jade took off down the umbilical that connected the planes to the airport. She hated these things. They bounced and moved with each step. It was worse when there were other people. She hurried to get ahead of Nick who'd probably make it shimmy like a dashboard hula doll.

As she neared the plane, she could smell warm summer air as it found its way through the seams, touched with a faint smell of jet fuel.

She loved that smell. It always heralded the start of a new adventure.

22:20

Jade settled comfortably into her seat. With her single tote stuffed beneath her, she poked her earbuds into her ears and hit play on the audiobook, *Foundations and Empire*, and closed her eyes. As soon as takeoff was over, she planned on sleeping. Tomorrow was going to be a long day and she needed the rest.

She felt bumbling and shuffling as her seatmate got settled away but never looked. She'd no intention of making a friend or having a conversation. A bump as her companion sat; elbow brushed against elbow. She tucked her arm in a little closer.

After a few moments she felt a gentle tapping on her arm. She ignored it. A few more taps. With a sigh she opened her eyes and turned her head.

"Hi." A smile with perfectly white teeth framed by a bushy greying beard greeted her.

"You."

"I felt really bad about before." Still grinning, the man held up a steaming Starbucks coffee cup before her.

Jade was at a loss for words.

"I didn't know how you like it so I brought creamer and sugar too." He held up a small brown back in his other hand.

"Wow. You didn't have to," Jade said. "Seriously."

"I did. It was the right thing to do. You looked like you were having a crappy day and I made it worse."

"You could have missed your flight."

"Nah, the kiosk was nearby. It only took me a minute."

Jade was floored. She'd had a terrible day, but this man had gone out of the way to make it better. She returned the smile and took the coffee from him.

"Thanks. I take it black, like my soul."

"So it looks like we're seatmates."

"Yeah." She looked at Nick from over the top of her coffee. "I'll be honest. I'm not great company. I hate night flying."

"That's okay. I hate flying."

Jade struggled with the idea that this mountain of a man being afraid of anything.

"I'd never have guessed she said." She paused to take a sip. "What brings you to London?"

"My Mum." Nick suddenly looked sad. "She's been sick."

"You're from England? I don't really hear an accent."

Nick laughed. "I was born there, so technically I'm British. My Mum's from a small village just south of London, my Dad is from Virginia so we moved back there when I was a kid."

"How on earth did they meet?"

"Dad worked at the US Embassy. My Mom at a coffee shop across the street."

"Seriously?"

Nick laughed. "Yep. Dead serious."

"What did your Dad do?"

"He was with the CIA."

"He was a spook?"

Nick laughed. "No, he was a clerk."

After a brief pause he continued. "So. You know my

name, where I'm from, and how my parents met. Do you have a name or will I call you random stranger number one?"

Despite herself Jade laughed. "I'm Jade," she said, sticking out her hand to for a shake.

"Pleased to meet you, Jade." Now that she knew he was from England she could hear an occasional hint of an accent with certain words.

"What brings you to London?"

"I'm participating in a martial arts expo."

"Wow! That's cool. Which martial art are you involved in?"

"Kenpo Karate."

"That's specific."

"It is. It was developed by the Shaolin monk…"

The two looked at each other and then leaned to get a better view of first class from the cheap seats. Something was going on up there.

"Cripes," Nick said. He'd caught a glimpse of a man wearing a tailored black suit. For a moment his jacket had flicked back and Nick had seen a SIG Sauer nestled in a shoulder holster. "Secret Service?"

"What?" Jade stood, trying to see over the tops of the seats before her.

"Looks like we've got some big wig on the plane."

"Can you see who?"

"No. Not clearly. I think it's a woman."

Jade sat back down."A woman, Secret Service, noisy attention grabbing boarding…" Jade paused for a minute, "Speaker Loehr?"

Nick looked down at his new friend. "She's in a wheel-chair right?"

"Yeah. Car accident left her paralyzed."

"That would account for the entrance. No matter how quiet the Secret Service wanted to be, it would draw some attention." Nick nodded. "Looks like we're in good company."

"You like her?"

"You sound surprised. She's tough, no nonsense, straight talking, and weirdly honest for a politician."

"I just figured you for a…"

"Conservative?"

"Well, yeah. Biker."

Nick smiled, a sad knowing smile. "I'm a member of a biker group that supports veterans. We do charity events, etc. We also have participated in the program that protects abused kids from their abusers."

"Damn, sorry, I didn't know."

"It's all cool. I thought you were rude and stuck up when I first met you."

Jade's jaw dropped open.

"Kidding!" Nick chuckled. "I try not to judge people."

Jade was still pretty sure she'd been insulted but was at a loss as how to respond. Was the insult that she had been rude, stuck up, or judgmental?

The plane lurched as it began to back away from the terminal.

Nick gripped the armrests and whispered, "Jesus protect me." And quickly blessed himself.

"It's okay, Nick."

"No, it's not."

"We haven't even started to taxi yet."

"Doesn't matter. This is a little tube of death."

Jade hesitated for a moment and then reached out, taking Nick's hand in hers. "I gotcha big guy."

23:12

"Ladies and Gentleman, this is your captain speaking. We've reached our cruising altitude of thirty-six thousand feet. I've turned off the seat belt sign, so feel free to move about. Just don't all go to the same side of the plane." He paused and a few people chuckled politely. "Your flight attendants will be around shortly with some refreshments. Our estimated time of arrival to Heathrow will be 10:30 AM. Please, enjoy your flight and thank you for choosing Allied Skies."

Jade looked at Nick. His eyes were shut and beads of sweat dappled his brow. She'd lost feeling in her fingers from how tightly Nick had been squeezing her hand.

"You okay?"

Slowly, he opened his eyes. "I'll live. I think."

He was an unhealthy looking colour as he looked around the cabin. There were lots of empty seats.

"At least it's not crowded."

Nick was a talker and Jade had found that irritating. He'd intruded on her self-imposed solitude. Now that he was so quiet she found she missed it. He'd broken up what had otherwise been a terrible day. She could have written a country song about it. Her original flight on Delta had been cancelled and Allied had been the only one that would get her there in time for the expo, but it was a red-eye and she'd have less than an hour to get ready after she landed. She returned home to wait for the next flight only to find her boyfriend and best friend making out on the sofa. He thought she had already left. She dumped them both on the spot. They'd both been trying to text or call her ever since. Messages of "I'm sorry!" or "I was an idiot!" kept lighting up her phone, but Jade had no intentions of responding.

"Fool me once..." She whispered.

"I'm sorry. What did you say?" Nick disengaged his hand and turned to look at Jade.

"Oh nothing."

"You look sad again."

Jade sighed. "I'm sorry I was a jerk to you earlier. You seem like a really nice guy."

"I am a nice guy. Or I try to be."

"You succeeded. I've had a rotten day and I took it out on you."

"It's alright. We all have those days. Man trouble?"

She nodded.

"Can I give you a hug?"

Jade nodded. She felt oddly safe around Nick and laid her head on his shoulder.

"We've all had relationships like that. Falling for some-one who doesn't deserve it."

"Thank you."

"I'm sure you'll meet the right guy. It will be the last guy you ever expected and in the oddest situation."

Jade pulled away and looked up at Nick, suddenly wary. "Is that what this has been about?"

Nick looked at her perplexed, "Huh?"

"Are you flirting with me?"

He looked a little shocked, then he laughed. "Outside of being old enough to be, at the least, an uncle to you," he lifted up his left hand and waggled his fingers, drawing attention to an ornate golden band on his third finger, "I don't think my husband would approve."

"Oh, you're married." Jade flushed bright pink.

"Yes ma'am. We've been together for over twenty years. Got married the day it was legal."

"Congrats."

"Thanks. Our kids stood for us." He pulled out his phone and showed her the photos. "That's Mark, my husband, and our two kids, Lucy and Jason."

"You have a beautiful family."

"Thanks." Nick was beaming with pride at his phone and Jade smiled. She hoped she could find that happiness someday.

They were interrupted by the attendant who provided them with drinks and a small pouch of chips. Nick had a whiskey, Jade a red wine. Hopefully it would help her get some rest.

01:05

Jade blinked owlishly. The cabin lights were dim. Blearily, she rubbed her eyes and looked at her watch. One am. She'd been asleep for just over an hour and a half. Next to her, David snored, blissfully asleep. He'd taken an Ativan with his whiskey and it had knocked him out cold. Her bladder reminded her of what had awakened her. She slipped over her companion and headed to the washrooms between economy and first class.

She was washing her hands when she heard the first pop, followed quickly by three others. Someone screamed. More screams. Jade dropped to the floor, putting the cabinetry between her and what sounded like gunfire. She'd grown up in New York; someone out there had guns and had used them.

Above the cries: "Everyone stay calm."

A heavily accented voice outside her door yelled "Sit down. SIT DOWN!"

"Russians?" she whispered.

The cries reduced to whimpers and mutterings. A

hand pounded on her door making Jade jump. "You in there. Come out. Now."

Heart racing, Jade stood and unlocked the door with trembling hands. The man outside shoved it open, driving her back against the wall. A folding shelf dug painfully into her shoulder and she cried out in pain. He reached in, grabbed her arm and shoved her out in front of him.

"Go. Sit down."

Jade stumbled ahead. She glanced back over her shoulder. Speaker Loehr was looking at her with wide eyes while one of the gunmen held a small white plastic pistol to her head. Her two Secret Service agents lay in their seats, blood trickling from the small holes in their temples.

"Crap."

She stumbled ahead and clumsily fell into the seat next to Nick. He put his arm around her and pulled her close.

"You okay?"

Jade nodded. The Russian stepped up next to them. "Wife?"

Nick nodded.

"Pretty. You keep her close. Das?"

"Yes, sir."

"Good."

The Russian turned and headed back to first class.

"What the hell is going on?"

"Not sure." Jade leaned in and whispered "The Secret Servicemen are dead."

"What?"

"Yeah. There's two more of these guys by the Speaker. They all have the same guns."

"They're plastic."

"Explains how they-"

The speaker crackled to life. "Myself and my comrades will be your hosts for the rest of the evening. I am Alexi. The gentlemen with the bags are Serge and Vlad." Alexi pointed towards a very young man, no more than twenty. "This detka,' Alexi said, grabbing the younger man by the cheeks and squeezing. "This is Pavel."

"Don't call me a baby."

"Then stop acting like one." The oldest of the men stood, holding Speaker Loehr roughly by her arm. Her legs dangled beneath her, wrists bound before her with a zip tie.

"This handsome man is Demitri. We are all members of the RFT and we now control this flight."

"RFT?" Jade whispered to Nick.

Nick shrugged his shoulders.

All of the men had the same dark, short cut hair and beards. Except Pavel. He was pale blonde, almost white haired and was clean shaven. They were dressed almost identically: t-shirt, hoodie, jeans or khakis and heavy boots. Each carried a small bag.

A woman to Jade and Nick's left had her cell phone out and was recording.

"You should not tell them our names," Demitri said, glaring and Alexi.

"It doesn't matter." Alexi continued. "Remain calm, stay in your seats, and everything will be okay. We are not here for you. Once we land and leave, you will be left behind."

He paused as Serge and Vlad started walking down the aisles, holding the garbage bags before them.

"Please put all cell phones, tablets, and laptops into my comrades' bags. You will get them back at the end of the flight."

"Put that away," Jade whispered to the cell phone lady. She stuffed it back into her purse and pulled out a white iPhone, which she dropped into the bag. As soon as Serge passed, she pulled the other phone back out and continued recording. Jade raised her eyebrows at the woman who just looked back grimly.

The seatbelt sign came back on and they felt the plane bank to the right while it dropped altitude. The TV screen before Jade had been defaulted to the map. She could see they were now flying at twenty-thousand feet and were headed towards Africa.

Somewhere behind them a child began to cry.

01:45

Most of the passengers had settled down. The woman across from them had stopped filming for now, but she was scribbling franticly in a notepad. She glanced up at Jade and then lifted the notepad "Reporter. *NYT.*"

Jade just nodded and leaned in to Nick's shoulder so she could talk quietly.

"Nick, I've been thinking, someone in Allied has to be part of this."

"I figured that. There's no way they'd have accessed the cockpit. Not since the changes."

Nick switched on the TV in front of him to CNN. A Breaking News banner was flashing slowly. The reporters had deadly serious faces as they talked about whatever was happening. A tickertape ran below them: "Marine One carrying POTUS Missing" followed by "Air Force One crashed, VP feared dead."

The two looked at each other and then back at the hijackers.

"What the heck is going on?" Nick muttered.

"Nick, how much do you know about the government?"

"Not much. Why?"

"If something happens to the President and Vice, the next in line to be president is the Speaker of the House."

Nick looked towards first class and then back at Jade.

"Crap."

"Yeah."

The reporter took a quick look around and leaned over to Jade. "What do you know?"

"Check the news," Jade replied before ducking back into Nick's arm just as one of the hijackers turned around.

Out of the corner of her eye, she watched the reporter read the screen. Her eyes went wide with shock. She looked back and Jade and mouthed "Oh my god."

Jade only nodded.

02:12

Jade leaned in close again. "Do you think they'll really let us go?"

Nick shook his head. He'd been observing the men move around. He'd watched them fiddling with panels, lifting floor plates and poking around, placing small grey squares of something here and there.

"No, I don't. I think they are going to blow us all to hell." He recounted to her what he'd seen.

Jade nodded. "That's what I think too."

"You sound remarkably calm."

She smiled. "Oh, I'm not. There's a little monkey in my brain running around screaming 'Climb a tree!' but panicking won't help."

"No, I guess it wouldn't."

Jade looked over at the reporter. She had stopped her note and video talking. She sat watching the small screen in front of her, her expression grave.

"So, what are we gonna do about it?"

"What do you mean?"

"Well, I don't plan on sitting here and waiting to get blown up. Do you?"

"No. I don't suppose I do."

Nick looked at the small screen to his left. The little plane icon blinked closer and closer to Africa.

"Whatever we do, we have to do soon."

"I've counted five hijackers, plus however many of the Allied Skies crew that are working for them."

Jade nodded. "So what do we do?"

"I have no idea."

The reporter leaned over. "What are you two whispering about."

"Nothing," Jade replied.

"Bull," the reported said. "I've been a foreign correspondent for ten years, I recognize two people who are planning something."

Jade and Nick looked at each other and flagged for her to slip into their row. With a quick glance Jade slipped over Nick's lap and the reporter slid in next to him.

"My name is Diana Swift."

"I've heard of you," Jade said. "You broke the story about the --"

"What do you think is going on?" Nick finally asked.

"I think this is a coup."

"A coup?" they said together.

"They sure as hell aren't our military."

"Think about it. If you wanted to take over our country, but didn't want to start a war..."

"Oh shi…"

"Yeah."

"So. President is missing. VP is dead. We are the only ones here that know what is going on." Nick scrubbed his hands through his hair, pulling wisps from his ponytail.

Jade sighed. "We gotta save Loehr."

02:41

"So, we're all clear, right?" Jade said, grateful for her paranoia that her luggage would be lost. She hadn't packed all her exhibition gear in her suitcase, so she had some things in her carry-on.

"Only the guy Pavel guarding the back. Serge and Vlad are patrolling our section and the last two are up with Loehr." Nick reached into his bag and pulled out a set of heavy rings that were linked together, slipped them on his right hand, and flexed his fingers. When they looked at him he muttered "Technically it's jewelry."

Jade was taking her time screwing her escrima sticks together. They'd been disassembled for transporting, but only took a minute to screw together. She also had a short baton and a very short ornamental blade. As she slipped each item from her bag, they looked at her with incredulity. She grinned. "I've got permits for all of them."

"I'll get the attention of the guy in the back. Hit him with this." Diana pulled out a personal taser from her bag. "You guys take out the two on patrol, then go after the ones guarding Loehr."

"That's the plan," Nick said with a nod.

Quietly, Diana slipped from her seat and headed towards the back of the plane while Jade and Nick moved into position. Nick crouched down in a row near where they'd been sitting on the right side of the 747, while Jade slipped over the middle row of seats to hide on the left side.

The guard was standing in the section that narrowed by the washrooms. Passengers looked up as Diana passed by; they were scared. She motioned for them to duck down and stay quiet.

When she was close to the hijacker's back, she turned and watched as Jade and Nick got into position.

"Excuse me?" she said quietly, standing behind the guard.

He turned, surprised at how close the woman had gotten.

"Back," he growled.

"I need to pee."

"I said move."

"Please? I really need to go," Diana pointed over his shoulder towards the bathrooms and put her knees together. As Pavel glanced over his shoulder to where she was pointing, Diana brought up the taser and slammed it in under his chin. He began to twitch and thrash as he fell to the ground. Diana had cranked the amps up to full. It was enough to stop a heart.

In slow motion Diana watched his finger twitch on the trigger. The gun exploded, sending bits of plastic and hot copper flying. The shrapnel dug into Diana's legs and she cried out in pain. Pavel fared far worse. The blast had torn his hand to pieces and he began to howl, drowning out Diana's cries. He tried to grab for the ruined hand, but his nerves were not under his control. Instead of protecting his hand, he banged it repeatedly against the wall until he blacked out.

Passengers joined in the screams.

When the gun exploded the other guards stood, except for Demetri, his only job was to guard Loehr and Alexi's was to guard Demitri.

Serge and Vlad brought their guns to bear on the commotion. Nick burst from the seat and, drawing back his arm, nailed the terrorist nearest in the face, driving the heavy rings as hard as he could. Bone crunched and Serge fell lifeless to the floor. As he hit the floor, his hand jerked and the gun fired. A clean firing, no explosion. The single .22 round that the gun carried blasted from the barrel.

Diana had started to kneel near the wounded terrorist when she felt something punch her in the back and push her forward a little. She staggered into a wall and slid to the ground. She reached behind her and when her hand came back it was covered in blood. There were people screaming, but they were very far away. Diana looked down at the terrorist she'd shocked. He was still twitching but his eyes were glassy. She looked into those empty eyes as she faded away.

Jade heard Nick fighting, but she was focused on her quarry. She broke cover from the seat she was hiding behind and brought one of her fighting sticks down, quick and hard, on Vlad's wrist. She heard bone snap and the small plastic gun flew from his fingers, sliding under the seats. He opened his mouth to scream, but Jade spun and slammed her other stick into the side of his head. She heard a crunch and he crumpled to the ground.

She heard the gun go off and turned. Jade followed Nick's gaze to the back of the plane, a horrified look on his face. Jade watched as Diana fell to the grown, a scarlet patch spreading across her white blouse.

They stood dumbstruck for a moment. Another bang

snapped them back to the now. Jade heard Nick cry out and saw him diving in between the seats. He held his left arm, blood seeping between his fingers.

"So, some of you do have courage."

Nick held a finger to his lips, then pointed to just behind him. Alexi was in the divider between first and second class. Jade nodded.

"Come now. Talk to me," he continued. "I suppose you are wondering what this is about?"

Jade kept low and headed towards the divider on her side. Cautiously she crept with the bathrooms to her back and the flight attendants' galley before her. She could see Alexi's legs. She leaned back to survey first class. All the flight attendants had been bound and gagged. They were sitting in a row up near the front. One man was bleeding from a cut on his forehead. The rest looked terrified but okay. Looked like none of them were involved.

One attendant nodded her head to Jades right. Jade looked and saw two pairs of legs. One was wearing heavy cargo pants and black boots, the other stockings and sensible loafers.

"I was hoping we could talk, but I see that you are a man of action, not words. I will tell you anyway."

Dave tied a piece of cloth around his wound and climbed over the back of the seats into the row nearest the divider.

"Your country, it is despotic. Capitalism has ruined it. Homeless haunt your streets like forgotten ghosts. Elite live in castles you call mansions, while the middle class act as fodder for the corporate grist. Today, the RFT will end that existence."

She crawled back to where she could see Nick. He looked over and saw her peeking around the corner. She pointed at where the voice was and then back at Nick. She then pointed to herself and towards first class. Nick nodded and got up into a crouch.

Jade slipped back around the corner, checked that the leader wasn't working, and then belly crawled past the galley. She could see the speaker as she passed, the man she figured was the leader. He was tall, about a foot taller than Jade's five-foot-three. His black hair was cut short and he was clean shaven. He was muscular and moved like someone who knew what he was doing. He was leaning into the edge of the wall as he spoke, trying to get a view of the compartment beyond.

She swallowed hard and crept past him and into first class.

"We've take action today. Your president is our captive. Your vice president, dead."

The other passengers cried out when they heard this.

Jade had moved into the row ahead of where the pair were sitting. When Nick made his move, she'd only have seconds to act.

"Alexi, stop talking and get back here," the seated man called to his comrade.

"Demitri, they deserve to know before the end."

"They deserve nothing," Demitri spat the words.

Alexi laughed. "Your country fell without a fight."

"No it didn't." She heard Nick roar and the sound of crashing as he drove Alexi into the galley. Trays and dishes rolled into the walkway. She could hear the two men fighting in the galley.

"Alexi?" Demitri stood up and leaned to the left, trying to get a better view of the galley.

Jade stood and stepped forward. Demitri had his back to her, but held a gun to Loehr's face. Jade reached out with one of her sticks and tapped the chair to her right. Demitri spun, moving the gun away from Loehr's head. She brought down her other stick hard, hoping to break his wrist, but Demitri sensed something and spun. Her stick missed and Demitri fired his gun.

Nick had Alexi on the ground with an arm around his neck.

Nick whispered in the hijackers ear, "We will fight you to our last breath."

Alexi's arms and legs were flailing as he tried to free himself. He had one hand tangled in Nick's long hair and was pulling hard. He found a glass carafe with his other hand and swung it up, smashing it into Nick's face.

Glass flew everywhere. Nick screamed as he released Alexi and grabbed his face, pulling glass shards from his cheeks. The two men stood and faced off against each other.

Alexi nodded towards Nick's vest patch and pointed to his own shirt which sported a grizzly bear. "Eagle versus bear. As it should be."

On his last word, Alexi dove into Nick's middle sending them tumbling towards the bathrooms on the far wall.

Air hissed from above Jade's head. The bullet had missed and had gone through the fuselage. Relief washed over her until Demitri pulled a large knife from his belt. It was at least eight inches long and serrated on one edge. He stepped forward, intent on driving the blade into Speaker Loehr, but Jade's sticks were there, battering and tapping him. Staccato hits, each one a little more stinging than the last as Jade built up momentum.

Demitri spun from his intended victim and turned towards Jade, forcing her to break off and step back. Crouching low and holding his knife at the ready, Demitri advanced.

"Little girl, go sit back down. I can forget what you've done."

Jade glared at him. "I sincerely doubt that. We just took down three of your men."

"Those men mean nothing. I fight for the cause. Nothing more."

"What cause is that?" Jade stepped back while Demitri stalked her. She gave up ground willingly, hoping Nick would rescue Speaker Loehr, giving Jade the freedom to attack.

Demitri made small experimental thrusts with his blade, which Jade blocked easily.

"I'll ask again," she said. "What cause?"

"The one thing Russia has wanted since the end of World War Two."

"Which is…"

"Global domination."

"Seriously?" Jade saw movement behind Demitri. She hoped it was Nick. She had to keep him distracted.

"Yes. We were once a great empire. We will be one again."

Jade took a swipe at Demitri's hand, which he easily parried. That was fine as far as Jade was concerned; she was only trying to delay him right now.

"And hijacking a plane and taking an old woman hostage is the best plan you could come up with?"

Demitri stopped walking and laughed. A real, honest

laugh.

"No, little one. There are cells all across the world activating right now. Taking key officials hostage or killing them. After tonight, Russia will rule the world."

Jade was floored. Demitri truly believed this. It sent a shiver down her spine and Speaker or no Speaker, Jade wasn't going down without a fight. She adjusted her grip on the sticks and began to spin them. No more retreat. Demitri paused, shocked as the young woman moved forward, her jaw set in grim determination. She moved fluidly. Demitri didn't even see the first few blows land. All he knew was the sudden pain flaring in his arm and hip.

Demitri crouched defensively and squared off against Jade. All she could see was the light shimmering along the blade's edge. While experienced in knife fighting, this was the first time Jade had ever fought anyone who actually wanted to hurt her.

"So why now?" she said as she paced around him, stepping in and testing his reactions.

"Governments of the world are destabilized."

Jade dove in and did a quick double tap on Demitri's knife arm. He yelled and stepped back, shaking his arm. He looked at her and grinned. "A challenge."

Demitri closed the distance quickly. He knew space was her friend and his enemy. Once close, he made a stab at her neck. Jade bent backwards, avoiding the blade, the tip of it scrapping across her collarbone. She stumbled backwards, landing on one knee. Her hand came up to her shoulder.

"You son of a-"

Demitri grinned. "Tich tich. Language." Jade was in a vulnerable position and Demitri planned on taking advantage of it. He closed, trying to drive his blade into her ribs.

Jade dropped to the floor and swung her stick, hitting Demitri on the ankles. It did little damage, but it made him step back. Jade rolled up onto her feet and back into a fighting stance, right foot forward, left back and turned slightly.

"You will not succeed," she said.

"Even if we fail, the other's will not."

It was Jade's turn to laugh. "You're nuts if you think people won't fight back."

"You will see."

"No Demitri, you will see." It was Nick. The fighters turned to look. Nick was standing there with a bruised looking co-pilot.

"The others are done. This plane isn't going to wherever you'd planned."

Nick shoved the bound co-pilot into a seat. "We've been in contact with a control tower. The Queen is safe, the German Chancellor is safe, the Canadian Prime Minister is safe. You lost."

"No!" he growled. "You lie."

"Tell him," Nick kicked the co-pilot.

"It's true," he mumbled through swollen lips.

In a rage, Demitri dove at Jade. He swung wildly, missing her completely. Jade swung her right stick at Demitri's head. He ducked and dove into her mid section, driving her back against a bulkhead.

"Oof." She felt his blade dig into her thigh and screamed. Pain made her angry and she brought her left stick down on his neck and heard a pop. Demitri staggered back.

Knife still in her thigh, Jade swung with all her strength, hitting Demitri on the temple. She felt the bone snap and he fell backwards.

Jade crumpled to the ground just as Nick reached her. He helped her to sit against the bulkhead.

"That was incredible."

"Thanks." She smiled wanly. "How'd you know?" She nodded towards the co-pilot.

"We knew there had to be insiders. I freed a flight attendant and she opened the cockpit door. Everyone else was tied up. It had to be him."

Nick waved to a flight attendant who came over and started bandaging Jade's wounds.

Jade laughed weakly. "Gonna call you Doc Watson."

Nick grinned and held up the plastic gun she'd knocked from Vlad's hand. "Found this. I thought it would help, but it's crap. Only holds one shell and Vlad already used it. So I went to my back-up plan." He held up his fists.

"Good plan."

"I thought so."

"The others?" It was getting hard to talk.

"Out cold. They are being tied up now."

"Good."

Jade's eyes began to close. "Nick?"

"Yeah?"

"I don't feel very good."

"I don't suppose you do." He helped lower her down and put a cushion under her head. "Rest now."

07:31

The plane landed safely in Portugal. Jade and Diana were rushed to hospital while the hijackers were escorted to a jail cell.

Nick took out his cell phone and made a call. "Nick checking in. Diana is down."

He paused, listening to the person on the other end."I will give a full report, but I wanted you to know the intel was right and all the operatives are in custody."

Another pause. "Thank you sir, but I was not alone." Nick looked at the flashing lights of the ambulances surrounding the plane. "There is someone I think you should meet."

Jennifer Combden

Jennifer Combden is a meteorologist living in St. John's, Newfoundland. She is a sponge for knowledge, and her love of learning is second only to her love of sharing that knowledge. Jennifer prefers to write science fiction, with a strong emphasis on the science, as a medium by which to explain complex ideas.

Combden's work will be recognized by longtime short fiction readers for her stories 'Sunny Days' and 'Immune' in *Sci-Fi from the Rock* (2016).

In May 2018 Combden won the monthly Kit Sora Flash Fiction prize for her short story 'Tarnished,' which went on to be featured in the *Kit Sora: The Artobiography* collection.

Sulfer Bridges

He stood back to admire the job he had done, crossing his arms with pride. Being the Senior Engineer for the sulfuric acid separator generally wasn't difficult, especially if maintenance was regularly completed, but he liked to go the extra mile and have everything shining. The machinery looked almost new, belying the over forty years it had been in operation. This was the first step in taking the Venusian atmosphere, extracting the sulfuric acid mists that surrounded the airships as they floated fifty kilometres above the surface, and processing it for the creation of oxygen, water, and other materials. This made him feel like an important cog in the larger machine that was their functioning colony.

"Christoff, you work yourself too hard." A light, Russian-accented voice came from behind him. Turning, he grinned.

"Davis, I keep telling you, call me Chris." He patted his friend on the arm in greeting. "And I work just hard enough."

Davis worked in oversight, but they had been in the same cohort - growing up as comrades. Their friendship cemented after Davis stayed by his side when he suffered the pain of being incompatible with his assigned pair-

bond. Given the small population, genetics had to be carefully decided, so even though they had separated she still
bore his children. She found someone else and moved to
another ship, and, for the sake of stability, he generally
stayed out of the way.

"Come, Anya made supper. And Alexei wants to show
you his latest project." Davis's middle son had become
extremely attached to Chris, showing a great aptitude for
machinery already. His surrogate niece and nephews had
helped fill the emptiness as well, and he often spent time
there rather than his quarters.

"Let me wash up, and I'll be right over." He said, grinning. He gave the machinery a last once-over, and then
left it to the night watch.

After thanking Anya for the delicious meal, he spent
the rest of the evening helping Alex. The kid had the basics of how the balloon that held the colony section up
worked--filled with breathable air at normal pressure it
floated simply by being lighter than the acidic air outside
it. Chris had issues with how catastrophic accidents and
incidents were dramatized though, and how they were
made to seem far more likely than was actually the case.
Chris chalked it up to safety drills overemphasizing how
dangerous it was in an attempt to keep everyone paying
attention. Assuring the child that even a fairly large hole
wouldn't cause the airship to instantly fall into the molten
surface of Venus, he explained the adult drills and how
quickly things could be repaired.

"We haven't survived here for this long for nothing!"
He laughed, clapping Alexei on the back.

"The drills are still important," chided Davis. "They
are part of our survival."

"Yes, yes," Chris acknowledged. "Trade with the other planets is slow, so there would be tremendous strain on the other airships before we could make a new ship from scratch. Better to just not lose this one!"

Soon it was bedtime, and Chris said his goodnights so as to not be a distraction.

He decided to detour through the garden on his way home to get some of his weekly required time in the grassy "Earth-like" area. It was considered necessary for mental health that all citizens spend time there, but he didn't see the point. Maybe the first colonists, having come from earth, missed being able to spend time in nature. But he, and those younger than him, just had stories. And to be honest, Earth didn't sound that great anyway. Still dealing with major pollution, all of its "nature" was confined to sanctuaries, and it also had areas you couldn't go into without protective gear. He did have to confess that the flowers smelled nice, though.

Time continued its march forward, occasionally punctuated by visits, repairs, and external maintenance. He found going outside most enjoyable, needing only an air tank and an acid suit. It was important to make sure the acid resistant coatings stayed intact or there would be more work later. While he only needed to check the baffles used for collection, he generally spent the length of his air inspecting and patching up the catwalk, too.

But today something was different. As he walked through the colony there was an air of stress. Higher-ups gathered in small groups, speaking in hushed whispers. Chris just tried to put it out of his mind. Politics held no interest to him, and even when decisions were made that he didn't particularly agree with, he generally acknowledged that it was for the good of the colony.

Days passed and stress levels increased to the point

that even he couldn't keep ignoring it. He left work early so he could meet up with Davis as he left his office.

"How are things up in the land of paperwork?" Chris asked, trying to get a smile from his friend.

Davis shook his head. "We should not speak here. Come to my home, I will tell you what I can."

With an uncomfortable silence, they walked the familiar path to Davis's apartment. Nodding to his wife, he gestured for Chris to come into his home office.

"You're worrying me, Davis. You're acting serious, even for you." Chris tried to inject some humor, but it fell flat.

"Christoff. I tell you these things in confidence, you understand? I am confident that you can pretend ignorance if you get called upon to advise." Davis laid a heavy hand on Chris' shoulder.

Not knowing what to say, Chris simply nodded. He lived a life of predictability, and the knot in his stomach told him that this wasn't going to be pleasant news.

"There is a ship coming. From Earth…"

Chris cut him off. "Yea, I suppose it is that time. But that's not unusual. Trade with earth isn't strong but we do have some." These ships took many months to travel the distance between the planets, and came infrequently.

Davis frowned. "I wouldn't bring you in here to speak of a supply ship. This is a human transport vessel."

"Wait, what?" He furrowed his brow. The initial colonization of Venus had apparently been met with ridicule by most of those involved in space exploration. Sure, it was technically challenging, but it had far less to overcome than many of the other planets and moons colonized. They were able to create their own oxygen for one thing, rather than depending on temperamental plants.

But after the initial establishment of the colony, immigration was completely closed.

Davis nodded as he continued. "Yes. So far, they have ignored all attempts to communicate, but rumor is that the ship is capable of carrying thousands. There apparently has been some contact with people on Earth who are sympathetic, but I do not know the details. I can only assume it is related to the nuclear fallout that occurred last year."

"Or any of the other disasters they keep having. But why us? After decades of being ignored?"

"I have no clue, my friend. But I know the Council didn't have a contingency plan for this so they are trying to form one quickly. If that ship is full…" Davis trailed off, lowering his gaze.

Chris could only shake his head. Standing in silence for a few moments, Davis took a deep breath and left Chris standing in his office. Chris took a few seconds to push this news to the back of his mind, and followed Davis. The rest of the evening was like any other visit.

When one of the Council assistants showed up a few days later while Chris was working on adjusting the efficiency of the condenser, he silently thanked Davis for the heads up. Getting a Council summons was rarely a good thing, but at least he had some idea of why he was getting called. There was an underlying sense of pride that he was indeed the most knowledgeable in this particular area, which also helped ease his anxiety.

He was led through the Oversight Office to a teleconference room. There was already one person there, fidgeting in her chair. He recognized her as one of the scientists who came by occasionally to tweak the catalysts and do other slight modifications. He nodded towards her, and she gave a tight smile. Chris sat in the chair indicated by the assistant, who hadn't introduced himself, and took in the blank room around them. It was clearly a conference room, and the blankness meant it was likely setup for video. The main Council were on one of the other airships, where most of the bureaucrats lived.

"The conference will start in a few minutes. As the Council recognizes that you have not had time to prepare answers, this will be primarily for information and assigning reports. In the interest of saving time I will be giving you the background." The assistant, who apparently had no interest in putting them at ease, tapped at his datapad.

"Am I able to assume you both understand the genetic growth plan?" He looked directly at Chris, who stopped himself from squirming. History was not his strong suit. He knew the colony started with 1500 individuals, and they hit 10,000 a few years ago.

"More or less? I know it was planned from the beginning, and the growth rate is specified." He answered as confidently as he could.

The assistant nodded. "And each airship has a specific capacity that it is intended to hold. We are still a couple generations away from having to decide whether to commence building a new airship or curb growth." He tapped at his pad again, then produced a stylus and handed it to Chris.

"This is a confidentiality agreement. The information you're about to hear is only to be shared with authorized individuals. Please sign." Chris gave it a once-over, and then scrawled his name before handing it over to the other woman who also signed.

Retrieving the pad, he nodded. "Thank you. This is

your briefing, please hold any questions for the conference."

"We became aware of an unscheduled ship on an intercept trajectory just over one month ago. They have indicated that they wish to seek asylum here but have not provided much more information. The class of ship is capable of carrying 5000, including crew, but rarely do they launch with maximum capacity. We are estimating a population of 3800 on board, but we have no indication of even the average age of those on board. The fact that they are refusing to share such information is leading us to assume that they would not be able to integrate into society without significant education. I will allow the Council to share the current possible contingencies." He finished quickly as his datapad pinged.

A screen lit up in front of them, and the assistant took a seat in the back of the room. Two individuals in an identical room appeared.

"Thank you for joining us, Dr. Erdos and Mr. Kotov. I'm Dr. Elizabeth Parker, the Chief Protocol Officer. With me is Dr. Dmitri Foster, Chief Engineer. Have they signed the agreement, Andrew?" She spoke tensely, but seemed much friendlier.

"They have, and basic specs covered." He replied.

"Excellent. Well I won't waste any more of your time. Essentially, the decision boils down to accepting their request for asylum, despite their lack of cooperation, or denying it. Obviously, the details are more complicated, and we are also considering allowing them to remain in orbit while we resupply them. We have no indication as to their fuel status, however, so our focus remains on the other two." She let out a sigh, rubbing her temple for a moment before catching herself.

"Dr. Foster, the floor is yours."

He nodded, and grabbed some printouts. "We will be focusing on if it is even possible to accommodate these individuals, given the assumptions previously mentioned."

The conversation went on for over an hour, with mostly Chris and Dr. Erdos speaking back and forth on current research and potential issues with implementation. Up until now, improvements had been incremental at best, and any significant progress would require a complete overhaul of the system. Not something that could be done in the less than two months they had before their arrival.

While not within his expertise, Chris felt compelled to question whether this would put them over current evacuation procedures. The plans called for there to be enough space on the other two airships for the inhabitants of the third. He was informed that capacity was being taken into account, but to focus on the task at hand.

"You may inform those you're working with that you've been assigned to develop a plan to quickly increase the collector yield, but the reason for doing so is to remain confidential," Dr. Parker warned. "I expect a report in a week."

Chris and Dr. Erdos affirmed their understanding, and the screen blinked out.

"So, Dr. Erdos, I think it might be the best use of time for each of us to gather what information we can and meet up in a few days." He attempted to project an air of confidence, while the knowledge of what they were doing created a hurricane in his mind.

"Ann. And yea, that makes sense. I don't have high hopes on my end though. You?" She replied with a frown.

"Call me Chris, and I'd have to check, but it might be possible to do a rapid refit if you have anything along those lines." He was visualizing the system, and the different sections that could be worked on simultaneously, against general safety procedures.

"Would be nice if these people had brought some materials to actually help expand our systems," Ann spat bitterly.

"We don't know the circumstances under which they left," he reminded her, but his voice lacked conviction.

"This room will be designated for you to work out of for creating your report," Andrew interjected. "Feel free to use it to confer with others as well." After deciding on when to meet up, Chris left Ann and went down to climb around the machinery.

Over the next three days he had accumulated dozens of blueprints filled with scrawls, half baked ideas, and an even bigger knot in his stomach. The airships had been meticulously designed to work a certain way. That was the case with the entire colony; everything had been planned down to the smallest detail before they had even left earth. The unpredictability of nature was even accounted for, with population growth tied to what resources were found and what trade was possible. It was not designed for hack fixes.

The day of their meeting, he arrived early to attempt to organize his information, hoping that Ann held the other half of the equations to make some of these ideas work. By now most of the colonists were suspicious that something was up, and it would be nice if the Council would make an announcement soon so he could stop pleading ignorance as to why he was having to do all this extra work.

Ann walked in, looking like she had barely slept since

he last saw her. She spread out a few sheets and a data-pad--much more organized than his side of the table. He hoped it was just conciseness, not a lack of progress.

"So, tell me what you have there," she said, dropping herself in one of the chairs.

"The only useful thing for certain is that it is possible to do upgrades to sixty-five percent of the system quickly enough that evacuation of the airship won't be necessary. That can be boosted depending on how quickly Agriculture can grow algae, but you're getting into high risk territory there. Additional baffles could be added if the speed of conversion is increased without much effort, but capacity will still be an issue. I have the designs here for a variety of potential upgrades." Chris had to stop himself from going into more detail that wouldn't mean anything to a non-mechanical engineer. He did slide over one of the blueprints that showed which sections could be worked on so she could match it up with her chemical engineering work.

The room was silent as Ann looked over everything. Her face fell as she input more information into her datapad, and she was shaking her head.

"Well?" Chris interjected, not being able to stand the stretching silence.

"One-point-three percent increase. Best case scenario so far," she said without looking up. "You make a good point about capacity, maybe if we can get things to work at high pressure..." she trailed off.

"I can focus on methods of increasing pressure allowances next. Any other ideas?" Chris asked, his heart gripping the thin line of hope there.

They discussed a few more details about the potential of partial upgrades and other technical aspects before agreeing to meet up again in a few days to get the report compiled.

This time around Chris was less coy about what he was doing, bringing in others for their opinions and ideas. He still had to refuse to answer why they needed to rapidly increase the oxygen and water production, which honestly was probably causing more worry but orders were orders. He assigned one of the kids who had only recently joined them to go over everything that had been compiled so far. Fresh out of school, he wouldn't be as tied down by how things were "supposed" to be done. Anything to give even a slight edge to their research. Regular maintenance was being neglected, but he'd worry about catching up later.

Armed with a few more ideas, he met with Ann again. Being that she was far more organized than him, she worked at compiling potential plans for the Council to consider. In addition, they included how effective it would be, time for completion, and risk factor. But even the most hazardous plan only had a less than five percent increase. A couple of plans did include an alternative that reduced oxygen output so more water would be produced, so they could be potentially combined with other departments. If these plans could be used, they just might be able to help the asylum seekers.

They submitted their report and were told to return to their regular duties. If anything, this confused matters more throughout Chris's department, but they got caught up on all the regular duties that had been put aside. After another week had passed, despite the growing apprehension, everyone just acted as if everything was normal. With each passing day, Chris grew more concerned. If any of the plans they had submitted were to be effective, they needed to be started as soon as possible. No other departments seemed to be doing anything beyond the status quo either.

Finally, just over a week later, the emergency screens lit up with a countdown, indicating a message was going to start. Chris and his coworkers gathered together to wait. The anxiety was palpable.

The screen lit up to show Harris Novikov, the Council Chair. A brief moment of silence passed before he began.

"Fellow colonists, as many of you are aware, things have not been business as usual as of late. We regret that we haven't been able to share the exact circumstances, but we will be explaining now." In the top right corner of the screen, an image of a transport ship appeared. It looked derelict, barely spaceworthy. He could only guess how glitchy and inefficient the onboard systems were. Just from this glance, he understood why the idea of letting them stay in orbit was unlikely to succeed.

"As we became aware of the ship's intention to intercept us, attempts to communicate began. They have labeled themselves asylum seekers but have refused to give details on personnel. Contacts on Earth have been unable to verify any additional information. While asylum seekers are not unexpected given the current problems facing Earth, their refusal to assist in preparations for their arrival is problematic. We have completed extensive research--based on the small amount of information we were able to glean from these people--on how to increase our population capacity quickly.

"It is with a heavy heart that we have decided we cannot admit them. We will be offering resupply to whatever extent we can spare, and allow them to remain in orbit. That said, we will be increasing security across all ships and outposts. To achieve this, there will be some people temporarily reassigned. These notifications will be sent out after this broadcast completes.

"While it seems cruel, the safety and health of those who have worked all their lives towards the success of our society has to be our priority. We are not willing to risk your lives." His voice droned on, explaining how to find more information and such.

But Chris's heart dropped. If the transport ship didn't end up being shot down, they would simply run out of oxygen. They would arrive only to find their deaths.

Erin Vance

Erin Vance is a graduate of the Memorial University of Newfoundland English Honors Program.

Erin won the Arts and Letters competition when she was just 14 years old in 2007 with her short story, 'Something White.' She is featured in the Nelson Literacy 7 Homegrown (Newfoundland Edition) with her poem 'Rough Draft.'

Erin wrote her Honors thesis paper, *Song of the Mockingjay*, on exploring the nature of Katniss Everdeen's agency in Suzanne Collins' *The Hunger Games* series. She is creative, spiritual, and loves reading, writing, and anything to do with words.

Erin is the co-editor of the From the Rock anthology series, which highlights Newfoundland talent in genre writing.

Erin is the editor-in-chief for Engen Books.

Cast Clutter Pack Murder

You know your life is crap when you have to share your bedroom with about a dozen other animals.

Something nudged Vico's foot; he peered down to see a mangy dog nose at his sock. His (or hers. Its? Whatever) tail thumped on the floor upon noticing Vico's gaze on it. Vico frowned at the bald spot on its left hindquarters and felt something twang painfully in his chest.

"Don't even think about it," he croaked. He shoved at the dog half-heartedly with his foot. "Probably covered in fleas," he muttered.

Above his head, a pigeon cooed, and another answered it. Another dog whined from underneath Vico's cot, and a third scratched at the wall. Something swatted his forehead and he lifted his chin to see a large black cat sitting by his left ear, one paw still raised. One ear was mangled, chewed nearly in half, and its fur was matted in clumps. It swatted Vico's forehead again.

Vico scowled at the cat, but closed his eyes. Cats would do whatever the hell they wanted; best to leave them to it.

There was a thud above his head and a flurry of wings flapping and a bird's squawk and the squeaking of rusting metal being forced to move. Some cat had jumped onto the pigeon cage again; a couple feathers landed on Vico's stomach. A dog let out another whine and another one barked twice. Vico swore under his breath and hunched his shoulders.

A low long beep sounded and then a voice said, "How are you, Mr. Baggio?"

Vico opened one eye and glared at the ceiling with it. "Peachy," he answered, only to be swatted by the cat again.

"Sarcasm does not become you, Mr. Baggio," the voice countered. It was female and human, although its cadence was slightly off in a way Vico couldn't describe. "We should be ready for you soon."

Vico opened the other eye and used his left hand to prop himself up. He dug his right elbow into the thin mattress for balance as he struggled to raise himself into an inclined position. "Finally," he groaned. "This place is a dump."

The mangy dog that had nosed his sock earlier whined as Vico struggled to sit up fully. It shifted positions, turning so it could rest its chin on Vico's right leg. Its chin was damp, and drool began to soak into his pants.

That twang vibrated in his chest again, and Vico scowled in compensation. "Dumb dog," he grumbled. "Can't you see I can't pet you?" After all, he didn't have an arm past his right elbow – just an ugly, red stump. Made it difficult to do much of anything, let alone give an abandoned dog a head scratch.

"That'll change shortly, Mr. Baggio," the voice said.

"*If* the surgery works," he countered, shooting the cat a dirty look as it slunk past him.

"It'll work," the voice said, rather mild for its conviction. "We have not spent the last three years in vain."

The dog beneath his cot chose that moment to shuffle out and pause at his right side, giving a full-body shake that forced Vico to turn his head away. The dog with its head on his lap whined again, and the black cat swatted at his left foot.

"The three human subjects previous to you have exceeded our original schematics," the voice continued. "I can now announce that we are ahead of schedule."

Vico raised an eyebrow even as he wiggled his foot away from the cat. "Wow, Miranda. You almost sound excited."

"I believe I'll gas you now," Miranda replied, voice still mild. "We have to maintain our secrets, you understand."

Vico watched as a white mist began to seep out of the walls, escaping from invisible vents about a foot off the ground. A dog began barking, the one on his left went back under the cot, the birds began flapping their wings, and a trio of cats began howling. "I hate you," he said evenly.

"I recommend lying back down, Mr. Baggio," Miranda said. "A concussion would be an unnecessary complication for our surgeons."

Vico swore again, but began the painful and slow process of reclining. The cat curled up by his foot, and the dog raised its chin off his leg only to place its front paws on the cot. Vico paused, half-reclined, and said, "No…"

The dog jumped up; if the cot hadn't been bolted to the floor, the three of them would have gone toppling to the floor. As it was, Vico was laid flat, the cat sat up and hissed, digging its claws into Vico's leg. He would have sworn except the dog had landed on his gut and all of his breath had escaped in a low *guh*. "Dammit," he wheezed.

"Don't worry, Mr. Baggio," Miranda said as the world began to grow fuzzy at the edges, the blur seeping into his vision like the gas seeped into the room. "You're in the hands of professionals."

The dog rested its head on the center of Vico's chest, and began creating a new damp patch.

Once upon a time, there was a war-

(and then another, and another, and another – or was it all just the next phase of that first one?)

-and some countries rallied together and some allied against, and a man who was not yet forty took his younger wife and his four children, and left his home. They fled their proud country still struggling to regain the glory they had held as the Roman Empire, and flew to that prouder country across the Atlantic. His only daughter and eldest son, despite their young age, remembered the smell of war, and the tension in the weeks leading up to their departure, and found freedom in the airship that took them across the sea. They remembered their old home, and found their new home lacking. They grew bitter and melancholy from their memories haunting them, and found they could neither settle roots nor stretch to the skies.

The eldest son grew up in-between wars – or in a calmer phase of that singular one – and joined the army for a cause he didn't believe in. But they gave him a gun and a purpose, and taught him how to fly, and that was worth the omnipresent taste of blood in his mouth.

He rose, both literally and metaphorically. He piloted a small airship called a Warnet – loathed the wordplay and loved the vessel itself. He captained four other men,

and the aching in his chest began to settle and soothe, even as his hands grew stained brown with dried blood.

Then he found hell.

(He was raised a good Catholic boy; he knew what hell was: fire and brimstone and never-ending screams.)

He lost half of his arm, he lost his ship, and in the losing, lost the only things keeping him together.

Two years later, he crawled back to the people who had cost him the closest thing to happiness he ever knew, besides that of his old, Italian home. They promised him a new arm and a new ship and something better than a gun. He accepted the offer, because a bitter, poisoned something was better than the gaping nothingness haunting him now.

Did he find salvation? Only in the same way Noah's Ark was: a rocky journey from one kind of survival to another struggle of the same, all the while surrounded by animals and their waste.

He missed his gun.

He had ten fingers again; it didn't matter that five were gray and glass with wires and softly pulsating blue lights – they were fingers that bent when he willed them too, and could reach out and pet that damn dog if he wanted.

"I see you've made a friend," Miranda said coolly, her eyes focused on the tablet in her hands.

Vico scratched the top of the dog's head and was rewarded with it closing its eyes. "Something like that," he said, eyes focused on the wires exposed where a diseased left leg had been, and a leg remarkably similar to his new right forearm was now. The other three legs gleamed silver in the artificial lights of the recovery room, and slowly pulsed blue light through the joint bulbs.

A soft *whump* sounded on his right, and he turned to see the large black cat paw at its cage weakly. Its mangled ear had been replaced with a silver one, with metal plating traveling down the right side of its face; its right eye was now laser-beam red.

"Of course, a secondary surgery will be performed in a week's time," Miranda continued. "The skin grafts are a much less complicated surgery, statistically speaking. There is only a 7% chance of rejection, and even then, we have not lost any subjects."

Vico glanced down at his hand, bent and straightened each new finger in turn. "Is the skin graft necessary?" he asked, voice quiet.

Miranda paused. "Objectively, no. Not in your case. However, all other human subjects have found psychological calm with the secondary surgery-"

"But I can refuse it?" he asked, turning on his heel. "Right?" he demanded, voice hard.

Miranda looked at him through her thick glasses. She was not a pretty woman, but she wasn't ugly either – her hair was neat but never styled, and her skin had the pale tint of someone who lacked Vitamin D. She was a little skinny, but Vico contributed that to the fact that he'd only seen her eat once, and that was while she was very distracted. Her face was average, her nose a little large, her ears a little small, and her lips pale pink. She was obviously female, but just as obviously lacked sex appeal.

"You may refuse the skin graft," she agreed, her voice calm. She looked down at her tablet and began swiping her finger across it. "Please be aware, however, that it will be noted on your psych analysis."

"Yeah, whatever," he said, turning back to the dog. He

reached through the bars of the cage to scratch the dog's head again.

"We've programmed those two as your captains," Miranda said. "Seeing as you seemed to have developed a bond already."

Vico paused in his scratching. *Programmed.* He swallowed the sudden bile in his throat and focused on the other issue: "I thought I was gonna have an airship."

"That is true; however, your ship will host four platoons – two terrain and two aerial. These before you comprise 4% of your land troops."

It took Vico a moment to do the math – fifty dogs and cats at his command.

"Your air troops are not finalized yet," she continued. "However, I believe it will be comprised of crows and hawks."

He closed his eyes for a moment and withdrew his hand. The dog whuffed out a breath, but didn't move. He shifted slightly in order to touch the cat's still outstretched paw. He couldn't feel the texture of its pads, only its warmth. The cat blinked back at him.

"No fish?" he said, one side of his mouth twisting up.

"We have been unable to successfully implant cybernetics into aquatic subjects," Miranda answered. "But research is still ongoing."

"I was joking," Vico snapped, looking over his shoulder at her.

She looked back at him. "I know," she said simply. She looked back at her tablet and turned, walking towards the doors. "I'll escort you to your new quarters."

He lowered his arm and followed, refusing to look behind him. "They'd better be nicer than the old ones," he grumbled.

Life is not a fairy tale, nor is it a legend that gets embellished with every new telling, old men and women gesturing to wide-eyed babes. Life is something you survive or you don't: easy as that. Life is something you go through alone, and on rare occasions it meets up with someone else's and you can walk it together. At least until something comes along and makes it all explode in your face.

He knows, objectively, that it is not his fault that he had to leave his beautiful home as a child – that war, a word that explains both everything and nothing, was the reason they had to leave. But he also knows that it was his fault that he had to leave the one he carved out with his bare hands until dirt stained the edges of his fingernails, and his knuckles were raw with blood and sweat and effort. He knows that he failed them; that he flew them straight into hell and that when he crashed, they all did too. He knows he dragged them through Purgatory, and he hopes that they found something better than he did on the other side.

(There is a part of him that is terrified of being in command again; because if he couldn't save a group of professional soldiers, how the hell is he supposed to protect a slew of unwanted, untrained animals?)

The dog turned out to be a girl – he called her Moxie. The cat was male – he called it Nero.

They never left his side, and they brought at least three other mammals with them at any given time. Moxie walked at his side, nudging at his new hand with her head when he fell still. Nero sat on his left shoulder, glaring at all that dared to look at him.

He had names for the other animals – he was up to nineteen dogs and thirteen cats, with more coming every few days – but they didn't sleep in his bed with him. Instead, the dogs slept against the walls of his quarters, curled up on blankets or cushions, with the cats claiming the long shelves that lined the walls, standing about four feet above the ground.

When Vico said, "Bed," they all went; when he named them, they answered. When they listened, his heart throbbed to the same pulse that his hand still flashed.

Then they gave him his ship.

It was… not what he was expecting.

"This is a passenger ship!" he snapped. On his right, Moxie was taunt and tense; on his shoulder, Nero was licking his front paw. "You gave me an airplane!"

Liu rolled his eyes and shoved his hands deeper in his pockets. It ruined the line of his uniform, but he wasn't the kind of person to care about those kinds of details. "Is that a problem?"

Miranda walked between them, her shoes clipping against the cement. Vico's newest addition, a falcon he had named Hermes, squawked a sharp cry at her, flying towards her.

"Hermes, return!" Vico snapped, holding out his left arm. The bird made a point of sweeping over Miranda's head as he turned (not that Miranda altered in her trajectory whatsoever), but came back, landing on Vico's wrist even as he continued arguing with Liu: "I was a pilot of a weaponized aircraft; this thing is useless to me!"

Liu frowned. "But, Baggio, you forget: you'll be carrying passengers."

All three animals looked at Liu; behind Vico, another

dog huffed out a breath.

Vico clenched his teeth and his mechanical hand. "I am of more worth than a cargo pilot."

Liu exhaled a long breath. "Baggio, you haven't even checked it out. Why don't you use your eyes instead of your mouth for once?"

Nero hissed. Vico turned on his heel and snapped, "Hermes, scout!" The falcon lifted off his wrist and glided towards the plane. Vico followed, snapping his flesh fingers once to call the two dogs.

The first thing he noticed was that there was no cargo hold: although the plane was long – likely three hundred feet – and fairly wide – maybe fifty feet – it was only about fifteen feet high. And that was standing on its wheels.

The second thing he noticed was the window – one single pane of glass that stretched about one hundred feet. The other side was identical.

The third thing was that there were no seats inside. Instead, it was designed a lot like his quarters: each side with a wide shelf about four feet above the floor, and a series of hanging cages – all open – stretching across the ceiling. At the very front of the aircraft was a pilot's cabin: one chair, a huge panel, and a curved glass window.

He looked over his shoulder and said, "Explore!" Nero hopped off his shoulder and two other cats mysteriously appeared, trotting the length of one of the shelves. Moxie went straight for the pilot's cabin, while the other dog, Hyde, sniffed out the floor. Hermes went straight into one cage and cried out again. The cage shook slightly with his weight; his talons were completely mechanical, as was his beak and the inside of his wings (supposedly).

Vico followed Moxie into the cabin and sat in the chair. He looked over the panel and focused on a small cluster of buttons.

"The cabin separates," he said.

"Yes," Miranda said behind him. He didn't flinch, but it was a near thing. "A hover unit."

He spun the chair around to face her where she stood in the open doorway between the cabin and the rest of the craft. "That's not very fuel efficient," he answered.

"Precisely 53% of this ship is constructed out of solar panels," she said. "There is a gasoline backup system for emergencies, however."

He rolled his eyes and spun the chair back around. "I was teasing, Miranda."

"I would appreciate it if you refrained from flirting with me, Mr. Baggio," she replied.

He peered over the panel and patted Moxie on the head when she settled at his side. "Yeah, well, you're basically the only girl who talks to me; so what's a guy to do?"

"Refrain himself," she said, her voice dry. "On another note, we should have your fourth troop's beginning formation by the end of the week."

Moxie's tail thumped against the floor. Vico said, "New friends. Oh boy."

Satin was a very quiet crow. She was brilliant and vicious and came with fifteen others.

Vico spent half of his free time playing mediator between the four troops. It wasn't too different from his army days, though, so he didn't mind. He just created new whistles, snaps of fingers, and sounds all of them could distinguish.

They trained a *lot*. He made different orders for different tasks, and learned that one-word orders worked best. They found out what each troop excelled at, and that there were divisions of tasks within each troop.

His room began to smell like animal fur, and he got accustomed to a large black cat sitting on his chest most nights. He wore a leather armband on his left arm for the birds to land on and take off from, and a black, leather vest for the cats to hold onto when they sat on his shoulders. He kept a couple of dog treats in his back pocket for a job well done.

Baggio the Shepard, a few of the young soldiers and interns called him; he swore at them and sent a bird flying at them with talons outstretched.

Once upon a time, he used to speak fairly good French. Seemed that hell had taken that skill from him too.

He sat outside a small café at a round table with a croissant and a coffee in front of him and Moxie at his feet. Three tables down, another dog, Juniper, was mooching off an elderly couple for their scraps. On the top of the next table's parasol, one of his crows peered around, eyes black and glossy.

Moxie put a paw on his foot and he lifted it in response, using his heel as a fulcrum. "Non, mon ami," he muttered. "Pas maintenant." She huffed, but moved her paw off.

Then came the crash.

Vico had heard a lot of crashes in his lifetime: aircraft, sea vehicles, bicycles, hovercrafts, and automobile; but he still flinched at the sound of metal crunching and brakes squealing. He wondered what kind of vehicle it was – hover or electrical, large or small – and made sure to reach down and touch his flesh hand against Moxie's nose. Around him, people were exclaiming in French and rising to their feet. Juniper looked over to him, and he gave a single shake of his head.

(She was only eighteen months, poor thing. Still full of beans and eager to please.)

"Une ambulance! Quelqu'un appele une ambulance!"

"Alright," he murmured. "Time to go." He stood up, snapped his metal fingers inside his coat pocket, and started walking, following the too-curious people that were headed towards the collision. If he looked up, he knew he'd see a crowd of birds, so he kept his eyes facing forward until he reached the site of the commotion.

It was a vehicle, small and electric and smashed into a light pole. There was a crowd of people swarming the car, and a couple of similar cars pulled up on the sidewalk nearby. Across the street, a small Persian sat licking its front paw. It glanced over at Vico, and then stood, running off into an alley behind it. Vico kept walking; he refused to loiter or glance around to check on his troops. Instead, he kept his eyes forward, even when he heard the soft hum of hovercraft ambulances.

Liu looked over the report, finger tapping on the screen, and nodded to himself. "One pedestrian, and both the driver and the passenger injured; police and two ambulances tied up for an hour, leaving ample room for our primary force to secure the cargo." He glanced over at Vico with just his eyes. "And all because a cat ran across the road."

Vico stayed at-ease. He'd have to give Starshine an extra treat today.

Liu slide his finger down, shutting the tablet off. "Well,

at least we know that works. On to Phase II."

If Vico were an introspective man, he wouldn't be in the position he currently found himself in. There would also have been a long period of time where he mused about the new arm and what it might mean to him later in life... But Vico wasn't an introspective man; it said so on his psych analysis.

(In case anyone was wondering, the arm was an incredible piece of machinery, and might have even been aesthetically pleasing had Vico consented to the skin graft. As it was, it was a silver skeleton, with transparent pieces visually exposing the wires (blue, red, and black) underneath while keeping everything neatly together. The joints were created with small spheres that flashed with softly pulsing light, to the same beat as his heart. It looked flimsy and fragile, but it was stronger than steel.

It would mean a lot to him later in life.)

Phase II was not well received by Vico.

"You killed my birds!" he shouted, storming into Liu's office.

Miranda glanced up and with a quick scan, tossed a small sphere onto the floor. It rolled to a stop between Vico and the desk, and created a barrier reaching from floor to ceiling and spreading about six feet across. It fizzled with electricity.

Liu raised his eyebrows. "What are you talking about, Baggio?" he asked.

"Operation Icarus," Miranda answered, already consulting her tablet. "It was a clue, Mr. Baggio." And she almost sounded kind, with the quick glance she darted his way.

Vico clenched his hands and wished he hadn't left his troops at the Infirmary; wished he could click his tongue and send a cat with outstretched claws straight for their eyes. Because she was right, dammit, she was right; he should have known, should have made the connection. But he hadn't anticipated four of his crows – Lillian, Jack, Frost, and Bimbo – to spontaneously burst into flames like hellish phoenixes as they flew through the hospital's windows. He hadn't expected kamikaze crows.

Liu looked at him and folded his hands on his desk. "Let me get this straight, Baggio: You're not upset that we set a hospital on fire, resulting in the causalities of eighty-nine civilians, but that we used your troops to start it."

"They're my birds," he gritted out.

Liu's eyes narrowed. "They're *my* birds, Baggio. Just like you're *my* soldier. And whatever I order you to do, you'll do; understand?"

"No!" Vico snapped, kicking the small sphere. It sent a shock through his body and a ripple through the barrier. It made his breath catch in his chest, and he gritted his teeth. "Why bother making these birds if you're just gonna blow them up?"

"Why do people make bullets; why do people create bombs?" Liu retorted, getting to his feet in one smooth motion. "To serve a purpose; and if the weapon malfunctions, then we will dispose of it. Do you understand *that*, Baggio?"

Vico swore once, kicked the sphere again, and limped out of the office.

There were three squads of cybernetic animals. Vico's Wolf Pack, as he called them, was the largest and most varied, but also the newest. They trained every day, and because of their size, roamed the entire base, often scaring the new recruits by running between their legs.

Isabelle Mason had named her squad the City Spies. It was comprised of twenty-five rats and fifty pigeons. They were used for surveillance mostly, and stayed in designated areas of the base. For some reason, not everyone liked rats slinking across the walls or pigeons cooing in their ear while they tried to eat their lunch.

Rudy Anderson had The Hounds – ten Dobermans as vicious and strong as tigers. They returned from missions with blood-soaked muzzles and white scars on their torsos. They didn't answer to anyone but Anderson, and always travelled as a complete unit.

On the whole, Vico, Mason, and Anderson stayed on their own, choosing the company of their squads over that of any human. They were not friends in the least, and only tolerated the presence of the other two. Vico's cats liked to hunt Mason's rats, and Anderson's dogs growled at Vico's if they came too close.

The squad was loyal to the squad. They didn't need anyone else, and they didn't like anyone else either.

His troops began coming with collars. The birds wore bracelets on their ankles, and the dogs and cats shook and scratched at the new additions around their necks. Vico was given the colour code, and started a new diet of bitter guilt and rage.

Red collars meant that they were kamikaze fighters – this suicide portion comprised half of his crows and five of his smaller hawks. Within a few weeks, a rotation developed where he lost at least ten birds a mission. While he knew he shouldn't bother naming them, he had a routine down now; and how do you discriminate against creatures when they hadn't done anything wrong? They were like children: innocent, eager to please, and often incredibly stupid.

Vico had broken a lot of lives in his time; maybe this was karma slowly breaking his heart.

Then Marshmallow, a fluffy white cat, came back to him with a yellow collar. While Vico knew, according to the colour code, that this meant she was a conductor of some sort, it wasn't until they had a mission where they were supposed to fry the databanks of a company that he understood what it meant.

Unlike the kamikaze birds, where there was nothing left but a pile of ash and frayed wires, Vico was forced to collect the carcass of Marshmallow. The hot, dark smell of burnt hair stayed in his nose for hours, and lingered in his clothes.

"We haven't yet successfully calculated the amount of electricity a body can hold," Miranda said, fingers tapping at the screen in front of her. Vico's hair was still damp from the three showers he had taken to get the smell off his hands. "Too much cybernetic material and the subject loses its nature that makes it so useful as a weapon. Too little, and the body burns from excess of electricity." She swiped a finger to the right, and when the screen blinked black for a moment, Vico could see her reflection. Her lips were curled up at the corners. "It's a fascinating experiment," she said.

Something curdled in his stomach.

Black collars were spies – with cybernetic eyes and

cameras installed inside. When he got that notice, he stroked a hand down Nero's back and said, "Does that make you a spy too? I remember that eye of yours."

Nero opened one eye – his real one – sent Vico a dirty look, and then closed it again. A few seconds later, he began to purr.

There were other collars, other jobs, other things that broke his heart, but Vico tried not to think about it. He compartmentalized. Soldiers died. It happened. It even happened under his control.

But somehow it was different when you fed the soldier by hand, and gave them an ear scratch, or cleaned them of their loose feathers, or brushed out their fur, and then sent them out to die.

Satin was pissed at him – but Vico didn't really blame her. Every week, she lost a portion of her troops, and Vico was the one ordering them. Still, she didn't have to peck his flesh hand every time he poured out her food; he was getting tired of walking down to Infirmary twice a day for disinfectant spray and a bandage.

He was walking back from one of those trips, rubbing at the bandage – the nurse was either new or grumpy, and hadn't wrapped it very tight, and it was lumpy and distracting and would be itchy in an hour – when he saw Miranda standing in a room by herself. This wasn't unusual, Miranda was about as social a creature as he was, but what was unusual was what was on the large screen she was standing before. It wasn't her usual charts and diagrams – it looked like maps and graphs.

He walked over to the door and opened it, stepping inside. He moved towards the screen and stopped at Miranda's left shoulder, taking in the information. It looked like some sort of shipping information, something coming from the States.

"Is there something you required?" Miranda asked, fingers tapping away at her personal tablet.

"That new nurse is terrible," he answered, eyes still scanning the screen.

"She doesn't approve of your personality," Miranda responded, eyes flicking down to her screen. "I do hope you're not suggesting we fire her."

"And why not?" Vico countered, rubbing at his hand again. The texture was weird under the robotic finger.

"If we fired everyone who disapproved of your personality, operations at this base would grind to a halt." She reached out to tap a finger on the large screen – it changed to a grid of the east coast of the States. "You don't have clearance to view this material."

"You're sure going out of your way to keep me from seeing this too," he said. "What's all this about anyways?"

"A new shipment," she responded. "This is for our newest squad."

"Another squad?"

"Domestic animals," she said, eyes flicking back and forth between the tablet and the screen. "Goats, pigs, sheep… We're hoping to move into another area." She tapped on the screen again. "However, this requires new equipment; each species has certain requirements, with a different criteria for effectiveness-"

"You're kinda sadistic, Miranda," he interrupted.

She paused, actually stopping mid-sentence. "I beg your pardon?" she questioned the screen, finger barely touching it.

"You love this," Vico said, no emotion in his voice. "You are taking animals, destroying their lives and the lives of innocent people, and all you can focus on is how to make them more effective, while keeping them as alive as possible."

She brought her finger to her chin, and slowly rotated on her heel to face him. "Mr. Baggio, sadism is defined as deriving sexual pleasure from inflicting pain on another individual," she said. "I am not inflicting pain for the sake of my own gratification; I am experimenting and working on a final solution of biological and cybernetic co-existence. If specimens are injured or killed in the process, that is merely a fact." She raised an eyebrow. "Pretending to care for something beyond the finished project seems like an excessive waste of energy to me."

Vico watched her face for an expression. "You're very cold, Miranda."

She rolled her eyes and turned back to the screen. "And your life is a clear testament that being passionate is an admirably characteristic." He clenched his metal fist, and exhaled slowly through his nose. She watched this reaction from the corner of her eye before adding, "Terran Engineering allows me to explore my research. They fund it without placing limitations on my work. What more could a girl ask for?"

Vico scowled, and said, "Yeah, well, explain that to my dead troops." Then he stormed out of the room.

And sometimes, when Nero felt the need to support his troop – usually while they were on the Ark, as Vico had taken to calling his aircraft – a huge orange and white cat named Fat Ass would hop up onto Vico's bed, and stretch out on his chest. Vico didn't really like not being able to breathe, so he'd give Fat Ass a swat, but Fat Ass seemed to take it as a sign of love, because he'd just roll over on his back.

The birds whispered above his head, chittering at each other, and grooming their feathers. There were a couple of soft thuds as a couple of dogs pawed at each other, trying to get comfortable. Moxie rested her head on Vico's leg, and huffed out a cloud of hot breath.

Vico stared at the ceiling, and used his metal hand to scratch at Fat Ass' stomach. He pawed at the metal, squirming until he fit a metal finger in his mouth. Then he began to chew on it. Vico sighed.

Miranda was correct about one thing: the metal forearm and hand was recognizable, and it did draw attention. People tended to stare at it, and then at Vico, with their eyes finally falling on whatever animal was hanging around him at the time. They avoided him; called him a robot, called him hotheaded, called him an animal, and didn't care about the contradictions of these names.

And Vico found himself looking in the mirror some days, and being unable to recognize the man he used to be. He kept himself clean-shaven still, mostly because the crows like to pull out his hair, and the dogs sometimes drooled on his face when they got too excited. But his hair was getting shaggy, and his clothes were no longer neat, and his smile was difficult to find now. He was used to the softly flashing lights of his hand, and accustomed to the way light reflected off his forearm, but sometimes reached out expecting to feel softness or coarseness, and instead only registering the heat of the object.

Once upon a time, he was Major Ludovico Baggio; for a while, he was simply Bags. Now he was Vico Baggio, with a leather vest, dog drool on his pants, and cat hair on his shirt. He scowled and grunted, snapped fingers and stomped feet. The only women who spoke to him were the nurses or Miranda, and the only men were the ones who gave him orders. He practiced shooting five hours a week, and snuck into the Weaponry on the third level, poking around without asking permission.

For all that he had a metal arm, he stuck close to the basics: his animals, his favourite outfit, and a couple of six-inch knifes and a semi-automatic handgun. They tried to make him use the handheld machine guns, the laser guns, the immobilizing pistols, and he refused. He liked the classics too much. But he loved the soft zoom of The Ark, the 3D screen for missions, and the hovering ability of the pilot's cabin. He got a hold of a hovercycle, and took the dogs for runs, and the birds for flights; shooting across fields at 60mph, with the dogs running easily at his side, and the birds doing lazy loops in the sky, waiting for a challenge.

The cats, well... Cats would do whatever the hell they wanted; best to leave them to it.

Apparently, the shipment that Miranda was so fascinated in was due to arrive tomorrow. Not that it affected Vico in any way, since him and his troops were being sent out to the Netherlands to cause an Air-Dock incident.

Vico stood in the doorway separating his pilot's cabin from the rest of the Ark, watching his animals settle in for the ride. He glanced down at Moxie, sitting at his side, and said, "Whadd'ya say, girl? Second star to the right, straight on 'til morning?"

She looked back up at him, and thumped her tail against the floor. Hermes let out a loud cry, and Satin pulled on his hair, plucking a handful right out of his scalp. When he turned to look into his cabin, Nero was sitting in his chair, grooming his genitals again.

"Dammed cat," Vico grumbled, stepping over. He swatted Nero up the side of his head, and hustled him out of his chair. When Nero removed himself, after hissing at Vico, Vico took his seat, and started pulling lever and pushing buttons.

First, he activated the solar panels, bringing energy to the engines; then he fired up the thrusters, following with the propellers in the back. Beneath them, the Ark began to hum, and the animals began to whine, and cry.

Moxie let out a single bark, while Hermes and Satin cried out in unison. Nero hopped up onto a shelf, and flicked his tail once.

The Ark fell silent.

Vico mentally reviewed the mission parameters, considered the three crows he was going to lose, the two cats and one dog that was supposed to ruin the computer system of the Air Control, and the five spy-hawks that were supposed to report back. He knew Liu and Miranda didn't understand why he had to bring all his troops for a simple eleven-man mission; but he didn't have to explain much to them. As long as the job got done...

He cracked the knuckles of his flesh hand, and wiggled the metal fingers. He said, turning his head to look down at Moxie, "One day, we won't have to answer to anyone. What do you think about that?"

And Moxie whined.

Bronwynn Erskine

An Ontario native currently residing in Newfoundland, Erskine is an avid steampunk enthusiast and acrylic landscape painter.

Erskine made her publishing debut in 2018's *Chillers from the Rock* with her chilling tale: 'Scarlett Ribbons.' She returns to *Flights from the Rock* with her new story: 'Feather and Bone.'

Feather and Bone

The maid servant attending Princess Ingrid this morning was one of the new ones, a timid little thing who'd served one of the local lord's many mistresses before the conquest. She was trembling so hard Ingrid could feel it through her hair as the girl worked with comb and brush--probably thinking about the rumours that were whispered through the back halls.

Ingrid wished she could send the girl away and braid her own hair; they would both have been happier that way. But Jacinda would have vapours if she appeared at breakfast with the only simple braid she could manage by herself, and probably have the maid punished as well. So she sat as still as her grey mood allowed, fidgeting restlessly with the rings on her fingers, but holding her back stiffly correct, and tolerated the frightened girl's work.

A rustle of curtains at the open window caught her eye in the mirror. The silhouette half shrouded behind them made some of her restless tension ease, and she smiled.

"Merla," she said, quietly so that the girl wouldn't startle. "One of my birds has come looking for treats. You remember I told you they wouldn't hurt you."

A single shiver translated itself from the maid's hands to the comb tangled in the princess's hair, but she managed to reply in a mostly steady voice. "Yes, milady, I re-member."

"Good. I'm going to call him over to sit with me while you finish up."

In the mirror, the girl's fair cheeks paled further. But she also nodded resolutely and went back to work with the comb. This one might be worth keeping on after all.

Ingrid held out a hand heavy with gold and jet, and hummed a bar of the calling song she'd learned from her mother as a little girl.

In response, the bird lofted himself into the air with a single powerful wing beat and glided silently across the room. He alighted before her on the dressing table. Talons as long as Ingrid's fingers gripped the edge, careful not to scrape the paint, and he ducked his red-stained head to her hand. His wickedly curved beak was meant for cracking bones and rending flesh, but he only mouthed gently at her skin.

"You're looking well, my prince," Ingrid crooned, stroking along the edges of the vulture's wings. "Have you been getting on well with the local flocks? They haven't been unkind to you?"

The bird replied with contented sound that was al-most a chuckle. A sound wild birds had never made in her hearing.

"Things are going well then, I take it? Perhaps the mountain flocks are cleverer than the lowland ones, if none of them have challenged you."

He stretched out his long neck and touched his beak to her temple. In her mind's eye, she looked down from a great height upon the jumbled rocks and ledges of a cliff side aerie. At least a hundred vultures nested there, their broad wings dark against the reddish stone, and every single one watched her soar closer.

The shared memory faded slowly when he drew back. Ingrid's body felt heavy and confining for a moment, without the freedom of wings to carry her aloft. She sighed softly and stroked the feathers behind the vulture's eyes.

"Definitely cleverer than the ones around Otterby," she murmured.

The birds there had been reluctant to accept him into their territory, and he'd fought several bloody challenges when he'd followed her there the first time her father had moved the court. He chirruped softly and nuzzled her hand, remembering her panic all too well. He was her oldest friend, and one of the few she had left who remembered her mother from before the accident. The thought of losing him still made her stomach ache as if she'd swallowed stones.

But it was hard for the truly wild creatures to challenge the massive bird who'd been fed from the time he was barely fledged on the delicacies of the king's table and the magics of the queen's solar. On that diet he'd grown to half again the size of his wild cousins.

Ingrid reminded herself of this daily, and more than daily when the court was settling into a new city. The local vultures might have glutted themselves on the bloodshed the army sewed before the advancing court, but they did not have the same advantages as her prince.

As if he knew the dark paths her thoughts flitted down, he stretched up again and touched her forehead with his beak. There was no sharing of memory this time, only the echo of her mother's kiss so long lost. Still, it was enough to wake the hot, tight knot of grief in Ingrid's chest. She leaned their foreheads together and closed her eyes against the traitorous tears that threatened to fall.

"Milady?" the maid asked hesitantly. "Is there anything else I can do for you?"

Ingrid blinked her eyes open. She hadn't meant to slip away into her grief for more than a moment, but it was clear that more time had passed. The girl had finished brushing her hair, then curled and pinned it into a complicated arrangement quite different from the maidenly chignon in which the other servants had always dressed her hair. She found herself staring into the mirror in shock.

"Did I do something wrong, milady?" Merla asked when the princess remained silent. Her reflection bit her lip and clasped her hands tightly in her apron, wringing the fabric nervously.

"No," Ingrid answered slowly, tilting her head a little to see the arrangement better. "No, it looks fine. It looks very nice. Just not what I was expecting."

The maid blushed a startlingly bright red. "I'm sorry, milady. I just thought. I should have asked, but I didn't want to bother you and I thought..."

"You thought what, Merla?" Ingrid asked, curiously fascinated by the way the girl's expression flitted from shy to chagrined to flustered and back.

"Well, with your birthday, milady. You're a lady grown now and not a little girl, and I thought I'd better put your hair up like a lady's." She looked near tears now, lips quivering and pale lashes fluttering as she blinked rapidly. Her voice was scarcely more than a whisper as she added, "I'll take it down and redo it if you'd rather, milady."

"No, it's fine," Ingrid reassured her.

"Are you sure, milady?"

The confection of curls bounced a little as Ingrid nodded. "It's a good thought; it just hadn't occurred to me.

Thank you for taking the initiative."

In the mirror, the maid raised wide, startled eyes and flushed a painful looking scarlet all the way to the roots of her sandy hair.

Ingrid stored the mental image away for future consideration and smoothed her own expression into the polite mask she wore in public. "That will be all for now, Merla," she dismissed the maid gently before rising from her seat.

A lady indeed. She'd realised, of course, and had been cognisant enough to ensure that her wardrobe was updated to match that new status. But it still felt unreal to look in the mirror and see a young woman with an artfully careless tumble of raven black curls instead of the girl with feathers and leaves poking haphazardly from her disheveled braids.

"This insistence that I'm a different person today than I was yesterday is awfully strange, my prince," she murmured aloud to the bird once they were alone. She gave him one more gentle scratch before rinsing her hands to remove any trace of the red dust he'd used to stain the feathers around his head and shoulders. "I'm likely to be busy most of the day, so you'll have to entertain yourself. I told the servants to open the solar windows for you, in case you decide the winds are too cool for flying and you'd prefer to laze by the fire."

In answer, the bird hopped down onto the chair she'd just vacated and began to preen the feathers under his wings. Smiling to herself, Ingrid took herself out of her dressing room.

Ingrid was profoundly grateful that breakfast was not

a court affair. There were still almost a dozen places set around the table as she entered, but most were occupied by members of her father's privy council. They could be granted a certain, limited amount of trust so that, on a normal day, there was at least one meal where she could allow herself some measure of relaxation.

At the head of the oblong table, in a pair of elaborate chairs that were not quite thrones, sat the king and queen. Her father, in stark black mourning with a thin steel circlet on his greying hair in place of the more elaborate crown she knew he hated. And her mother, a silent ghost of her former self, dressed in white like a virgin bride in spite of the way it showed up the unhealthy pallor under the natural brown tone of her skin.

Jacinda sat in her accustomed place beside Ingrid's mother. She was first duchess and the hostess of the king's court, and served him in other positions as well if the rumours that had reached Ingrid's ears held any truth. But she was not queen, and her perpetually pinched expression spoke strongly that she never allowed herself to forget this fact.

Across from her, next to the empty seat at the king's right hand that Ingrid would take, the minister of war had been displaced by a young man whose vivid scarlet doublet stood out among the court's perpetual mourning greys like a cardinal among sparrows. Or a fox among hens.

Ingrid disliked him immediately.

She entered, as was her custom, with no more announcement than the sweeping rustle of her heavy skirts, but the young interloper looked up immediately. He rose and graced her with a deep bow, and Ingrid couldn't think of a single pleasant thing to say to him. She should welcome him to the court, she knew. But his very presence grated at the edges of her nerves like salt to a raw wound. It was all she could do to bite her tongue and hold back the acid words that churned in her stomach.

She curtsied, slow and graceful as Jacinda had taught her, but she was quite sure her expression was as stormy as the grey velvet of her gown.

"Her royal highness, Princess Ingrid i Madartoll," Jacinda announced her with stiff formality. "Princess, may I present Lord Etienne des Marais, Marquis of Cormly, come to pay his respects to your father."

To pay his respects indeed. Ingrid knew why he was here, and she hated him for it. She wished she was permitted to bring the vulture with her inside the keep's halls. Let this simpering peacock try and pay court to her under her prince's baleful black glare. That might almost be worth enduring the marquis's company.

Unaware of her thoughts he let his grip on her hand linger longer than was strictly necessary as he bent to kiss her knuckles. "Had I known her highness's beauty so far exceeded the rumours, I would have come sooner," he murmured. The words sounded to her like an actor's on the stage, practiced and certain but with no true feeling behind them.

"I'm quite aware of what the rumours say about me, Lord Cormly," Ingrid told him, and was pleased to see his grey eyes widen a fraction in alarm. "So you may be sure I take your words in their full measure."

He looked a little panicked, though he struggled to hide it, and Ingrid allowed her smile to widen a trifle.

Her father was frowning when she turned away from the marquis and stepped close to kiss his cheek. "Be nice, sunflower," he whispered in her ear. "At least give him a chance."

"Yes, Father," Ingrid replied demurely, knowing that he would hear the lie but would not call it out in front of so many witnesses.

She stepped behind him to come to her mother's side, and leaned down to kiss her cool cheek. "Good morning, Mother. You look lovely as always," she said.

The queen's head turned, her garnet-sheened lips smiled. She even rested one tiny, bird boned hand on her daughter's velvet sleeve for a second, but her deep black eyes remained as blank as the finely crafted doll she resembled. Ingrid closed her eyes and kissed her mother's cheek again, and forced herself to ignore the faint scent of wilting roses that always clung to her mother's cool skin.

She retreated to her seat between the king and the marquis and fixed her eyes firmly on her plate, though its contents held no appeal.

By the time the morning session of court ended, Ingrid felt as if she might scream. The court's usual business had been interrupted time and again by courtiers who insisted on bringing up her birthday. They plied her with gifts and compliments that weighed her down until she felt chained to the earth as tightly as Gilded Hearnet, Lord of Fallen Stars.

As a little girl she'd loved the attention, but it had soured over the years. Every year she grew older and her mother did not, the weight bore down heavier. It wouldn't be long now until she was the elder of the two of them.

She slipped quietly away through the concealed door behind her father's throne, nodding to the pair of guardsmen who stood outside it. "If my father is looking for me, please say I've retired to my rooms to meditate and will rejoin the court for supper," she said quietly.

"Yes ma'am," the guard on her left replied with a reg-ulation perfect salute. He was scarcely more than a boy, cheeks still carrying traces of baby fat, and his enthusiasm drew a small but genuine smile to her lips.

The guard on her right raised one bushy eyebrow in a brutally scarred face. "And if we need to know where you are in the event of an emergency, ma'am?" he asked without inflection.

Ingrid glanced his way for a second. Grey had begun creeping into his red-brown hair at some point and the wound that had cost him his left eye had never faded in its healing from the first angry red, but he stood as tall and straight as he had years ago. She remembered, viscer-ally, how he'd smelled of leather and aftershave that day. She remembered pounding her tiny fists against his broad chest, drenched in blood and howling with grief too great for her child's mind to encompass, as he dragged her from her mother's side. She remembered clinging to him, perched in the saddle before him as the guard closed ranks around her, horse hooves pounding through the night as they abandoned the compromised palace at Dolcollette.

"I'm going to walk in the gardens, Sol," she replied quietly.

He nodded slightly, saying "Very good, ma'am. Enjoy your meditation."

She heard the younger guard whisper something as she continued down the corridor, but didn't bother to lis-ten. Sergeant Solomon could make his own decisions in what he told his subordinates. He was one of the very few people she trusted completely, and she wouldn't insult him by fretting over his choice.

There was a door leading into the gardens only a short walk down the hall, and she managed to slip outside without meeting anyone else. She waited until the door was firmly shut behind her before letting herself sag against the cool stone wall. Too long spent in the formal audience hall, where the stuffy air was perpetually choked with tallow smoke and a hundred competing perfumes, always left her head pounding like a regimental drum.

She drew in great lungfuls of the crisp, late fall air. Eyes closed and face tilted up towards the frail sunlight, she finally felt the tension easing out of her body.

The rush and whisper of small wings alerted her before the first starling alighted on her shoulder. She held up her arms and opened her eyes to watch the flock descend around her. They landed on her shoulders and arms, on her hands, even in her hair, and wrapped her in the bright joy of their delighted chatter. She let it wash over her and breathed it in as greedily as the fresh air, and let herself surrender just for a few moments to the memory of happier times.

The starlings weren't her creatures to call, but they came anyway. They'd been her mother's flock. Some days, she could almost hear her mother's sweet, clear soprano in the flock's chatter. Those were good days, and also bad ones. Today she heard only the cheerful calls of half tame birds greeting someone who regularly fed them.

With that thought in mind, she unfastened one of the doeskin purses that hung from her belt and stepped away from the door a little way before scattering the first handful of seeds. The starlings erupted from her hair and clothing. They fell upon the offering with the eager gluttony of all small birds, squabbling and shoving.

Ingrid had worried after her mother's accident that they wouldn't find enough to eat if left to fend for themselves. She knew better now, but she still fed them. They were friendly little things, and her father's court would turn a blind eye to far more eccentric habits in its princess than feeding starlings.

She gave them one more handful, then returned the pouch to its place and started walking.

The gardens were quiet and empty once she'd left the flock behind with their meal. Most of the leaves had turned brown with the approach of winter, and the courtiers who might have strolled there in finer weather had all migrated to warmer venues. Even the ornamental white gravel of the path hardly made a sound beneath her soft soled slippers.

It crunched loudly, however, under a pair of heavy boots that approached down an intersecting path. A moment later she caught a flicker of red through the faded leaves of a climbing rose. The marquis, of course.

Ingrid clenched her hands into fists for a heartbeat, then forced herself to relax and smile with the proper amount of graciousness in her expression as the young man came properly into sight.

He bowed in greeting and smiled in a way that almost reached his eyes. "I do hope I'm not intruding, Your Highness, but I couldn't help noticing your departure. I thought this might be a good opportunity to beg a few moments of your time."

"A few moments," she allowed in a neutral tone. "I find court meals a trial most days. They're very loud."

A handful of starlings alighted in the bare branches of a poplar sapling not far from her left hip. Snatches that were half words interspersed their more ordinary chatter now, and their small dark eyes watched her attentively.

"There's more birds here than I expected for the season," the marquis observed. He was frowning faintly, watching the starlings instead of her.

Ingrid shrugged. "I feed them when I walk in the gardens. They often follow me about." Both perfectly true statements, if not nearly the whole truth.

She shook a few seeds into her palm and held it out, immediately getting three of the boldest starlings perched on her fingers. They ate the seeds, but without the usual jostling between them.

"How delightful," he replied. There was a hint of something that might have been real pleasure in his eyes. "I raise kestrels and gyrfalcons at home. I envy them, truth to tell. I envy the freedom they must feel in the skies."

"I envy them the simplicity of their lives," Ingrid admitted, stroking their dark feathers with a fingertip. She hadn't meant to speak such a fragile truth aloud, and certainly not to this man who was all but a stranger. She hadn't spoken so freely to anyone in years.

An odd light-headedness had come over her as they spoke. Not the smothering sensation she got sometimes if she'd been indoors too long, but a sort of floating lightness not unlike the time she'd pilfered a bottle of wine from the kitchens and gotten drunk. She hadn't enjoyed the sensation then.

The marquis stepped in and laid a hand on her elbow to steady her when she swayed ever so slightly. "Simplicity is such a rare luxury, isn't it, Your Highness," he agreed, so close she could see hints of blond in his brown lashes and feel his breath on her cheek.

He was far too close for propriety, but she couldn't make herself look away.

"It's a pleasure to discover we have so much in common," he went on. His voice had an almost musical rhythm to it, not entirely unlike the calling song. "And such a shame as well. I'd like you to walk with me, Princess, and listen very carefully to what I'm going to tell you."

He turned to lead her towards a secluded corner of the garden that was popular among courting couples when the weather was fairer. As he did so, his sleeve brushed past the birds still perched on her hand.

With wild, raucous shrieks they leapt into the air. The rest of the flock followed from all over the garden, wings slashing at the air and voices raised in cacophonous fury.

Abruptly, Ingrid's fascination with the marquis's voice fell away. She shook herself as if she'd just awakened from a daydream and looked around.

The starlings had gathered in a wild flurry of tiny wings. Their individual screams blended eerily to form a single voice that hissed the words of a binding song. Ingrid could taste its power on the back of her tongue as she added her own voice.

She hadn't worked more than the most basic of magics since the aftermath of her mother's accident. The words felt heavy and clumsy on her lips at first, but the melody vibrated in her bones and begged to be released. With a sigh, she let it fill her lungs.

The sere brown vines of the climbing rose and the naked branches of the poplars twitched. They reached for the marquis with grasping fingers, snagging at his clothing.

Without noticing, Ingrid had taken control of the song. Her voice filled the garden from the deepest roots to the highest branches, and she was one with its slow, deep power as the song faded slowly from the air. The air she breathed was alive with the scent of clean earth, and the faintly bitter tang of leather polish.

Four royal guardsmen had arrayed themselves between her and the struggling form of the marquis, where he stood bound in branches before her. There were another four behind her. Sunlight dripped like honey down the blades of their lowered pikes and burnished the leather of their gauntlets to a tawny gold.

"I hope we aren't disturbing your meditation, ma'am," Sergeant Solomon rumbled at her left hand. "The birds seemed agitated this morning, and I thought there might be something you needed."

The magic had brushed aside cobwebs she'd allowed to form about herself, and she felt as if she looked on the world with clearer eyes than she had in long years. The sky and garden seemed less faded. Even the uniforms of the guards were closer to the silver blue of her childhood than the washed out grey she's seen them this morning.

And there were other birds besides the starlings. Her vulture prince loomed in the branches above the marquis's head, his red stained feathers looking positively gory in the bright sun, with his cousins circling silently above. Crows and pigeons crowded every window ledge, and a lone mountain eagle perched atop the courtyard wall surrounded by a court of lesser hawks and falcons.

Ingrid shook her head in awe and turned her gaze back to the marquis. He'd gone still now, wide eyed and panting slightly under the vulture's unnerving glare.

"Thank you, Sergeant. Your initiative is appreciated," she told Sol slowly, laying a hand briefly on his shoulder to steady herself in the reality of his presence before stepping past him.

He followed as she approached the pinioned marquis, a step behind and a step to the left like a well trained guard dog. Or a soldier shadowing his commander. The baby-faced guard from the corridor mirrored him on Ingrid's right.

The marquis's even features had lost some of their handsomeness in the snarl that now twisted his lips. He spat on the ground as she approached, then reeled back as far as the tangled vines would allow when the young guardsman's pike pressed into the hollow of his throat.

Even the gleaming blade at his throat wasn't enough to silence him, however. "Unnatural witch," he growled with teeth bared like a cornered beast.

Ingrid raised an eyebrow. "Coming from the man who just attempted to ensnare me with witchcraft, I'm afraid I don't quite grasp your issue with me," she said.

He flinched when she raised a hand, but she merely spread her fingers for a handful of starlings to land on. They trilled the melody of the calling song and jostled each other good naturedly.

"Is this the witchcraft you find so unnatural?" Ingrid asked with her head cocked to one side like a starling herself.

The marquis sneered. "Fur and feather, scale and skin, root and branch, and quickening breath," he recited in a kind of sing-song, the rhyme all children learned of the domains of Aria of the Feathers, Queen of Witches, and Lady of the Morning Mists. "Quickening breath, not the grave's still shadows."

There was a gleam in his eyes, pupils wide as the Gardens of Night, and he looked past her to the guards who'd formed a loose protective arc. "Do you know what she's done? What she is?" he demanded of them. "Do you?"

Ingrid's heart lurched to a halt in her chest and her throat was suddenly as dry as the dust in the mausoleum where they'd laid her mother out after the accident. She could taste the cloying memory of wilting roses on the back of her tongue as if it was yesterday.

A short chuckle from just behind her left shoulder made her jump. When she looked Sergeant Solomon was smiling, sharp edged and without humour.

"Of course we know, you idiot pup," he replied, deep voice rumbling in his ruined throat like a rockslide in the mountains. "Who do you think has kept watch for wraiths and witch hunters all these years? Who do you think has dealt with fanatics like you and kept the court in hand while we waited for the rightful queen to come of age?"

The sound that came from the marquis's mouth was too choked to understand, even if Ingrid's mind hadn't been reeling.

"The rightful queen?" she whispered.

Sol nodded curtly. "Forgive an old soldier's bluntness, ma'am, but after what he done to your royal mother the king rules only by your sufferance. The guard know who was responsible for winning the Polgren Wars, and who would have let those savages run roughshod all the way to the Sunken Sea. Her daughter is the one who belongs on the throne."

She turned to look at the rest of the guardsmen arrayed about her. The nods they gave her were grim, shoulders set and eyes unsmiling, but they were certain.

"Say the word, ma'am, and the guard will rise with you," the sergeant said grimly.

"We'll bring you your crown," the young guard on her right added, a gleam in his eyes. "Along with the head of the man who's wearing it."

Her voice came out a shaky whisper she hardly recognised. "I never thought about whose crown it was after mother's accident." She paused, bit her lip. "After her murder. It's long past time I learned to call it what it was."

"You were only a child then," Sol reminded her gently. "No one can blame a child for her grief."

She glanced towards the seething marquis. "I think he does," she whispered.

The sergeant shrugged. "Easily remedied, my Queen. Easily remedied. Just say the word."

She studied his face. The sturdy set of his jaw and the muddy brown of his single eye. The way he met her gaze unflinchingly, as so many people had been unable to do since that day. After an interminable moment of hesitation, she nodded.

"Yes."

The word hung in the air for long seconds, held aloft by a power that had nothing to do with her mother's songs.

The young guardsman's pike bit home, quick and gleaming bright as the marquis's blood welled red around it.

All around the courtyard the birds leapt aloft with raucous cries, the first heralds of Queen Ingrid's reign.

John Burnham

John Burnham is a professional bush pilot and flight instructor originally from Denver, Colorado, currently living in Red Deer, Alberta. He is an accomplished author with more than ten story credits to his name, including 'Alternate Meats' in *Red Deer Living*, 'Decision Time' in the poetry anthology *Across the River*, and 'The Girl With Forever Eyes' in *Moon Magazine*.

He is the author of *The Kitten Burgler*, a crime novel published by Strategic Books, and is co-author of the short story collection *Change*.

John is a member of MENSA, IONS, and The Orchid Society of Alberta. His interests include palaeontology, astronomy, comparative religion, cosmic evolution, and -- of course -- writing.

Halley's Comet

I park the airplane, hoping this was my last flight of the day. As I walk toward the office, visions of supper dance about in my head. Unfortunately, the office atmosphere is stormy as I walk in. The visions of a pint and a steak sandwich at the pub fade as I watch the superintendent stomp about. Something has gone awry in the field. In the Canadian north, that usually means work for the pilot.

The supe's face is red as he turns toward me and snarls, "Can you believe that goddamn, stupid, son-of-a-bitch?"

"What particular goddamn, stupid, son-of-a-bitch are we referring to?" I ask.

"Carl! How anyone could be so stupid? I'm gonna take a pair of rusty side-cutters and make a gelding of him."

Construction foreman Carl Sutter left here three days ago with a four-man crew and equipment to prepare a gas well drilling site. The roads would have become poorer and the going slower as he pressed into the undeveloped Canadian bush. During the last day, he would not have been on roads at all -- just trails through the trees. He should be at the site now. "What's his problem?" I venture.

The supe runs his hands through thinning hair as he raises his head and closes his eyes. "Propane! That stupid klutz is out of propane!"

My voice is incredulous. "Out? Clear out of propane?"

The supe lowers his head. He's beginning to calm down; the rant has had a cathartic effect. "Not out, he has about fifteen percent left in one bottle, but the other two are empty. Empty! Can you believe that? He leaves here with two empties!"

I do some math in my head. The skid-shack Carl and his crew will live in for the next several weeks is heated by propane stored in hundred-pound bottles. What he has left won't last until morning. "You got any more headed his way?" I ask.

"Of course I do. Whaddya think I am, some sort of freakin' ninny? I sent the fuel truck early."

I ignore the question and ask, "How early?"

"Coupla hours ago."

We look at each other. We're both calculating. The answers aren't nice. It will be around thirty-six hours before the fuel truck gets to Carl. The best scenario means he will be without propane -- and heat -- for twenty-four hours.

The supe's voice is husky as he asks, "What do the weather-guessers say for tonight?"

"Minus thirty."

We continue to look at one another. We can't leave Carl and the boys out there in subzero weather without heat. The supe falls into an uncharacteristic silence. Even though it will take the truck another thirty-four hours to get to Carl, I can be there in a little over two. We both know what has to be done. The supe can't tell me to do it, because it's illegal. His eyes betray an inner plea. I nod, turn to the phone, and dial the

loading dock. "Ernie, this is Jay. Please fill a hundred-pounder to sixty percent."

"Carl?" Ernie asks.

"Yeah."

"You're the man," Ernie replies enthusiastically. "It will be at the bird in five."

"You have it filled already?"

"Yeah, thought things might shake out like this. I even cinched the vent a little."

Carrying propane cylinders in an airplane is like hitting on Mother Superior. You just don't do it; nor do you want to. These hundred-pounders are fitted with a mechanism to vent off excess pressure. Raw propane wandering around in an airplane cabin is a recipe for turning the whole works into a fireball. That's why I asked for the cylinder to be under-filled. It's also why Ernie did something that may have disabled the vent.

On my way out of the office complex, the restaurant cook meets me with two thermoses of hot coffee. I'm surprised and touched. Even that crusty old bugger wants to have a piece of helping Carl.

Clad in parka, mitts, and pack boots, I taxi to the runway with the propane bottle strapped to the floor behind me. I don't intend to turn the cabin heat on because I don't want to warm the damn thing.

Takeoff into the inky sky is uneventful. I don't climb very high because the bottle's tendency to vent increases as the air pressure decreases.

There is no moon, but the stars are out. Their light makes things directly below quite visible. As usual, it is a bit hazy, so fewer stars are seen as one looks from the zenith downward. Somewhere ahead, the darkening sky merges with the velvety black of the forest below. There isn't any horizon.

The main road going out into this part of the oil patch crosses beneath me several times as it weaves through the hills and avoids the swamps. Soon, it gives way to narrower roads that branch out to serve existing facilities. Eventually, these peter out and the cut lines for seismic work are the only evidence of man. Following this labyrinth of roads, almost roads, and goat trails made Carl's journey more than twice the length of my straight-line path.

Airplanes make strange noises at night. During the day, all you hear is the roar of the engine, but at night, you hear -- or think you hear -- squeaks and groans. To-night, I'm hearing the fsst, fsst of a propane tank venting. My rational mind tells me it can't be happening. I'm able to ignore it until I smell the damn stuff. I flip the cabin light on and turn around to look at the tank. I don't see any fog from the venting. I pour myself a cup of coffee. I don't hear any more venting or smell propane as I sip the warm beverage. Obviously, it's all in my mind. And, what the hell anyway, if there is a little venting; there isn't any source of ignition. I'm okay either way.

Suddenly, I'm blinded by a shower of sparks from beneath the instrument panel! My heart stops. I can hear the fsst, fsst of the tank venting. The smell of propane is strong! I can see the airplane turning into a ball of fire re-sembling Halley's Comet (the matter of comets not actu-ally being balls of fire doesn't concern me at this point).

I shake my head and concentrate on what the instru-ments are telling me. My mind is reeling. I try to think as another shower of sparks lights up my feet. I reach under the panel and produce more sparks as I touch a dangling wire. I check the instrument panel. Everything seems to have power. Which wire is loose? Another shower of sparks and more propane odour scrambles my brain. Thinking is difficult. I have to do something. I scan the breaker panel and pull the one for the cigarette lighter. Minutes pass without a spark. I reach under the panel and bat the loose wire around. No sparks. It must have come off the back of the cigarette lighter. I take a deep breath and sit back in the seat. There will be no Halley's Comet tonight.

According to my calculations, I should be nearing Carl's camp, so I select the company air-to-ground frequency on the radio and key the mike. "Camp six, this is Alpha Bravo Zulu."

My earphones come alive. "Jay! God, I'm glad to hear your voice." Carl's not much for radio discipline.

"Camp six, Alpha Bravo Zulu estimates your position in ten minutes. Can you show lights?"

Up ahead, a small lake comes alive with vehicle lights. As I get closer, I can see that Carl has plowed the entire length and positioned everything with headlights along the edge.

A few minutes later, Carl rushes up and opens the door as I'm shutting the engine down. "Jay, I can't tell you how much I appreciate this," he pants.

"No biggie, bud," I say, "just get that damned thing out of my airplane." The last is unnecessary. Carl's guys are already hauling it through the door on the other side.

On the way home, I relax. I've shed my parka and mitts. With the heat on full blast, the cabin is toasty. I'm working on the second thermos and thinking that this is why I love the Canadian oil patch. Robert Service wrote poetry about the men who moil for gold. I don't think anybody will ever put the adventures of the men who moil for oil to verse, but it's the same deal. Our common enemy is the cold. Facing this formidable foe brings out the best in us. Alone, each of us would lose the fight -- we have to rely on one another. Carl knew he wasn't alone out there. He knew the rest of us would do whatever it took -- legal or not -- to get him some propane.

Peter J Foote

Born and raised in the Annapolis Valley of Nova Scotia, and the son of an apple farmer, Peter studied archaeology in university. He is employed as a boiler and refrigeration operator, is an active Freemason, and runs a used bookstore (Fictionfirst Used Books) out of his basement in his spare time.

Through FictionFirst Used Books Peter strives to support the written word community, which he does by sponsoring the monthly Kit Sora Flash Photography Fiction prize.

Believing that an author should write what he knows, many of Peter's stories are a reflection of his personal life.

Peter's work has twice been awarded the Kit Sora Flash Fiction Prize: once in March 2018 and again in September 2018.

Peter holds the distinction of being one of only three authors to be featured in all the modern *From the Rock* collections to date.

Stowaway's Luck

"Brynjar?"

"Aye, Captain Ylva?"

"There seems to be a disturbance at the bow, please see to it, I dislike conflict on my ship."

Brynjar looks to his Captain who is scanning the skies and KNOWS she hasn't so much as glanced towards the front of the ship in half an hour. Grinning at the almost magical abilities of his captain, Brynjar puts on his first officer's face and goes to investigate the disturbance.

"Osvald, if I catch you anywhere near my kit bag again I'll toss you over the side as dragon bait!" roars Gudfrid as she grabs her shipmate by his leather jerkin.

Adam's apple bobbing, the Viking warrior stares down at the petite woman with fire in her eyes threatening him, and replies: "I swear I haven't been near your stuff, don't blame me if you can't remember what you ate after getting into the mead."

"Are you saying I can't hold my drink?" Gudfrid hisses between clenched teeth as she pushes her crew mate towards the rails of the airship. The rest of the crew just watch the drama play out, many of them stopping rowing, and excited voices calling out bets who will come out on top.

Just as Osvald's legs hit the airships railing, Brynjar wades through the sea of bodies, his massive arms swinging to clear a path, heedless of the chins or noses in his way. He grabs each by the shoulder, his scarred and twisted hands like vices that squeeze until both Gudfrid and Osvald yield.

Strong arctic winds blow the braided beard of the first officer of the Skripi, revealing teeth broken in too many fights, but the wind is no match for his bellowing voice. "What in Odin's name is this? We have dragon sign and you're arguing like we're safe on land!" A savage shake causes their heads to snap backward. He continues: "Well? Speak!" and glares at the pair.

As Osvald opens his mouth, Gudfrid hurries to get there first: "This piece of dry rot..." she stabs a finger into Osvald's chest, "has been stealing my honeyed fruit when I've been up on deck at the oars, and I want it to stop!"

Brynjar's eyes narrow. He gives their shoulders an extra squeeze, causing a gasp of pain from both before replying. "There are two options. One, you two work the same shift and take the same breaks, or I dangle you BOTH by the thumbs over the side as dragon bait, your choice." And to punctuate his statement, he gives another squeeze and something pops in Gudfrid's shoulder, she clenches her teeth.

Brynjar's knuckles go white. "Same shift works for me," Osvald hisses, and Gudfrid gives a quick nod. Brynjar releases the pair and slaps them on the back. "There, I knew we could settle it, and your new shift starts NOW, so get to those oars." Once Brynjar sees the pair scramble for their empty bench and pull on the oars of dragon rib, his cold stare takes in the audience who scramble back to their benches.

Nodding to himself, and giving the crew a broken-toothed grin, Brynjar goes to report to his Captain.

"Now, what was that all about Brynjar?" asks Captain Ylva

"'Tis nothing important, just two crew arguing about petty theft, the normal squabbles on a voyage. I dealt with it."

"I'm sure you did, Brynjar, but this isn't the first complaint about theft, correct? And all the dragon-sign we've been having isn't doing our nerves any good."

Rubbing his bearded chin, Brynjar replies: "We're outside our normal route. That's bound to have people twisting in their hammocks."

"True, but I think it might be something else. Here, take the rudder," Captain Ylva says. "Close your eyes. Open yourself to the world around you, let it fill you as mead in a cup." Captain Ylva says, her voice sounding far away.

Brynjar does his best, though flinches when Ylva whispers: "There, do you feel it?"

"Nah, Captain, nothing than the normal smells and sounds of the Viking airship. What am I missing?"

Captain Ylva's voice takes on an ethereal lilt as if she were speaking from a hundred leagues away. "Forward hold, light-footed and small. Doing her best to stay hidden and quiet, but I feel her."

"I could believe you're touched by dragon blood, Captain, but you're saying we have a stowaway? It's been over a week since we set sail. A stowaway couldn't have kept hidden that long on a ship this size."

"Nonetheless she has, and is the cause of the food

thieving and the repeated dragon sign," the Captain says as she scans the skies and squints into the darkening clouds around them.

"Do you want me to take care of the stowaway, Captain?" Brynjar asks, as his hand slides to the dagger at his belt.

"That won't be necessary. I'll handle it. Take the rudder and keep on a course away from those clouds. Go over them if you must," Captain Ylva says as she gives the darkening clouds an intense stare before making her way to the ships lower level.

Ylva allows her eyes to adjust to the gloom of the hold and allows the Touch to flow through her again. Brynjar might tease his Captain about having the legendary "touch", those rare individuals imbued with a drop of dragon blood; Ylva knows it to be true. For most of her life, she's had the ability to feel the world around her with senses that a normal human doesn't own. Around lots people it overwhelms her, only in empty skies does she feel at peace. That peace has been elusive on this trip. They had dragon sign while land was still in sight; the crew murmured that it was an omen. The thieving of food started soon after. Never much, but everyone craves honeyed fruit and sweet cakes, and the crew noticed.

She's felt the presence of the stowaway for days and hoped she'd make herself known once they were away. Life seldom goes the way we wish; we will have to do it this way. Captain Ylva thinks to herself and slides through the shifting maze of hanging equipment and gear filling the hold of the *Skripi* without a sound, her steps as sure and graceful as a dancer, her only light the banked coals of their hanging fire pit.

Feeling the ship rise, Ylva knows Brynjar is trying to

skirt the coming storm rather than fly through it, but wonders if that will be enough. Worry about that later, focus on the task at hand. Ylva stops in front of the forward cargo hold.

Captain Ylva enters the pitch dark hold, knowing where each coil of rope, barrel of tar, and roll of dragon hide is located; the smooth sailing of the *Skripi* depends upon it. "Child, come out of there."

No movement, not a sound other than the creak and the groan of the ship, yet Captain Ylva can feel the heartbeat of her stowaway quicken in fear.

"My name is Captain Ylva, and I don't allow stowaways on the Skripi. You make yourself known now and face my fair judgment, or I send first officer Brynjar to force you out and believe me, you don't want that to happen."

For the space of three breaths nothing happens, then Captain Ylva hears the scratch of fabric, and a small pale face leans out from a bundle of dragon hide and blinks. "You... You're the Captain?" a small girl says and wipes her nose on her stained wool jerkin.

Trying not to smile, Captain Ylva puts on her voice of authority and says: "I'm not used to having my word challenged by any snot-nosed little boy!"

"Hey! I'm a girl, just like you!" the girl says as she steps out to face Captain Ylva.

The spirit in this one! Father Odin blessed this child! A grin shines through on Captain Ylva's face.

"Aye, I see that now, child. Now come out of there, and let me get a good look at you." Stepping aside, the child edges past the Captain, careful to stay out of arm's reach.

She's nothing but skin and bones. Starvation like this takes months. Someone has treated this child poor. Captain Ylva thinks and does her best to keep her anger off of her face.

Once out of the hold, Ylva sticks out her right arm and says: "My name is Captain Ylva, and this is my vessel, the Skripi. We are on a voyage of discovery. What is your name?"

Eyeing the Captain, the young girl grasps Ylva's forearm with her own grubby hand and says: "I'm called Sassa after my Nan, and I want to crew with you."

Her tone neutral, the Captain responds: "It's rare for me to take a stowaway as a crew member, and never children. You best tell me your story, child, but not down here; on the deck so the rest can hear your tale and meet the thief who has been raiding their sweet treats."

With that, the confidence that Sassa just displayed, evaporates into the cold air.

"By Odin's missing eye!" says Brynjar, his eyes wide as he watches Captain Ylva escort Sassa onto the deck of the Skripi. "Captain, you know better than most the dangers of a child on board ship. Their minds attract the dragons like a drunkard to a cup of mead," Brynjar exclaims, and, as if naming the fearsome beasts, he scans the cloudy skies looking for them.

"Brynjar, calm yourself, you're scaring the crew," Captain Ylva hisses between clenched teeth. The blush that stains Brynjar's face as he tugs his vest smooth confirms he heard her. With her second-in-command back under control, Captain Ylva looks out at the sea of faces sitting at their oars and sees them staring back at her and the child by her side.

"This is Sassa and likely the reason some of your belongings have gone missing." Feeling the young girl slide behind her as the crew murmurs, Ylva reaches down to put a comforting arm on the child's shoulder. "But, there hasn't been one of us who hasn't been down on their luck and done things they aren't proud of. Right?" As eyes soften and look to the deck and feet shuffle, the mood of the crew shifts. "Sassa has asked to crew with us, and, as Captain, the choice is mine, but seeing as you all have a grievance, I think it's only right we hear her story."

Giving the young girl a gentle push forward, Ylva says: "Speak now, Sassa, if you want to crew with us we need to trust one another."

With tear-rimmed eyes, Sassa nods and speaks: "Hi, um, I'm Sassa and I'm sorry I took your food. I had a loaf of bread when we left port, but I didn't know voyages are this long, and once I stole I knew I couldn't come forward and I got scared." Sassa stammers to a stop and wipes her runny nose on her sleeve.

Osvald yells out while still maintaining his steady rhythm on his oar. "Yass, where be your kin? Have you no parents?"

Ylva feels the tension that had been loosening within the child build again, and whispers: "Just tell the truth. We all have ghosts in our past. Talking about them helps."

Her voice stronger, Sassa continues: "My parents died of the rattling cough two winters ago, and my Pa's brother took me in but he... hurt me." Sassa hugs her chest with her arms and draws her knees together. Several faces among the crew darken, but remain silent as Sassa continues. "And he made me sleep with the dogs, which wasn't so bad, I like animals. Anyway, last spring during the lambing, one of the old yews was struggling, and I could see the black ring all around her." Sassa doesn't notice Captain Ylva start in surprise. "Just like was around my folks before they died. I tried to tell my uncle she was in trouble but he won't listen and when she died, he blamed me and said I put a spell on her and came for me with a knife. He would have gotten me if it hadn't been for the dogs. They bore him down. I ran and ran. His screams chased me for days."

Sassa shrinks, as if telling her tale took more out of her than the lack of food, and finishes in a weak tone: "I've been running ever since. I always loved the tales of the dragon ships sailing the skies. So when I made it to town and saw your ship at port I snuck on when that one," Sassa points to Gudfrid, "was trying to load the chickens and they were running everywhere."

The crew laughs at the memory, and even hard faced Gudfrid cracks a smile and says: "I wasn't born to be a farmer."

The tension broken, Sassa finishes: "I'm a hard worker, and this is my twelfth summer and almost an adult, and I so want to sail the skies..." trailing off as her young eyes take in the oars tipped with dragon wings, and the balloon of sewn dragon hide keeping the wooden ship aloft.

Pulling the young girl against her in a comforting hug, Captain Ylva speaks, her commanding tone slicing through the cold wind and grabbing the whole crew.

"Sassa will do the cleaning chores of those she stole from and I'll decide about offering her a place in the crew afterward." Raising a hand to forestall the arguments she could see on the lips of many. "And the myths of children being bad luck and drawing dragons to vessels is just that: myths. Remove them from your mind. Now, back to your oars. That storm is still on our tail and I mean to stay ahead of it."

Once the crew is back at their task, Captain Ylva directs Brynjar and Sassa around her place at the rudder and says: "We three need to talk."

Her light-hearted tone gone, Captain Ylva pins Sassa with her eyes. "Tell me about this black ring you saw around your parents and the sheep."

"Cap'n? I don't understand," Brynjar begins. Ylva waves him to silence.

"Well?" Ylva raises an eyebrow.

Swallowing hard, the young girl replies, her voice meek. "My Uncle said I was lying, but I wasn't, honest. Sometimes I can see a glow around people and things around me, but I can't control it. If a person is about to die or is sick, the ring is black or maybe red, most normal people and animals are green or blue, but I can't see colour around myself, even when I look at my reflection in a puddle." Seeing the Captain and First Officer exchange glances, some colour comes into Sassa's cheeks as she says: "You're like everyone else, you think I'm lying but I'm not!" A stomp of a foot against the deck punctuates her sentence.

Her blue eyes as warm as a glacier, Captain Ylva speaks. "Have you always had this ability?"

Giving her head a shake, Sassa says: "Nah, only since, since I passed into womanhood." The last words are a mumble as she speaks into her jerkin.

The smile that crosses Captain Ylva's face melts the frost there a minute ago, and she directs the stowaway to the stern and points to the sky. "Tell me, Sassa, do you see anything behind us?"

With a seriousness belaying her years, Sassa grabs the

railing with her dirt-encrusted hands and leans out, Brynjar watches with a puzzled expression.

"There's a yellow ribbon twisting out behind us. Is the ship making it, or are we riding upon it?" Sassa asks.

Brynjar surges forward, jostling Sassa. "What is the lass on about? There's nothing out there but a cloudy sky!"

"Sassa, to answer your question the *Skripi* is riding upon the ribbon as you call it. It's a band of warm and calm air to ease the strain upon our balloon and the rowers," Captain Ylva says. "And to answer your question, Brynjar, the girl has the Touch, just as I."

With Sassa handed over to Gudfrid to find clean and warm clothing and something to fill her empty belly, Captain Ylva watches her wide-eyed first officer as he struggles to form words.

"You be telling me, Cap'n, that the Touch is real? I thought it was just something to help fill a storyteller's mead cup."

Captain Ylva eases the rudder of the *Skripi* away from the edge of the oncoming storm and watches Brynjar look over his shoulder at their back trail, no doubt wondering if they are still on the yellow ribbon.

"It's real, Brynjar, though less than half of the stories are, and don't bother asking me about the dragon's blood because I don't know. It happened to me like it did Sassa when I entered womanhood. I saw halos around people and creatures. My Grandpa believed me, he said his Grandpa had the Touch and helped me come to terms with it."

At seeing the confusion on her first officer's face, Ylva

tries to explain. "Seeing that a sick baby will die wears down your soul. But you see a lot of good things, too. A new baby rooted in a mother's womb, the rain coming to thirsty crops. You can see but do nothing else. There is no control. At a young age, I left home and have been sailing ever since. The peace of the skies has become my home, and I shall never leave it."

Her tone turning serious, Captain Ylva finishes. "Forget what I said to the crew Brynjar. What I'm about to repeat is what's told to newly minted captains. Children attract dragons as the stories say, their young minds have a spark of wonder within them that's lost when we become adults. Most think dragons are mindless animals good for being harvested to create airships. That's a lie. They're intelligent, but we can't understand them. They could be attacking us out of spite for killing their kind, or see us as desecrators of their dead. No one knows. What I do know is that if a child is onboard an airship the dragons will try to take her," she says, meeting her first officer's eyes. "Do you understand? They take children alive. We must protect Sassa."

It's a far different scene below decks when Ylva goes down an hour later. Having set Brynjar on a heading she hopes will keep the *Skripi* ahead of the brewing storm, she descends and finds her crew caring for their little stowaway.

The pale and dirty child that stood before the crew of the *Skripi* above is no more. They have replaced her dirty and tattered jerkin with one that Ylva recognizes as Gudfrid's; sleeves rolled up to her elbows, and the hem hanging below her knees. Her face scrubbed, Sassa is jamming roast chicken into her mouth as her wide eyes try to watch everything the crew is doing around her.

At least the crew seems to have forgotten their concerns about a child being bad luck for the moment. I hope that holds out. Captain Ylva thinks to herself as she weaves her way through her crew, ducking her head to avoid the low ceiling and swinging oil lamps with an ease born of years in the skies.

Crew members make room for their captain around the table. Ylva sits across from Sassa with a sigh, rolls her shoulders, peers at the stowaway's meal, and asks: "Is that the chicken I was saving for lunch?"

Sassa's eyes grow big and she drops the drumstick from her hand. Ylva's smile takes the sting out of her words. With a wink, she picks up the fallen drumstick and takes a large bite as several members of the crew chuckle at the young girl's discomfort.

"I jest, child, honest. We are more family than crew and we tease each other as a family is wont to do. Now, have you had your fill?" Sassa nods as she hurries to chew her mouthful of chicken.

"Good, now gather up some more chicken, a loaf of bread, an apple in that basket, and take it up to first officer Brynjar for his midday meal." As Sassa scrambles to do the captain's bidding, she freezes as Ylva speaks again. "If you ask him nicely, he might show you how the *Skripi* works." And if she had been hurrying before, now she moves as if the shore patrol were chasing her, and bounces off the legs of crew members to do as bid before rushing up the ladder, a knotted napkin filled with food clenched in her teeth.

Once the young stowaway is above decks and out of earshot, Captain Ylva reaches for her own apple, selects one that isn't too wrinkled, and bites into it. Chewing, Ylva scans the faces of her crew and lifts an eyebrow, shuffling feet and throats being cleared are the only replies.

"Spit it out," Captain Ylva says around her mouthful of apple, and after a pause, Osvald speaks.

"With all due respect Captain, are you going to let her stay?"

Captain Ylva puts down her half-eaten apple and makes eye contact with everyone willing to meet her gaze. "And why shouldn't I?"

Osvald realizes he's become the de facto spokesperson for the crew. To his credit, his voice is clear and strong. "It is your ship, Captain Ylva, and we your crew. You've always treated us fair, but you know it's bad luck to have a child on board. You've heard the same stories how young minds call dragons and attack ships carrying them. 'Tis not safe, Captain." Finished, Osvald nods his head to his captain, voices around him murmur in agreement.

Her chin in callused hands, Captain Ylva says in a calm tone: "What would you have me do? Throw her overboard? It is my right as Captain and she stowaway."

Rubbing palms against leggings that leave sweat marks, Osvald counters: "No, Captain, she's a good lass and treated poorly. If her Uncle was here, there's not one of us that won't chop his hands off for what he did. No, but maybe we could return to port. I'm sure we could find a place for her in town, those who would treat her right."

Nodding as if considering the suggestion, Captain Ylva stands, the scrape of the bench on the floor sharp and piercing. "It would take us a week to return to our last port and there's no guarantee we could find someone to take her in. I'm not prepared to forget her crime as a thief and stowaway aboard this ship. I'm surprised that you lot are. She has told me that she's entered womanhood and therefore isn't a threat to the ship."

Looking into the faces of her crew in the dim confines of the hold, Ylva thinks to herself: *I hope to the gods I'm right!*

"... and we braided each one of these lines with a narrow strip of dragon hide. We need that strength to hold the balloon to the body of the *Skripi* otherwise it would float away."

Brynjar's voice floats down to Ylva as she stands at the base of the ladder and a smile crosses her face. *He plays the tough, bitter old man, but Brynjar likes her, I can hear it in his voice.*

Lounging against the ladder Ylva listens as Brynjar continues: "We waste no part of the dragon. They are too hard to kill for it to be a sport. Our oars are its ribs tipped with parts of its wings to row when the winds aren't kind. The sun going through the dragon hide balloon keeps us aloft, and the rudder arm is a leg bone. We burn the head and heart and scatter the ashes in the sky so it might always fly. But to honour its sacrifice, we carve a wooden dragon head at the bow to lead us on our voyages."

Ylva strains to hear the next words spoken by Sassa. "You've... you've SEEN a live dragon? I looked for them at the port, but only saw seagulls." The disappointment in the young girl's voice is clear but doesn't stop her from continuing. "Do you think Captain Ylva will let me stay? I so very much want to fly."

Something tugs at Ylva's chest as she remembers her first time among the clouds, the escape from the constant bombardment of the Touch, and she knows she will find a place for this little stowaway on the Skripi. She places her hand on the ladder rung but pauses as she hears Brynjar answer.

"Truthfully, child, I don't know, but I will say this. Captain Ylva is the best Captain I've ever sailed with, fairer with the crew than we deserve. I won't worry yourself too much. Now, let me be asking you a question, do ya see this halo around everything... even me?"

"Not always. I can't control it. Healthy people like you have a soft green glow, the air is a river of colours, bands of yellow and gold around us, and those clouds are blue and purple." The girl's voice lowers as if speaking to herself, and Ylva risks a step up the ladder to hear her continue. "But I don't know what those flashes of silver are riding on bands of yellow. I've never seen that..." the child's voice takes on a dreamy tone.

"Damn!" Captain Ylva curses, and rushes up the ladder yelling *"Dragon sign!!! Take your posts!"*

The words are still ringing in the ears of the crew as Ylva leaps up the last rung onto the deck.

Ylva weaves herself through the sea of shouting crew who are stumbling to take their places at the oars, craning their necks to search the sky for the danger their Captain has heralded, and hurries to stand beside a confused Brynjar at the rudder.

"Captain? Dragon sign? Where? The lookouts have seen nothing since sunup," Brynjar says, though tilts his head in puzzlement as he notices that Sassa hasn't moved from her place beside him.

Pointing without looking, Captain Ylva says: "There. And at least six, coming fast." As she grabs the rudder from her first officer, and throws the *Skripi* away from the direction she pointed, forcing everyone to grab something. Brynjar's massive arm steadies Sassa.

"Six!!! I've never heard of that many all at once. What could they want with us?" Brynjar exclaims. Then, as if answering his own question, looks at the young stow-away. "Captain? What do we do?"

Ignoring her first officer, Ylva uses her free hand to shake Sassa and says: "Sassa, answer me?"

As if drowsy with sleep, the young girl mumbles: "Captain? Can you hear them? They're calling, it fills my mind, I can't think..."

"Sassa, listen. It's your imagination drawing them, like a moth to a flame. I need you to do something for me, ok? Do you know your numbers?" A slow nod answers the Captain's question. "That's good. Now I need you to count along with me ok? One, two, three..." After a brief hesitation, Sassa begins, the struggle clear in her voice.

Throwing a hurried glance to the skies and seeing that the dragons are now visible to the naked eye, Captain Ylva curses and yells to Brynjar: "Get the crew to lash themselves to their oars and seats, there's no way we can outrun nor stave off six dragons. Our only chance is to head into the storm and hope to lose them."

"Into that!" Brynjar says, his eyes wide as he looks at the storm they have been skirting. "Thor himself has created that storm, you would have us fly into it?"

"It's the only way! The magic, the unbound vision of a young mind is like honeyed fruit to dragons, they can't control themselves," Captain Ylva shouts as she steers the *Skripi* towards the frothing storm on the horizon.

"Captain!" Brynjar yells and puts his hand to the knife at his belt. "I can do it fast and clean, the lass won't feel a thing."

"No! This is my ship and am I her Captain, and my

word is law. We will protect Sassa from the dragons and sail this ship to safety. Is that clear Brynjar?"

His eyes welling up with tears, the first officer of the *Skripi* shakes his head and removes his hand from the knife. "Curses! I knew children were bad luck!"

"Do as I ordered, secure the crew, we are about to take on the god of thunder." Captain Ylva says through clenched teeth. Captain Ylva kneels down and faces Sassa, and smiles when she hears "twenty-nine, twenty-ten, twenty-eleven"...

"That's it, Sassa, you keep counting and you'll be fine."

With a prayer to the gods hoping she didn't just lie to the girl, Ylva draws the trembling girl against her, and with a length of cord lashes them both to the rudder post just as the first splashes of rain strike their faces and the shriek of the dragons reaches their ears.

"The crew's all lashed to their oars, Cap'n, and rowing as best able. These winds make it difficult," Brynjar shouts to Captain Ylva from his place on the crew deck, the rain already having soaked his vest, his beard flapping in the wind.

Leaning into the wind, Captain Ylva nods and yells back: "Good, now get yourself to the bow and keep an eye open for trouble."

Brynjar pauses and looks over his Captain's shoulder at the approaching dragons before meeting Ylva's eye and nodding. His bare feet slap across the wet wooden deck, and Ylva watches her first officer and friend fade into the slashing wind and rain of the storm, comforted that the green halo around him is as strong as ever. *May Odin protect you, my friend.*

Knowing she's done all she can, Ylva focuses upon her

duty, and grabbing the rudder weaves the *Skripi* through the violent throes of the storm, doing her best to steer the ship along the shifting bands of yellow, orange, and red of air that only one of the Touched can see. The bands are being twisted and slashed by the more violent winds of the storm and they have just entered its fringe.

Bone rudder handle nestled in her armpit, Ylva looks into the face of the young girl tied to her. Whether it's the storm, the approaching dragons, or the girl's tenuous grasp of counting, Sassa has stopped fighting the call of the dragons and is staring open-mouthed behind them.

"Sassa! Come on, girl, fight it." Ylva shouts over the raging wind.

Maybe the young stowaway heard the Captain, and maybe not, but Sassa's lips mouth: "They're here," and Captain Ylva sees a flash of scales and wing above them.

"Archers, pick your targets. Rowers at double speed!" Captain Ylva yells and sees the men and women of the *Skripi* strain to pick up the pace, as the handful of lookouts draw short bows and loose arrows at the scaled dragons.

The odds of them hitting a dragon in this, let alone injuring one, are as likely as Thor coming to our aid, Ylva thinks to herself, as lightning arcs through the sky, mocking her. Savage forks of blue light dance all around the *Skripi*, highlighting the silver dragons as they dart around and under the tossing ship.

"Rip..." Ylva feels the *Skripi* drop, and her years in the skies knows they are in trouble.

Curses, The balloon! Either the stitching let loose or a dragon talon did the job. Captain Ylva leans as far as she can, wind whipping her hair as tries to see the damage. Instead, she sees a dragon streak towards them. Knowing that the creature is after Sassa, Ylva does the only thing she can and covers the girl with her own body. Dragon talons rake Ylva's back and as darkness consumes her she hears Sassa yell for Brynjar.

Pain, burning pain. Is the ship on fire? Where's Brynjar? We must organize the crew to combat... combat. Dragons! and with that, memory floods back into Captain Ylva and she struggles to open her eyes.

She takes several moments for her eyes to focus, but when they do, Ylva sees Brynjar beside her, his brow sliced open and bleeding. "You're hurt, Brynjar!" Ylva exclaims and attempts to rise, but burning pain down her back makes the world lose focus.

"Aye, Cap'n, as are you. I've bound your wounds as best I can in this storm, but we should get you below decks."

"No! Get me on my feet, we have a ship to see to," Ylva says through clenched teeth. Brynjar puts his hands under the Captain's armpits and lifts. Sharp gasps of breath blow against his ear until Ylva says: "Stop, put me back down." And the pair collapses onto the wet deck.

"Can't... can't feel my legs, you need to take the rudder..." Captain Ylva slurs her words, the world losing focus. "Sassa!" she cries and looks around only to find the frightened girl hugging the rudder, unhurt.

"The lass is fine, Cap'n, but the dragons slashed the balloon and still hound us. What are your orders?" Brynjar asks, his face pale and not all from his injury.

A lazy smile crosses Captain Ylva's face as if she were deep into her cups, and waves the young girl to her. Sassa kneels in the pool of blood and rainwater around the captain and Ylva grabs her hand with trembling fingers.

"I need you, Sassa. You need to help Brynjar get us through this storm. Stick to the yellow and orange bands if you can, red if you must but no darker. Do you understand?" The last words are a whisper as Captain Ylva slips into unconsciousness.

Wide-eyed, Sassa looks to Brynjar and shouts: "This is all my fault. If I hadn't snuck aboard, this..."

Brynjar's rough hands grab the girl and give her a shake that causes her wet hair to snap like a whip. "Enough of that. The Cap'n gave an order and we will follow it." As if to punctuate the desperation of the situation, the *Skripi* is flung sideways and the cry of the dragons rings in their ears.

Brynjar drags Sassa back to the rudder like a bag of potatoes and shouts over the wind: "Which way?"

Soaked to the bone in her borrowed jerkin and shivering, Sassa looks at the crew lashed to their oars, at least as frightened as she, before looking down at the woman who showed more compassion to her in the past day than anyone in the past year.

Something breaks within the girl and in the act of breaking, Sassa is remade a woman. The fear is distant. She's stronger, more focused than ever before. "I'm dragon bone, tougher than iron and lighter than wood," Sassa says to herself and places her hands upon the rudder alongside Brynjar's and says: "This way," and with that the dragons' roar in anger and fly out of the storm, the mind calling them no longer a child's.

"Lass, wake up, we're safe." A familiar voice brushes Sassa's mind, and a big bearded man with broken teeth, soft eyes under a bandaged brow floats in front of her and Sassa blinks, coming back from the waking trance that has consumed her for hours.

With effort, Sassa forces her hands to release the bone rudder. Her sun-dried jerkin stiff and scratchy as she feels the life returning to her body, though her head feels like it's filled with wool from her Uncle's farm. The words register as she mumbles: "Safe?"

"Aye, lass, the storm lasted most of the night. The sunrise chased the last away."

Awareness returning, Sassa feels the sun on her face, and the clear blue of the sky around the ship, and then the harrowing journey of the night before crashes upon her. The flashes of lightning and the peel of thunder deafening them; the mad flight as they fell, as the storm tossed the *Skripi* like a rag doll; the pain as their ears popped, as Sassa did as the Captain Ylva ordered and steered the ship...

"The Captain!" Sassa exclaims, and grabs Brynjar's arm, her tiny hand dwarfed by his massive arm, but nonetheless he grunts at the strength within it.

"Here, Lass," Brynjar points to a wrapped body laying atop a rower's bench. His voice hoarse, he continues. "She's still with us for now, but her time grows short. If the blood loss wasn't bad enough, the dragon strike broke her back. We can do nothing for her. Say your goodbyes while you can."

Stunned, Sassa allows Brynjar to lead her to where Captain Ylva lays under the care of Osvald, whose red-rimmed eyes and shaking head let her know Brynjar spoke the truth and that Captain Ylva is dying.

Kneeling on stiff joints, Sassa brushes aside a wisp of hair from the Captain's cheek and has a dim memory of her mother doing the same to her years ago. Captain Ylva must have felt it; her eyes open and focus on Sassa. The smile that fills Ylva's face makes the tears Sassa had been holding in run free.

"Easy, Sassa, it's all right. I lived my life as I wanted and have no regrets."

"But this is all my fault. I made the dragons come. We wouldn't have fled into the storm if I hadn't snuck on board." Sobbing joins Sassa's tears and Captain Ylva finds the energy to lay a comforting hand on the girl's head.

"We don't know that for sure. This wasn't our first dragon attack. No one knows what draws them to our ships." Captain Ylva lies to Sassa as her breathing becomes laboured. Osvald and Brynjar exchange a sad look, as the first officer places his hand on the young girl's shoulder.

With a smile at her first officer, Ylva continues, forcing herself to say these final words: "Brynjar says you saved the ship...that you kept to your post...and guided us out of the storm." Captain Ylva closes her eyes, her breath rattling in her chest, bubbles of blood forming at the corners of her mouth.

A squawk causes everyone to jump, as a seagull lands on the railing beside them.

Captain Ylva opens her eyes and laughs. "Stowaway's luck". And with that, her laboured breathing stops and her eyes stare sightlessly into the sky.

Eyes still wet with tears, Sassa watches as Osvald wraps the Captain's body in a piece of dragon hide. The deed done, Brynjar nods, and Osvald joins the others who are throwing the furnishing of the ship over the side to disappear into the ocean below.

"Wait, what are they doing?" Sassa stammers, wiping her tears with the cuff of her jerkin.

"We're falling. The damage to the balloon is too great to fix. Our best chance is to toss any unnecessary weight and hope for land. And it appears the Cap'n was right once again. Your stowaway's luck is with us."

Seeing the confusion upon the drained child, he adds: "That gull," and points to the seagull that is still preening its ruffled feathers, "is a shorebird. And even if he got blown around as we did in the storm, all we need to do is follow him and he'll lead us to land."

As if hearing the pair talk about him, the seagull squawks, and takes to its wings.

Putting his arm around the girl's shoulder, Brynjar says. "Let's go follow him, what say you?"

With a forlorn look at the wrapped remains of Captain Ylva, Sassa turns to Brynjar and nods.

With everything not nailed down tossed over the side, except for the rowers' bench in which Captain Ylva still lays in state, the crew of the *Skripi* watch as a rugged coast grows closer.

"What shoreline is that, Brynjar?" Sassa asks from her place beside the first officer at the rudder.

Squinting, the first officer shakes his head. "I don't know it, too many trees, not enough snow."

"So where are we?" Sassa asks, her earlier confidence sinking as fast as the ship.

"I don't know. It might be a newly found land. We'll know more soon enough. It's coming up fast," Brynjar says as the bow of the Skripi brushes the waves and becomes a vessel of water rather than air.

The oars are manned and, while not meant for water, do the job of bringing the ship to the gravel shore. The crew scurries off with the last of the food and water, and with the *Skripi* released from their weight it struggles out of its water-bound prison and drifts out of reach before any can secure it.

"The Captain!" Sassa cries, staring at the stricken ship which still holds its captain.

"I think the *Skripi* has one more trip in her and wants her Captain aboard," Brynjar says as the crew and their Stowaway watch as the *Skripi* takes her Captain on her final voyage into the evening sky.

Lamenting Father

Why Father? Why Icarus?

What caused you to disappear before I even hatched? I had to fight my way out of my shell alone, my small fingers striving to chip away at the hardened shell, the splinters cutting my fragile feathers. It comforted me, waking up within my shell to the song of your voice singing to the stars at night. The warmth radiating as you and Mother snuggled close around my shell in our nest.

What of Mother? Do you not care of the heartache you are inflicting upon her? The home in the bluffs the two of you built from branches woven together with seagrass is barren of your warmth and affection. The comforting down my shell rested upon has dried and blown away leaving me to languish in a skeleton of branches. She devotes her days to soaring through the cliffs and valleys of the land you came from and out over the unending water which circles this island searching for you. Don't you accept any sense of responsibility? I know you cared for her once. Only true love can force her to go without food for so long, allowing her once vibrant and rich plumage turn into the dull and tattered mess it is now.

Mother has forsworn taking another mate; you must have realized Eagles mate for life. She has faith in finding you – that you are just over the next ridge or injured and trapped in one of the many coves of our island. Young I might be, but the Human in me wishes she would listen to the others and consider you dead. Existence is so short if we spend it alone. Has she cut herself off from the Eagle family by giving her love to a delicate and fickle Human?

Is it because of me? That I'm not of the race of Human as you, nor the Eagle of Mother? Or is that I'm a girl that drove you away? Is the great hero Icarus embarrassed that he fathered a daughter? My sword arm is as strong as any man's. Or did the thought of the life growing within this broken shell at my feet disgust you so much that you couldn't stay and look upon me? Has the life that your love created, a young woman with wings and arms, become a poison in your soul? Do you see me as an abomination, a child of two worlds?

I lay here scared, frigid, and alone, in the neglected remains of the nest you helped Mother build high in the mountains, but I will not let that stop me. I may be young and unable to fly, and I sense that my life will be a solitary one. A living thing, part Human and part Eagle, a woman of wing and feather with no people to call my own. You must realize the isolation ahead of me, how it feels to be an outsider, you with your wings of feather and wax.

Why Father, why Icarus, did you abandon us? Maybe I'll never know the answer, and I will not waste my life searching for you. Once I'm strong enough to fly, I will leave this place and chart my path, and fly to the top of the world.

Jennifer Shelby

Jennifer Shelby was born in Halifax, Nova Scotia and currently resides in Hopewell Hill, New Brunswick. She is the author of many works of short fiction, including 'Mrs. Coleman's Backyard Refugee Camp' for *Andromeda Spaceways*, and 'Toby's Alicorn Adventure' for *Cricket*.

Borrowed Wings

Darina discovered the wings of a luna moth in a scattered pile of leaf litter. At first she thought they must be the wings of some poor, dismembered fairy. After some research she knew better, but she couldn't shake the feeling they were connected, somehow, to the Wee Folk.

That summer Darina found wings everywhere. There were butterfly wings in parking lots, in ditches, and along the streets where she rode her bike: each one a grim memorial to a fragile being embedded in a grill or smeared across a windshield. She tucked them into paperbacks and pedalled them home, safe inside their literary sarcophagi.

She captured her collection within the sticky pages of an old-fashioned photo album. She labelled them with slips of paper, recording the date, the place she found them, and each wing's Latin name. She kept the pages on a bookshelf that sat above her bed and showed them to no one. They became Darina's dark and special secret.

One night in autumn, she awoke to a flurry of half-broken fairies ransacking her bedroom. They wailed as they searched frantically for her collection of wings. Darina calmed the fairies with soft words and a lullaby. She bade them to hold still while she worked with a bottle of glue, a sewing needle, and a thread of spider silk. One by one, slipping out of her window, the fairies flitted off into the darkness, whole again on borrowed wings.

Sherry D. Ramsey

Sherry D. Ramsey writes speculative fiction for both adults and young adults, and is one of the founding editors of Third Person Press. She has published over thirty short stories nationally and internationally, and her award-winning debut novel, *One's Aspect to the Sun*, launched in 2013. It was followed by two sequels, *Dark Beneath the Moon* (2015) *Beyond the Sentinel Stars* (2017).

Some of her short stories are collected in *To Unimagined Shores* (2011) and *The Cache and Other Stories* (2017).

Ramsey has co-edited six anthologies of regional short fiction with Third Person Press. A member of the Writer's Federation of Nova Scotia Writer's Council, Sherry is also a past Vice-President and Secretary-Treasurer of SF Canada and is currently SFC's website administrator.

Unquiet Skies

Collie glanced down as the rocky ground fell away beneath them, the chill wind of the upper currents lifting his hair. He loved this moment when powerful wings pushed them up toward the blue and white promise of the sky. The height wasn't scary, although there was little enough in his perch to keep him from tumbling into empty air. The ripple of powerful muscles underneath his legs felt a lot like riding a farm horse, and he clenched his knees for balance. The land spread out below, unrolling craggy brown and green expanses streaked with blue, dissolving into crinkled edges where land met deep, dark blue sea.

What's the word on the racers?

The voice sounded in Collie's head, deep and feminine and half-amused, with just a trace of concern. Collie had never quite gotten the hang of communicating mentally, so he answered aloud. The wind tore his words from his throat, but the dragon would hear.

"Four teams coming, so I've heard. One from as far away as Australia! But who wouldn't want to take a shot at ten thousand pounds sterling?"

Do you think one of them will make it? They'd climbed high enough now that Collie could see all of northern Newfoundland below, one long peninsular finger stretching north to almost touch Labrador. He'd surprised Miss Bell on last week's geography test, drawing the coastline of the Dominion on his slate with the finest accuracy his unwieldy chalk would allow. Later he'd berated himself for showing off, hoping she wouldn't find his extensive knowledge too suspicious, but she'd only given him a smile and a "Well done!" when she saw it.

Collie screwed up his face as he answered Awdwith. "It's near two thousand miles to Ireland," he said. "That's a lot of gasoline, and gas is heavy."

But eventually, someone will do it, the dragon mused, and this time Collie heard sadness bloom in her voice. *We won't have these skies to ourselves for much longer.*

Sudden fear clutched Collie, a cold, slippery thing winding around his heart. He pressed his palms, cold even inside their thick leather gloves, to the sides of the dragon's neck and hunched his shoulders to draw the collar of his jacket up to his ears. "You won't leave, will you? You're still safe enough. No-one's ever going to be interested in the middle of the island. There's nothing there!"

Awdwith's smile was in her voice. *If I've learned anything, it's that humans eventually go everywhere, and drive all others out. But don't fret. I'm not going anywhere yet.*

They grew quiet then, keeping their thoughts to themselves as the dragon's powerful wingbeats carried them north. Eventually, the dragon glided down to settle on the westernmost of the Horse Islands, windswept, barren, and empty. Collie clambered down from her back on the top of a craggy cliff and settled himself to watch as the dragon cruised high above the waves, hunting. When she spotted prey--a seal or large fish--she'd dive like an osprey, leathery wings tucked back, arrowing down into the water after her prize. Collie licked a pencil stub and sketched her--flying, circling, diving--in an old notebook Miss Bell had given him when she noticed him doodling on his slate one day. Not drawing Awdwith, of course--he'd never let anyone else see his images of her--but a quick sketch of his dog, Bridey.

Collie tucked the notebook back inside his jacket as Awdwith returned and set down on the rocky crag. She settled her bulk next to him, her back stretching taller than his father's six feet even when she hunkered down. He'd only ever measured her length with his eyes, but he guessed she ran a good twenty feet from nose to tail, her head twice as big as that of any draft horse. Now she shook her iridescent green scales dry in the sun, long tongue snaking out between ivory-white teeth as she licked her lips with satisfaction. *Time to go home?*

Collie made no move to leave just yet. "Even if someone wins the *Daily Mail*'s contest, we won't get much air traffic here--least not for a long time," Collie said, looking out across the waves to the dark, unbroken line of the distant horizon. "It won't be like Ireland and England, planes zipping everywhere. You wouldn't be driven away again. Who'd want to fly here? It's only the challenge that has some people fired up. Someone will do it just to prove it can be done and then everyone will forget about flying to Newfoundland. Folk 'round here won't have it, anyway. They're sea folk, born and raised. They won't have do with airplanes flying overhead all the time."

Awdwith pulled her long, toothy mouth into what Collie knew was a smile. *What about dragons flying overhead all the time?*

"But you told me they can't see you!"

Awdwith shrugged, muscles rippling under sea-green tinted scales. *I can deflect their attention most of the time with a glamour, she agreed. But that's because most folks are as you say—focused on the water and earth below, not the sky above. If that sky gets too busy...* She let the words trail away, joining Collie in pinning her eyes to the roiling water. Then she seemed to shake herself, and rose to her feet. Her claws clacked and scratched on the bare stone. *But we'll worry about that later,* she said. *Climb on. I should get you home before you're missed.*

"Win's looking out for me," Collie said. His younger sister would make excuses if anyone looked for him, just as he did for her when it was her turn to visit the dragons. But he clambered aboard Awdwith's broad back again.

They flew in silence over the myriad tiny outports clinging to the coast like burrs on a sock; the spring-budding stretches of forest; the countless wind-tossed lakes; the rough, eroded crags of the dwindling Appalachian range. As Awdwith descended to the human-free expanse of the interior, where the dragons had taken refuge, Collie spotted Win in the clearing. She held a hand to her brow, peering up against the sun to find them. Win clutched her coat close around her neck against the cold March wind, as tendrils of dark hair, come loose from her braids, whipped around her face. She waved, and Collie raised a hand in answer. Why was she here? Ma would surely notice both her children missing.

As Awdwith glided to a smooth landing, claws rasping on stone, Win ran forward to meet them. Her cheeks were pink from the wind, and the freckles dusting her nose stood out against her pale skin. She patted Awdwith's neck as Collie slid down from the dragon's back, feet jarring against the hard ground. "Win? What's wrong?'

Win's blue eyes were wide with a mix of excitement and trepidation, her thin voice breathless. "They're here," she gasped. "The racers are here. And two of them are staying with us."

Collie and Win's parents ran a small lodge on the outskirts of St. John's. Not the kind of posh hotel you'd find in the heart of the city; if your business brought you to St. John's from one of the smaller towns or outports and you couldn't afford the city rates, you might stay at The Pearl. Over the front door, a painted sign showing a bright white pearl settled comfortably on an open oyster shell creaked slightly, wind or no wind. For the front tavern, Ma cooked and Da served simple hot meals and beer in the evenings, and breakfast for guests in the mornings. Ma, Da, Collie and Win lived in the first floor apartments tucked into the back of the house. Upstairs, five guest rooms boasted clean linens and scrubbed wood floors. Behind the house, two cabins with tightly chinked log walls, woodstoves and voluminous piles of blankets could accommodate more travellers. Da had been a fisherman once, of course. But a careless deckhand and a stray line had led to a leg caught up and twisted painfully out of true. It never did come right again, and Da complained that his limp had ruined his sea legs. When Da's uncle in Harbour Grace died and left Da his boat, Da sold it and bought The Pearl. What had been a run-down boarding house, he and Ma had transformed into what Ma called "a respectable house where anybody's mother might be happy to stay."

Standing a hundred and fifty miles inland from The Pearl now, with one hand on Awdwith's neck, Collie asked, "Who is it? Why would any of the racers stay with us?" A mix of trepidation and excitement tugged at his stomach. He knew the thrill of soaring higher than most folk could ever imagine, so he felt a certain kinship with the daring transatlantic racers.

Win grinned. "Da says it's because they're building their plane in a field in Mount Pearl, and they want to stay somewhere close. All the planes are coming crated in pieces, and they have to put them together here."

"We'd better get back. Ma'll be in a tizzy."

"She's all right. In the kitchen setting a pot of chowder to simmer and making biscuits for supper. But Da wants us on hand in case they need anything."

Go ahead, Awdwith said. *Don't feel bad if you can't come for a few days.* She reached out to give him a gentle nudge on his shoulder with her nose, the equivalent of a dragon hug. *Be off, now!*

Collie nodded and gave Awdwith's neck a quick pat, her scales leathery and faintly warm under his palm. "We'll send word with Latchet once we know what's happening." He and Win crossed to the eastern side of the clearing where a cave mouth gaped, its dark maw tucked under an overhang of craggy stone. Inside, the cave opened to a network of tunnels where the dragons made their home. The mouth was just large enough for Awdwith to squeeze her bulk through, wings folded close against her back.

Just inside the shadow of the cave mouth, Latchet stood with his arms crossed and a cranky look sketched across his sharp-featured face. Every inch of his two-foot frame radiated discontent. "Messenger-boy now, am I?" he grumped as Collie and Win approached.

Collie grinned, undaunted by the faery's display of bad humour. "Go on with you, Latchet, or your face will freeze like that. What'll it take today to get in your good graces? I've got bread or coin. Your choice." He pulled a pair of copper pennies from one pocket, and one of Ma's bread rolls--fresh-baked that morning and still wrapped carefully in oiled paper--from the other. The yeasty fragrance escaped the paper, scenting the air.

Latchet held his grimace for a moment longer, and then his features softened and he broke into a smile, reaching for the roll. He shook his head and pretended to sigh as he opened the delicate paper wrapping. "It's not fair to play on an old man's weaknesses, you young scallawag," he said. He sent them deeper into the cave with a nod. "The door's clear, get on home now," he added. "Leave a note in the stable and I'll see my lady Awdwith gets the message."

"Thanks, Latchet!" Win patted the little man on the shoulder, and Collie followed his sister into the cave. Against the western wall leaned a low wooden door frame with a door hung in its center. The frame stood perhaps four feet tall, the bottom edge pulled out six inches from the wall so it wouldn't topple. It might have once led down to a root cellar, and bore a layer of faded blue boat paint, cracked and peeling with age and weather. Since Latchet had said the coast was clear, Win lifted the door latch and pulled it open. As she did, the world around the edges of the frame--the cave wall, the floor, the outline of the frame itself--blurred and wavered. Collie stared at the space as he always did, but the faery magic concealed the details of how a door stood by itself against a wall could suddenly lead to somewhere else.

In this case, the *somewhere else* was the tiny stall at the back of The Pearl's stable, stacked with bales of hay cunningly arranged to hide the cave door's twin. The door in the stable sported green paint instead of blue, but no matter -- they were identical in every other detail. The scents of hay and horse met them as Win slipped through and

Collie ducked his head to follow close on her heels. As usual, a journey that would take days across the island's rugged interior landscape was accomplished in a few heartbeats. Collie closed the faery door behind him and made sure the hay bales hid it from view.

"I'll tell Ma you're getting things ready in here," Win told him. "The racers want to stable a couple of draft horses for hauling equipment and suchlike."

Collie nodded. "I'll be in soon."

Win raced off to the house, braids flying, and Collie made a quick survey of the state of the stable. He tended to keep it in readiness for occupants simply to make it unnecessary for his father or anyone else to poke around inside. He shook some fresh straw into two stalls, filled the water buckets, and emerged into the back yard. Before he could reach the back step, however, the thump and rattle of an approaching horse and wagon echoed off the buildings, and he stopped to watch the road. Sure enough, a pair of Clydesdales, snorting but docile, turned in next to the house. They stopped in response to a few swift tugs on the reins by the driver, a man of perhaps thirty with a shock of dark hair above a narrow, smiling face. The wagon behind him held stacks of wooden crates, the words SOPWITH/HAWKER stencilled in dark letters on each one. A second man sat next to the driver, perhaps a few years older, with straw-coloured hair and blue eyes. Both were red-cheeked, although bundled well against the frigid spring air.

The driver tied off the reins and clambered down, greeting Collie with a smile and an extended hand. "G'day, mate. Can you see my nags get some water? We're expected, but I'll be hauling the wagon out to Mount Pearl before we bed them down for the night."

The man's accent was unusual, but Collie worked out what he'd said. Collie shook hands with him and nodded. "'Course, sir. I'll bring them a bucket and a mouthful of hay to keep them happy."

"Good lad!" The second man had climbed down from the seat now as well, and he nodded in a friendly way to Collie. The two strode into The Pearl.

Win came flying out the kitchen door as the horses snorted and Collie turned to fetch a bucket from the stable. His sister never walked anywhere. She ran, she skipped, she hopped. "Is it them? They're here?"

Collie nodded toward the overloaded wagon. "Look at the crates. It's them all right."

"Here, I snuck you a couple of biscuits," Win said, handing him two warm lumps wrapped in a cloth napkin. "You gave away your after-school snack to Latchet, I'll wager."

Collie grinned and took the biscuits. "Thanks, you're right." He pulled one of the biscuits from the napkin and took a bite, pleased to find the soft inside of the biscuit smeared with melting butter. The second he tucked in his pocket for later...or for Latchet, should the need arise. It was wise to be prepared to bargain with or appease the faery folk at any time, Collie had learned in the course of the past year. And Latchet, displaced from his native soil to follow the dragons he served, was considerably less cranky than Newfoundland little people were rumoured to be. Collie had fought a boy at school once, when he'd been taunted that his father's limp was due to a poorly-healed fairy blast. Ever since he'd met Latchet, Collie had been tempted to ask the little man for the truth about that-- whether fairies really could strike a person and cause horrible things like bones and hair to spew from the wound.

But he'd never summoned up the courage. He much pre-
ferred his father's injury to be wholly mundane.

Collie shook himself from his reverie and came back
to the present as the horses snorted behind him. Then as
Win scooted back to the house, he went to fetch the water
and hay for the beasts, wondering what the arrival of the
racers would mean for them all.

Weeks passed at The Pearl, as the winter's chill refused to loose its hold and concede to spring. Collie grew
to like the racers, although they spent little time at The
Pearl unless the brutal weather left them no choice. The
younger man, bluff and easygoing, had instructed Collie
to call him Harry, although that seemed too disrespectful-
-Collie generally opted for "sir," which the racer accepted
with a wry smile. The older man with the lilting Scottish
accent was "Commander," which seemed to suit him and
his more reserved military bearing just fine. They spent
most of their days at the makeshift airfield, first oversee-
ing teams in the clearing of land for the airstrip, then un-
packing the many crates of aeroplane parts, and finally
testing and assembling them. They returned to The Pearl
most nights for supper, tucking into whatever Ma laid
before them with hearty appetites and appreciative comments that made Ma beam. Later, they'd burn lantern oil
long into the night as they pored over maps and plans
and technical drawings. Despite a gnawing feeling of dis-
loyalty to the dragons, Collie listened avidly to many of
their discussions, twice almost slipping up by interjecting
a comment that would have betrayed his far-too-intimate
knowledge of the joys of flight.

He and Win did not neglect the dragons, although

they couldn't visit as often as they usually did. The Pearl had gathered in another handful of boarders; technicians hired by the racers and a brace of newspaper reporters who hung on Harry's every word and followed him around like pups. Occasionally he'd don his sheepskin-trimmed jacket and leather helmet and pose for pictures with the partly-constructed biplane to appease their need for news on the racers' progress. The presence of the racers at The Pearl also drew more locals than usual to the tavern, eager to hear of each day's events. Ma and Da were thrilled with the brisk trade, but with so many people around, it was difficult to find a moment when one of them didn't have a chore for Collie and Win. Even harder to slip out to the stable unnoticed and disappear for hours.

But Awdwith and the others deserved to hear what news there was of the racers' progress as well, so Collie managed it as often as he could.

"They're close to a test flight," Collie told Awdwith one sunny April afternoon as they soared above the Avalon Peninsula. "Heard them talking about it last night. It might be wise to keep to the ground for a couple of days."

Awdwith snorted. *And what if we'd like to eat?* she asked in a tone that, even though her voice appeared only in his mind, conveyed an obvious measure of sarcasm.

"Well...you know what I mean. Hunt the forests," Collie said, a little stung. "Just stay close to home, I'm thinking."

Awdwith sighed. *I know, and I'm sorry. I didn't mean to snap. I know you mean well.*

"I'm just worried," Collie said. "What if they saw you? There's more news hounds here than I've ever seen in my life, and I don't think they're so focused on the racers that they wouldn't be distracted by a clutch of dragons."

Awdwith chuckled and arced into a slow glide, drifting down through the clouds. *I'm sure you're right about that.*

They heard it at the same time--the insistent buzz of an engine as it laboured to climb. Some of the racers--either The Pearl's boarders or one of the other teams--had taken to the air.

Collie tapped the side of Awdwith's neck. "Turn! Turn and climb! Get back into the clouds!"

But the dragon seemed to be in a contrary mood. *Relax*, she said. *They won't see us. I'll stay well above them. I want to see the plane. Don't you?*

Instead of swooping up and away, she dove further, following the sound of the nearby plane. Collie scanned the sky, hoping he could steer Awdwith away if only he knew what direction "away" was. It had to be below them still--the sound was not entirely directionless, even here with the winds battering his ears from every compass point. Collie peered down, his gaze darting to the left and right of the dragon, leaning forward along her neck to see past her outstretched wings.

Finally he spotted it, the moving t-shaped dark spot below them on the right. It was closer than he would have liked, but he felt a thrill shiver its way down his back. Whoever this was, they were making history.

Clumsy-looking thing, was Awdwith's observation. *They've not yet managed to overcome that hurdle.*

"Be careful," Collie pleaded. "You've seen planes before, now can we go?"

I'll keep to the upper wing blind spot, the dragon insisted. *Even if they look up, they won't see us. And I've put the glamour on.*

"You said that isn't foolproof. It might not work on

someone who's already up here in the sky."

The dragon had no answer for that, keeping pace above the buzzing plane. Collie shook his head in frustration but said nothing more. The dragons had survived the coming of manned flight to the British Isles and migrated to Newfoundland without detection, so perhaps she knew what she was doing.

But a little voice whispered that perhaps the dragon was tired of hiding, too, which might be fueling her recklessness.

The plane below them circled out over the eastern shore of Conception Bay and curved inland over the peninsula again.

"They're turning back," Collie said, "we should head home, too."

Are they yours? the dragon asked. *Your racers?*

Collie peered down at the plane, but from here he couldn't tell. Without distinctive markings, one biplane looked much like another from this vantage. "I don't know," he said. "It could be; they said they were ready for a test flight."

He looked down again and realized that as they'd talked, Awdwith had slipped slightly behind the plane. With horror, Collie saw the pilot's dark leather helmet tip back, looking up. He couldn't make out features in the goggle-covered face, but he saw the jaw drop and sensed the jolt of shock as the man saw them. Now the distinctive shape of the pilot's sheepskin collar and the pale band of white along the helmet's front brim were visible, and Collie knew without a doubt it was Harry, and behind him the Commander. Intent on his instruments, however, the Commander didn't look up. The plane wavered in its course along with the pilot's attention, now fixed on them.

As Collie feared, the dragon's glamour had failed to hide them from the aviator's gaze.

"Awdwith! He's seen us!"

With wordless, powerful strokes of her wings, the dragon veered up and away, taking cover in a bank of low-hanging clouds that had drifted up from the southwest. Collie lost sight of the biplane and the pilot's open-mouthed wonder as the clouds enveloped them like a thick, wet blanket.

"I could Blast him," Latchet offered gravely as he joined Collie, Win, and Awdwith in a discussion of how to deal with the problem of Harry. "No-one would believe the word of a man who'd been elf-struck. I could tempt him to the woods and lose him for years."

Collie shook his head. "It's been three days now, and he hasn't said a word to me nor anyone, far's I can tell," he said. "The newsmen have been all over him since then on account of his test flight being the first ever to take off from here. But not a whisper about Awdwith. He gave me an odd look that night when he came back to The Pearl... studied me every chance he got. But then he smiled and tipped me a wink."

The moment had been strange, Collie's heart flapping like a fish on a rock and sweat beading his back as he moved about the inn, trying to act normal and waiting for the racer to say something. But he hadn't; the airman had smiled and winked and then went on as if nothing had happened. "I think he's of a mind to keep quiet."

Latchet paced across the cave, small hands clasped behind his diminutive back. "I don't like it. I don't trust it."

"He's got bigger things on his mind," Collie said, and

the faery-man turned on him.

"*Bigger* things?" he bellowed in a voice surprisingly large for his small frame. "Bigger than *dragons*?"

Collie winced, but held his ground. "Ten thousand pounds and a place in history as the first transatlantic flyer? For this man, that's bigger. Bigger than a faery story that no-one might believe."

Awdwith stirred, and Collie hoped his words hadn't hurt her. But it was true. For all his worries about discovery, the flight attempts were the talk of the day. Rumour had it that the first real attempt at a crossing was mere weeks away. Now that the worst had happened, it felt less dire than he'd feared. He knew these newsmen now. It was unlikely any of them would actually believe Harry's tale if he told it, with no proof to present. They'd say he'd flown too high or knocked his head or mistaken a bird for something else. Harry was bluff and easygoing, but he wouldn't be anxious to appear a fool.

Latchet stopped pacing and crossed his arms. "I dinna like it," he said, his Old World tongue more pronounced in his agitation. "He kens too much. If we quieted him, perhaps the rest would leave, into the bargain."

Collie frowned, but Awdwith spoke before he could. Her quiet voice filled the cave. She so rarely spoke aloud that the musical tones felt more like magic than the fact of her existence.

"No, Latchet. Many thanks for wanting to help, but Collie is right. They'll not leave any way but to try their machines, and nothing that happens to one will dissuade the others. If Collie thinks his racer can be trusted, I believe him."

"Bah!" Latchet snorted and stormed off. Collie watched him go with trepidation, then turned to Awdwith. In the dim interior of the cave, her scales shadowed the dark, shimmering green of the deep sea, but her yellow eyes caught the light from the entrance, burning like lanterns. She stretched her mouth in her approximation of a smile and nodded to him.

He hoped her trust, and his, was not misplaced.

Later, Collie thought it had been. He was alone in the stable, settling the horses for the night and checking their water buckets. A flickering lantern shadow alerted him to the presence of someone else. He turned to see Harry leaning against the wall just inside the stable door, hands in pockets. He regarded Collie as if he were a puzzle piece and Harry was trying to decide where he fit.

"Evening, sir," Collie managed. He wondered if Harry would hear his galloping heart. "Got the horses all tucked up for the night."

"Thanks, mate." Harry paused, then said, "That *was* you, wasn't it?"

Collie tried to still his heart and stay collected. "Was what, sir?"

Harry pursed his lips and strolled to the nearest stall, patting the big horse's flank as if considering his next words. "You've got fairy lore here? Pixies, elves, that sort of thing?'

"Well, sure," Collie said, swallowing. "If you believe that stuff."

Harry grinned and pulled a hand out of his pocket. He held a balled-up handkerchief, which he carefully opened to reveal one of Ma's dinner rolls. "Never go walkabout without a bit of bread on my person, I don't," he said. He shook his trousers and coins jingled in the pocket. "And a bit of coin as well. Fairies where I come from have a nasty streak, you know. Some say it comes from being transplanted away from their woodland magic to a place with bush magic...but I don't know about that. Seems half the creatures in Australia would as soon kill you as look at you, so maybe they fit right in." He shoved the bread back in his pocket and met Collie'e eyes.

"What I'm saying is, unless I miss my guess, you've got a bite of bread and a pair of coppers in your own pocket. And if it was you skimming the clouds with a creature we both know shouldn't exist--I didn't see it. I would have loved to, mind you, but I didn't." He winked at Collie again as he laid a finger beside his nose and said, "Mum's the word, mate. I'd just like to know I'm not mad as a cut snake."

Slowly, Collie put his hand in his pocket and pulled out the biscuit he'd filched from the kitchen this morning and showed it to Harry. He shook his own pocket to let the coins inside jingle and gave Harry a tentative smile. "Her name's Awdwith," he said.

Harry slumped against the wall and closed his eyes, blowing out a long sigh. When he opened his eyes, he smiled. "Thanks, young Collie. I didn't feel I could risk the Commander's life if I'd gone off my nut."

"You won't say anything?"

Harry shook his head. "I won't. I'm jealous, of course, but I have my own flying to do. I won't interfere with yours. It won't leave this stable." He stuck out a hand and Collie shook it, feeling safe for the first time in days.

The following month flew by as if carried on Awdwith's wings. No-one talked of anything but the racers, and Awdwith and the other dragons, amid some grumbling, took Collie's advice to stay earthbound as much as possible. More test flights followed, not only by The Pearl's racers but the other teams as well, and the risks of taking to the sky seemed too great. Harry might have agreed to keep silent, but it was too much to expect that other flyers would feel the same way.

Finally, though, the day came when The Pearl's team--as they'd come to be called--were ready to make their attempt. Excitement had built as the teams raced to be first into the air. It was Harry and the Commander who declared themselves ready to take to the skies over the Atlantic. Win, Ma, and Da went to the makeshift airfield to see them off, but Collie had another idea. He slipped out to the stable and through the door at the back, emerging into the cave with an echoing shout for Awdwith. He found her already outside in the clearing.

"They're going," he said breathlessly. "I want to watch them."

Awdwith bared her teeth in a smile. *I thought it was too risky*, she said.

"Not today. There won't be anyone else about, and Harry already knows about you."

His friend does not.

"Please, Awdwith," Collie begged. He wasn't sure if she was merely teasing him or taking her revenge for days without a tasty seal.

Well, don't expect me to fly all the way to Ireland, she said grumpily, but she extended a front leg so Collie could scramble up onto her back. He caught a twinkle in her enormous golden eye as she turned her head to watch his progress, and he grinned his thanks at her. Once he was settled at the base of her neck--the only part of her back narrow enough for him to straddle--she leapt upward with great strokes of her wings. They were airborne.

They circled lazily for a time, concealed by clouds and riding the updrafts. Today of all days, people would have their attention turned heavenward, and Collie didn't want to test the strength of Awdwith's glamour. Eventually, though, they heard the buzz of the engine far below, and knew the Sopwith had taken to the sky.

Following the sound, Awdwith banked to the east, pointing her nose over the Atlantic, where the closest land lay some nineteen hundred miles distant. After some minutes, she dipped below the cloud layer and glided, slowly descending as Collie searched the sky for sight of the biplane. They spotted it finally, still nosing upward, its Rolls-Royce engine doggedly thrumming to keep the plane aloft.

"They're away, and they're the first," Collie breathed. "I wonder if they'll make it?"

It's a cold, wet landing if they don't, Awdwith observed. *Shall we follow them a while?*

"I thought you said you didn't want to fly to Ireland," Collie teased, but inwardly he wanted nothing more than to make sure Harry and the Commander were off to a solid start.

I don't, she assured him. *Which is not to say I couldn't. I've done it in the opposite direction, after all.*

"What if the Commander sees us?"

We'll stay well behind, Awdwith said. *They're looking ahead, not looking back.*

And so they did. Collie kept his eyes on the tiny airplane ahead of them, glancing down now and again at the deep blue waves unfurling below. The late afternoon sunlight sparked diamond dazzles across the surface of the water, making Collie squint his watering eyes. Awdwith's wingbeats fell into a rhythm--three long strokes and a glide just as long--that embedded itself in his head, endlessly repeating like a stuttering heart. *Whoosh, whoosh, whoosh, pause. Whoosh, whoosh, whoosh, pause.* Time slowed and then ceased to have meaning as the world shrank, encompassing only himself and the dragon, the buzzing plane ahead, and the endless rippling water below.

Collie didn't know how long they'd been flying when he realized his hands had gone completely numb inside his thick gloves. He blinked and roused himself with a shiver. The sky overhead had darkened to a deep violet black. Stars pricked the firmament above them, and a waning gibbous moon peered over the horizon to Collie's right. The ocean had long since lost its shine, now undulating deep and dark and secretive.

"Awdwith? Where are we?"

Somewhere over the Atlantic ocean, she said, something strange in her voice.

"Stop joking. I'm freezing. How long have we been flying?"

The dragon hesitated before answering. *Hours. I've… lost track.*

"Ma and Da will kill me," Collie said, his teeth chattering. "They won't know where I am. We'd better turn back."

Here, Awdwith said, and Collie felt heat flood through the dragon's scales beneath him. Grateful, he pressed his cold hands harder against the dragon's neck, fingers prickling as sensation returned. Welcome warmth spread through his legs and up his spine. His stomach growled — supper was long past. He fumbled in his pocket with one cold hand, easing out the scone he'd taken that morning in case Latchet needed mollifying, and took a bite. It was thick with plump currants and just about the best thing

Collie had ever tasted. He was about to ask again about turning back when he heard the change in the Sopwith's engine. The steady buzz of the motor rose to a whine, and Collie knew without needing to see the craft that it had nosed into a dive.

At the same moment, Awdwith said, *I smell...something hot.*

"Let's go!" Collie gasped. "They're in trouble!"

As if astride a horse, he dug in with his knees, urging the dragon forward. Awdwith snorted, but picked up speed, her massive wings scooping air.

The whine of the Rolls-Royce engine cut off abruptly, and Collie's heart froze in mid-beat as well. Clinging to Awdwith's neck, he leaned forward, straining to see into the darkness ahead, but the moon rode too low to shed light on the little plane.

Then with a cough, the engine restarted, laboured for a minute and then evened out. Collie sat back and drew a long breath. "Can we get them in sight?"

Wordlessly, Awdwith thrust forward, abandoning the leisurely, energy-conserving glides. Another moment of searching and Collie spotted the telltale glint of moonlight reflecting off the wide vertical stripe on the Sopwith's tail. It climbed, recovering from the dive, and was flying steadily. As they drew closer, however, Collie smelled what Awdwith had scented earlier; the hot, acrid odor of overheated oil or some other fluid. All thoughts of asking Awdwith to turn back fled. Win would think of something to explain his absence--and if not, Collie would take his chances.

Twice more the Sopwith dove, twice more Harry cut the engine and restarted. He must be undertaking the maneuvers to try and fix whatever ailed the engine. A blockage, perhaps, or some other issue he thought he could reset. Awdwith edged closer until Collie felt sure her glamour couldn't possibly hide them, should the Commander turn to look back. He didn't, though; both men were entirely consumed with trying to fix the unknown problem. Although the darkness had shrunk their world even further, Collie knew they must still be long hours distant from the coast of Ireland.

Then the engine choked out again, and Harry's shout of frustration carried back to Collie. He knew what it meant. This was no tactic, not this time; this was a failure. The imminent dive would send the plane spiraling down out of control into the dark and icy waters.

"We have to help them," he heard himself whisper. "What can we do?"

I can't carry them, the dragon said, even as she shot forward and down, angling under the plane. *It's too big, too heavy.*

Of course she was right. The plane was as big as the dragon, if not bigger.

They were close enough to hear Harry's frantic attempts to restart the engine. They produced only coughs and sputters, and then a repeat of the same futile sounds.

"Can we buy them time?"

Watch your head, the dragon said, but she didn't explain.

The dragon surged beneath the plane, whose nose had just begun to tilt forward. Awdwith brought her head up behind the landing gear, long neck snaking out to its fullest extent. She heaved her wings, shoveling air, forcing the airplane up and forward. Collie ducked and flattened himself against the dragon's neck to avoid being hit by the fuselage. One of the men in the cockpit whooped, while the other bit off a scream and turned it into a lurid oath. Collie thought he knew which was which. So much for keeping secrets from the Commander.

Level again, the plane glided as the engine coughed and wheezed.

But it didn't catch, and the nose began to tilt downward again.

I can't do that many more times, Awdwith said, but she circled around and tried again. It bought them another attempt at restarting the engine.

To no avail.

"Just get them down in one piece," Collie breathed. "It's all we can do."

For the space of a few heartbeats, the dragon flew in silence, wheeling aft of the plane once more. Collie wondered what she was thinking. For a frightening moment, he thought she might refuse. After all, if the Sopwith crashed and the men inside her were lost, might not the others give up the quest?

Collie knew it wouldn't stop them. And the dragon had said as much herself.

Hang on, Awdwith said. *There's a ship. Not too far.*

She angled in underneath the fuselage again, tucking her head behind the Sopwith's wheels. This time she didn't heave, but let the weight of the plane settle against the top of her head. Collie felt her strain as she took the extra weight, and pressed his hands against her neck as if he could add his strength to hers. Above them, someone knocked twice on the right-hand side of the plane. Collie wondered if they might be trying to direct her flight, but Awdwith was already arcing in that direction, carrying them further south.

A ship, the dragon had said. The shipping lanes must

lie that way.

Collie wasn't sure how far they flew, the dragon delaying the plane's descent as she carried them ever southward with a slow, measured cadence. On the upstroke, her wings brushed the tips of the biplane's own lower wing. Once, Collie caught sight of both men leaning over the side of the cockpit, staring down at the labouring dragon with bemused wonder. Harry retried the engine twice, but the rank scent of overheated fluid filled the air almost immediately and he had to abandon the idea. Every beat that took them south also carried them closer to the dark menace of icy waters below, the dragon unable to overcome the demands of gravity.

Then lights appeared, twinkling out of the blackness ahead. Low to the water, they suggested a long, narrow shape, and with them came the low churning murmur of a steamer. Awdwith angled toward it. Collie wondered how close she'd dare.

A knock sounded from above again, and Collie looked up to see Harry looking down. He'd pulled off his goggles and gave Collie a wry grin. The pilot threw a thumbs-up sign and touched the brim of his helmet, saluting Collie and the dragon. Collie knew what he meant. Thanks, and it would be all right to set them down now.

Awdwith must have somehow understood the same thing. They were skimming mere feet above the waves, and Collie wondered for a heartbeat how they'd get out from underneath the plane. He hoped the dragon didn't plan to dive with him clinging to her back. But with a final heave, the dragon pushed the plane upward and darted to the side, clearing the fuselage and the tips of the wings before they descended. Her own wingtips breaking the surface with almost inaudible splashes, the dragon retreated into the darkness, keeping low, hiding her bulk against the dark ocean. Behind them, Collie heard the splash as the Sopwith ditched. Men's voices carried across the water, raised in shouts and exclamations, and he knew the ship's crew had spotted the downed plane. Harry and the Commander were safe, if disappointed. They'd live to fly another day.

I must rest, Awdwith said. Pain laced her voice, and Collie felt guilt clutch his heart. The dragon flew on only a short distance before alighting softly in the water. She spread her wings to the sides like floating canvas sails, and Collie had to pull his knees up to keep his boots dry. He put a hand on her neck, stroking the scales.

"Thank you," he said simply.

I'm sorry I can't get you home quickly. Win might prevail upon Latchet to help with your parents.

Collie wondered exactly what that might mean, but decided not to ask for details. Some faery magic was best left unexamined. He did have a question for the dragon, though.

"Awdwith, how did we end up here? Why did you follow them for so long in the first place?"

The dragon had settled her long neck across the surface of the water, letting it bob gently with the undulations of the current. She turned her head slightly to regard him with one yellow eye. In his mind, he heard her sigh.

I thought you wanted to, she said. *But it was more than that. I was truly curious to see if they could do it. And if they could, I had a strange compulsion to witness it.*

"Well, so I did, I suppose," Collie said. "But you might have warned me."

I didn't know if I would help them, should they need it, the dragon went on meditatively, as if he hadn't spoken. *Part of me wanted them to fail. It was...a test. To see if I would make the right choice.*

Shocked, Collie said, "But you could have told me no and followed them on your own. Why bring me along?"

The dragon smiled, moonlight wrapping around sharp, white teeth. *Perhaps to be sure I wouldn't choose badly. To see I'm still fit for human company.*

Collie hugged his knees as water lapped around the bobbing dragon. Her scales warmed faintly under him again, dispelling the sea's chill.

"If the next team makes it...you won't leave, will you? Not yet? The skies might get busier, but it'll take a while."

Awdwith shook her head, sending wavelets rippling out across the water. *Not yet, no. The island is big. The skies are still quiet. And the ocean offers many... possibilities.*

They floated there, Collie and the dragon, drifting in the currents for a long time, as the moon rose high overhead and traced a silvery pathway for them, leading home.

Amanda Labonté

Amanda Labonté lives in St. John's, Newfoundland, where she gets much of the inspiration for the characters and places about which she writes. Though she knew she wanted to be a writer since the eighth grade, it was many years before she finally walked into a creative writing class and found a new home.

Her first novel, *Call of the Sea*, won critical acclaim in her home province of Newfoundland. The first book in her *Supernatural Causes* series gained Bestseller status on Amazon in September 2017.

As the co-owner of an educational business and mother of two she spends much of her day with kids of all ages. They give her some of the best reading recommendations.

The Triumph

Lady Hazel Winchester adjusted her bonnet as she headed through the downtown streets toward the London dock. A weak sunlight streamed through the ashy clouds overhead, not quite touching the lines of people heading to work for the day.

She was still two blocks away when she saw the massive balloon of the airship loom in the distance.

Nothing stood out quite like a military ship.

As she reached the docklands, the smell of fish and salt assailed her nostrils.

"Wotcher miss!" a young male voice called, and Hazel lifted her skirts just in time to skip over a broken mast lying in her path.

She mixed in with a stream of passengers disembarking from a ship from France for a few yards, then dodged a group of young men unloading barrels from a trading ship.

The tall ships grew sparser and so did the people as she reached the end of the docklands. An eight-foot tall wrought iron gate, complete with spikes, marked the entrance to the military section of the dockyard.

A clockwork mech with a large round head and a military uniform stood guard, his squat body making him look like a heavy-booted giant had stepped on a tin soldier.

Hazel pulled a pass card out of her reticule and stuck it in the mech's hinged mouth. There were a series of clicks followed by a punching sound as the card was spit out and the gates swung open. Hazel walked through, careful to keep the skirts of her day dress from catching on a pointed iron spike.

"Can I help you with something, miss?"

Hazel looked to her right to see a young naval officer hurrying toward her. She pointed at the airship balloon which now hovered overhead.

"I'm here for the tour."

"The tour?" the officer repeated.

With a sigh, Hazel pulled her press pass out of her reticule and handed it to the officer.

"You're Lady Hazel?"

"I am."

"My mother loves your articles."

"Glad to hear it," Hazel said.

"The rest of the reporters are straight ahead and to the right."

"Thanks," Hazel said, fighting the urge to point out that she probably could have found her way without his directions.

She put her pass back in her reticule and headed off. As she rounded a corner, *HMA Triumph* came into full view. Hazel paused for a moment to get the full impact of the ship.

The gondola, or vessel, rested in the water in full navy and gold perfection. Its figurehead stared proudly ahead, a winged woman who was ready to guide them through the clouds.

The *Triumph* could almost be mistaken for any other

naval ship if not for the massive white balloon hovering over it, attached to the masts instead of sails. Once the aether engines started that balloon would pull the ship into the air, ready for flight.

Hazel heard a clicking noise and turned to her left to find her friend and photographer Matilda Martin standing next to her, capturing the airship in all its glory.

"What do you think?" Matilda asked, taking the gold and mahogany camera down from her face and looking at Hazel.

"It's quite impressive."

"It's smaller than I'd imagined," Matilda said, pushing a stray curl under her bonnet. "Not the balloon part, but the ship."

"On an airship that part's called the gondola. And it's the biggest HMA to date."

Matilda wrinkled her nose. "I think I was expecting a full size navy ship attached to a balloon."

"Then you'd have been disappointed with the early models. They were barely bigger than dorys."

"I assume this isn't your first time on an airship then?"

"No," Hazel shook her head. "But those were just pleasure cruisers. Nothing like this."

"I forget sometimes that you're a lady," Matilda laughed. "Of course you were probably a duke's guest on pleasure cruise."

Hazel half smiled. "It was an earl, actually."

The two women walked forward, joining the line of reporters on the dock waiting for the tour to start.

"You in the right line, ladies?" A man with a crooked nose raised an eyebrow. "I don't think they're serving tea on board today."

The man next to him laughed and though Matilda visibly bristled, Hazel didn't bother answering. She eyed Matilda's camera instead.

"Do make sure you get a photo from the upper deck when you get a chance," Hazel said. "The view of the city should be impressive from up there."

"Already planning on it," Matilda said, messing with the lens on her camera and holding it up to her eye. She had a bag with more parts slung over her shoulder. Hazel had no idea how the contraption worked - Matilda had constructed her own device - but there was no mistaking a print by M. Martin.

"I'm glad Mr. Walters sent you with me," Hazel said. "Last time I had Benny and he wasted his plates on a group of tavern maids and had nothing left for when we made it to the event."

"Never fear." Matilda patted her satchel. "I never run out of materials."

As the line of reporters began moving toward a gang-plank, Hazel frowned. "That's the cargo bay. We're not entering through the main deck."

"There's probably a good reason." Matilda looked around Hazel to get a better view of where they were going. "Have you heard who's doing the tour this morning?"

"No," Hazel shook her head.

"Captain Merritt Lancaster."

"Really?" Hazel turned to look her friend. "Whose wrong side did he get on to have to do a job like this?"

"I think the Navy wants to make sure we all walk away with a positive impression. They had a hard time justifying the expense of a new airship."

Hazel looked up at the massive white balloon that

would keep the ship afloat while the aether engines propelled it through the air.

"Her Majesty was completely in favour of the purchase," Hazel said.

"Maybe," Matilda agreed. "But I heard Parliament was a bit more divided."

"Stupid Parliament," Hazel said. "I should have known about the debate. When are they going to let women in the press gallery?"

"Probably when we force them, just like everything else."

The line continued moving forward until Hazel and Matilda found themselves at the end of the gangway with a young officer ready to greet them. They handed over their press passes.

"Straight ahead, ladies," the officer said after looking at their credentials. "Have a pleasant day."

The gangway led to the cargo bay of the airship where barrels and crates labeled with everything from flour to aether powder lined the walls.

Hazel and Matilda went to stand with the dozen other young men who were there for the tour. Based on their accents, Hazel figured a number of them had come in from out of town for the day to report on the newest addition to the British fleet. An officer walked toward them from the other end of the bay. Hazel recognized him from the dozens of pictures she'd seen in the papers. Captain Merritt Lancaster, defender of the Empire.

"His photograph doesn't do him justice," Matilda whispered, holding up her camera.

A flurry of flashes went off, capturing a smiling Captain Lancaster in his glory. Once the photographers finished, he began speaking.

"Thank you all for joining us today," Merritt started, his cheery voice echoing off the solid walls. "It's my pleasure to show off the *HMA Triumph*."

Two more officers joined the captain, and they began their tour in earnest.

"I had you come in through the cargo bay so that you could all experience the ship from the bottom up," Merritt said, leading them toward a rounded doorway. "Let me assure you it only gets better from here."

They went up a staircase into the galley, its long wooden tables already set for dinner.

Hazel figured it could easily feed two dozen officers at once.

While the captain called the cook out to give examples of the daily menu and Matilda set up to take a photograph of a sample meal, Hazel studied the oil paintings on the wall. They were all of various battles during the Great Sea War.

The first two showed the English triumphing over the crew from the Americas, but the third depicted the battle of Greenland and the sinking of *HMS Glory*. It had been such a staggering defeat and such a waste so close to declaration of the truce.

"Perhaps you want to be taking notes?" The crooked nosed reporter came up behind Hazel. "Won't your lady readers be most interested in what the officers like to eat?"

There was a general burst of laughter from the reporters around her and Hazel saw Matilda straighten, ready for a fight.

"Actually," Hazel said, "I think the *London Daily* readers will be most interested in the torodial engine. But by all means, if you need more time in the galley I won't stop you. Which of the country papers have you come in from anyway?"

There was a snicker behind her and Hazel turned around to see the captain cover his mouth and cough. She wasn't certain, but she could have sworn he winked at her.

"I was under the impression the engine room was off limits," crooked nose said.

A Chief Petty Officer hurried into the galley and went up to Merritt. They had a quick exchange before the captain addressed the group.

"If you'll excuse me for a moment," Merritt said. "Officer Shaw will show you the next section and I'll meet you on the deck."

"The next stop will be the visitor's deck," Shaw said. "If you'll follow me."

The reporters lined up and followed Shaw out of the room. Hazel and Matilda joined the end of the line.

"How do you feel about taking a detour?" Hazel whispered.

"Really good," Matilda said.

Watching the line move up the stairs, Hazel and Matilda went around the corner toward the centre of the ship.

"What are we looking for?" Matilda asked.

"The engine room."

They crept through the hallway and arrived at a large round door edged in brass.

"Do you hear that?" Hazel asked. "The door is humming."

"It's not the door," a familiar voice called. Hazel felt her cheeks start to burn as she turned around to see Merritt standing behind her.

"We seem to have gotten lost," Hazel said, clearing

her throat.

"Somehow I doubt that," Merritt said, grinning as he opened the door and walking into the vibrating room. "All I ask is that you keep this room off the record."

Hazel braced herself to see the ship's engines but instead found herself in a room with floor-to-ceiling brass tubes.

"This is the communications room," Merritt said. "It not only receives and sends messages via telegraph, but also has an intra-ship communication system."

"How does it work?" Hazel asked.

"Vibrations. The Chief of Communications can use the tubing to get from one part of the ship to another. It isn't necessary for everyday use, but when in the midst of battle it could be of the utmost importance to get a message from the cannon deck to the wheelhouse."

Hazel ran a gloved finger over one of the tubes. It made a faint ringing sound.

"It's aether lined," Merritt added.

"It's quite the innovation," Hazel said. "Are you going to send us back to the visitor's deck now?"

"Not quite yet."

Next to the communications room was a door with a large wheel instead of a door knob. Merritt turned it twice counter clockwise, then once back. The door swung open.

At first, all Hazel could see was gold.

"As you know, only pure metals can conduct aether," Merritt said. "And this is the largest engine of its kind so there's a lot of precious metal in this room."

The engines were the centrepiece of a circular room,

towering a good twenty feet above them and culminating in a solid gold sphere. A walkway with a railing wrapped around the room, letting engineers and visitors manoeuvre around the engine.

Even though the engines weren't currently running, the walls and railings still glowed from the aether residue.

"Are you sure I can't take a picture of this?" Matilda asked.

"You'd never do it justice," Hazel whispered.

"Not to mention, we don't need the plans getting out."

"How does it work?" Hazel asked, stepping closer to the engine.

"It's a state secret," Merritt said, then he smiled. "Also, I'm not an engineer."

Hazel looked down. The engine stack went right to the lower deck.

"You must know something," Matilda said.

Merritt pointed at the gold sphere above them. "I know when that starts turning there's enough force created to bring this whole vessel into the air."

"How splendid," Hazel said, her eyes on the sphere.

"I'm a glorified pilot though," Merritt continued. "This is all the work of engineers. My job is to keep us in the air and make sure the aether smoke is properly ventilated, away from the helium in the air balloon."

"It sounds dangerous," Hazel said.

"We're soldiers," the captain shrugged. "That's our job."

There was a tapping behind them and two naval officers entered the engine room.

"We're ready for the demonstration," one of them

said.

"Excellent," Merritt clapped his hands together, then he turned to the Hazel and Matilda. "Now ladies, I really must insist that you come with me to the upper deck."

With one last look over her shoulder, Hazel followed Merritt and Matilda up the stairs, through the main part of the ship to the deck. The other reporters were already there chatting in small groups while the photographers took pictures. Matilda started setting up her camera next to the railing.

"You're going to want to wait about five minutes," Merritt said. "Trust me on this."

As he spoke, the decking beneath their feet began to vibrate and Hazel hurried to join Matilda, holding onto the railing as the balloon began to pull the gondola up out of the water.

"Where are we going?" Hazel asked as Merritt joined her at the railing.

"Does it matter?" Matilda called from behind the camera lens. "This is bloody brilliant!"

"It's just a short demonstration," Merritt said. "We'll putter around London and then back down in time for tea."

As the city grew smaller and smaller below them, Hazel couldn't help but remember the purpose of the airship.

"It's truly remarkable," Hazel said, catching Merritt's attention. "But I wish it wasn't a battleship."

"You don't think the British Navy deserves the best?" Merritt asked.

"We're at peace," Hazel said. "The Americans haven't attacked in over a decade. The war is over and the working people need food not warships."

Merritt looked out over the city of London, the tower looming in the distance. "Perhaps we're safe for now, but we were caught off guard once before."

A shiver ran down Hazel's spine. She'd grown up with the stories of London being set on fire, of men and women screaming in the streets from toxic rains pouring down from American air balloons.

"In the event the Americans get any ideas of coming after us again," Merritt continued, "we're going to be ready. They won't take us by surprise. Not again."

Nicole Little

Nicole Little is an award-winning short story author from St. John's, Newfoundland. Her previous writing credit, "Sweet Sixteen," won the June 2018 Kit Sora prize. She has also placed in the Writer's Alliance of Newfoundland and Labrador "A Nightmare on Water Street" contest, October 2018.

She is a mother of two.

On a Wing and a Prayer

Mei Ya was filled with sorrow. Her new friend, the whistling thrush, had flown off during the storm and had not returned. Her father, loud and stern, shooed her outside to play; he had no time for her childish tears. She wandered through the maidenhairs, calling for the little blue bird, but he did not come. Bereaved, she sat in the circle of golden trees and watched as their fallen leaves danced upon the wind. At dusk, she slowly made her way home.

Bàba rose before dawn to tend the yaks and, once he had gone, Mei Ya dressed swiftly in the cold. An idea had come to her in the night as she had drifted off to sleep in her cot, and she was eager to begin.

She hurried outside to the rear of the hut, where indigo leaves grew in wild abundance, and filled the pockets of her tunic to overflowing. Humming to herself, she plunged her hands into the icy waters of the creek, collecting two smooth rocks. She nodded to herself. Yes, they were perfect. The tip of her tongue betwixt her teeth, she roughly ground the indigo leaves together, just as she had seen the merchants do at market. She kneaded the pulp into an old strip of blanket that she had ripped from her bed linen and grunted in satisfaction as the faded gray-white began to turn blue. She rinsed it in the creek and laid it out to dry. She was a patient child and to pass the time she softly sang the cradle songs she remembered from her Māma, while she neatly unraveled the hems of her skirt. At last, meticulously, using those small bits of thread, she tied the cloth to short thin sticks of bamboo, tethering it all with a long length of cord; a most elegant tail. Pleased with her creation, she dashed at full speed through the millet fields, laughing; her long, tangled hair trailing behind her in the breeze.

A sharp tug -

And oh, but it was flying; soaring!

A splash of brilliant color across an ashen sky.

Her squeals of astonishment and delight brought her father scurrying from the hut. Fearing his anger as he neared closer, Mei Ya tried frantically to reel it in but her little arms were not strong enough.

"What is this?" Bàba thundered. "What have you done?!"

"I wanted my friend, the bird, to return. I… I think he is lonely too. I have made this for him."

"Yes, perhaps", he conceded, his voice softening with wonder. "You have done well, daughter of mine. What is it called?"

Mei Ya paused for a moment. "I think it will be called a kite!" she said.

And so, it was.

Far Out

Nose pressed against the window, I gazed with unconcealed interest as my fellow travelers bid tearful goodbyes to their loved ones out on the tarmac. I had already boarded eagerly; the first to do so. I was leaving nothing behind that was worth crying about. I only felt relief.

I sat back in my seat, secured my harness, and gaped in wide eyed wonder at my surroundings. Everything was high-tech, polished and ultra-modern, and though I hated to admit it, most was far beyond my comprehension.

I was still shocked to be here. Me, Audrey Melrose, sitting aboard the Madonna 61. The much-hyped civilian inhabited spaceship would be the first of its kind to travel to another planet. It was a technological marvel, and everyone wanted in on it. The manifest bore names of some of the world's top scientists and experts in the fields of astronomy, biology, and terraformation. No expense had been spared, and like anything done on such a grand scale, the expedition needed more and more money to get off the ground. Consequently, a few thrillseeker celebrities, and at least one professional athlete, had been able to buy their way on board. But everyone else was ordinary like me. A streetwise foster kid who had just aged out of the system, plucked from obscurity and thrust into the spotlight; my name randomly chosen by an automated system along with 159 others.

We were about to make history.

We had known our world was dying long before the authorities finally acknowledged it, but by then it was too little, too late. In order to save our species, they had to set their sights farther than ever before... to the stars. Surely ours wasn't the only planet capable of supporting life. Time was fast running out when they finally made a breakthrough and by then, relocating was the obvious, and only, solution for survival.

Shortly after we had been notified of our selection and had passed all the requisite physical and psychological examinations, we were taken on an extensive tour of the ship. It was thrilling but just impossible to take it all in. I had been assigned a small anchored pod on one of the lower levels and, given my poor social skills, I expected that I would spend much of my time there. The accommodations were stark and white: a small room with nothing more than a bunk, a small built in bookshelf, and a desk with a chair. I overheard a few mumbled under-the-breath complaints at the simplicity and lack of comforts, but I was thrilled to have something that was all mine. It was not lavish by any means, no, but it was clean and safe and warm, which was more than I could have said for most of my foster homes. It even had a tiny window: my very own personal planetarium.

I watched openly now as the others embarked. We were "a broad cross section of society" they had exclaimed at the orientation and, yes, it certainly seemed as though we represented all walks of life. It had also been announced, with much fanfare, that as an added incentive we would receive education and training in a field of our choice as we journeyed through space. Upon our arrival there, we would be expected to use the skills we had learned en route to help establish the first settlement, so that others could eventually follow. It was exhilarating but overwhelming to be a part of something so huge.

Now here we were, the moment we'd been waiting for: launch day. There was a tense excitement in the air. We could feel that we were perched on the precipice of something magnificent, and there was no going back. There was uneasy chatter, bursts of nervous laughter and the worriers – there were quite a few -- anxiously poured over the information packages we'd found on our seats. I picked up my envelope and ran a finger along the flap to open it. I pulled out the hefty bundle of papers and sifted through them absently. Satellite photos of our destination spilled across my lap – my first look – and I stared in stunned silence. This was going to be my new home.

"Good morning all! Welcome aboard the Madonna 61!"

As the applause died down, I shifted my focus to the steward who would now instruct us as we prepped for flight.

"… you are tutelaries of the new world, giving hope to all those left behind. Your dedication and sacrifice have not gone unnoticed. And so today you will embark upon a journey of infinite possibilities! Destination: Earth."

Carolyn R Parsons

Carolyn R. Parsons is a full-time writer and radio personality residing in Lewisporte, NL. She has contributed to *The Central Voice*, the Saltire network of papers, and *Downhome Magazine*. Her books include a poetry collection, two novels and a collection of short stories. Her 2017 novel, Charley through Canada, attained bestseller status on Amazon.

Carolyn is a founding director of Literary Events NL, an organization that provides Newfoundland authors a forum through which to share their work, debuting with the highly successful 2017 Canada 150 Literary Tour NL. She is also on the Board of Directors of the Writers Alliance of Newfoundland and Labrador (WANL) as the representative for Central/Burin. She was a contributor to 2018's bestselling photography book, *Kit Sora: The Artobiography*, with her flash fiction: 'The Doorway Home.'

Her most recent novel, *The Forbidden Dreams of Betsy Elliott*, was released in February 2019.

You Know When You Fly

March 12, 1921

"How'd you get away?" Jimmy whispered to Charlie who shut the first stage door behind him. He walked the length of the salt-scented building where Jimmy had slid the other door, the one leading out to the wharf, open just a bit more than a crack.

"I never brought in a turn of wood or shoveled out the henhouse so fast. Is it come yet?" Charlie bounced up and down, his body bursting with excitement.

"No. I don't think it will. I don't see nobody on the tickle at all. You think if it was really coming we'd see somebody out there." Jimmy jammed his head through the slot again so that only his face showed through on the other side. The cold air assaulted his cheeks.

"Let me see!" Charlie ignored Jimmy's pessimism and tried to pull him away, but Jimmy stood firm.

"No, you kneel down, I'm not budging." He pulled out, shoved Charlie back with one hand then squeezed his cheeks once more back into the crack between door and frame and stared straight ahead.

"You don't think he's coming?" Charlie had risked a good trimmin' if he was caught out of the house except for work. Last week he'd caught heck for chasing Mrs.

LeDrew's cat until the poor thing jumped into the well. They did manage to extricate it before it froze to death or drowned, but it also rendered the water undrinkable, a big cause for concern in March month when only the deepest of wells weren't frozen solid like the tickle. So Charlie'd been bound to the house, his workload doubled, and he'd been forbidden to go watch the landing. This was the real punishment.

"Not because of the weather. Tickle's froze up solid. She could land there fine," Jimmy said.

There'd been talk of a thaw. A robin had pitched on the ridgepole of the Bown's store on March 7th causing Mr. Alec Bown to declare an early spring was upon them.

"Nah, b'y, nar chance it'll happen. I allows the tickle will be all abroad by the end of the week," Old Alec had predicted. But the robin must have been lost or stunned because here they were, March 12, 1921, with the tickle still froze and a landing imminent. Turned out robins were no better harbingers of the weather than his creaky old joints. If anything, the weather was colder and that was just fine by Charlie.

The boys had a good spot from where to watch the excitement. Jimmy's father's stage was located directly across the tickle from the Robertses' premises. It had poked out over the tickle, clung there like it belonged, for two generations. The large wharf stretched out into the white expanse of ice that ran towards the east so far as Fogo and west so far as Twillingate. The tickle itself was narrow, running between the north and south islands and made a good, natural runway for an adventuresome aviator wanting to stop in to drop off the mail and locate the seal herd.

"They says Fred Roberts is going out to meet her hisself," Charlie said, settling onto the floor, his face pressed to the narrow opening to wait.

"He's able to do some good with just one arm. I bet he saw lots of planes over there in Europe in the war. They say the plane that's coming here is the kind they used back then, same thing only now for spotting seals instead of dropping bombs on Germans." Jimmy's voice over Charlie's head was wonder-filled.

"It's a de Havilland. DH-9 to be 'xact. Over in Botwood they got two more planes, Martinsyde with a Rolls Royce engine in her and a Westland Napier. I wonders if poor Mr. Roberts might be frightened to death of the planes seein's he saw them in the war killing people." Charlie sniffed, a drip falling from his nose. He wiped it away with the warm cuffs his mother had knit for him and kept his gaze to the sky. He had never laid eyes on either one of these machines but he memorized all he could about anything to do with flying.

Several men were on the Robertses' wharf now and there were more walking down the road in that direction along with, what appeared to be, several women.

While Charlie stared at the sky like it was going to turn into diamonds, Jimmy pondered planes dropping bombs. He wouldn't admit it in a million years, but the reason he wasn't out sitting on the edge of the wharf waiting wasn't because his father told him not to. It was because deep down in his ten-year-old gut there was a fear of this mighty flying thing that would be coming soon to their place. He didn't know what to expect, nobody he knew ever saw a picture of a plane before, much less saw one up close and 'longside.

"I'd fly one if I could," Charlie said.

"I would, too!" Jimmy declared, not to be outdone. The

odds that there would ever be the chance to do so made him brave enough to pretend. His stomach clenched in a knot at the idea of being up so high, though. Sure, he didn't even like it when he had to walk out on the flakes in summer to check the fish. The height of them, dangling over the water, held up by stilts, made his stomach do strange flips, and queer feelings ran up his middle at the memory of standing on the trembling platforms. He glanced over at them, now banked full with snow and gulped. Nope, he wouldn't be flying that's for sure.

"I'd fly one so high I'd see the back of the gulls!" Charlie declared.

"I'd fly out over the ice, find the ducks and shoot them all," Jimmy said. Afraid or not, he wasn't going to be outdone.

"You can't shoot and fly a plane at the same time?" Charlie laughed as he eyed just such a duck in the distance.

"Oh, how did they shoot the Germans then?" Jimmy asked.

"They dropped bombs of gunpowder on 'em."

"No they didn't," Jimmy said. "They shot them."

"Don't be stund. You can't shoot a gun and fly a plane altogether. You'd make the plane shake and she'd fall down onto the ice. I think they can hammer guns on though, but that's different. Planes falls easy. You got to bide still in them. You don't see ducks shaking all about when they flies. Planes is the same. They needs special guns that don't shake her much. If you shoots at ducks with machine guns you'll blow the ducks to bits. Ducks can't be cooked in bits."

"You don't know nothin' about planes," Jimmy said, giving Charlie a nudge with his foot.

Charlie would have done more than tap Jimmy back on the leg. He would have told him he knew more about planes than almost anybody around though he was guessing at much of it, but he realized then that the black speck in the sky he had thought was a duck was getting closer and bigger. It was not moving like a bird at all, but rather like something blowing in the wind. And he could hear a sound, too.

"You hits me again…" Charlie said.

"Shut up, Jimmy. Look!" He pointed with his mittened hand to the sky where the black speck had transformed into a box.

Jimmy looked down at Charlie's head. "You think that's it? It's square. Don't they have round fronts?"

"I think they can have all kinds of fronts. Look it's turning, see the things to the sides, that's the wings. That's it. That's the plane!" Charlie jumped up, knocking Jimmy back. He slid the door open and stepped out onto the wharf. It was covered in ice and he slipped a bit but grabbed a rail. There was a rim of blue water around the wharf over top of the ice, the crystal blue of Jimmy's eyes and the clear March sky. It ended a foot or so off from the edge and then it was straight on solid right across. Charlie stopped, gauging the distance.

Could he make it? Before he could decide, a voice bawled out from high on a hill behind him. "Charlie, you laddio! If I gets a hold of you, you'll get a trimming like you never had before."

Jimmy moved back from the doorway at the voice. His first glimpse of the plane had sent him into a terror far bigger than he had expected. His friend's old man, known for his lack of patience, and freedom with the belt with his youngsters, didn't help much to calm him. Jimmy backed up in the stage and when he was about halfway from the wharf door, turned, exited the building through the main door, and made for the house, the roar of the plane terrifying as though it were flown by the devil himself come to take Jimmy into the fiery pits he learned about in church.

Panicked, he kept going until he was inside. Soon Jimmy had his boots off, coat thrown on a hook, and had blown past his baffled mother who was sewing in the parlor until he was in the room he shared with his three brothers. Once there, he flattened himself to his stomach and wriggled under the wrought iron bed, safe, he hoped, from the gunpowder bombs that were surely going to rain down upon them at any moment.

Meanwhile, the plane's engine chugged overhead as the de Havilland 9, flown by Major Sidney Cotton, circled the tickle. Clem -- Charlie's father -- was closing in on the stage. Nearly all hands were coming out of their houses except those terrified of the racket and a few who pretended it was no big deal and instead knit, rocked and peeked through panes of glass at the aircraft.

The tickle might be froze solid but it was far from smooth. Still, by the way she was lined up and getting lower, it looked like the plane might land.

Charlie shot a look at his father, who was on the hill but closer, checked the incoming plane, sized up the distance between wharf and ice, and backed up.

"Charlie!" His father's voice bellowed and he knew he'd never see the light of day again until voting age once his father caught him. Given that was going to happen anyway, he'd do his best to see the plane land before his imprisonment. He backed up further on the wharf right to the door. He heard footsteps rattle on the outer walkway., But before his father reached the stage door, Charlie took off in a run as fast as he could. When he reached the edge, he leapt into the air.

Over the moat of ocean water that surround the wharf he flew, barrelling through the chilled air, the wind in his face, weightless for just a few moments before he descended. He landed on his feet with a thud and rolled away from the wharf. As he did he caught a glimpse of his father, fists raised as he came to a full stop at the opening of the wharf door. He pulled it all the way open and stepped out onto the platform.

Charlie picked himself up and tested for injuries. His knees felt scraped and his ankle was a bit out of sorts but it was nothing too bad. He started walking off from the shore then picked up speed as he realized he wasn't hurt much at all. Charlie knew his father wouldn't make the leap. He'd have to go back up and around and come onto the ice a different way. It would give him enough time to get across the tickle and in line with where the plane was set to stop. He had to go just far enough that it would be hard for his father to catch up, but not so far as he'd be in danger from the plane landing on him.

The plane's engine roared louder and louder, like a million claps of thunder all at once. It was loud enough to shake the ice under his feet and to rattle the panes of glass in the windows of the saltbox homes that lined both sides of the tickle.

I don't know how they can get near the seals with all that racket. They'll all dive off the ice and overboard, he thought lowering himself down, covering his ears and watching from a spot that felt about perfect. Across the north side of the tickle, men stood on that side of the ice too, waiting, like he did, as the marvelous, man-made machine set lower and lower, quivering and shaking in her descent until she was closer than a gunshot away. Finally, in no time, her runners made contact with the ice and she bounced and slid forward for a distance until she came to a full stop just off from Solomon Roberts' wharf to the north, and where young Charlie lay watching from behind a small knob of ice to the south.

Once she was silent, Charlie stood and walked towards her, eyes on the marvel before him. Large letters: G-something. A gust of wind blew snow in his face so he couldn't see the rest. Call letters. He knew that much. Her tracks streaked in the snow, perfect trails that indicated a skilled aviator was at her controls.

Men had made themselves into birds using machines, Charlie thought. What magic! Not a single man had ever flown until 1903 when the Wright brothers had done so for a mere 12 seconds, and already, not even twice as many of Charlie's lifetimes, they were everywhere, even on Main Tickle, Change Islands. He couldn't believe it. What a time to be alive!

Charlie rubbed his nose and glanced back, expecting his father to be in close pursuit but instead he was still back on the wharf. It appeared he'd forgotten all about chasing his runaway son, lost like so many others that day in the marvel of seeing their first flying machine up close.

He closed in on the plane, walking around her front. The men on the north side, Solomon Roberts and his crowd mainly, had reached the pilot and were shaking his hand as he pointed to the plane and laughed.

A woman walked up to the pilot. "I'm the post mis-

tress, Miss Scevior, I'm here for the mail?" Charlie overheard her say.

"Yes, ma'am," the pilot replied in a voice that was different from their own but not much like the Canadians or
Americans who visited on occasion.

"Australian," Charlie said out loud, then he covered
his mouth with his mitten. His face, already reddened by
the cold, deepened to a shiny scarlet.

"Why yes, young man, I am. Are you familiar with
it?"

"It's…" Then Charlie remembered that his mitt covered his mouth, removed his hand and started again. "It's
on the other side of the world and has kangaroos." He
said before whipping his hand back over his mouth.

"Indeed it is." The pilot sized up ten-year-old Charlie
and reached out and tugged the top of his wool cap at its
point. "Nice cap you have there."

"You, too."

Major Cotton smiled and said, "It's for pilots. Perhaps
one day you'll get one and fly?"

Charlie nodded. He had no more words left. All the
thoughts and questions he had about planes and flying
flew out of his head as he considered that he'd just met a
real, honest to goodness pilot and was standing by a real,
honest to goodness plane. He stared at it all as Major Cotton helped the postmistress get the mail.

"We saw seals not too far out from here," Major Cotton said to the men. "We'll radio the information to the
sealers and they'll head straight for them. Next year, we
hope to have a fleet of planes out just looking for seals to
save them the trouble."

Charlie stood there unnoticed as the men gathered

around and the lady left with the mail. He eavesdropped on every conversation. The men chatted, sized up the plane, looked at her engine, marvelled at her wingspan and shook their heads in wonder at it all. Many children stood along the shore, as curious as he was, but forbidden by the parents to go see up close.

By and by, the pilot was invited along for food just like every stranger always is, though this one seemed to be just a bit more special than most.

"Charlie!" His father's voice carried across the tickle and the boy lifted his hand for a wave to him. Then he turned away from the plane and started a slow trek back to the other side, heading towards a safe place to get ashore. Every so often he glanced back. She was still there. Still magnificent. Each time. Sure, he was doomed to a good long punishment but he didn't care much in that moment, so happy he was at the entire day.

The wind was in his face as he made his way back to the south island, the plane abandoned and quiet behind him as everyone repaired to their own houses to talk of the magic of such an event. A few would call it an evil and several more would call it a miracle. Not him. He'd call it science and progress. He'd memorized every word the pilot said and repeated it over and over in his mind. Lift. Altitude. Acceleration. All big words plus many more that together described flying. He wondered if the gulls had to remember all these words. Perhaps he shouldn't throw rocks at them anymore if they were that smart. Mrs. Le-Drew's hens, though, were too stund to fly. They were fair game. Just like her cat.

When he finally opened the door to go in, his mother met him and grabbed his coat and boots. There was no sign of his father.

"Do you *like* a trimmin'?" She asked as she fussed around him, giving him a thick slice of white fluffy bread, slathered in more molasses and butter than she usually spared. She was making up now for the trouble he'd be in the once.

"Did you see the plane? I talked to the pilot feller," Charlie said. "Jimmy ran away but I went over and talked to him. Did you see?"

"Yes, I saw it through the window. It was a fine bit of fun for a March day, but none of the other youngsters nosed in like that. People will think you're wild as the loo, running across the ice to see a plane and think we are, too, for letting you. But tis 1921 and modern times are here, even on this island I suppose. We wouldn't see a speck of mail until June with the ice like this, but now p'raps there'll be a letter from Nan for us."

"I'd like to be a pilot in a plane some day. I bet I could fly."

"If you want to you can," his mother said. The door swung open and Charlie's father entered with a big dust of snow before him.

"He can't do nothing for about ten more years after what he done today. Get to your room and think about if t'was worth what's to come," his father said.

Charlie took off, his head in the clouds, in a plane somewhere in the future. What was a trimmin'? Just a moment of hurt that was worth all the moments of dreams yet to come.

///

September, 1940
The flames enveloped the entire fuselage and the plane went into a spiral, twisting and dropping from the sky.

Charlie felt a pang for the pilot. Enemy or not, he didn't like knowing a man had just died. But it was either the Nazi or him, so he let the feeling go through him then beyond. The German planes made a roaring sound as they whirled past him. He hung on, his hands firm on the controls, his eyes unwavering as he dipped his aircraft, ready to engage again. Then he saw them turn away, one by one, retreating from this battle, though he didn't fool himself that they'd not be back. They'd only run low on fuel, the distance they had to fly before engaging with the British their greatest weakness.

He navigated his Royal Air Force spitfire back towards the air strip. He prepared for landing, mentally judging the distance and speed required for a smooth end to this flight. He knew this plane like he knew his own face in the mirror. Perhaps a bit better he mused, remembering the nick he'd given himself with the razor that morning.

He thought of Jimmy as his altitude decreased. He'd been injured at the front and sent to a hospital to recover. His mother was going to give him an update soon on his condition. His injury had been minor but he'd contracted malaria and wasn't doing well.

Charlie manoeuvred the aircraft so that it aligned with the runway then brought her forward onto the smooth surface, greasing her on with barely a bounce. He slowed the plane down then taxied her to the hangar where she'd be checked and readied for another battle on a different day. He opened the door and exited, unsnapped the strap of his flight helmet and let it dangle a moment before tossing it into his seat. He climbed down and was met by a young man he recognized as a new mechanic.

"Sir, glad you're back safe and sound. The Germans took off?"

"Yes, same as always, keep 'em at bay until they run out of gas. Got one of them though."

"Good for you sir! Um, sir, I got a letter for you from home. I was told to bring it to you straight away." He reached into his pocket and pulled it out, handing it to Charlie. He saluted and, at Charlie's nod, walked away. Charlie had brothers in the army and navy and a letter from home wasn't always good news. He'd leave a fellow alone with his mail, just in case.

"Thank you," Charlie said, a moment too late. He walked over towards the exit, waving at the men who worked there fixing up planes that had been damaged in battle. Some were so dented and twisted it looked like they'd never fly again but the mechanics of the RAF never gave up on a machine until they had tried everything.

Once outside, and free from the eyes of others, he pulled open the envelope, ripping the seal off and hauling out the paper within. His mother's pretty handwriting filled both sides of the single sheet. His heart fluttered as he read the words he expected would come but hoped against all hope, wouldn't.

Poor Jimmy. He'd been so brave as he signed up. He'd thought the worst that could happen was he'd be without an arm like Fred Roberts, and he was ready to sacrifice even a leg to protect the world from Hitler. Instead he'd died of Malaria, picked up in Asia where he'd been stationed to fight the Japanese.

"Damn," Charlie said, hitting a fist off the side of the building.

"Sir, are you okay?" a small voice asked.

Charlie wiped a hand over his nose and sniffed before turning. A young boy stood there in a double breasted overcoat and jaunty paperboy hat.

"Oh yes, just working off some energy. That's a nice hat you have on there." He flicked the brim of the boy's cap and smiled. He must be one of the crew's kids he figured.

"I'm not supposed to be here. Mom sent me away from London to not get bombed. She'd not be pleased much at all if she knew I was here where the bombing planes are."

Charlie was about to scold the child for disobeying then stopped. "Why are you here if you're going to get in trouble?"

"Sir, because I wanted to ask a real pilot a question. Are you a real pilot? You're wearing a Sidcot so I think you might be."

"Yes. I am." Charlie's face broke into a smile. "You know the Sidcot?" He referred to the warm aviation overalls that pilots used to keep them warm while up in the air.

"Oh yes, I do. I heard of that before, sir."

"I once met the man who invented this suit, a lot time ago when I was about your age. Major Sidney Cotton, inventor of the Sidcot Aviation suit. We'd all freeze up there without it. What's your name? And what's the question young fella?"

The boy's eyes widened at the story and he gulped, in awe of Charlie. "I'm Michael and I want to know, sir, when did you know you *had* to fly?"

Charlie noted the boy's phrasing. It wasn't "want to fly" but rather "*had* to fly."

The obvious answer was that day when the plane landed on the tickle. It was then that he'd decided he had to fly or he might as well die. But the child deserved more. He cast his mind across the sea of his memories and caught the precise one that answered the child's inquiry best.

It even surprised him to realize that it was not the plane landing on the tickle, nor the pilot who had taken a moment to make the day special, like he was doing for young Michael now.

It was the moment when he had jumped over the wharf, his body hurtling through space, the landing calculated but not guaranteed, the rush of the air past his body as he flew forward over the strip of water at the foot of the wharf, landing on his feet then going into a roll to spread the force from the impact. He remembered the moment like it had just happened. It was his first flight.

Charlie heard the rumble of a spitfire on approach bringing another man back from doing his duty against the tyrants they fought. He cast his eyes to the sky, grateful that his comrade was safe. He could still watch planes all day. He remembered the letter and Jimmy, now gone, who hadn't stayed and who had been teased mercilessly after his older brother told everyone that he'd hidden under his bed in fright at the sight of the plane.

"Sir?" The boy tugged his jacket, pulling him back to the present with his perfect London dialect.

"Michael, I knew I had to fly, the first time I flew," he said. He glanced at the paper in his hand. "My friend Jimmy, however, for him it was different. He never wanted to fly. He was afraid so he joined the army. Which for me, seems a lot scarier."

"I wouldn't want to be like Jimmy and never fly! That must be sad," the boy stated, eyes as large as saucers.

Charlie folded the letter and shoved it into his pocket. "Oh, no worries son. It's okay. Jimmy is flying now. Higher than any of us and without a speck of fear. Come on! You want to sit in a spitfire?"

He took the young lad by the hand and when they got to the aircraft the mechanic grinned at the pair.

"New recruit sir?"

"Yes, a real flyer this one." Once they were near the plane, he picked up the boy, who was as light as a feather, reached in and grabbed his hat, took the boy's hat off and plopped his own on the child's head.

Then, he wielded him in his two hands, lifted him and spun him around so that he was flying through the air before he stepped up to the door of the spitfire and set him down, plop, in the pilot's seat.

The boy squealed, his delighted laughter spreading across the hangar bringing grins to the men's faces.

"There you go, son, you just flew, now you should know if you have to fly."

The boy looked up at him, eyes wide with wonder. He looked at the panel, around at the gears, touched nothing.

Then young Michael looked straight ahead, his mind in the clouds, his eyes sparkling with the bliss of one who knows his destiny.

"Yes, sir," he said, his voice soft but sure. "*Now* I know I have to fly."

Afterword
Matthew LeDrew

The From the Rock series celebrates the best of us. The best that we have to offer. In the past we have shined a light on the best of science fiction, fantasy, horror, and dystopian stories; and now, flights and stories regarding aviation. I believe this to be our best collection yet, as it combines our best storytellers with our best impulses as humans: the impulses to explore, to overcome, to imagine, and to invent. These were the impulses that, one hundred years ago, led us to the first flights.

This anthology is unique in that it unites many of the genres that came before it in this collection, unifying them with a common theme. There's something here for everyone.

Airfields make up some of my fondest memories. My grandfather was a well-known flight enthusiast, bringing remote planes with small cameras on them to abandoned airstrips and watching as they soared off into the distance until they were mere specks on the horizon. Long after I'd stopped seeing the planes, he'd look into the distance with squinted eyes and just know.

My wonder led me to stories, and it is with great pride that I announced and published this collection, finally bringing these two together. Through the invention of aviation, as through the invention of stories, we see the heights to which the human imagination can soar.

Big thanks to editors Erin Vance and Ellen Curtis, as well as guest-editor Dr. Lisa Daly. Also, large thanks to Brad Dunne, who helped at the last minute with some editing duties.

Matthew LeDrew
Publisher

ON THE COVER

This year's amazing photo cover artwork was shot and modeled by Kit Sora of Kit Sora Photography. Sora is known for evocative and emotional imagery that draws on fantasy symbology for inspiration. She often uses herself as the model in her work and explores themes of body image, folklore, and self-esteem in her art.

The photo was taken using practical effects on the rocky cliff-sides surrounding Signal Hill in St. John's, Newfoundland and Labrador.

The practical effect of the paper airplane was accomplished by Kit Sora crew member Drew Power making a paper airplane and then copying the measurements of each piece onto foam board, then carefully painting the blue and pink lines of the page onto the larger version to match the original.

A hole just large enough for Kit Sora to fit through was then cut in both halves of the faux-paper plane, and assembled around her.

If that sounds like the artist strapped herself into a kite and then climbed out onto the rock-face of one of the most dangerous cliffs in our country just to get a good shot... yes, that's what she did.

We asked her many, many times how she was going to accomplish the shot. Green screen? Photoshop? Maybe a picture taken from a rented drone? She kept shrugging and saying "We'll go to the side of a cliff and take it" in her usual chipper tone. We laughed and laughed.

...

...

That's a one-hundred meter drop to jagged rocks and ocean below her.

Kit remains adventurous and intrepid for her passion, like the early aviators this picture pays tribute to.

Engen Books would like to thank Kit Sora for her work on the cover to this book, and encourages everyone to check out the full-length collection of her work *Kit Sora: The Artobiography*, released in December of 2018.

Kit Sora:
The Artobiography

Available now from Engen.
Soon in paperback!

The early years of **Xander Drew** as he struggles with the evils of his small rural hometown of Coral Beach, Maine. Cursed with the heart of the Womb and the gift of seeing the world around him for what it really is, Xander must learn the hard lessons about the nature of humanity to traverse the minefield of criminals, gangs, and abusers that stand between him and ultimate happiness -- but most of all that **sometimes it takes a monster, to catch a monster.**

"THE WRITING OF ITS GENERATION- - VISUAL, TO-THE-POINT AND IN-THE-MOMENT."
- *The Northeast Avalon Times*

The Coral Beach Casefiles series by Matthew LeDrew:

Book One: Black Womb (February 2019)
Book Two: Transformations in Pain (March 2019)
Book Three: Smoke and Mirrors (April 2019)
Book Four: Roulette (May 2019)
Book Five: Ghosts of the Past (June 2019)
Book Six: Ignorance is Bliss (July 2019)
Book Seven: Becoming (August 2019)
Book Eight: Inner Child (September 2019)
Book Nine: Gang War (October 2019)
Book Ten: Chains (November 2019)

Epilogue: The Long Road (December 2019)

For more information, please visit

www.engenbooks.com

FLIGHTS

FROM THE ROCK

A COLLECTION OF SHORT STORIES
EDITED BY CURTIS, DALY & VANCE

In 1919, the first transatlantic flight took off from the island of Newfoundland.

Celebrate the landmark 100 year anniversary of this historic event with twenty-seven stories that thrill, inspire, explore, and soar through the imagination.

Featuring the work of Sherry D Ramsey (*One's Aspect to the Sun*), Amanda Labonté (*Call of the Sea*), Carolyn R Parsons (*The Forbidden Dreams of Betsy Elliott*), and more!

Edited by Erin Vance, Ellen Curtis, and aviation historian Dr. Lisa Daly, this collection showcases the invention, imagination, and prestige that brought us to the skies. From alternate histories to adventures for lost planes, steampunk tales to modern epics, this collection has it all!

www.ingramcontent.com/pod-product-compliance
Lightning Source LLC
Chambersburg PA
CBHW051939240626
47153CB00005B/1554

* 9 7 8 1 9 8 9 4 7 3 0 5 4 *